LORD OF FIRE, LADY OF ICE

MICHELLE M. PILLOW

Michelle M. Pillow® - MichellePillow.com

About Lord of Fire, Lady of Ice
MEDIEVAL HISTORICAL ROMANCE

"She found herself unimpressed with him, having expected more of the legendary man—Brant. Lord Blackwell. Brant the Gladiator. Brant the Vigorous. Brant the Flame. Brant the Viking Hero. Della snorted in unladylike disgust. More like, Brant the Thorn in my Arse!"

Lady Della the Cold-Hearted

Lady Della despises all things Viking. They may rule the land, but they will never rule her. Unfortunately, her father doesn't seem to agree. To prove his continued allegiance to the Viking king, the Ealdorman of Strathfeld betroths his only daughter to a respected Viking Lord—a warrior whose legendary prowess isn't reserved for the battlefield. Fighting the newfound craving in her body and the unwelcome fire in her heart, Della must choose between everything she knows to be true and the one thing she never expected…

Lord Brant of Blackwell, the Fiery One

Lord Blackwell is as fiery on the battlefield as he is in his passions. He has fought valiantly for King Guthrum and has earned the respect of the nobles. When his overlord offers the hand of his beautiful daughter and the right to inherit his lands, Blackwell can hardly refuse. However, he soon discovers that his noble bride is anything but the meek and mild woman he envisioned for his wife. One minute she's kissing him back, the next she's swearing to do whatever it takes to dissuade him from their marriage. Can his lust for life and his new bride melt the ice that surrounds her heart? Or will Lady Della the Cold be this warrior's undoing?

Featured Titles
FROM MICHELLE M. PILLOW

Historical Romances

Maiden & the Monster
Emerald Knight

Medieval Fantasy Romances

Realm Immortal Series
King of the Unblessed
Faery Queen
Stone Queen

Author Updates

To stay informed about when a new book is released sign up for updates:

michellepillow.com/author-updates

Acknowledgments

There are many people who contribute to the making of my books: editors, line editors, proofers, the fantastic street team, Pillow Fighter fan club members, assistants, a best friend who listens to the endless plotting and re-plotting, cover artists, a wonderful (talented, smart, beautiful, creative, talented, smart, awesome…) child who doesn't question mom's choice of yoga pant attire during deadlines, formatters, the pizza delivery kid, distributors, the spreadsheet king who has been an invaluable help behind the scenes, reviewers, coffee bean growers, that other pizza delivery kid, cover artists, bookstore employees, the new The Raven Books marketing dude, convention workers, Rocky who is convinced my shoulder is a scratching post, Bella whose definition of work is to snore, Winston, Annabelle, the stray/feral cats who had babies in my yard (no, wait, they were a cute 'n fluffy distraction so they didn't help), and then finally you the wonderful readers.

Without all of you, I would be lost. Thank you.

Author Note

Late in the 8th century, Vikings (also called Danes and Norsemen) raided and plundered the English coast. By the end of the 9th century, they were a powerful force that reigned over the Anglo-Saxons, settling and ruling much of England—including Northumbria, York, Mercia, and East Anglia. The Danish King Guthrum wanted Wessex—the only territory left to conquer. Though they fought, no side claimed victory and Wessex's borders remained intact.

In 871, King Aethelred of Wessex was mortally wounded at the Battle of Martin only to be succeeded by his brother, King Alfred (known now as Alfred the Great). Even with a new Anglo-Saxon king, the Nordic army was vast and none could predict how young Alfred would fair against them. For those Anglo-Saxons living under Viking authority, it was a hard time. In a land torn by war, ruled over by fierce warriors, it wasn't wise to change allegiances.

Ealdormen (later to be called Earls) were the chief magistrates, leaders of armies, and the highest ranking nobles of the period below the king.

This period of time is commonly known as The Dark Ages. Though the events surrounding this story are based on the history of the time, the main settings, characters, and situations are purely fictional.

STRATHFELD CASTLE,
NORTHUMBRIA, 871 A.D.

"METHINKS my sire has lost his bloody mind! It would seem this man is truly a barbarian."

Wrinkling her nose, Lady Della lifted her chin haughtily into the air, trying to hide her apprehension beneath a composed expression. Under the long skirts of her blue overtunic she tapped her foot, staring across the main hall to where her father spoke to their Nordic visitor. She took a calming breath and then another, doing her best not to let her aggravation show.

I am a lady, she thought with a feeling of resentment curling through her entire being. *I am above him.*

Her fingers worked against her waist in frustration, causing the fine linen of her gown to crumple beneath her hold. She concealed her scorn under an icy mask of indifference. It was an old habit, one she'd cultivated through years of practice. The dirty Viking glanced around the hall, paying her no mind. However, she watched him intently from the shadowed end of the stairwell, taking in his every gesture like a falcon waiting for a sign of weakness—something, anything she could use against him.

The warrior laughed, nodding in agreement at something the Ealdorman of Strathfeld said. Lord Strathfeld was her distinguished and honored father, though Della was hard pressed to think so highly of him this day. Her irritation deepened as the grating sound of the warrior's merriment only continued.

Grumbling under her breath, she said, "We may have to show allegiance to the heathens, but this goes too far."

"M'lady," her faithful servant scolded. Della didn't take offense to the light reprimand in Ebba's tone. They had known each other for too long, though not exactly friends, they were as close as a maid and her lady could be. "It's not yer place to question yer sire's wishes. He has good reason fer this match or else he would ne'er make it."

Della gave the maid a stiff smile. Feigning nonchalance, she stepped out of the shadows to edge closer to where the men talked. Though she strained her ears, she failed to make out a single word they said.

"Yea, he has his reasons. He thinks by making me wed this barbarian, it will ensure an alliance with King Guthrum in case there is to be another war. With Aethelred so recently in his grave and his brother, Alfred, just named his successor, times are uncertain, especially with Wessex so close to falling under Viking rule."

The entire time she spoke, Della kept her eyes coolly on the warrior, taking in every detail of his figure. She found herself unimpressed with him, having expected more of the legendary man—Brant. Lord Blackwell. Brant the Gladiator. Brant the Vigorous. Brant the Flame. Brant the Viking Hero.

Della snorted in unladylike disgust. *More like, Brant the Thorn in my Arse!*

"M'lady?" Ebba tilted her head in confusion, causing her short, black curls to bob as she moved. She imitated her mistress by pulling at her own clean, white apron.

"Yea, he has his reasons." Della glanced wearily at the maid, who really had no understanding of politics. The noblewoman didn't know why she bothered to explain them as she turned her eyes forward once again to her intended.

The Norseman was dressed as if he'd just come from battle, still wearing his shirt of chainmail. Della was surprised he hadn't rushed boldly into the hall, brandishing his bloodied sword, calling out Nordic curses to his pagan gods. She couldn't help but wonder how many Anglo-Saxons the barbarian had killed. By reputation, it was many.

Della was predominately of Saxon heritage, though not directly related to those in Wessex. Would Lord Blackwell's anger toward the race be transferred onto her in their marriage? The only reason her father retained his title was because of a single drop of royal Viking blood in their ancestry, from when the heathens had first come to Briton. That and her father had proven himself a loyal and valuable man to his Viking overlords.

Briton had been ravished by wars for several hundred years, perhaps since the beginning of time itself. Wessex to the south raged against the Vikings to the north. Her Northumbrian home was in the middle of it all, firmly held by their Viking rulers. No matter how she secretly wished victory for the Wessex king, it wasn't likely her traitorous prayers would be answered. In truth, Della wasn't sure the Christian God could hear prayers said in a pagan land.

The world will always be at war so long as men are in it, regardless of my marriage to Brant the Thorn! Della fumed inwardly.

The barbarian lord nodded as her father pointed up into the high rafters of the main hall. Whatever it was they talked about, it looked to be a serious conversation. Della turned back to her handmaid. "Times mayhap are uncertain, but my cousin, Sir Stuart of Grayson, could well man this keep. Methinks he would make a more likely choice in husband and father to my children."

Ebba giggled and Della wondered at the knowing look in the girl's eyes. "Yea, Sir Stuart is handsome. Would yer sire consider him?"

"Nay," Della admitted with remorse. *Nay, he thinks naught of Stuart. He is more interested in his political intrigues and an alliance with Stuart is not politically advantageous. He would rather see me married to a murdering, lecherous boor of a Viking than let me find true happiness with a man who would stay out of my way and let me run my keep!*

"It's a shame." Ebba licked her bottom lip. "Perchance this Viking husband will not be so bad. It's rumored he's good with his sword, both in bed and out."

Della suppressed a groan at the younger girl's crudeness. It was no secret Ebba already had many lovers in her young life. She had never even been alone with a man, except for her cousin, Stuart. They'd been childhood friends, though she hadn't seen him for many years. She didn't love him as a woman loved a man, far from it, but he was safe.

The marriage bed terrified her and wasn't a prospect she'd been looking forward to experiencing. Della knew if she would've been permitted to marry Stuart, he would've let her out of that particular marital duty. In turn, she would've let him keep as many mistresses as he desired so long as he was discreet and out of her way.

She determined it best to change the course of the conversation before her fear of the marriage bed was discovered. It was easier to be in charge of men and servants if she showed no weaknesses. Della knew what the men called her behind her back—"Della the Cold-Hearted" or, for short, "Della the Cold". Long ago, she'd taught herself not to care so long as they showed no disrespect to her face and did as they were commanded.

"Do you think this Viking has even seen the inside of a keep? I heard it told they sleep outdoors on their ships. Mayhap right next to the cattle." Della gave Ebba a pointed look.

"M'lady!" Ebba's cheeks turned red and she grabbed a piece of her cropped black hair, twirling it around her fingers. She kicked the worn tip of her shoe into the herb-scented rushes that lined the floor. "Mayhap he was just at battle. Mayhap he rode through the night to get here on time."

The maid gave a romantic sigh, no doubt believing the whispers of Lord Blackwell being a glorious war hero, a valiant *knight-errant*. It was said he was a man of distinguished valor on the field of battle and those war-hardened men who fought against him ran at the mere sight of him and his fiery sword. However, Della knew how the scribes liked to exaggerate. Eyeing the Norseman now, she frowned. He wasn't so frightening.

Besides, Della thought ruefully, *he might scare grown men but he would assuredly meet his match in a woman.*

"Yea, and mayhap you should marry the nefarious barbarian and I could be your handmaid." Della understood Ebba had no knowledge of the conspiring that ran her mistress's life. All the servants could seem to understand was the work of their daily existence. Della tried to change that by teaching them the ways of the world, for she believed that everyone deserved to be enlightened. She found most of them didn't want her lessons.

Ebba scrunched her face at the prospect of being a fine lady. "Nay, it's too much to ask. Abovestairs he would break me with his very size."

"More like he would stifle you with his odor," Della noted wryly. Ebba giggled again. Though, the handmaiden had a point. Brant was indeed a big man, even for a Viking.

"Yea, it's a sad truth. Lord Blackwell is not known for his cleanly ways."

Della stiffened, as the soft words drifted from behind her. The sound curled the hairs on her neck to standing. She'd only changed the subject to keep Ebba from probing too much into her future husband's carnal appetites. She hadn't meant for anyone else to hear her barbs—especially not someone with a Nordic accent. Her heart fluttered and she felt sick at being caught, but she couldn't let her anxiety show.

Proudly straightening her shoulders, she turned to the man behind her. Heat rose on her cheeks and she hoped he didn't see it, as she eyed the man who dared to interrupt their conversation. Giving him a chilly stare, it was too late to back down from her viperous comments.

"Yea, it is." Her hard tone crackled over them like breaking ice. No one would know it, but the more nervous she became the harder her voice was, the icier her expression.

"M'lady?" Ebba whispered. Della saw the maid from the corner of her eye, but refused to pull her gaze from the barbarian's. The servant swayed back and forth, clearly wanting to be dismissed. Ebba gave a cautious glance to the large man and took a step back. "M'lady?"

"Yea, Ebba?" Della's head was forced back to look up at the man. His light blue eyes held a rigid formality within their depths, though his words had carried some vast amusement. Della found herself suddenly grateful he wasn't to be her intended. She thought her fiancé was big, but this one gave her reason to pause.

"M'lady?" Ebba insisted once more, tugging lightly on her mistress's sleeve. The barbarian raised an eyebrow and Della's frown deepened.

The noblewoman drew her gaze away first. "Ebba, get you to the kitchen and tell Isa about our guests. Mayhap they would like a draught of mead after their travels."

"Yea, m'lady." Ebba gave a small curtsy and scurried away in relief.

"Do you know Lord Blackwell?" the Viking warrior asked when they were alone. His low voice dripped over her like heated syrup—thick and warm and wickedly sweet. For a barbarian, he was well pronounced despite the heathen accent. He hadn't moved, but with Ebba gone Della lost some of her confidence. She didn't like being alone with him.

She was by no means a short woman and yet this man still towered over her. An unsettled feeling curled in her stomach at his nearness, taking her by surprise. She took a step back to put some distance between them. His mouth twitched up in obvious amusement and she was compelled to run. Not many people could frighten her by their mere proximity.

I am a lady. I am above him. The words were less convincing than before.

Purposefully, she gave a slow, dispassionate

glance over the length of his attire, refusing to let him know he unsettled her. It was a mistake. Looking at him only made the feelings worse. The flexible chainmail shirt he wore ran across an expansive chest, the heavy links molding into the folds of his muscles. An unfamiliar fire worked its way through her, causing a shiver to run the length of her body.

Repulsive, Della thought, hoping to convince herself she meant it.

From the look of his shabby clothing, she presumed he was part of Blackwell's *hird*, the retinue of fighting men who served under him. His crossed arms and widespread stance effectively made an unbreakable barricade. Under his threadbare long tunic, she detected his thighs were like the trunks of two large oaks and his arms like their immense branches. It occurred to her if she were to try, she wouldn't be able to wrap her arms around his upper body.

Della saw how this man would make a formidable opponent on the field of battle and off it. His hair hung loose, in the typical Viking style, to just below his shoulders with two braids plated into it behind the ears and banded with thin strips of leather. He had trimmed blond whiskers over his jaw. She looked at his eyes, momentarily lost in the clearness of their depths.

Come on, girl, wake up! He is a lecherous Viking!

The barbarian raised his eyebrow and an amused corner of his mouth wrenched up higher than before.

She grudgingly noticed the attractiveness of his lips under the short beard.

"Do you know Lord Blackwell?" he repeated. "His manor lies not far from here and you speak as if you are acquainted."

Blessed Saints! She chastised herself, annoyed at having been caught staring like a dimwitted fool.

"Nay. It's only by his inflated reputation that I know of him." Her icy features remained purposefully blank, though she was hard pressed to keep the hauteur from her voice.

The Viking nodded and Della wondered at his unwarranted concern. As he stepped forward, a lock of his long hair fell across his shoulder. The braid on the left side of his head appeared to be a dark shade of red, while the rest of his hair was lighter blond. It reminded her of a streak of fire burning through a golden field of wheat. It was said that Vikings were able to bleach the color from their hair with soaps, though she had never seen it done.

"Do you ride with Lord Blackwell oft?" Trying to sound uninterested, she turned to watch her father and intended. She decided to ignore the fact that the man to her side wasn't properly introduced.

Leastways, mayhap I can discover a few things about my intended.

"Yea, oft enough," he answered, his tone serious. "It's almost like we are the same person."

Della scrunched up her nose at his enigmatic words. "And you have fought together in many battles, I presume?"

"Yea, and sometimes we even sleep by the same row of cattle," the man whispered mischievously.

Della paled and refused to look at him. She was about to question him further when she saw her father turn to her with a look of satisfaction. Nodding her head stiffly in the ealdorman's direction, she acknowledged his interest.

"Lord Strathfeld is a good man." The Viking prevented her from asking more. There was a yielding respect in his voice as he spoke. "He has truly proved his worth in battle."

"Yea, my father has fought in many battles," Della said.

Those battles were the reason for her hasty marriage. He'd fought bravely several months ago at the Battle of Martin, where King Aethelred had been brought low, and had caught the notice of King Guthrum. Together they had formulated a plan to help ensure Strathfeld's continued allegiance to the Viking clans. Their arrangement was simply to unite the prominent Strathfeld line in marriage to a Viking noble and have male heirs of mixed blood produced to join the people. Her father had readily offered her up to be a political sacrifice. Not only did he seek to assure peace with King Guthrum, but he also wanted to ensure continued loyalty between his manor and the neighboring Nordic manor of Blackwell. So it came to be that she was betrothed to Brant of Blackwell, Viking Barbarian.

A jarl, Lord Blackwell was one of the few nobles truly descended of pure Norse blood. Generations of raiding and pillaging the land had given way to Norsemen taking Saxon brides and the children of such matches were considered Viking by birth. If her father had been a pure or even half Viking, he would have been Blackwell's better. Lord Strathfeld was richer and had more land. However, by Viking law, the circumstance of Blackwell's birth made him more powerful than Della's father.

While he is titled, it does not make him noble. He is still naught more than a Viking barbarian, a Viking barbarian who is soon to be my husband.

Della closed her eyes as a wave of disgust rose in her chest. Taking a deep breath, she steeled her nerves.

"M'lady has a look of distaste. Do you feel ill?"

She sensed the man kept his emotions well-guarded and couldn't tell if he disapproved of her earlier remarks regarding her intended. His stony expression puzzled her. She could usually sense what others were thinking.

Mayhap he is as displeased by this match as I! It's likely he does not care for the Saxons as much as I do not care for the Vikings. Mayhap I can convince him to persuade his friend to leave before the nuptial vows are spoken.

Della turned her most charming smile to her unknowing ally. She ignored his surprise at her sudden change in attitude toward him. "Methinks this marriage between our people is a mistake. Perchance, it is the same for you?"

The Viking's eyes narrowed and shot flames in her direction, but he kept quiet.

Della took his silence as a fervent agreement. "I do not wish to marry Lord Blackwell and it's obvious you dislike the match as well. Perchance you can whisper a few words of discouragement into my intended's unsuspecting ears. It would be well worth your while to do so."

"And what would these whispers say?" The Viking leaned closer, his face devoid of emotion as he scratched at his beard.

"They would say I love another, that I would not be faithful. They would say I carry the bastard child of Stuart of Grayson in my belly. They would say aught you would see fit." Della's tongue edged the line of her upper lip in nervous agitation. She barely believed the lies spilling from her mouth. But she didn't care, for they could be disproved when it was discovered she carried no babe. "I care naught what the whispers say of me, only that they meet their purpose."

"It would appear that m'lady has little care for her reputation, nor for the reputation of her betrothed, to speak thusly of herself." The Viking's lips pressed together into a thin line.

Was it possible she'd been mistaken in her assessment of him? He didn't appear as daft as she first assumed and he didn't seem pleased at her intention to overthrow the betrothment. Jutting her chin up in defiance, she said quietly, "I care naught of his lordship's reputation. If you are a true and loyal friend to him, you will warn him against me. Do you understand my words?"

"Yea, I understand." The Viking lowered his head and leaned his face into hers.

Anger glowed like embers of fire in his gaze. He didn't take her veiled threat lightly. Narrowing her eyes, she returned his hard stare, not about to back down now that she'd stated her case. What did it matter if she got along with a barbarian who owed allegiance to her future husband? If this charade of a marriage took place, her first act would be to dismiss the knave at her side and turn him out of the castle. Her heart pounded loudly in her ears as she stared into his steely gaze. Even before the battle of wills had started, she somehow knew she was to be the loser.

Contemptuously, she withdrew her gaze from his and noticed his fists clenching and unclenching at his sides. Suddenly the size and power of the man before her grabbed hold of her senses and she knew she'd stepped too close to the flame. Taking a hesitant step back, she debated as to whether she should turn and run.

"Do you leave so quickly?" Brant asked in low, exact tones as his future wife backed away from him. He wanted nothing more than to wring the life's breath from her traitorous, unfaithful throat. Her passionless face gave no emotion away.

No wonder you are called Della the Cold-Hearted. Methinks you lack all passions, even fear.

Brant watched the woman's unwavering composure in awe. She was a beautiful creature, or would be once the ice melted from her features. She looked too young to possess so much self-control, though she was old by marrying standards. He estimated she could be no more than one and twenty years.

Brant hadn't meant to overhear her conversation with her handmaid. He'd thought simply to introduce himself, for it was clear she thought his seneschal and good friend, Gunther, was he. But when he caught her cutting remarks about his heritage and cleanliness, he couldn't help himself. He had teased her to teach her a lesson about gossiping. Though now he saw there was to be no end to her insults. The damned Anglo-Saxons always insulted what they didn't understand and it seemed his bride was no different. He'd hoped since she was a lady, a position allowed her by the very race she now scorned, she would see the wisdom in their alliance.

Brant took a menacing step toward her. He usually would be against striking such deliberate fear into a woman, for he knew they were naturally apprehensive of his large size. He always tried to treat womankind with a gentle hand and, after they got to know him more intimately, they never complained. But this frustrating woman wasn't fearful of him. In fact she seemed damned near indifferent. Could it be the rumors about her were true? Did she truly feel nothing?

Do you understand your mistake now, little schemer? Brant took another step, closing the distance between them. He noted in grim satisfaction the way her pulse quickened at the base of her slender neck. *Nay, you are not immune to my anger, you just shroud it well.*

"Do you leave before being introduced to your future master?" Brant forced a hard smile as he fingered a lock of her waist-length blonde hair. He smoothed the submissive strands gently between the pads of his thumb and his forefinger. She wore a simple blue gown, the fine linen embroidered at the edges as to befit her station. By looks alone, she would make him a good wife—someone warm and soft to hold during the night, someone to slake his desires when they arose. First, she must learn to submit to him. He had a feeling she wouldn't take kindly to being commanded. Lifting the soft lock of hair to his lips, he kissed it lightly before whispering, "For make no mistake, Lord Blackwell will be your master."

"No man will ever be my master." She snatched her hair from him and threw it over her shoulder in contempt. "And you will do well to unhand me in the future lest I tear off the offending appendage."

Brant's smile widened at her show of defiance. He was going to enjoy taming her obstinate ways. Underneath her icy façade was a fiery passion just waiting to be released. Even through his anger, he had to confess, he was drawn to her unpleasant temperament. And he had worried that his bride would turn out to be an unexciting wife who couldn't hold his attention.

"I will not be commanded! Not by my father and certainly not by your fellow barbarian over there."

Della turned her chilly gaze in the direction of Lord Strathfeld.

"Of that you can be certain, m'lady," Brant whispered mockingly to her, as he followed her eyes. He felt more than saw the small shudder of apprehension that radiated through her body. A lazy smile settled on his lips, though his insides were kindled in a temperate rage. His future father-by-marriage nodded his acknowledgment as he made his way toward them. Gunther followed closely behind him. Della's hand trembled as she grabbed the dress at her waist to still her fingers. He turned and gave an agreeable smile to Lord Strathfeld. "M'lord."

"Ah! It is good that you are getting on." Lord Strathfeld nodded worriedly to his daughter, his look of concern belying the pleasure in his words.

"Argh," Della huffed under her breath in aggravation.

Lord Strathfeld raised a brow at her anger and shook his head in disapproval. Leaning into his daughter, he warned none too quietly, "Della, this is no way to act before your intended. Would you have him think you are no lady?"

Della looked scornfully at Gunther and held out her hand to him. "It is a pleasure, I'm sure." The words barely escaped her bared teeth.

Gunther looked at Brant in confusion and then took her hand. He bowed gallantly over it. "M'lady."

Brant felt a small pang of irritation as Della moved to Gunther's side. She took up his friend's arm and turned a self-important stare to him.

"Della?" Lord Strathfeld coughed. He motioned to the man whose arm she held. "Have you met Gunther? He will be replacing Edwyn as seneschal here after I am gone. I was showing him the improvements Edwyn made here in hopes that he would see fit to continue them."

Brant watched in grim satisfaction as Della turned to Gunther in horror.

"Seneschal?" she mouthed as she dropped Gunther's arm. Her eyebrows shot high on her face, adding to her icy charm.

"Yea, m'lady." Gunther let her hand slip from him as he turned to Brant, not even trying to hide his amused smile. "Brant, did you introduce yerself?"

"Lord Blackwell?" Della gasped and turned her head sharply to look at him. Realization dawned in her amber eyes.

"M'lady." He bowed and offered his hand to her.

"Oh!" Della opened her mouth in shock. She jerked away from him as if he were poisonous. "You are a detestable, unspeakably miserable lout! How dare you not reveal yourself to me?"

Gunther chuckled and soon all the servants in the hall were doing the same. Della turned around in dismay, quickly making her way abovestairs.

"It would seem you did not make a favorable impression on her, Blackwell," Gunther said in amusement. "And to think we left the fighting behind us. Perchance you are just too much Viking fer her."

"Yea, perchance." Brant gave a wry smile as he

stared at the place his bride's feet had disappeared from. *And perchance the battles have just begun.*

"M'LADY?" A knock sounded on the door, following the maidservant's words. "M'lady, it is me, Ebba."

"Come, Ebba." Della sat on her bed with her back to the door and kicked the bottom of her shoes against the nearby stone wall in frustration.

"M'lady? What are you about?" Ebba eyed her with concern, tilting her head to the side as she investigated the source of the hard thuds.

Della sighed and dropped her feet to the floor in order to stand. Leaning against the cold stone of the wall, she pretended to look out the narrow slit window. "What news from my sire?"

"They are done with the negotiations. Lord Blackwell has announced his intention to marry you in front of yer father's men and yer sire has named him his heir pending the marriage." Ebba eyes shone with excitement. "And yer husband—"

"Nay, future husband, Ebba. He is not my husband yet," Della corrected tersely. *And if I can help it, he will never be.*

"Yer future husband," Ebba amended before rushing on. "He gave yer father the *handgeld* in good faith. It is said he paid a princely sum fer yer hand. It's said King Guthrum blesses this match so that the manors of Blackwell and Strathfeld can become one."

Della shivered at the maid's words. She doubted it was truly a 'princely sum' Brant paid, for her future husband didn't clothe himself like he had many coins. Already, she knew Brant would become Ealdorman of Strathfeld upon her father's death, as well as remaining Jarl of Blackwell to combine the titles. She'd hoped her hasty words of being unfaithful would have dissuaded her suitor. It wasn't to be. The men had actually gone through with the dealings. The last splinter of hope left her.

"Begone, Ebba," Della said dismally into the window. She refused to turn lest the woman see her nervousness. Ebba was a good servant and an admirable companion, but she was still a servant and prone to gossip. Della didn't want her childhood home knowing the full extent of her displeasure over the marriage, at least not yet.

"Ah, m'lady?"

"Yea," Della finally moved to look at the woman. There was something to the maid's tone that worried her. It was rare that Ebba didn't do exactly as told.

"It is to be a Viking wedding."

Nay! How could my father have agreed to that?

"Perchance I did not hear you?" Her voice croaked and she was sure her heart nearly stopped beating.

"Yea, m'lady. It's to be a traditional Viking wedding. Lord Blackwell was insistent on that point. Though, it will be presided over by a Christian priest as well, so it will be binding in everyone's eyes." Ebba took a step back.

By All the Saints! A pagan wedding? A shaking started in her stomach, only to make its way to her heavy limbs. It wasn't completely unheard of, but she'd just assumed they would follow the local customs. She took a deep breath, mortified by the news. *You will not get away with this, Brant the Fiery Thorn!*

"What else?" Della demanded, feeling that Ebba was hiding something from her.

Ebba shook her head in denial.

"Ebba?"

"Naught else, m'lady." The woman's voice was weak.

"Leave me." Della didn't believe her, but it didn't matter. Whatever else there was, it wouldn't compare to a pagan wedding.

EBBA TOOK a deep breath as she hurried down the hall, away from her angry mistress. Lady Della looked fit to kill at the news of a pagan wedding. All in the manor were well aware of her ladyship's abhorrence of the Viking people. It was no great secret.

Ebba ran faster, eager to get away before she could be called back. She'd lied to her lady, but what else could she do? She wasn't going to be the one to inform Lady Della that Lord Blackwell demanded her maidenhead checked.

"Gunther, I'm pleased you have agreed to stay on with me," Brant said in their native speech. It was early in the day and they were alone in the main hall. He grabbed a wooden goblet from the high table and took a long drink of mead. Smiling secretly to himself, he let visions of Della storming up the stairs brighten his mood. She had a chilly disposition, even more so than rumored, but there was fire hidden there as well, just waiting for the right tinder.

He looked around the quiet room, knowing it would all be his. Someday soon, if Lord Strathfeld was to be believed. The old ealdorman sensed his time was near. It was always sad when a good soldier and leader passed on.

Strathfeld's hall was made of stone and not wood like so many manors were. It once had been a Roman fortress, plundered and then refortified by the Anglo-Saxons, and was now sitting on Norse land. Many of the walls still reflected the old stronghold, making

Strathfeld a strange blend of old and new. By all standards, it was impressive.

"Yea, where else was I to go?" Gunther answered in the same language. He too took a drink. "But with my rich and noble friend."

Brant studied the main hall. The room showed the large extent of the wealth he was to inherit along with the title. The nobles' table sat high before the rest of the long hall, with the other tables and benches lower for the servants, soldiers, and freemen of the keep. On the far end, separated by curtains, were the sleeping pallets for the soldiers. True to Viking style, a large stone fireplace had been built into the middle of the hall, excellent for producing heat, but it did little in the way of light. To compensate, candles made from animal fat and beeswax were placed along spikes in the stone walls. Next to the main hall was the kitchen with a fireplace of its own for cooking.

He'd already explored much of the home. Abovestairs there was a separate chamber for the lord and lady of the keep, with narrow slits in the floor so one could peek down onto the guests to make sure everything was in order. Lord Strathfeld had informed him that the chamber had never been used and that it was where he wished Brant to stay. There were smaller sleeping chambers—one for Lady Della, one for the ealdorman, and a few for honored guests. There was even a small room for sewing set up with looms and cutting tables. Many homes didn't have such fine accommodations and often the lord and lady slept in the hall with everyone else. Brant looked forward to the silence of sleeping away from the men.

Directly outside the kitchen were the castle gardens and a small fruit orchard, and beyond that were the pens for animals to be slaughtered in the fall. The old fortress itself set high atop a motte of earth and rock. It towered a good fifty feet above the bailey. In front of the castle was the bailey yard, which was surrounded by a large wall made of both stone and timber, and in turn was surrounded by a large ditch and wooden palisades for reinforced security. By some ingenious plan, the servants' chambers were built into the bailey wall to utilize space and to better keep watch in times of conflict. The only way out of the keep was through the front gate and over a stone path that was surrounded by water on both sides. Contained within the inner bailey were the exercise yard, a small chapel, the stables, a couple barns, a few workshops, and a small brewery.

Brant knew from his travels that the castle was one of the most innovative of their modern age, both in discipline and in design. Lord Strathfeld had taken great care in the planning, utilizing many of the ideas from the southern kingdoms. Brant had been in awe of it since he had first detected its magnificent fortress walls from the distance.

Setting the goblet back down with a thud, Brant wiped his mouth on the sleeve of his dirty tunic. He was still amazed by how quickly this change in his life had been brought about. One day he fought a war, the next he was inheriting land so vast he could hardly imagine it. He knew the reason Lord Strathfeld sought him out as a suitor for his daughter was because his Viking blood was pure, he had a valiant war record, and he lorded over a small piece of land next to Strathfeld.

"Yer off to sea, Brant, row back to shore." Gunther laughed as he patted Brant hard on the back.

A sharp pain radiated through his body at the friendly gesture, bringing him again to reality. He'd been struck in the lower back a month ago during a small skirmish and the wound still pained him some when disturbed. "Yea, this a good place. Strathfeld's land will make a good addition to Blackwell Manor. Mayhap we can finally rebuild Blackwell to what it was before my father's time."

"Yea." Gunther grinned, winking at a passing maid. The girl blushed before hurrying across the empty hall to the kitchen. "It is a good place, this Strathfeld. Do you e'er remember so many pleasing young maids in one stead? If yer new wife does not take to you, you can have many a pick fer a bedmate."

Brant laughed in appreciation. He knew well that he could have as many mistresses in the keep as he liked and his new wife couldn't protest. But he also knew what his unfaithful father's ways had done to his mother. She'd taken her own life when he was only ten years old. Brant had no desire to flaunt his indiscretions. He secretly wished that he could find some sort of happiness in marriage—even if it wasn't the fabled love of his people, *inn makti murr*, the mighty passion.

Brant shook himself from his deep thoughts and turned to an amused Gunther. "I see much that needs to be done with the fortifications if this place is to continue to be impermeable."

"Methought I saw some walls on the east boundary were made of wood. They could be fortified with stone. There are enough rocks lying around to easily do it." Gunther continued to use the language of their ancestors. A servant came to refill their goblets. Her red hair spiraled out of her head in a disarray of pleasant curls and she had wide green eyes. When Gunther spoke, she stopped, looking at them in confusion. "I do not see why that section was not yet done. Though, it's said Lord Strathfeld has spent little time here nigh on these last years and that his daughter has managed the keep in his absence."

"Lady Della would know little about maintaining a stronghold." Brant crossed his arms over his chest and stretched his legs before him. The servant didn't move and he realized she didn't understand them. He motioned her forward. Without much thought, he easily switched to the Saxon tongue. "Though she does maintain a clean keep."

"Nay, m'lord. It's because of the spirit." The servant looked at him. "She will come out if the manor is filthy. Have you not heard?"

Brant smiled at her superstitious ways. "Nay, tell me. Who is she?"

"The spirit of the Roman lady who lived here when the home was built."

"And what does she do?" he asked.

"She cleans, m'lord," the servant answered in all seriousness.

Brant and Gunther laughed.

"Nay, sweetling, it's not you we find amusing." Gunther also switched easily to the Saxon speech as he leaned forward. He touched the young maid gently under the chin. "Methinks you would just let the cleaning spirit work."

The maid smiled at Gunther's charms and swayed back and forth on her feet in girlish shyness. "Nay. It was tried. After a sennight, she tore the manor to bits with her rage and we ne'er tried again fer fear she'd take after us next."

Brant chuckled even harder as Gunther nodded in earnestness.

"It's a grave thing you reveal to us, sweetling. Perchance, you can tell me more later?" Gunther lowered his voice suggestively. "Mayhap, tonight?"

"Yea, m'lord." She curtsied before turning to leave. Gunther let out a belch and pounded himself on the chest. The maidservant glanced back with a small jump, giggling as she scurried off.

"There has been little need to mind the castle walls. The fighting has been away from here." Gunther resumed where the conversation had been interrupted.

"Yea, but it will not always be so." Brant rubbed the bridge of his nose. Spirits were a serious business.

Not that Brant believed in them, but because the people who served him did. "Mayhap our spirit will fix the wall. It appears she has little to do inside."

"Yea, and mayhap she'll get angry at our sloth and tear it down."

Brant chuckled and hit his friend hard on the shoulder. "Yea, mayhap."

"It appears m'lady does not get much credit fer her work." Gunther stretched his arms. Seeing a gathering of dust on his sleeve, he patted it from his shoulder with a hard smack. The particles rose into the air and drifted in the narrow rays of sunlight.

"Perchance, she does," Brant mused, watching the dust settle.

Gunther lifted an eyebrow and then shrugged his shoulder. Spotting the informative maid across the hall studying him, he winked, giving her his most charming smile.

Brant had given his temper a moment to cool after his first meeting with Lady Della. Even he had to reluctantly admit that his bride had a charming vivaciousness to her. Most men would not dare to stand up to him in opposition. He liked the idea of a wife who could hold her own. It meant she would be strong enough to last through hard times. Once he won her loyalty, she would make a great ally. Though he would have to do much to curb that wayward tongue of hers in the future, for it was not right for a wife to holler at her husband in front of servants.

Maybe she was just nervous, or irate that her father hadn't asked for her consent before the decision was made. Regretfully, there had been no time for such concerns. He had seen many unhappy marriages because a lady wasn't consulted before the agreement, not that a consultation would have changed anything. But the gesture often assuaged feminine pride. He would just have to make it right by her on the wedding night, prove that he had some sense of good manners.

He suppressed a groan at the prospect of the coupling. It had been a long time since he was held in the gentle arms of a woman. Sleeping next to an army of men was hardly as pleasant of a diversion.

"What was that about earlier? Lady Della did not appear taken with you." Gunther nodded to a serving wench with black hair as she went abovestairs. He shot her a come-hither smile. "Perchance, you have lost yer charm."

Brant watched his friend in amusement. Gunther never stayed in one place long without some company to share his bed. Unlike Brant, who preferred to keep a steady mistress.

"It would appear m'lady has an aversion to Vikings—something to do with the way we smell and sleep out of doors with cattle." He sat up and finished his cup of mead in several long gulps and then rubbed his eyes in aggravation. They'd been riding all over the countryside for the last several sennights and had yet to have a day of peace and quiet. He'd hoped that would have changed when he finally arrived at Strathfeld. It wasn't to be. "Yea, she even tried to convince me not to wed with her.

She said she carried Stuart of Grayson's bastard child."

Gunther choked on his mead as he gave Brant a horrified look. "*Gods Bones!* She did not say that. What if it is so?"

"I do not think it is," he answered softly. "Besides, I have ordered her checked by the midwife."

"You didn't!" Gunther's laugh echoed in the hall as he pounded his fist on the arm of his chair. "Methinks the Lady Della will not take kindly to that."

"She left me little choice in the matter. Though, I have yet to tell her father." Brant let a small smile lift the corner of his mouth. Lord Strathfeld had informed him that his daughter wished to be married to Sir Stuart, but she hadn't seen him nigh on the last five years. It was too long of a time to be carrying a man's babe. Unfortunately, he had no way of knowing how many people she'd told her lie to. This was the only way to ensure Della's reputation and his own.

"What are you going to do about her aversion?" Gunther's laughter subsided for a moment as he took a quick drink.

Brant re-crossed his ankles and adjusted his arms over his chest. "It's already done."

"What?" Gunther's eyes narrowed in anticipation.

"I told Lord Strathfeld my ancestors demanded I have a traditional Viking wedding. He didn't care either way, just so it was done."

"You didn't." Gunther laughed louder, unable to

believe the audacity of his friend. "I don't believe you. How traditional?"

"My friend, it is my wedding day. We are going to do it right." Brant grinned as he imagined the look on his intended's pretty face as he made her drink from their *kasa* filled with mead and goat's blood. He wondered if his dainty bride would refuse and then he thought of the many pleasurable ways he could punish her.

"No one has used the traditional ceremonies nigh on the past hundred years."

"Nay, there are a few tribes to the far north," Brant answered. "Besides, the Saxons don't know that."

"Well, m'lord, it would seem someone has just informed yer bride of the change in nuptial plans." Gunther looked to the stairwell in feigned concern as he settled more deeply into his seat. It was apparent he had no intention of missing the upcoming fray.

Brant followed his friend's gaze. Not surprisingly, there was his bride storming across the main hall in their direction. Even in her wintry fury she was lovely. Rushes were kicked up in her rage and the dark-haired servant quickly moved behind her to smooth them down once more. He nodded his approval of their quick attention to detail. It said much of how his future wife ran the keep.

Or the spirit.

He knew the moment her gaze alighted on him and felt the chill of her icy stare from across the room. Suddenly he frowned, disapproving of her second public display of anger.

"Lord Blackwell," Della fumed at him from below as she made her way up to the high table. Once on the raised platform, she placed the palms of her hands squarely on the table to stare him down. Brant smiled and moved as if to look down her bodice. Della gasped and straightened. Her hands flew to cover what little cleavage showed before fisting stiffly at her sides. He shot her a devilish smile. Her face tightened until it looked as if she might crack. "May I have a word with you?"

Brant studied her for a second, pretending to ponder his answer. She was an enchanting creature despite the constant icy restraint on her face. Her eyes were the color of prized Viking amber and hair was of the lightest spun gold. Earlier the locks had fallen freely to her waist in waves of pleasing softness, but now she had it bundled tightly to the back of her head and held into place with a circlet of gold chains. He had a feeling it was to keep him from fondling it again.

She grabbed a fistful of her long blue dress at the waist and held it in her clenched hand. Her foot tapped as she waited impatiently for his answer. He tried not to let his amusement show. Finally, he nodded once to grant her permission.

Della took a deep breath and lowered her voice. "Perchance I may have a word with you in private, *m'lord?*"

Brant hid his delight at her mocking restraint,

again pretending to mull her request over in his mind. "Nay."

Her jaw dropped and her eyes rounded in bewilderment. It was clear she was rarely refused anything. Bristling as Gunther laughed, she shot a deadly look to his friend. To her credit, it quieted the man's laugh to a chuckle. She turned her thorns to him once more.

Brant realized only he could detect the small changes in her emotions. To anyone else in the hall she would appear cool and calm. He watched her mounting fury and wondered how far he could push her before she exploded. Would her passions be as easy to rise between the bed linens? He found it peculiar that he wanted to demand control from her a moment before and now he couldn't seem to stop himself from provoking her anger.

She wasn't as frigid as she would lead him to believe. There was a wealth of passion in her, just waiting to be released. Perhaps, when he showed her the pleasure of the marriage bed, she wouldn't be so adverse to his presence. Brant suppressed a grin. She might even beg for it.

DELLA GLARED at the obstinate man, despising his highhanded treatment of her and thought, *You are not Ealdorman of Strathfeld yet, Brant the Thorn, you Viking barbarian! This is still my father's keep.*

"Must I insist?" She clenched her teeth.

"Insist all you like, but the answer is nay. I am

content where I am." He looked obnoxiously smug. She watched as he lifted a lazy hand to his beard to scratch at his chin.

I'll bet he is infested with fleas, she thought in dismay, *and I will have to clean the rushes daily because of it.*

She raised her chin and her voice, not caring that Gunther was there to witness. "Very well, I *refuse* to marry you. I'd rather live my life as a pauper, scrubbing the garderobes. I care not for you or your pagan customs. Is this clear enough for you?"

Brant snarled. He shot to his feet, slamming his palm flat onto the high table. "Methinks it's about time I had a talk with my lady bride."

Her jaw dropped as she took a hasty step back. She placed her hands defiantly on her hips and didn't look away. But, even so, she knew she had talked too out of turn. His dark fury poured from every movement. She cursed herself for again daring to step too close to the flame. He stalked around the table until he was well upon her. His fists were hard balls at his sides, attesting to his ire. Without pause, he grabbed her about the waist and threw her easily over his shoulder.

"Oomph." Della felt the wind rush from her lungs as she landed hard against him. He then leapt from the platform like a raging beast to the main hall floor. Della screamed and clutched at his back for support. Much to her amazement, he didn't drop her. His feet found easy footing in the rushes. Screaming, she demanded, "Let go of me, you oaf. How dare you treat me like this? I am Lady Della of Strathfeld. I am a lady!"

Brant's arm blazed a liquid heat into her stomach as he adjusted her on his shoulder. Della dangled helplessly over his back, pressed intimately against the heat of his body. Her waist fit next to his thick neck and he held her steady with one arm wrapped around her upper thighs. Della didn't move, noting in astonishment how gracefully he walked for a man of his size. Then, hearing Gunther's hearty laughter, she came to her senses. She pushed her arms on his back and wielded herself up with a cry of fury.

Brant grunted like he was in pain as she hit him. He stopped at the foot of the stairs and grabbed her butt with his free hand. Giving her cheek a hard squeeze, he warned, "Hold! Or I will likely drop you on your hard head."

Della instantly let her arms fall and did as he commanded. A strangely devious and unfamiliar response started in her stomach at his arrogant handling and she felt the familiar way in which his hand caressed her backside. For a moment, the touch mystified her into silence. The heat of his grip sent scorching waves of fire through the two layers of linen she wore.

Della stiffened as she realized he was carrying her to the bedchambers. Tears instantly came to her eyes and she began to shake. The weight of his hand deepened on her sensitive bottom. Her thighs tightened and she became hot as an unusual throbbing started in her core. She squeezed her eyes shut, preparing to run as soon as she was let down, and prayed her quivering legs would carry her.

He moved his hand from her backside to push open his chamber door. Then, with a hard jerk, he kicked it shut behind him. The door vibrated with a decisive thud. He carried her across the chamber and effortlessly tossed her onto the feather mattress. Standing over her, he crossed his arms to make an impenetrable barrier with his body. His eyes silently dared her to run.

Della shivered. Hurrying to her hands and knees, she backed away from her potential ravisher. She dashed the shameful tears that slipped from her eyes. Brant watched her edge to the side of the bed, a look of hot passion on his face.

"You are naught more than a dishonorable barbarian," she yelled, terrified by the animalistic way he looked at her. It was like a starving man watching a loaf of bread.

"And you are a spoiled shrew," he fired back.

"Miserable lout!"

"Aggravating wench!"

"Heathen!"

"Battle-axe!"

"Wretched boor!"

"Enchantress." He softened his tone and smiled when her mouth dropped open with no reply. "So, there is a way to silence your foolish tongue. I could quickly show you more effective ways to draw a compliment from your lord husband."

Enchantress? Della swallowed uncomfortably. No

one had ever said such a thing about her, at least not to her face. She cursed herself for the pleasure she felt at the compliment. "You are not my husband."

"Yea, not yet, but I will be soon enough. There are a few things we need to get straight between us if this is to be a happy marriage."

She eyed his devilish looks. He still wore the same long tunic he had been wearing earlier, only he had removed the chain mail. His clothes were threadbare and bewailed a want for a woman's touch. They lacked fine embroidery at the edges and the material was old, not at all fit for a leader of men and the future Ealdorman of Strathfeld. She wondered why the poor quality of his clothing didn't bother her as much as it should. Or why she suddenly felt compelled to rip the tunic from his chest to see what was hidden beneath.

"If it is happiness you seek, m'lord, mayhap you should seek another wife. It's not too late." Her low whisper sounded ominous. "For you will not find happiness with me."

He studied her for a long time. Then, as if trying to be reasonable, he said, "Mayhap, you judge our marriage too harshly and out of turn."

"Nay." She reached to pull at the material that hung from the top canopy of the bed and entangled her foot. "It is you who judge me out of turn. I refuse to be married to a Viking. The whole race of you murderous heathen barbarians can rot. Call me a traitor. Do whatever it is you do, but I'd rather hang than—"

"I am afraid, m'lady, you have no choice in the matter, for it is out of your hands. You will be Lady Blackwell or you will suffer—"

"Are you threatening me?"

"Either you wed with me two days hence or you die a pauper."

Della understood instinctively that the man before her wasn't lying. He would ruin her if she refused him, and not only her. There were a lot of people living in Strathfeld Castle and the surrounding lands, a lot of people who depended on her—Saxon people. No matter what she felt, she couldn't be selfish. Lifting her chin as she stood on the other side of the bed, she wasn't willing to be humbled by his threats. "Yea, I will marry you then, but heed my words. It will be rape the night of the wedding and every night thereafter you seek your husband rights. I will never lie with you of my own free will and I will fight you every time you try to take me. My body will not bear you a child. I will seek the help of the midwife if it becomes necessary. If it's happiness you are seeking, it will not be at my hand."

"And you heed me, *lady bride*. I will tolerate your bad temper no longer. You will treat me with the respect due your lord husband, both in public and private." Brant moved around the bed and stalked toward her. He backed her against the stone wall and placed his hands on either side of her head. His chest rose and fell in aggravation. "And if you ever try to rid your body of my child, I will be rid of you in the same manner. Only I will not be as kind, for it will be a painfully drawn out death. Do you understand?"

Della nodded, breathing heavily at his nearness—partly because she'd never been studied as intently by a man and partly because she found herself enjoying his perusal. His heady scent engulfed her senses as she tried to back away from him, tried to bury her body in the unforgiving stone. He smelled of sweat and horses, of mint and the earth, not at all unpleasant like she'd first insinuated.

"Do not," she whispered, afraid that he might ravish her to prove his power over her.

Brant threw back his head in mocking laughter. He glanced down at her breasts and licked his lips as if wanting desperately to taste them.

"What?" she demanded as her cheeks colored with hot embarrassment. She pushed against his chest. He didn't budge. "Why are you staring?"

"I have never raped a woman and I never will. Women come freely to my bed, as will you given time. I will make you plead me for my favors." He leaned in closer and lowered his voice. His warm breath covered her neck and her chest. Her eyes strayed to his lips. She smelled the mead on his breath, and saw the hard texture of his firm mouth under the whiskers. "I will touch you in passion until you beg for my embrace, nay, the very length of my sword thrusting within you. And when you carry my heir, you will birth him and you will be a mother to him."

"Perversion," Della swore, even as she shivered at the hidden promise in his voice. It was clear he meant what he said. She'd heard of such carnal pleasure whispered by the maids of the keep, but she'd also seen firsthand how unpleasant the mating act could be for a woman. In her mind, the pain outweighed the pleasure tenfold.

Then why did she keep looking at his lips? Della self-consciously licked the side of her mouth as she glanced up into his piercing eyes. She wondered what his lips would feel like against hers. Her body's response to him defied the logic she knew to be true.

This is one of your pagan curses you are casting over me!

Della realized her hand lay motionless on his chest above the steady beating of his heart and she hastily snapped it back. Clenching it into a fist to resist touching him again, she couldn't erase the feel of his heartbeat on her palm. He was so close, so real. She lifted her chin, stubbornly refusing to rise to his taunting. A small smile formed on his lips.

"Yea, I will not consummate the marriage until you beg me." His sensual whisper held untold promises. He tilted his head so his parted lips settled by the curve of her neck, not touching her save for his breath falling hot and heavy against her flesh. "And when I am done touching the full span of your person, beg me you will."

"I will never beg for you." Her words had lost a bit of their chill.

"Nay?" Brant asked against her throat.

Della shook her head. She felt the brief shift of his mouth, as if he smiled, but he didn't move his head. With his forefinger, he touched her neck, lightly massaging over her pulse several times. When her heart quickened in response, he slowly moved the finger over her collarbone.

"Mayhap you are mistaken. Your skin is as soft as I've imagined it to be and warm. You are not the icy maiden people whisper about, are you?"

Della shivered, unable to move. His lips drove her mad with their teasing, airy caresses. Her heart was so loud she barely heard him and her mind centered over the feathery brush of his finger. It sent a fire coursing through her blood. Maybe he hadn't even spoken. Maybe she'd imagined it. Her hips shifted toward him of their own accord.

What was she doing?

Brant took advantage of her confusion, drawing his finger down the low collar line of her dress. Della arched her chest into him. She couldn't think, couldn't fight. His breath continued to fan her throat, making her pulse race out of control, like the thunderous hooves of wild stallions. Short whiskers tickled her flesh, not unpleasant, but a distinct contrast to his soft breath. He spread his palm over the top curves of her breasts. Her nipples peaked and strained against the linen of her gown. He was so close, so warm. She wanted him to explore more of her body. She wanted him to touch her.

He flicked his tongue over her pulse. At the same time, he delved his hand into the front of her tunic. Moving his fingers over her hardened nipple, he caressed her breast.

Della arched fully into him and let out a moan of

surprise. No one had ever dared to stand so close to her. Never had she been touched so boldly. Her arms had a mind of their own as they moved to rest weakly on his mammoth chest. She felt his hand as if it was everywhere, sliding over her flesh beneath her gown. Clasping her thighs tight, she wondered at the sudden dampness between them.

Brant's smile broadened against her throat and she heard his small chuckle of victory. She was too far gone to care. Somehow he managed to lift her breast from her tunic to better cover it with his fiery palm. Della let out a cry as air hit her chest. Hot kisses moved down her throat to sting her collarbone. Licking her skin, he groaned as if reveling in her sweet taste. His beard tickled her and she shivered.

Her hands twisted in his tunic and she pulled him closer, wanting to feel more of him. He moved his agonizing kisses lower onto her breast. Suddenly her nipple was in his mouth and a burst of light and color lit up her closed eyelids.

Della ran her fingers into the neckline of his tunic, innocently caressing the muscles she found there. Her hands shook with the force of the new emotions that flooded her. She didn't understand what was happening to her body, didn't think she wanted to. All she knew was that she couldn't speak and she couldn't beg him to stop.

Brant released her nipple and pressed his arousal boldly against her center heat. Growling, he lifted her by the butt, forcing her legs to grip his waist. Della gasped at his strength as he held her against the wall of the bedchamber. Through their clothing his hardness ground into her.

"Methinks you do not find me such the wretched boor now, m'lady," he said aggressively against her throat. Her lips stung with longing, but he refused to kiss her. "Beg."

Della heard the word through a fog. It brought her up short and she stiffened against him in anger. "You miserable toad. Let me down before I scream. How dare you do this to me? I loathe your touch. You have no right to fondle me so."

Brant instantly let go and stepped away. Della jerked in surprise, barely catching herself from falling on the floor.

"Methinks you have already screamed aplenty, lady bride. Or do you forget so quickly what came out of your mouth a moment before." Brant didn't wait for her reply before storming angrily out of the chamber.

Della watched him go, somewhat disturbed by what his words implied. Had she been screaming at his nearness? Had she let him touch her so wantonly? Shivering, she knew he was right. She had acted shamelessly in his arms. The remnants of the flames he'd lit inside her coursed through her limbs and she quickly covered her exposed chest.

Tears ran over her cheeks. Turning her face into the wall, she pounded the stone with her fist until her skin was bleeding and raw. His whispers had exhilarated her and tormented her at the same time. He represented everything she hated, but she couldn't stop herself from wondering what his hands had meant with their mysterious promises.

Curse you, Brant the Thorn, and your pagan ways.

BRANT STORMED the halls in disbelief. The mass between his thighs strained, begging for attention. He could still see her clearly, Della's image burned into his brain to torment him. Several strands of her hair had come loose at his rough handling and fell sensually over the exposed breast. Her skin was the color of fresh cream.

Temptation raged inside him and it took all his control not to turn around, throw her onto the bed, and take her in his passion. He wasn't used to denying himself such pleasure, especially when he had every right to take it. Only the look of utter terror on her face had stopped him.

Brant sighed in frustration. He couldn't understand her distaste for him, no matter how hard he tried. He'd hoped things could be cleared between them, but her prejudice was blatant. She judged him by the ancestral blood that ran through his veins and not his merits. It was strange that she had such distaste for his heritage, for many of the Northumbrians were of mixed blood between the Anglo-Saxon and the Norse. Although it was well known she came from an almost purely Anglo-Saxon background, he knew that her own heritage had some Norse blood. Besides, Northumbria belonged to the so-called heathens.

Though his raging arousal still wanted to debate the fact, Brant didn't think he could bed her now if he wanted to. He was too angry. But his fury was as passionate as his desire and he felt a strange war begin to wage within his depths. He'd felt her reaction and witnessed her innocent desire. She didn't understand what her body was doing, just as he knew she couldn't begin to control its response.

Brant groaned. He'd acted purely on instinct. His body desired her so much. It just had a hard time deciding whether it desired to ravish her or to throttle her.

Good thing he hadn't kissed her lips. He knew if he felt her sweet mouth he would be lost and then Odin help him. His self-control threatened to abandon him as he stopped and looked back, tempted to finish what was started. He forced himself to continue down the stairwell.

Beg.

If it had been any other maid, his command would have been met and eagerly so, but she wasn't just any maid. She was Della the Cold and she was to be his unwilling wife.

"*M'LADY!*"

The shout of a small boy carried over the loud main hall. Della looked up from where she'd been staring at her trencher to see Rab running across the floor toward the high table. The manor had come together for the morning meal, except for a few servants and guards who were on duty. Hearing a small sound, she glanced at Gunther on her right in distaste. He was licking grease from his fingers. To her left was her father, whom she refused to talk to out of principal, and on the opposite side of him was her intended. Lord Blackwell had chosen not to sit by her and they enjoyed the morning meal in relative hostility. She was relieved to have time to get her emotions under complete control and didn't want to have a repeat of their last meeting. Stretching her sore, raw hand, she grimaced. She shouldn't have taken her frustrations out on the wall.

Rab gasped for breath, his thin shoulders heaving

under his worn, brown tunic. Seeing the lower tables filled with soldiers, he skidded to a sudden stop, almost slipping in the rushes. Nervous, he eyed the gathered hall. Most of the knights continued to dine, ignoring the rambunctious lad. Suddenly, his gaze found Della and the boy seemed to relax.

"Rab, what is it?" Della couldn't help but give him a fond smile, knowing that he'd come to her in such a panic and not to one of the men. It just proved who the people thought was in charge.

"Go on, boy, out with it." Lord Strathfeld's voice was gruff. Chunks of half-chewed meat flew from his mouth at the command, some of it landing on her trencher. Della stiffened in her chair, gripping the arms for support. The hall quieted and all turned their attention to the boy.

Rab flinched. "Raiders, 'long the south section. Two o' the freeman…"

Della's breath caught in her throat, her body instantly weak with worry. She started to stand, instinctively wanting to ready her horse and ride out. Sensing movement at her side, she stayed seated, reminded of who was in her hall. Gunther looked at her thoughtfully. Brant didn't move as he watched the boy in silence. Her father frowned. If it was only her, she'd have ordered the men to their horses, but with her father home she didn't have the authority to do so.

Rab continued, "They're dead, m'lord. Burned alive!"

"To the exercise field, tell Roldan to ready the

men. Go now, boy!" Lord Strathfeld shot to his feet, the chicken he'd been eating still in his hand.

Della pushed her food away, no longer hungry as her mind raced with the news. Who had been killed? She knew most of the people who worked the land, if not all.

"M'lady?" Gunther asked quietly. "Do you know that child?"

"Yea," she answered in distraction. "That is Rab, a foundling boy. I let him help around the manor. His mother was killed by raiders years ago, when he was still a babe."

Gunther furrowed his brows, but said no more.

Sensing Brant's hot gaze on her, she turned to him. His attention made her nervous and she resented that he could unsettle her with just a look. The man was a stranger and yet his face was burned into her thoughts. All night, as she sat awake staring into a fire that reminded her of the red in his hair, she'd tried to think of ways to end the betrothment without hurting her people. She'd come up with nothing.

Brant was the first to look away. Lifting his cup, he drank the remainder of his ale and set the empty goblet on the table. Standing, he said, "Gunther, I will ready twelve men to ride with Lord Strathfeld. You stay here, lest you are needed. It is unwise to leave the manor unguarded."

Lord Strathfeld nodded as he dropped the chicken. "I am sorry to tell you, but this happens quite often. You might as well see the worst of it.

Besides, the ride will give me a chance to show you the extent of the south portion of Strathfeld land."

"Nay, father," Della interrupted with false pleasantness. "The raids only started again since you made known your intent to betroth me to Lord Blackwell. Edwyn and I had the raids under control. Aside of petty thievery, such things only occur once a year, and always during winter when traveling bands of rovers raid for food, not lives."

Lord Strathfeld grumbled under his breath about meddling women, but said nothing. He turned toward the door leading to the bailey yard. "I will meet you and your men at the stone bridge outside the gate, Lord Blackwell."

Her intended waited until the ealdorman was well from earshot. Then, turning slowly, he scowled. Della forced herself to meet his hard expression.

"Would you like to explain that comment, m'lady?" Brant's fists were tight at his sides.

"There is naught to explain, m'lord. It's just an observation that someone is not pleased with our match." She gave him an innocent look and his eyes narrowed into dangerous slits. "Or that someone wants to make the match appear more necessary than it is."

"Methinks m'lady would do well to watch her tongue," Brant warned, "lest I be tempted to watch it for her."

She snapped her mouth shut, but her eyes shot icy thorns in his direction.

"Gunther, stay close in the event your services are

needed," Brant ordered, "and keep Lady Della company. Make sure she stays out of mischief."

It is not I who needs the watching, you miserable boor.

Della clenched her teeth, but said nothing. She hated to admit that even now she wanted to touch him. The fact only served to enrage her more.

Gunther nodded. It was obvious he didn't look forward to the task of playing nursemaid to a sharp-tongued woman. Brant stormed off, following her father out into the bailey.

"M'lady, if I may offer some advice?" Gunther asked.

Della turned her icy stare to him. "Yea?"

"It's not wise of you to be too public in yer dislike of my lord. He is a generous man, but methinks you test yer limits too boldly." Gunther smiled at her. "It would be too bad if he were to make public his example of you."

"And if I may?" Della smiled back. She tried to stay angry, but couldn't in light of Gunther's puerile charm. The man had a way about him, even if he was part Norse. By the look of him, he had some Anglo-Saxon blood in him as well.

"Yea, m'lady." Gunther nodded in mock seriousness.

"It's not wise of you to take the attentions of too many maids at once. They are not likely to enjoy the competing. Methinks you test *your* limits too boldly."

Gunther's eyes rounded in obvious surprise at her astuteness and he laughed. "Yea, m'lady, mayhap you are right."

DELLA SPENT the day showing Gunther the grounds and introducing him to the people who worked them. As the soon-to-be seneschal, he needed to know how things were expected to run. She didn't want Lord Blackwell to think he could change their highly effective system once he was ealdorman. Della had worked too many hours to perfect it.

Besides, to her delight, she found out that Gunther was indeed only half Viking. His other half was Welsh and not at all offensive. She turned to smile at him as they passed the blacksmith's workshop.

"Old Alston has been blacksmith here since before I was born." She nodded to the man who turned a brilliant piece of metal over the hot coals. His hands were deftly precise, even in leather gloves. Behind him a large stove burned, making a wave of intense heat come from the half-enclosed building.

"M'lady." Alston waved hurriedly before turning back to his work.

"How is your throat?" She gestured with her hands to illustrate what she asked. "Have you been taking the honey?"

The old man nodded and waved to her with a smile.

She turned back to Gunther. "Poor Alston had a bad throat and could not talk for a fortnight. Finally, the midwife said to make him take two spoonfuls of honey a day until his voice came back. I don't know if it helped, but his voice did eventually start to come back." She again walked. "Oh, that man there, the one with the absurd covering on his head. That's Boothe. He's in charge of the stables and fancies himself an inventor of clothing, thus the headdress. The man he is talking to is Lamar. Lamar is the groundskeeper. Lamar's twin brother, Lamont, works in the kitchen with Isa. Lamar and Isa are married."

Gunther stopped, a look of widespread amusement on his face.

"What?" She put her fists defensively on her hips.

"It's remarkable how you know everyone and how they are connected. I know some ladies who do not even know the names of the servants who wake them in the morning."

"I have no respect for those women. I love the people who work here and would die for any one of them." She refused to be embarrassed by her convictions. "And, methinks, they would die for me."

"And Rab?"

"Yea, and Rab. While he is a foundling, it doesn't mean his life is less important than a child who has parents." She sighed in frustration, realizing she was getting agitated.

Gunther only smiled and continued to walk beside her in silence. He offered her his arm and she took it politely. Nodding to a few people, she inquired about their health and their families. Suddenly, she stopped and turned to him. "Why does Lord Blackwell lighten his hair? Is it a custom of his?"

"What?" He tried not to laugh and failed.

"His hair. Why does he lighten that red streak into the side of it?" She bit her lip. "Is his hair blond or red? And does the dyeing take him long to do? It seems a shame to waste much time on it, for there is naught to be done for him."

Gunther only laughed harder. Patting the hand that rested on his arm, he ignored her pointed attack on Brant's attractiveness. "That is not bleach, but how his hair grows. His mother named him Brant, meaning 'one of fire' because of it. They say he came from her belly in a blaze and has gone fiery to many women since."

"I see." Her jaw tightened as she got his meaning. Appalled, she thought, *Wretched, lecherous barbarian!*

Gunther cleared his throat, evidently having forgotten for a moment that he spoke to a lady. He had the decency to look embarrassed and started walking again, forcing her to continue on. "Would m'lady be so kind as to show me the work being done to the bailey walls?"

"Most certainly," Della answered stiffly, her good mood dampened. She wondered at the burning sensation in her chest as she thought of Brant with other women. Then, with a decided shake of her head, she determined that it most assuredly could not be jealousy.

Della spent most of the day with Gunther. Considering he was a loyal subject to Lord Blackwell, he was a pleasant enough companion. He'd been surprised at her knowledge of the fortifications. When she'd shown him the additional plans she'd designed for the castle, he seemed almost unable to accept that she, and not Lord Strathfeld, had designed most of the keep.

What is it with men? Why do they think they are the only ones with brains? And most of them with skulls so thick you could not even use their heads for carrying water.

Brant and Lord Strathfeld had been gone since the morning. She was glad they were away chasing raiders. It meant she didn't have to face her intended. She didn't think she could control herself quite yet. Invariably when she thought of his willful embrace, her body would grow hot again and she'd be plagued with unfamiliar sensations.

Damned pagan curse!

Judging from the information she'd gotten out of Rab, there was a terrible fire in one of the cotters. An elderly couple had been killed in the flames. Della was saddened by the news. She knew well the location of the fire and could deduce that her father and her intended would be returning shortly. Not wishing to be around when that happened, she hid in her room.

Ebba's loud knock sounded again on the door. Della had been ignoring it in hopes that the servant would think she slept and leave her alone, but the knock was persistent. Trying to hide her ire at being interrupted, Della stood and slid on a tunic to conceal her nightclothes.

Since it was still early in the eve, she hadn't yet

tried to sleep. Della hardly ever slept at night, or at all for that matter. It had been that way since childhood. Presently she'd been staring into the small fireplace, bemoaning her future in self-pity. If it were up to her, she would have continued to do so undisturbed. Ebba knocked again, louder and more insistent.

With a heavy sigh, she unlocked her bedchamber door. Her stomach was tied up in nerves. She'd locked the heavy oak to keep Brant out, lest he get it into his mind to keep his word and try to make her plead for his favors before the nuptials. Although, a nagging part of her doubted a mere lock would keep the barbarian out if he wanted to come in.

"Yea, Ebba?" Della was aggravated as she pulled open the door and looked out into the hall. She froze, seeing the white face of the young maid. "Ebba, what is it? What has happened? Is it my father?"

"M'lady, I'm sorry," Ebba said quietly.

Alarmed, Della looked behind the woman. A few torches lit the dim hall to reveal a small gathering of people. Amidst the throng was her father. She sighed with relief to see him. But then her eyes drifted to the grim countenances of Lord Blackwell and the few servants who stood behind him, and finally she detected the midwife, Serilda. The woman smiled at her. Della didn't care for the woman and took the smile with a sense of foreboding.

"Begone, Ebba," Della hissed. When the maid scurried from her sight, she put her hands to her hips and turned her cold, proud gaze to her father. "What is the meaning of this deception? Why send Ebba to bring me from my chambers? I would have answered your knock as readily as hers."

Lord Strathfeld scowled as he pushed his way into her bedchamber. He didn't answer her outburst. Brant followed the ealdorman inside. Della fumed, watching them in disbelief. Her mouth fell open as her father halfheartedly searched the bedchamber, as if looking for someone.

"What is the meaning of this deception?" Her virtue had never been in question as far as her father was concerned. Not even after he spent months away from the keep, leaving her to manage the household alone.

"Della," Lord Strathfeld's voice was strained. He refused to meet her eyes. "It is whispered that you are with child."

Blessed Saints! Blackwell thinks I carry Stuart's bastard. Is he so dimwitted to not understand a scheme when he hears one?

"I…" Her words trailed off. She glared accusingly at Lord Blackwell who stood with his arms crossed blocking the door. Not taking her eyes off him, she answered, "I am not."

So you thought to fill my father's head with nonsense today while you were out. Della gritted her teeth. She should have insisted on going with them.

"Tell the truth now and you will be spared the brunt of my wrath, tell me false and you will be punished." Lord Strathfeld shook and she knew he was holding back his anger. "It's a very serious matter, Della, so I will ask again. Do you carry a child?"

His words washed over her to form a pair of cold clamps over her heart.

"Nay!" She ignored Brant and turned to her father, grabbing his arm. "Nay, father. You know I don't lie. I'm not with child."

"I know for a fact that your honesty is undeniably in question," Brant said from behind her.

"Father, I do admit to telling one falsehood. I told Lord Blackwell that I carried Stuart's babe." She heard Brant's angry breathing and imagined his eyes piercing like daggers into the back of her skull. He shut the door, keeping her words from reaching the gossiping servants. Della didn't care who heard her. She was desperate. "It was foolish of me to do so, but you have to believe I did what methought I had to do for the sake of my future happiness. Nay, for the sake of my future sanity. I would that you reconsider your choice in husband for me. Why not let me marry Stuart? He is blood. He is the rightful heir to your title. King Guthrum has no reason to question our loyalty."

Having stated her argument, she dropped her hand from his arm. She didn't need to turn around to feel the fierce sting of Brant's presence smoldering her with his anger, as she purposefully continued to ignore him. The Viking king did have reason to question her loyalty to them as a race, but not that of Strathfeld's people or her father's, or Stuart's for that matter.

"It's a grave thing you have said, my daughter," the ealdorman stated when the couple refused to speak to each other. He looked at Brant and then at his daughter before sadly shaking his head. Walking to the bed, he sat.

For the first time, Della noticed how tired her father looked. He appeared old and battle-worn. His taut skin was drawn and gray against his once-virile face. It was as if he'd been ailing for some time and she'd just now noticed. Chewing on her bottom lip, she fought the sudden onslaught of tears as she realized how fragile her father had become. She'd been too self-absorbed in her own troubles with Lord Blackwell to notice.

Lord Strathfeld cleared his throat, appearing uncomfortable under his daughter's scrutiny. "And it's a grave thing to go against the wishes of your sire, but soon you will no longer have to answer to me. You will answer to your husband and I will gladly relinquish the control to him, for you are a willful child, Della. You always have been."

"Father, please—"

Lord Strathfeld held up his hand and shook his head. "Nay, daughter. This is something you need to hear. Your cousin is not an honorable man. Why you so foolishly throw him your affections is beyond my understanding. I have warned Lord Blackwell of Stuart's designs and he is willing to honor my wishes in that your cousin will not set a foot inside this keep while I still live. It will be up to your husband if you are to ever talk to or accept Stuart as a guest after I am gone."

Della looked at her father in astonishment. He

never before had cause to attack her character or that of her cousin. It had to be the barbarian's influence.

"Mayhap your willful ways are of my doing. You were not raised with the gentle hand of a mother. Mayhap I should have remarried for you to have an example to live by, but that is all in the past. It is too late to change." The ealdorman turned somberly to Brant. "Perchance you will remember that in the future when she acts out of hand. For it is not all her fault."

"Father?" Della had never seen him act like this. His words carried a surreal finality to them.

"Nay, Della." Lord Strathfeld stood. He refused to look at her, instead choosing to stare at the closed chamber door. "It's a grave thing you have done, trying to convince Lord Blackwell to renounce the betrothment. You will have to live with the consequences of your actions."

"Father?" She backed away from the two men. The fire grew hotter behind her and she stopped. Not daring to look at her intended, she whispered, "What do you mean to do?"

Lord Strathfeld looked wearily to Brant. "That is not for me to decide."

"What are you going to do to me?" she asked Brant, not bothering to hide her fear. Looking up at him through the sweep of her long lashes, she waited. He watched her intently, his face red with irritation. Her gaze moved to the firm set of his mouth. "Would you consummate the marriage now? In front of witnesses no less?"

"Nay," Brant answered. Relief flooded her, but she hid it quickly beneath an icy mask. The frown between his eyes deepened.

"Would you not marry me?" She was unable to keep the hopefulness from her voice.

"Nay, should you prove to be a maiden, we will be wed. If not…" Brant took a step toward her, his fists clenching and unclenching in an unmistakable effort to control his anger. "If not, we will discuss it at that time. But, make no mistake, we will still be wed."

Della nodded, well aware that he was letting her off easy. Legally, he could kill her for her insults to his reputation and no one would think less of him. He would only have to pay her father her worth as compensation and women really weren't worth much in the eyes of the law. Or he could marry her first and then kill her. He would owe nothing and he would still be Ealdorman of Strathfeld. Della paled at the thought. There were many ways for a husband to rid himself of an unwanted wife.

Brant turned to Lord Strathfeld and nodded. The ealdorman frowned, but didn't naysay the silent gesture. Della wondered what they were up to.

"So we are to wait then? To prove I'm not pregnant?" A calm relief came over her at the idea. It would be well over a fortnight before her woman's time happened again. It meant she had more time to prepare herself for the tragedy that was to be her life. With more time another out would present itself.

"Nay, the wedding goes on as planned providing

the outcome of your checking is satisfactory." Brant's expression shone with determination.

The relief drained slowly from her limbs to be replaced by first dread, then repulsion, and finally outrage. "You would not dare."

"Della!" her father warned.

"Yea, m'lady, I would dare much. It's time you were put in your place. I will not tolerate a faithless wife, in words or deeds. Heed my warning now." He stormed toward her and grabbed her by the arm. "If ever I catch you even thinking of playing me false, I will beat you repeatedly within an inch of your life."

She glanced at her father for help, but he shook his head and moved to go. The sharp bite of Brant's hand closed on her arm like a vise. Her father opened the door and waved the midwife and two servants inside the bedchamber to witness.

Father? Father, please don't leave me with him. Father? Father!

Della watched with wide eyes as Lord Strathfeld turned his back on her and shut the door behind him. Glancing at the servants, she didn't really see them. She wasn't sure what torture Brant had planned for her, only that it couldn't be good. Della turned her pleading gaze to the unyielding man at her arm. It would be useless to beg him and yet she tried. "Please. Don't do this, m'lord. Give me a chance to make it right."

.   .   .

BRANT'S RESOLVE slipped at Della's soft plea. He read the innocent fear in her eyes and in that moment was completely certain she was pure. But she'd put herself into this predicament. He had to have her maiden status proven. For when it was, all would think her dishonorable words were a desperate defense by a bride nervous of the wedding night. Such a thing would be laughed at and forgiven. If he did nothing, everyone would think ill of her and his children's legitimacy would always be wondered at—no matter if he claimed them for his own. And worse, they would think he was less of a man. Soldiers wouldn't follow a man who couldn't control a mere woman. They wouldn't trust him to be a strong leader.

"I am ready, m'lord," the midwife, Serilda, called from the bed.

He knew it was too late to stop the inspection. Without answering Della's plea for mercy, he stiffly dragged her to the bed by her arm. "Della, lie still. It will be over quickly. If you move it will hurt more."

She shook her head and tried to back away from him, but she couldn't wrench her arm from the force of his grasp. Her lips trembled. Again her words were a soft plea that only he could hear. "Don't do this. Please, don't."

"Turn yer backs," Serilda instructed the two maids bearing witness. "M'lady, lie down on the bed."

Brant waited until the maids complied, aware that his bride had no intention of moving. Her face had iced over with a look of foreboding. Her limbs stopped shaking and her eyes were eerily dry. He searched her cheeks for tears. Surely an alarmed woman would wail and cry out for mercy. There was nothing in her features, just a blank wall.

He led her to the bed by her unresisting arm and helped her to sit. Then he gently laid her on her back. Her behavior frightened him. Never had he thought his obstinate bride would become so docile, her breathing shallow and slow. She remained motionless as her eyes stared into the ceiling and then past it. The midwife lifted her dress.

Nay, Ice Princess, stay with me.

Brant couldn't help himself. His eyes hungrily devoured her as Serilda lifted her gown to expose her ankles, the delicate curve of her calves, the creamy white skin of her inner thighs. She was beautifully formed—not too athletic, not too soft. He wondered what it would be like to have her legs wrapped about his waist as he thrust wildly into her. The thought instantly brought to mind the day before, when he had been very close to doing just that.

Brant sighed as he touched her arm. She didn't respond, didn't seem to notice him. His heartbeat quickened in panic. He poked her harder and still she didn't move. Not even to flinch. When he lifted her arm slightly, it dropped once again to her side—lifeless.

The midwife kept Della's nightgown over the tops of her thighs for the sake of modesty, though the rest of her legs were laid out for view. Her feet were as still as stone, her legs didn't kick. She was like a corpse.

Serilda took a small, white, square piece of linen and handed it over to him for inspection.

Brant sat on the bed and edged closer to his bride. He nodded, acknowledging the linen was unstained. Again he caressed Della's arm in hopes of eliciting a response. He was disappointed.

The midwife took the cloth and wrapped it around two of her fingers. Spreading Della's legs a bit, she shoved it unceremoniously inside the noblewoman's still body. He frowned at the deliberate motion and unnecessary roughness, but there was nothing he could say. All words died in his throat.

Della let out a soft moan and moved her hand close to her temple to clutch her fingers open and shut on his arm. Her eyes rolled back into her head before she closed them. A single tear fell silently across her cheek.

Brant held her hand as the midwife worked, his heart going out to her. Her fingers kneaded into him. But, despite her suffering, she didn't let another sound escape her lips. Not knowing what to say, he delicately rubbed the pad of his thumb across her wrist. She felt so small and fragile and weak, nothing like the defiant woman who had faced him down but a moment before.

Finally, after what seemed like an eternity, the midwife withdrew the linen and held it up for his inspection. A small red stain glared at him from the square piece of material. He nodded, not saying a word. The midwife stood without drawing Della's dress down to cover her legs. Brant let out an exasperated sigh and quickly covered her thighs before the midwife called the maids to examine the cloth.

When Brant leaned back to look at Della, she glared accusingly at him. Her face was drawn and pale as she ripped her fingers from his hand. Without saying a word, she turned away from him and curled into a ball.

Brant moved to the door. He nodded to Lord Strathfeld, unable to get out more than a whisper. "It's done. She is pure."

Serilda held up the cloth for the ealdorman to see. Lord Strathfeld nodded and turned without speaking. He slowly made his way down the hall, looking nothing like the great war hero he was.

After the maids and midwife left, Brant shut the door and turned to the immobile woman on the bed. She hadn't moved. A small shudder racked her body, but she let no more tears fall from her cold eyes.

"Della?" His words were very soft as he went to her side. He leaned closer to better see her face, staring down at her. The faintest hint of where her tear had fallen showed on her cheek. He reached to brush the trail from her flesh, but her cold words stopped him.

"I will never forgive this." She rolled away from him.

Nodding, he realized she couldn't see the gesture. Stiff and awkward, he sat on the bed. He lifted his hand to her back and tried to comfort her. She pulled away from him, cutting him off. His hand fell to his lap and all words died before they were spoken.

It had been his intent to punish her and instead he felt as if he punished himself. Moving quietly, he left her, feeling guiltier than he ever had in his life. The image of her small, shuddering body haunted him. Exhausted, he closed the door to her chamber and moved down the hall to the stairwell. Then, hearing a noise, he stopped and listened. A hushed sob echoed from her bedchamber. The noise only added torture to his guilt-laden soul as he made his way belowstairs.

4

A WARM BREEZE swept over the bailey to stir the wayward strands of Della's hair, molding her tunic gown over her body. The glint of steel caught her eye as she gingerly fingered the cold metal of the new sword she'd been given to hold during the pagan ritual. It was a fine weapon with intricate carvings in the hilt. She only wished she knew how to wield it correctly. Mayhap then Brant would not be smiling so vaingloriously next to her.

"How hard could it be? Lift and swing," she mumbled to herself, moving it slightly so it drifted back and forth like a pendulum. "Lift and…swing."

Brant glanced briefly at her in amusement, a small smile curling beneath his short beard. Della snapped her mouth shut, realizing she'd muttered it loud enough for him to hear. He turned back to her father.

It was their wedding ceremony. Both of them had been bathed first in hot water and then again in cold, dressed, scented, and finally marched out into the bailey to stand before witnesses. Della found it odd that they were outside the chapel, rather than in it.

More pagan nonsense.

Brant wore a clean tunic, though it too lacked the proper embellishments of nobility and was cut in the barbaric style of his people. Belted at the waist, it fell to mid-thigh. The long sleeves were rolled at the wrists. She wondered why a man in his position didn't order adequate clothing sewn. Surely he had servants at Blackwell Manor who could have attended to it. It was embarrassing for him to be dressed so on this day and thus a vexation for her.

Della had avoided confrontation with him since he'd brought the midwife to her chamber. She was still sore, deep inside. Serilda's touch had been anything but gentle. Invariably, when she thought of it, Della would shudder with revulsion and feel violated anew. Though she had partly brought it on herself, she found it much easier to blame her intended. She had seen Brant only once since that time, briefly, while dining, but luckily their guests had started to arrive and she had not been forced to endure his presence.

"In light of the betrothal two nights past, Lord Blackwell did present me with the *handgeld,* or the *mundr* for our Viking guests." Lord Strathfeld stood next to Brant and shook his hand in confirmation of the receipt of payment for the hand of his daughter. "And as due to him, I present my daughter's *heiman fylgia,* her dowry."

Della turned an unamused stare to her father as he pronounced the Norse words, but said nothing. He didn't notice her displeasure as he smiled benevolently over the gathered throng. She had also refused to talk to him, feeling very much betrayed and very alone.

Della knew there was no turning back. The betrothal agreement between her father and her bridegroom was as binding as the marriage itself. If she were to refuse, Brant would have a legal claim to her father's land and title. Even if Lord Strathfeld were to refuse, King Guthrum could easily give it to Blackwell for him. She lifted her chin as she felt Brant step closer. The tangy scent of mint and rosemary drifted off his body. Della self-consciously edged away from him under the pretense of adjusting her sword.

"Since the death of my unborn son, I have only a daughter to leave my worldly possessions to. So, in light of my death, she will receive Strathfeld and all of its holdings to be held and managed in good faith by her husband, the future Ealdorman of Strathfeld." Her father paused in his speech, coughing and pounding himself on the chest.

Della clutched her hands together around the tang of the sword at the mention of her brother's death. A terrible ache stirred deep inside, almost choking her. She stared boldly forward, not letting her anguish show. The tears crystallized in her eyes before they ever had a chance to completely thaw. In truth, none would ever know if the babe had been a girl or boy, only that it had died along with her mother. The horrible memory stiffened her resolve against her soon-to-be husband.

"With the consent and blessing of our King Guthrum, I name Lord Blackwell, future Ealdorman of Strathfeld, the *only* heir to my title." Her father finished with another handshake to the bridegroom to seal the pact of trust.

Della stiffened as the witnesses cheered behind her. She adjusted her head rail of white gauze. Over the rail, she wore a crown of small purple flowers entwined with a halo of wheat. A wayward stalk kept poking the side of her head, causing her irritation to grow, and her mind drifted from her father's words, as he continued to speak.

Her wedding gown was new, but simple. It had been a gift from the serving maids and a surprise for Della, who was touched by the unexpected present. She hadn't bothered to order a new overtunic made for the occasion. It was edged with soft, pale blue embroidery and had wide sleeves that only went to her elbows. The bodice was snug and the skirt swung out over her hips to rest just above her ankles. Her undertunic was older, but still in fine shape. It hugged tight at the wrists, showing, along with the bottom hem of the skirt, from beneath the overtunic. A rounded neckline fit across her breasts, exposing the tops of them more than she would have liked. She caught Brant ogling her chest. Narrowing her gaze, she glared defiantly at him. His smile widened by small degrees.

If Della had been given her way, she would have

worn a gown of mourning, but Ebba had hidden the dress she'd laid out. Della also refused to talk to Ebba.

All of a sudden, Brant turned to her and grabbed her hand. Della choked down her surprise. She hadn't been listening to the ceremony. The formalities were over with and it was time for the exchanging of vows. His warm, large palm closed over her trembling fingers as he lifted them to his lips. Kissing her hand lightly, he stared deep into her eyes. Della could swear she felt his tongue flick quickly over her knuckles. He rubbed her wrist with the pad of his thumb, a trait she was beginning to associate with him. She shivered despite herself.

The fire of his touch started at her fingers and worked itself down her arm. Her heartbeat quickened. For a moment, she forgot who she was as she looked into the light pools of his eyes. They were the color of the heavens on a clear day, just after sunrise. She inhaled a ragged breath as his smile revealed perfectly straight, white teeth. His nose was proud and his lips...

Mmm, his lips. Della groaned inwardly as she remembered the feel of them on her breast.

The sun reflected off his long blond hair, making the red streak look as if it were a trail of flames. Rays of light glistened on his sun-bronzed skin. It was the first time she had looked at him with the aid of bright daylight. He was as handsome as rumored, which probably meant he'd had as many women as rumored.

Was it not Gunther who said he was born with a fire

between his legs? No doubt he has many mistresses awaiting him elsewhere.

Good, let him have his mistresses! Della shook herself back to reality. It would mean that Brant, the fiery one, would spend less time demanding his husband rights and more time in the arms of other women. Lifting her chin in defiance, she arched a brow and dug her fingernails into the back of his hand. If the marriage bed was anything like what she'd experienced at the hands of the midwife, she wanted no part of it.

Brant's eyes narrowed in displeasure, but his angelic smile stayed intact. He squeezed her hand tighter, causing her fingers to flex out in pain. Tears sprang to her eyes.

Gunther stepped forward and handed Brant an old sword, which he took in his free hand. Turning back to Della with the weapon he presented the hilt to her. She eyed it with a sneer.

"For our oldest son. To be kept in trust by you until he is old enough to wield it. And to then be passed on to his wife and in turn our grandchildren. It is a symbol of our ancestors and the continuation of the bloodline. May we be blessed with many, *many* children." His voice was strong and confident as it rang over the onlookers. The Vikings cheered in approval and the few Anglo-Saxons who attended peered at each other in confusion over the strange declaration of words.

Brant grinned impishly as he let go of her hand so she could take the offered sword. Her fingers throbbed as she tried to grab the heavy hilt. The unexpected weight of it brought the tip crashing to the ground. Della dragged it to her side and a few men chuckled behind her. Her bridegroom smiled his irritating smile.

Brant watched her expectantly as he held out his hand to receive her sword. Della took a deep breath, all the while cursing his pagan ways. Using her wrist, she hugged the old sword to her waist and flexed her fingers. Her hand throbbed as the blood slowly returned to the crushed appendage. Staring at him for a long moment, she lifted the new sword to him blade first.

Brant gave her a look of warning and she in turn gave him an expression of innocence. Her tone even, she repeated the words that she had been forced to memorize earlier. "And for you, m'lord, a symbol that I am no longer my father's, that I am yours. For you to protect me in times to come and in turn to protect our *child* and our home."

BRANT'S SMILE WIDENED, hiding his relief that she hadn't refused to speak and thus cause another scene. In truth, Della didn't speak the traditional vows of the exchanging of the swords, but he thought the ones he'd made up for her were more appropriate. They were to be a reminder of his expectations of her. Only Gunther, who chuckled quietly behind him, noticed the alteration. He tried not to let his amusement show as the crowd hushed for the couple's exchanging of vows to satisfy the church.

Digging into the pocket of his tunic, he grabbed a ring and slipped it onto the hilt of his new sword. He studied her for a moment, feeling guilty for what he had put her through and cursing the midwife for not being a little more sensitive to his bride. Della was a maiden after all. He wondered if she was still sore from the examination.

Would you let me soothe that ache, Ice Princess?

His bride was indeed ravishing—except for her constant icy scowls. For a moment, he'd thought he had seen her softening toward him. But no, he admitted to himself in disappointment, it was clear she held no tender thoughts of him. In time, he hoped her angry heart would calm so they may live peaceably together. Although divorce was traditionally accepted amongst his people, it was not allowed so readily by the Christian church.

"I, Lord Blackwell, future Ealdorman of Strathfeld, take thee, Lady Della of Strathfeld, to be my wedded wife..." He continued with his vows, watching Della's face as he spoke. She didn't move.

When he was done, Della took the ring from the hilt of the sword and slipped it on her finger without looking at it. She shot him an expression of annoyance. Brant tried not to be hurt by her blatant disinterest in his gift. Swallowing visibly, she repeated his words back to him in a hushed voice. After she had spoken, the crowd was quiet, obviously not knowing she'd finished. A priest cleared his throat and held up his arms. Saying his quick blessing over Lord and Lady Blackwell, he bade them to kiss and seal the union. Della paled, her eyes traveling to his lips.

Brant leaned in to Della, watching as she shot a sidelong glance to her father. Lord Strathfeld started coughing. As Brant moved his lips to join with hers, she sharply turned her head to the left, causing him to miss her mouth and instead kiss the tip of her ear. He grated his teeth in irritation as he heard the assembly chuckle with laughter. Grabbing her by the shoulder, he was intent on giving the crowd a good show.

"Nay!" Della struggled against him, unable to break his grasp. She sought his gaze, panicked as she pushed at his chest. "My father!"

Brant glanced to Lord Strathfeld in bafflement. The older man's face had turned a grotesque shade of yellow. His lips were edged with blue. The ealdorman fell forward. Brant let go of his wife. She rushed to the man's side to catch him, getting pummeled by his heavier weight.

"Father!" Della eased the man to the ground the best she could. The head rail was knocked from her hair so the strands flew freely in the breeze to tangle around the fallen man. Unmindful of the damage the dirt did to her wedding tunic, she kneeled on the ground. "Please, someone get help."

The throng of people burst into chaos. Brant motioned to Gunther, knowing he'd understand his silent command to go after Serilda. She was the only one at the castle who had knowledge of the healing draughts.

Kneeling beside his wife, he lifted Lord Strathfeld out of her arms. Della stood, hovering next to her father. Brant noted her stricken features as tears worked their way into her eyes.

"Della, let us get him inside." Brant kept his voice soft.

He motioned to some nearby soldiers for assistance. After they hoisted the fallen ealdorman up, Brant helped to carry the man abovestairs. Glancing back, he saw a tear slip down Della's face. A maid picked up her headpiece and several more hurried forward to try to dust off her gown. She grimaced as she shooed them away, moving to follow her father.

DELLA WAS A MARRIED WOMAN, despite the minor formalities they had yet to complete. For the most part, the worst was over—at least publicly. She'd given her word, bound herself to the barbarian. In doing so, she'd assured her noble place, assured protection for her people, assured the Viking king would look upon them in favor. And she'd assured that happiness would never be hers.

After Lord Strathfeld's collapse, her husband had carried her father abovestairs to his bedchamber. He didn't look well and Serilda had said he might not last the night. Lord Strathfeld had been insistent they hurry back belowstairs and finish the formalities, so none might later claim the marriage was not legal before his death. Della hated to leave his side, but with his insistence she had obeyed. Already, she'd upset her father enough in the last several days and now berated herself for not talking to him. How selfish and foolish she had been not to see past her own anger and insecurities.

When she came down, the feasting had already begun. Gunther had been good enough to tend to the guests in their stead. She could see how he was a good man to have around, despite his numerous liaisons with the servants.

Brant made a few polite announcements regarding her father's health and for once she was glad there was someone to take over for her. It didn't mean she liked her barbarian husband, but even she could admit to being grateful. She didn't know what she was going to do without her father. He was the only family she had left, not counting Stuart. For all she knew, her new husband would forbid her from ever seeing her cousin again.

Not that his forbidding will do any good, she assured herself.

Plastering a false smile on her features, she stood at the high table, looking over the feasting wedding guests, pausing to nod regally to her father's friends as they lifted their cups in her direction. She let her gaze travel over the crowd and concentrated to keep her agony from her face. In truth, she didn't know many of the guests. There were the servants, knights, and a handful of nobles who'd fought with her father. She even could distinguish a few of the men who fought under Brant, Vikings all of them. They had been lurking about the manor since her husband's arrival.

The eve wore on mercilessly. Her muscles were bunched into hard knots and it felt as if her stomach was on fire. Several times one lord of something or the other would venture to the high table to give words of congratulations and ask the proper questions of the ealdorman's health. Della said nothing as Brant dutifully answered the queries.

Traveling minstrels played a lively tune, prompting some of those in the hall to dance. Others drank and gamed with vigor. She directed a withering look at a few of the maids who brazenly consorted with the robust male visitors. Della could not stop them from finding a bed partner to share the night with and they would not seek her approval before doing so.

Men at the lower tables devoured the feast, spitting the bones and waste onto the floor like mad dogs. The rushes were already soiled and she knew the stone beneath them would have to be limed, a horrible chore that would take all of a morning to complete. She shivered in disgust, having worked so hard to keep her home clean only to watch her hall destroyed.

A grim-faced man standing in the back of the hall caught her attention as he glared at the guests. He was the only person not visibly enjoying himself. Della nodded to him and smiled.

"Who is that?" Brant asked suspiciously.

Della grimaced as he addressed her, refusing to look at him. It didn't help. She could still see the piercing gaze of his blue eyes clearly in her mind. "Perchance it is another lover. Would you like to have me checked again this night? Mayhap Serilda did not do it good enough the first time."

"Della," Brant warned.

"He's my father's seneschal, Edwyn, and he is just arrived from visiting King Guthrum. My father had him personally deliver the news of our impending nuptials and the completion of the betrothal agreement, as per request of the king."

Brant nodded, visibly relaxing at the explanation. He didn't comment on her abrupt tone.

"And afore you accuse me of aught else, Edwyn is an honorable man. He's only a friend to me and has helped me to manage this keep while my father was away." She shot her husband a sidelong look from beneath her lashes. "Besides, he's rather aged don't you think?"

Gunther interrupted their conversation and drew Brant's attention away from her. She didn't understand the words they spoke in their shared foreign tongue. Ignoring them, she discreetly motioned Edwyn to her side. The older man nodded and made his way to the high table.

"Edwyn, it's good you are back with us." Della presented her hand to him, which he took briefly.

"M'lady." Edwyn nodded.

"Have you been to see my father?" Della's question came out in a rush, belying her uneasiness. She kept her features calm in case anyone looked at her.

"Yea, m'lady. He bid me to bear witness to the completion of the ceremony and report back to him." Edwyn sighed. She forced herself to look over the hall with a slight smile she didn't feel. "It would seem he is not doing too well. I told him to seek the help of healers nigh on three sennights ago, but you know yer father. He would not hear of it."

"You knew he was sick?" Della was unable to keep the pain from her voice. She moved an unconscious hand to his arm. "Why did you not tell me?"

"Lord Strathfeld was wounded at Martin. We thought he would heal, but after a time, the wound just got worse. M'lord has been fighting to see this day and is very proud of you. No one was told of the illness. He was afraid if the news was revealed before you were wed, Sir Stuart might try to intercede and make a move fer the title. And, m'lady, Lord Strathfeld is well aware of yer fondness fer yer cousin."

Della nodded as she fell back into her seat, weak with the realization of her father's scheme. Finally it made sense to her—the hasty engagement, the push for a quick wedding, her father's desire to please the Viking king. In her father's mind, he was protecting her from an uncertain world. She knew Lord Strathfeld believed that they had a force to reckon with in the new King of Wessex. And she also knew it was impossible to change political loyalties at this juncture. Her father had agreed to the marriage to ensure she had the protection of the Viking armies behind her if the war was to spread itself into Northumbria once more.

For if Lord Strathfeld's dying act was to give his title to a respected warrior of the Viking army, then King Guthrum would remember him kindly, and in turn, would feel a debt to keep his daughter safe. This arranged marriage wasn't because her father actually liked the Viking barbarian at her side.

Nay, perchance he doesn't favor him over me at all. He was only trying to protect me. What a sweet, diligent father I have and what a poor, ungrateful excuse for a daughter I have been.

Tears welled in her eyes and Edwyn quickly sat beside her. He leaned to her, refusing to touch her lest the guests or her new husband construe his attentions as unseemly. "M'lady?"

"Oh, Edwyn, I have been such a spoiled child." Shutting her eyes tight, she lifted her balled fist to her lips and bit her knuckle hard to keep from crying.

"Nay, m'lady, Lord Strathfeld knows well yer reason fer not wanting to marry a Norseman. He understands the pain you still carry in yer heart and is sorry fer it." Abruptly Edwyn sat up and looked over her shoulder. "Mayhap this is not the time to discuss such private matters, m'lady."

Della nodded, realizing her husband must be listening.

"Della?" Brant confirmed her suspicion.

"Yea, Lord Blackwell?"

Brant laid a gentle hand on her arm. Edwyn nodded in approval of Lord Blackwell's concern. Della frowned at the seneschal.

"Is all well?" Brant asked.

Della didn't have the energy at the moment to fight his touch. She took a calming breath before turning to him. "Yea, m'lord, all is well."

Brant studied her watery eyes. Slowly he nodded, accepting her answer.

"M'lord, you stare like a commoner. Mayhap you could direct your eyes elsewhere." Della snapped to her senses and pulled her arm away. Her weakness embarrassed her. She stood up to face their guests and imagined she could feel Brant glaring at her. He would not like her public show of distaste. After a few moments, he stood and moved as if to talk to her.

Della ignored him and lifted up the wedding *kasa*. She studied the bowl-like vessel. It had two large handles on each side and a strange Viking symbol of a hammer engraved into it. It looked very old, even for bronze, and had already been filled with dark ale when she'd arrived at the high table.

It was customary for the bride and groom to drink from the same cup for four sennights after the nuptials, at least whenever they were together at the high table. Usually the one larger wedding goblet was set before them with liquor, but they were permitted to have their own smaller goblets. It was a formality only, but one that must be adhered to, otherwise the wedding was not considered legally binding.

The crowd quieted some in respect to watch the couple. She nodded to Edwyn, who had once more made his way to the back of the hall, before presenting the cup to her husband. Brant's strong fingers lightly brushed hers as he took the cup from her. Della felt the unfamiliar shiver begin in her hands, only to work its way to aflame her stomach with a strange kind of fire. He held the two handles as he took a small taste. A look of confusion passed over his face and he hesitated before swallowing.

Once he set down the cup, Della picked it up to hurriedly take her drink. The ale was thick and overly salty. She set the *kasa* down and turned to Brant, who studied her with a look of extreme repentance.

"Would you explain the drink, m'lord?" The salty taste still stung her mouth and she wished another drink were nearby. "Is it another pagan custom? Perchance made from sheep dung and grass?"

Brant shook his head. A somewhat mischievous smile curved his lips. "Nay, m'lady. It is made from the sow's blood that was sacrificed in honor of the Norse Goddess, *Freyja*, to bless our union with many children."

"Do you waste a good sow for such purposes?" Della fumed.

"Nay, it is being eaten by the wedding guests." Brant didn't take his eyes off her.

Then the truth of his words hit her. He had made her drink sow blood? Della turned to the *kasa* and then back to Brant. All tender gratitude she had been feeling for his help with her father, though it had been little, slowly slipped away.

"You are a despicable, detestable, miserable boor." Della kept the pretense of a smile on her features. "I will not drink this for the next two fortnights."

At her words, Gunther, who was still to her husband's side, turned a disapproving look to Brant. It was obvious he didn't think much of Della's sharp tongue.

"It is only required this one time." Brant strained to suppress his amusement. "Besides, it could have been a goat."

"I would see my father this night."

"Your father insists we finish so there can be no doubt as to our union. I gave him my word and I will keep it."

"Could we please get this farce over with?" Della turned from him in dismissal.

"Noble guests," Brant announced, stopping her. His tone had turned serious. "We are grateful you have shared in our day. It would appear we are to leave the festivities early. My new bride is anxious to…" He paused. Della couldn't move. "To make the match binding."

The meaning in his words was clear and the inebriated crowd cheered out lewd suggestions as Della's face turned red. Mortified, her mouth opened as her eyes darted to Brant. A smug look lined his features.

If you, m'lord, want a battle of the wills, then you have just met your match in a woman! Della swore she would repay him for this insult.

A crowd of giggling, eager women rushed the high table before she had a chance to rebut his claim.

Hands grabbed her, pushing and pulling as they led her from the great hall. She didn't recognize some of their faces. With the suggestions of the men ringing loudly behind her, the women forced her toward the stairwell.

"*Della the Cold*, it seems her ice has melted after all!"

"If it's too hard a task, m'lord, I would be willing to do it fer you!"

"Nay, Lord Blackwell knows well how to sheathe his sword!"

"It would seem Lady Blackwell has heard that as well!"

Della was repulsed by their blatant disrespect. They kept up with their vulgar remarks, only shouting louder once she disappeared into the stairwell. The women giggled at the overbold men, a few even whispering their own unblushing suggestions for the bride. A persistent wave of hands pushed at her, forcing her toward the bedchamber. And, ringing loud above the entire commotion, she heard the irritating sound of her husband's lusty laughter.

"IT WOULD APPEAR the maiden has not softened yer mood."

"I would be better off with my mistress in Jorvik." Brant said to Gunther, even as he stared at the stairwell. He had tried to let her outbursts pass unpunished, for she had much on her mind with her father's illness. Clearly, she hadn't been told of Lord Strathfeld's condition beforehand. But as she'd tried to walk away from him as if she were too good to be in his presence, he couldn't help the plan that formed in his head. No matter how sorry he felt for her, he could not allow her public insolence to continue. There were too many eyes on them, too much at stake. One wrong look, one wrong act on his part and he would have more headache then he needed. If it had been anyone else but Gunther, he wouldn't have admitted his irritation over Della's actions. "My bride is a shrewish wench."

"It's not so bad—" Gunther laughed at the skeptical look Brant gave him, drawing curious attention to them. Lowering his tone, he said, "She is more beautiful than rumored and I should think you would like a bit o' fire between the linens."

"Yea, she is beautiful, but her beauty does have an awful spite to it." Brant took a pitcher from a passing maid and lifted it to his lips, gulping down the contents. When he finished, the maid was giggling. Handing it back to her, he said to his friend, "I am sorry for her sadness over her father, but I will not disrespect the wishes of a dying man to ease the displeasure of a quick-tempered woman. I promised to make this union work. The shrew is about to meet her match."

5

DELLA HUDDLED BENEATH A THICK COVERLET, teeth clenched in apprehension. The women, unfamiliar with the abovestairs of the keep, hadn't thought twice about following her direction to her own bedchamber and not her husband's. Though she'd protested every step, nothing she said could have spoiled their good humor. They giggled at her attempts to stay their hands as they quickly, and with surprisingly expert skill, undressed her. One plump, elderly woman even pinched the flesh of her backside.

She had never been seen naked by so many curious eyes and had tried to cover herself with her hands. When that didn't work, she'd taken one of her sleeping gowns from her trunk. The act only seemed to amuse the women more, as they laughed harder and suggested she wear nothing at all.

With the women gone, it was only a matter of time before the men arrived with Lord Blackwell. Seconds blended with minutes until she had no idea how long she waited. Every slight noise made her jump with alarm.

The bedchamber was uncommonly cold even with the fire blazing in the small hearth. Within the flame danced images so haunting that she couldn't look away. The first was that of a fiery red streak through pale blond. Then of her husband's supple lips under his beard and his clear, summer sky eyes behind the sweep of his lashes. She tried, but could not banish him from her thoughts and she hated herself for it.

What is wrong with me? I refuse to be attracted to a Viking. I cannot be. Another thought occurred to her and she slapped the flat of her hand against her temple. *The drink!*

"The lout has woven one of his pagan spells over my senses," Della said to herself in vexation. "That loathsome, ignorant son of a pig! That...that... *Argh!*"

That is why I still smell his scent of mint and horses, of earth and man. He put me under a spell!

Hitting the padded straw mattress in frustration, she shivered anew. The memory of his scent drifted over her as if he were there. She bit her lip, rubbing the top of her thigh through the coverlet. The spell tempted her to accept what it offered and, for a single moment, she let the thought of her husband over-whelm her.

Closing her eyes, she gently touched her lips with the pads of her fingers. She wondered what his mouth would feel like against hers. What untold promises did his hands hold for her, as he caressed the entire length of her form? Had he not said he intended to do just that?

Della ran her hand over her cheek and down her throat, imagining that it was his caress touching her. The erratic beat of her heart sounded in her ears. An ache started in her body, an unfamiliar longing that set a fire within her stomach and caused her thighs to tingle.

From the back of her mind, she heard a faint scream. It was her mother's voice, telling her to stop, to fight the curse he put over her. She jolted at the terrifying sound. It was so real that it drowned out even the loud crackling of the fire. Balling her hand, she forced herself to remember her mother's face, to hear her cries for help. A tear slipped over her cheek. Time had faded much, but the impression of her mother's death, the knowledge of it, was still there. She'd been young when she witnessed it, but not so young as to forget that Viking barbarians had killed the woman. And now her father was in the other room, dying. She should be with her father, not sitting on a bed waiting for her louse of a Viking husband.

She twisted the ring Brant had given her around her finger, not taking it off. A thin band of bronze with a polished piece of amber in the middle was an odd choice in wedding bands. Most noblewomen received thin threads of gold and large jewels. The weight felt awkward on her finger, like a shackle. It would be a constant reminder that she now belonged to her husband—from daughter to wife and no say in between.

Part of her irritation was because the king would not let her inherit the responsibility of the manor, despite the fact she'd been solely in charge of every decision for the last five years. Della knew every inch of the keep, every page of every ledger, every villager, every animal, and every season. She knew every child, every illness, and every memory. And now everything was being taken from her.

After what seemed like both an eternity and a second, she heard the boisterous throng of men leading her husband to her. Della cringed as they opened the door to Brant's bedchamber. She should have been waiting for him there, but she could not bring herself to leave the comfort of her room.

Mayhap the oafs will get lost, she hoped.

"Nay, it's empty!" a man crowed. His drunken words echoed loudly over the clamor of men. "Mayhap the Lady of Ice has melted away completely."

You drunken lout! Della felt like screaming. She nestled deeper beneath the coverlet. It wasn't her fault she had to be tough to run the manor. How else would the men follow the direction of a mere woman? Tears rushed to her eyes anew. *I'm not cold-hearted. I'm not!*

The men came nearer and their insults grew as they encouraged each other on, remarking on her icy nature, claiming how Lord Blackwell best be careful lest she freeze parts of his body off. The last drew a heated debate between them on whether she would melt or Brant would freeze.

"Methinks the maiden is hiding from you, Brant!" Della recognized Gunther's taunting voice.

She clutched the linens and held them to her chin, the texture rough against her palm as she agitated her fingers. Keeping her eyes on the door, she willed the men to lose their way, but eventually the light from their torches shone beneath the frame. They'd found her.

Della refused to look as the door was thrown open. A gush of cool air filled the room, making her stiffen in dread. For a long time, she didn't move amidst the robust jests. When finally she looked, she saw her husband. Some of the men were pulling at his tunics, baring his strong stomach and sides.

She sucked in a deep breath and held it, letting her eyes roam from his delectably flat stomach, up his muscled chest, to his thick neck. For a man of his large size, there wasn't a single ounce of fat on him. A small trail of darker hair grew seductively below his navel, leading a downward path into his tight fitting braccas. His feet were bare.

Unsure, she quickly brought her gaze to his face. He had the same aggravating smile that often graced his lips when he looked at her. The men pushed at Brant's back. Her stomach turned, fear choking her as he loomed forward.

"Into bed with you," Gunther yelled, drunkenly wielding his goblet like a sword as he forced Brant to the bed with the tip of his empty cup. Turning to Della, he winked audaciously.

To her horror, she realized her inebriated husband swayed on his feet, appearing very close to passing out. She wrinkled her nose in disgust. The action only made him laugh as he suggestively wagged his brows.

"Do you fret, Della?" Brant slurred. He stumbled to the right only to be caught by a toothless peasant and pushed back to standing. His hands strayed to the waistband of his braccas and he slid his finger along it, drawing her eyes over his rippled stomach. "It will be fine. I will not be too drunk to tend you proper."

The men cheered their approval. Her eyes rounded. She watched his inept fingers fumble with his lacings. Much to her relief, he gave up his task and swayed once more to the right.

"Nay," was all she managed to get out. She felt the blood draining from her face as she lifted her hand to keep him back.

"It will be fine," Brant said, his slurred tone trying to soothe her. He blinked slowly, frowning at her deathlike grip on the coverlet. "It's only a few drinks I had."

"Nay, more like a few dozen!" one of the men offered with a bawdy chuckle.

"A groom could little refuse a toast." Brant stumbled toward the bed. "Come give us a kiss, lady wife. I have a fire in my belly for you to tame."

"Nay. Methinks it is more like a fire in your addled brain," Della spat.

"You'd better tame the wench, m'lord, lest she eats you alive!" Gunther chortled uncontrollably as he fell against the frame of the door.

"Nay, Gunther, it's what I want. To be eaten alive." His smile softened. "It will be an agonizing death, but worth it if done by those pink lips. What says you, lady wife? Would you like to dine on my naked flesh?"

Her mouth fell open at his words, knowing there was a hidden meaning in them. She just wasn't sure what that meaning might be. Brant leapt onto the bed, straddling her with his massive legs. The weight of him pressed her down into the mattress. The intoxicated men fell all over themselves in fits of laughter. She tried to glare at them, but she couldn't force her eyes away from Brant as he swayed above her. It became clear the drunken crowd had no intention of leaving and missing the show.

Brant grabbed her roughly by the shoulders and pulled her mouth to his. Whiskers scratched her face and she wanted to push him away, but her hands were trapped against his chest. A startled moan escaped her as his lips moved sloppily against hers. She clamped her mouth shut and a trail of his spit trickled down her chin, dripping onto her cleavage. She tried to jerk her head to the side to loosen the hold he had on her. The movement only encouraged Brant to rub his slobbery mouth more insistently. Only when he was ready to let her go was she able to slip her mouth from his.

Brant drew away to the cheers of the onlookers.

Della wiped her wet mouth on her sleeve. Her husband looked quite pleased with himself, as she shuddered in what could only be defined as revulsion.

"Methinks she likes it!" Brant hollered. The men cheered louder.

"Mayhap, you should let me try, m'lord. Methinks she would like it better!"

Della grimaced at the possibility, for the man who said it was a fat, balding creature with only one tooth in his mouth and that one was close to rotting. Unconsciously, she leaned closer to Brant's chest. His muscles tightened in surprise before he wrapped a protective arm about her shoulder. As she trembled next to the warmth of him, she saw a slight smile curl his lips before he pushed her to his side, twisting his body to keep her from view of the others.

"Methinks not," Gunther said at her reaction.

"Begone!" Brant shouted in drunken ardor. He waved his free hand toward the door, not letting go of Della. His shoulder pressed her cheek. "Enough show fer you this eve."

The men grumbled as Gunther ushered them out, shutting the door, but it was clear by the uproar that they still stood on the other side. Della fiercely pushed at Brant's arm. He chuckled as he turned his attention to her. Gazing down at her, his eyes intent, he let her go.

"Take off yer gown, lady wife," Brant demanded loudly. "Let me see yer—"

"Get off me, you lewd oaf," Della screamed,

interrupting his vulgar words. She swatted at his wandering hands. "Begone!"

The men pounded their amusement on the door.

"Take it off or I'll spank yer bony arse!" Brant moved to pull at her gown again. "Would you like that, lady wife? To be spanked?"

The men cheered and Della heard Gunther urging them away. Brant leaned forward and gently nuzzled her throat. His whiskered mouth tickled her skin in light caresses. This time his lips were dry as they kissed her, gentle and light. Della let out a yelp of alarm and pushed, to no avail, against his fixed shoulders. His caressing mouth was oddly enticing against her, much like his hands had been. Her eyes rolled back in her head in a near swoon.

Nay, more, she groaned inwardly.

"Pagan!" This time she didn't push as hard against him. Her arms weakened to his touch and her head swayed to the side in submission. Lashes fluttered low over her eyes, almost flitting completely shut, until he suddenly stopped. Della blinked in momentary confusion.

Sighing, he leaned back to study her face. A devilish smirk lined his lips. "So tell me, lady wife, would you like to be spanked?"

"What?" she whispered. His blue eyes studied her attentively. He wasn't drunk at all. "How dare——"

"Nay, Della." Brant laughed, holding his hands up in defense as she swatted at him. Chuckling, he tapped her gently under the chin and climbed off her.

"Enough of your sharp insults. They are disagreeable and make my head swim."

"Why would you try to humiliate me like that?" She pulled the linens once more to her chin. Tears came to her eyes and she tried not to feel the disappointment that surged forth. "You use me for the merriment of your friends."

"Oh, my darling little Ice Princess." He looked at her as if the answer should have been obvious. "So the bedding would be believable. So your reactions would be real. Do you think you could have gotten over your aversion of me long enough to pretend to be a loving wife?"

"You could have told me," Della fumed, not liking his nickname for her. "I understand what is at stake. I'm not a fool. Not like you, Brant the Thorn in my Arse!"

"Methinks not, lady wife." He smiled. "Though if it is me in your arse you are interested in, I should be most willing to comply."

"Nay, you disgusting pig. It is a sin to even think such thoughts." She slapped at his hand as he reached toward her and gave him her most withering look. "And quit calling me lady wife, it is annoying. I'm done playing your sick, heathenish games. I would see my father now."

"Have you forgotten about the bedding? The others will notice if we leave too quickly." Brant was unruffled by her protests as he leaned to nuzzle her neck. "As long as we have to wait, would you like to beg me now for my touch?

Mayhap another kiss? I promise I can melt your ice with my fire."

"I will never beg for your touch and, as to my ice, there in naught your fire can do to it. My ice could easily put out your flame. If you don't believe me, try putting a torch in cold water sometime. See which comes back the victor." She again swatted at his playful hand and moved away from him to stand beside the bed. "You will have to ravish me."

"That could be arranged, since you seem to be so fascinated with the prospect." His tone was low and exact. The smile faded from his eyes, replaced by irritation. "Shall I use a knife to keep you to my will? A sword? Battle-axe? Large stick?"

"You would not dare." She took a hasty step back. The room was suddenly too small.

"Mayhap I will just use my heathen, brute force. Do you think you could fight me off?" Brant shifted to his knees, presenting her with his broad, naked chest. Muscles rippled under his tanned skin and she gulped at his leering expression. "You are the one who said I was naught but a barbarian. Shall we see all that I am capable of?"

She stumbled back, her mouth gaping open. It would be impossible to fight him off. He would crush her if she were to try.

He held his arms wide. "Come, sweet Della, soothe the fire in my belly with your pleasantness. I long for the honeyed melodies of love that fall so freely from your wifely mouth and the tender passions of your touches—"

"You are a lewd man to discuss such things at length." She covered her ears. "Can you think of naught else?"

Throwing his head back, he laughed dryly and dropped his arms. When he finished, he gracefully slid from the bed. Della shivered as he loomed toward her. If he attacked her with his 'brute force' there was nothing she could do to stop him. She came up against the door, pulled her hands from her ears and blindly searched for the latch.

"Nay, I don't think I would have to ravish you." He moved his fingers to her rapid pulse, stroking her chin with his thumb. "If you would but give me a moment, I could show you all of what your body is capable. I could show you how mistaken you are about my touch."

"I don't understand you." Della shivered at the sensual caress and forgot what they had been arguing about. Her mouth suddenly feeling dry, she licked her lips. She hadn't enjoyed his sloppy kiss, yet she found herself oddly drawn to try it again.

Had his lips been so inept on my body? Why had I not noticed?

"It would appear I'm not such the barbarian." He growled, dropping his hand and putting space between them. "For I have never brought an unwilling maiden to my bed and you, lady wife, are the most unwilling I have yet to behold."

Confused by his words and by the disappointment that unfurled in her at his withdrawal, she shook herself back to reality. She should have been happy that he was showing self-control. But she wasn't.

Brant smiled when she didn't speak, but the expression was bitter. He picked his tunic up from the floor. "They think I'm drunk so it's been long enough. Let us attend your father before my barbarian instincts come back to me and I'm forced to grant your wish."

He didn't look at her again. He nudged her aside and grabbed the latch, forcibly swinging the door open. Della stumbled out of the way at his abrupt departure. He stormed down the hall. Grabbing a plain overtunic from her trunk, she slipped it over her head.

"Stupid barbarian."

BRANT STALKED barefoot from the bedchamber, not bothering to see if his wife followed. His entire body shook with the force of his rage and with the power of his unfulfilled appetites. As far as everyone was concerned, the wedding was completed. No one would question their union.

Though he was tempted to find a maid to relieve his desires, he knew he couldn't. He would have to take care of the matter himself, quickly, before he went to see the ealdorman. Still aggravated, he went to his bedchamber. This was not how a wedding night should be.

THE EALDORMAN'S bedchamber smelled of pungent herbs, animal fat, and the smoke that curled from pots of burning incense. Della stood just inside the door, trying not to choke on the overbearing odor. She waited as Serilda gathered her healing draughts. The woman blocked her view of her father and Della shifted, trying to get a glimpse of him under the soft glow of candlelight. The room was quiet, save for the movements of the midwife. After what she had gone through at the woman's hand, Della found it difficult to look at her. Serilda strolled past and she heard the woman giggle, but the moment was so brief she wasn't sure it actually happened.

Della became aware of Brant's presence close to her back. She hadn't seen him in the passageway as she went to her father's chamber and had been surprised when he wasn't already there. It was odd, but she drew some comfort from his presence, like a newfound strength within herself.

She hesitated before stepping into the darkened room, only turning to glance at Brant when she could no longer feel his heat. He'd changed his tunic and put on a pair of shoes. As Serilda closed the door, Della continued to move toward her father. There was much she wanted to say to the dying man, but it was impossible with Brant in the chamber. Her father's eyes were closed. She shivered. The ealdorman had somehow been reduced to a fraction of the healthy man she'd spent most of her life idolizing. Why hadn't she suspected the truth? How could she have not seen it?

The lights were dim to help her father sleep. Edwyn stood in the shadows. The old seneschal's intense grief added a grim finality to the moment.

"Sire?" Della leaned to take her father's hand and tenderly rubbed her thumb over the thinned, almost translucent skin. Her eyes drank in the pallor of his graying flesh and the blue of his lips. His chest rose in shallow breaths. She closed her eyes briefly to the pain rolling through her.

Lord Strathfeld grumbled and opened his eyes. "Yea, daughter."

"Father, why didn't you tell me?" She was unable to help the quivering of her lips as she spoke. Resting her forehead on the bed, her voice was muffled by the mattress as she continued, "I could've taken care of you. I would've gotten you all the help you needed."

Lord Strathfeld's soft laugh turned instantly to a cough. When he could speak again, he answered, "It's because you would carry on so, my stubborn child, that I did not tell you."

Unshed tears lined her eyes when she looked up. "I am so sorry for—"

"Nay, daughter, hush." His movements feeble, he stroked her cheek. "I already know all that. Have you not been my daughter all your life?"

Della nodded and tears spilled over. She swiped the moisture from her eyes. Her lips curled into a brave smile.

"Now, give me peace. Tell me that the wedding is done. Tell me you are truly man and wife." Lord

Strathfeld coughed again. When she didn't answer, he groaned and tried to push himself up on his arms.

"Yea, it is done," Brant answered for her, putting a comforting hand on her shoulder, "and it will remain so."

Lord Strathfeld sighed, an expression of peace coming over him as he took his new son at his word. Nodding in satisfaction at his daughter, he hushed, "Good. Good."

The warmth of her husband's palm soaked through her gown and she let his hand rest on her, not daring to show distaste in front of her father. She had given him enough grief over the marriage.

"And you, daughter?" Lord Strathfeld narrowed his eyes, as if trying to focus on her in the dim light. "Are you still angry at my choice?"

"Nay, father," Della reassured him. Edwyn's gaze caught hers in the dimness and he nodded in understanding. Her friend knew what she was about to do and approved of it. She closed her eyes, begging forgiveness for the lie she was about to tell to put her father at ease. "I'm truly happy in your choice. I did not mean to act ungrateful. I was only nervous about this night and it made me waspish and quick to anger."

"Nay, Della. You have always been quick to anger." The ealdorman touched her face. Then, finding the effort too fatiguing, he let it drop once more to the bed. Della made a weak noise, her heart heavy. "But you have naught to fear any longer. Lord

Blackwell will make you a fine husband. He will protect you and our people."

How can you be so sure? Della thought, but she said nothing. Hesitant, she moved her hand to cover Brant's, stiffly patting it. Lord Strathfeld smiled weakly in approval.

Her flesh was chilled against his fiery touch. He ran his thumb over the side of her finger and she stiffened in response. Knowing her father watched, she pulled on his arm, her gaze imploring him to kneel beside her. Brant looked surprised by the request, but he joined her on the floor.

Dropping his hand, she wrapped her arm around his waist. She stroked the strong muscle of his back through the thin tunic. He returned the embrace, his arm gently winding around her waist, as he brushed his lips across her temple. Della didn't move, didn't look at him again. The tender gesture took her by surprise and she drank in his comfort. The ealdorman smiled contentedly, happier than she ever remembered seeing him. Their affection was having a heartening effect on the dying man. He was finally completely at peace over his decision.

I am doing this for my father. I feel naught for him. I feel naught for him. I feel naught…

Della exhaled, soft and long, not wanting to admit she was lying to herself as she leaned helplessly against her husband. She was so confused, so lost. She was losing her father and the one man she was supposed to hate was the one man she found herself drawing comfort from. Brant's heat warmed her and a strange sensation coursed through her blood at the embrace. It was a sensation that hadn't anything to do with the one his kiss inspired. It was different, gentler.

Della shuddered as her father closed his eyes. She withdrew her arm from Brant and laid it on Lord Strathfeld's chest. The declaration of all she wanted to say welled inside her, but she couldn't speak. Her eyes trained on the rise and fall of his shallow breaths.

The chamber was quiet and even the low fire refused to crackle. Della didn't know how long she kneeled at her father's side. After some time passed, Lord Strathfeld covered her hand with his own callused one. She could feel his weakened heart under her palm. He opened his eyes to gaze at her.

"Don't be sad for me, sweet daughter," he whispered. "I have lived a good and honest life, and I have lived to see you happily wed. Soon I will see my sweet Evelyn and my son. You remind me a lot of your mother. You have her strength. I love you, Della."

"I love you," Della mouthed. After all the years since her mother's death, his thoughts were of her still. A small smile alighted on her father's face. She felt the strength of Brant's arm around her as Lord Strathfeld's heart stopped beating under her hand. For a stunned moment she waited, willing his chest to rise, willing the thump against her hand, but the ealdorman's heart did not beat again.

"*Nay!*" She threw herself onto her father's chest with a painful sob. "Father, don't leave me. I cannot bear for you to leave me, too."

Edwyn stepped forward and closed the lifeless eyes. He kept his hand over the ealdorman's face for a moment and said a brief prayer.

"The priest," Della began as the man drew his hand away.

"Has come and gone," Edwyn assured her.

Della cried harder, gripping her father's overtunic as she hugged him close. She felt so alone and didn't know what she was going to do.

"Della," Brant whispered, unable to resist holding her. He pulled her forcibly off the dead body and into his chest. She was so small, so fragile, as she trembled in his arms. To his surprise, she didn't pull away from his touch. Her words of contentment to the ealdorman had come so easily from her and the sleek feel of her hand as it covered his callused one had been so gentle and soft. He held on to that moment, when all her anger toward him was gone.

A soft lock of her herb-scented hair brushed his jaw and Brant ached with a craving he could not name. It was more than the passion of the flesh—though he did have that aplenty. She touched him willingly, her eyes worried and scared, and it was clear she didn't know the effect she had on him. Her innocence only tortured him more.

As the brave woman, who had fought and aggravated him at every turn, was reduced to tears, he felt a large part of his anger toward her fade until all that remained was the sorrowful regret for the things he had done to her.

"All will be well, Della." Brant didn't know if she heard him. "I will take care of you. I will take care of everything."

6

A SENNIGHT HAD PASSED in a devastating blur since the death of Della's father. Brant had left her alone to grieve, choosing to sleep in his own chamber and leaving her to hers. He reminded her a few times that he slept nearby, lest she needed anything. Della had to admit she appreciated her husband's help. He made all the funeral arrangements, had taken care of the wedding guests turned funeral guests, and had given her the space she needed to recover from the shock.

Della hadn't gone to the hall too often since the tragedy. She went to the funeral and to the solemn meal after, sitting frozen before the prying eyes of those gathered. Aside from the first night when Brant held her, she hadn't cried again.

Della had actually been shocked to find that it had been Brant who held her and not Edwyn. She hadn't heard his words, but for the soothing sound of his low murmuring voice. For a moment, when her sobs subsided, she looked up into his concerned blue gaze and she became aware of his body pressed tightly against hers.

Although his eyes were kind, his face was that of a pagan Viking and she recoiled from him in horror. He didn't resist as she pushed him away. Only after running all the way back to her own bedchamber, and having left her husband a safe distance behind her, did she realize that she'd overreacted. But he didn't mention it, so neither did she.

Brant had been kind enough to make excuses for her absence and even remembered to have food sent to her chamber. Della smiled wryly every time she thought of it. She hated to admit it, but his kindness did much in thawing her heart toward him. He wasn't behaving as she imagined a barbarian should behave.

In light of the mortality of life, she looked at her marriage in a new way. She still didn't like her Viking husband, or the fact that she had been forced to marry him. But she was an adult and it was time for her to let go of the childish dreams of how she wanted things to be. She was married and it was time to make the best of it.

The nightmare of her mother's death would never leave her, nor would the hatred she felt for her husband's people because of it. So she came up with what she felt was an ingenious plan. Della decided she would fund her husband in his travels. Perhaps he could even take a mistress with him and only come back if the manor was in trouble and he was needed. Many noblemen campaigned away from home and wife. Della smiled sadly at the idea. She'd never really wanted to be married, but with this new plan it might not be so bad. It might even be like it had been before, when her father was away on campaigns and she was in complete charge of the keep. Of course there was still the consummation to deal with and Brant's help to stop the raiding would be nice.

It was early morning and Della doubted anyone would be stirring in the castle. She always awoke before the sun rose along the horizon. The remainder of their guests had thankfully left the eve before. She didn't like so many visitors and hadn't been introduced to half of them, not that she really cared. The endless line of nobles had blended together in her head until she could no longer pick them apart in her mind's eye. She'd already determined she didn't wish to meet Brant's friends. To her thinking, the less their lives intermingled the better.

Della took her time dressing, stopping to scrub her face in the basin of cool water Ebba had left out. She'd decided to forgive the girl for her part in the checking. It was hard for Della to stay mad at her. Besides, if she didn't forgive the maid, Ebba would have spent the next century on her knees pleading with her. Della laughed aloud at the memory. Ebba had actually laid down in front of her chamber door, refusing to leave until Della spoke to her.

Fully dressed, Della moved to her bed and picked up her sewing. The black linen was the finest in the manor. She'd spent her time in seclusion sewing clothes for her husband, as a thank you for his help.

She doubted she could have managed the keep half as well in her sorrowful condition.

With a few deft strokes, she finished the stitching and bit the thread with her teeth, completing the final touches on the braccas and undertunics. In total, there were six pairs ranging in colors from brown to black to one white undertunic. Della had taken much more care to decide his overtunic colors. She wanted what would look best on him as Lord of the manor and new Ealdorman of Strathfeld. Black was for his dark heathen nature. Brown because it was a service-able color that matched everything. Dark blue for it would complement the light blue of his summer eyes. Brownish-red was for his 'fiery' disposition. And two white because every nobleman needed a good white tunic.

The only thing she had left was to appliqué the embroidered silk onto the edges of the overtunics. Once finished, he would truly look like a nobleman worthy of the title her father had left him. Della gave a sad smile as she examined the large shirts. She used to sew such things for her father. Being awake twenty hours of the day left a person with a lot of extra time.

Knowing she didn't have the materials needed to finish them, she decided to search out Quinn. He was the only one she trusted when it came to overseeing the sewing. The man wielded a needle and weaving loom like a knight wielded a sword and shield. This wouldn't be the first time she had awoken one of the servants before dawn to help her.

Della honed many skills within the night hours.

She'd designed the castle, learned to play *hnefa-tafl*, had perfected her reading and penmanship, and had even taught herself to dance. Any lesson was better than staring through the darkness at the fireplace waiting for the dawn, although she had done her share of that as well.

Sighing, she gathered the overtunics into her arms and carried them to the door. Before stepping into the hall, she hesitated. Her eyes strayed to Brant's closed door. She wondered if he slept there and if he was alone. Then shaking her head, she frowned.

"I hope that he finds someone to fill his nights." Hugging the material closer, she didn't look at his door again as she hurried by it. Her feet soundlessly moved over the stone in search of Quinn. She didn't want to admit she was excited to see her lord husband well-dressed. Muttering in irritation as she walked, she said, "I am only sewing for him so as not to be embarrassed by his appearance. I care not what he looks like. I care not if he likes the gifts."

Even as she said the words, she heard her own laughter mocking her from the back of her mind.

***

"OH, YEA, THIS IS TRULY MARVELOUS!"

Brant stopped, not sure whether he could believe his ears. He tilted his head and listened again. Silence. Scratching his freshly trimmed beard, he shook his head with a short, weary laugh. He'd been on his way to the exercise field when he swore he heard his wife's excited voice coming from one of the empty chambers. Looking back down the hall to where her chamber door was shut, he studied the hard wood for a moment. Then, not hearing anything else, he moved again toward the stairs. His wife was no doubt still in bed.

He'd scarcely seen Della since the evening of her father's death, but he soon came to realize the affection she showed him had been only an act to please a dying man. For a moment, her act had been convincing.

Brant could still feel her slender body in his arms, clinging to him, as she cried into his chest. He'd stroked the soft length of her hair, his fingers tangling in the tresses. And, when finally he pulled back to look at her face, she'd stared up at him in stunned surprise.

Pausing near the stairwell, he closed his eyes. He could still see her beautiful lips as they trembled in question and the dark sweep of her moist lashes as she looked at him. And he knew well the exact instant she recognized who held her. Her eyes had been swollen red with the heat of her grief, but their amber depth shot their ice accusingly at him. She ripped herself from his embrace and visibly shuddered in repulsion at his touch. The look she gave him burned eternally in his mind.

Her words of contentment had been a lie, yet part of him held on to her tender display. His heart physically ached when he thought of it, remembering the gentle caress of her hand, the innocent way her head nuzzled on his chest. Just as soon as the manor started to settle, he was going to find out just what he had done, or hadn't done, to bring on her aversion to him and his people.

He had overheard her talking with Edwyn at the wedding feast about there being a pain in her heart and that being her reason for not wanting to marry a Norseman. Brant perceived he hadn't done anything at all, that in fact it was some deep hurt from long ago that kept his wife from him. Though he discreetly asked, no one said a word about her past. He was no fool to hope for love in an arranged marriage, but he knew they would be sexually compatible if she would just let her damned self-control go. And she was just the kind of stubborn woman a man would want next to him during the hard times.

Though he wanted it, Brant wasn't sure he even knew what love was, or if it existed for a man—for a woman, of course. Women were always going on about love. It was something that came to them naturally. Women nurtured, suckled. Men were a harder lot, bent on wars and fighting. Brant couldn't see how a warrior, such as himself, could fight and kill, yet love and nurture at the same time. The traits were too conflicting in nature.

"Oh, yea. Oh, yea, that's it!"

Brant's eyebrows furrowed in ire as he came to a stop at the top of the stairwell. That time he definitely heard his wife's voice. Spinning around, he strode back along the passageway. A slow rage consumed him at the sound of her pleasure.

Here I have been trying to find ways to please the wench and it sounds as if she is getting pleasure elsewhere!

Brant narrowed his gaze as he heard a deep male voice reply to his wife's exclamation. "Oh, yea, m'lady, this is truly the most marvelous..."

He couldn't listen to anymore. Focusing in on the chamber door from whence the sound came, he charged the thick wood. A low growl flew from his lips as he slammed open the door without drawing the latch. He didn't hear it crash through the blood rushing in his ears.

The chamber was lit by a single torch, set up with a weaving loom and several cutting tables. A half-woven tapestry of red and blue had been started on the loom. In the corner, behind it and sitting in a chair, was a slender man with a wide smile of satisfaction curling his thick lips. And leaning over the offending man's lap was his wife.

The man jolted at the sound of the wood smashing on stone, the reaction slightly delayed. Brant cleared his throat and the young man leapt to his feet, clutching black material to his stomach.

"Quinn, hold still. And whoever is making that noise, cease. You are going to wake the manor." Della stood up and turned, no doubt expecting to scold a servant. "My lord husband will not take kindly to your disquiet. It's likely he is still in bed —"

Brant raised an eyebrow.

"M'lord!" Della gasped in surprise. Her round amber eyes sought his and she quickly hid her hands behind her back. "What are you doing? Coming in here like that?"

"You, out!" His voice was hard as he directed his deadliest gaze at the young Quinn. He couldn't believe that his wife, who was supposed to be in her bedchamber grieving and denying him his marital rights, was giving adulteress pleasure to someone else. And a servant no less!

Brant's chest heaved as Quinn hurried from the sewing chamber. He didn't take his eyes from Della. She paled, not daring to move.

"Really, Lord Blackwell, that was not necessary," Della said. "Quinn will undoubtedly keep running until he arrives at the coast and there he is likely to get on a boat and sail away."

Brant took a step toward her. "Nay, lady wife, I find it was quite necessary. I will slaughter that little piglet later, but first I will attend to you, adulteress."

"Adulteress? What have I done?" Her long, dark lashes fluttered over her eyes. Brant wasn't swayed by her confused, innocent expression. A sewing needle and spool of thread dropped from her hands. Glancing around the chamber, she gradually made her way from behind the loom. Her gaze darted to the door, as if calculating her chance for escape.

"I catch her and she still asks me what she has done," Brant said in disbelief.

Della again looked around. "Who are—?"

"What do you think you were doing in that man's lap, Della?"

"You think that I? And Quinn? You think that I

would…with Quinn? A servant?"

"Yea, I saw you. Do not deny it!" Brant finally got enough control over his anger that he trusted himself to move closer. "I warned you that if you ever played me false I would beat you within an inch of your life. Do you remember?"

"Yea, you said repeatedly. How could one forget such a threat?" Though she tried to look brave, she trembled violently. Her hand sought the support of the wooden loom and she leaned into it. Then, as an angry heat rose over his features, she stumbled back, nearly tripping on Quinn's abandoned chair. She nudged the chair out of the way. "I have never played you false. I swear to it, m'lord, on my own life."

"I will have no more of your lies." His hands fisted. There was no place for her to go.

"I swore to be honest to you and I have been. Except for my earlier deceit, which I have paid fully for I might add, I have never lied to you. I have never made you the fool." Her back hit the stone wall and she began inching along it as if to get farther from him. Her eyes pleaded with him to believe her. "I don't wish to be with any man, *ever*. Methinks copulation is a distasteful, disgusting act of which I wish never to be a part."

Bewildered by her words, he kept moving toward her. Against his better judgment, he glanced over her slender frame. Even in anger, he found her the most beautiful of women. "Methinks there is much wrong with your statement, lady wife. Have you forgotten your Sir Stuart?"

Della rolled her eyes heavenward. "My father married me to an imbecile. You do not have a brain in your head if you still think I want Stuart. I only wanted what he promised me five years ago before my father encouraged him to leave Strathfeld to seek his own way."

"And what was that, pray tell?" He stopped to study her, torn by the fire coursing in his blood. The warrior in him wanted to take. The man in him wanted to seduce. The lord in him wanted to demand. For the moment, he did none of those things.

"To only have to lie with him in the marriage bed once, to both consummate the union and to get me pregnant so that we may have an heir. He said he could give me a draught so I would not feel it. Indeed, so I could sleep through it. And I told Stuart he could have a mistress after it was done, so long as he was discreet with her." She lifted her chin in victory, her expression proud. He knew she was being honest, for who would say such a foolish thing unless they believed it? "And so long as he kept her from becoming with child. It would not do to have bastards about the manor. It would not be fair to the mistress or the children."

Brant made his expression blank. In truth, he was fascinated, if not slightly dispirited, by her claims. She looked down at his chest, gulping visibly as she tried to press harder into the stone. Her breathing deepened and her fingers worked against her skirt, clutching the material tight. He took it all in, reading that which she would not say.

"I…" She swallowed, turning her attention over his shoulder, refusing to meet his gaze. When she continued, the hope in her voice was palpable. "I'm willing to offer you the same, m'lord, though instead of mistresses here, mayhap you would like to travel with them. It is a very noble pursuit to travel and Strathfeld is rich enough to send you about the world thrice in the utmost comfort. I could continue to manage the keep as I always have, and if there was a war or if you were needed, then I would call you home. I swear to take no man to my bed, if that worries you, though it's of no concern to me. After the one time we, ah, consummate, I will be pregnant and I promise to be a good mother to the child, like you decreed. I do not hate children. In truth, I would love the child and be an extremely good mother."

"And what if I wanted to see the child?" he ventured carefully, amazed at how much thought she'd given the insane plan.

"I would write you with the news of the birth. I would write you every sennight with news if you so wished it, though to me that would be excessive. There is no need for you to be around while I brought the child up. My father was not around when I grew up, except to stop in and check on the manor. It could be the same for you."

Della smiled and hope shined from her eyes. He stood motionless under the amazing strength of her expression. If her happiness were not stemmed from a desire to be rid of him, he would have basked in the beauty of it. Raising his hands to rest on his hips, he waited patiently.

"I'm glad you are considering it, m'lord," she said, assuming he was. "I promise to never speak ill of you to the child. I will tell him all the battle tales I hear of you, even the embellished ones. I will tell him you are a great hero. I know you have reasons to doubt my word, but truly, it can be trusted. Just ask anyone. I'm an honorable woman."

The torchlight flickered over the span of their silence. Her lashes dipped to hide eyes that drowned in aspirations of victory. Brant couldn't move. What could he say to her? Where did he start? Why did she hate him so much and wish to be rid of him?

She dared a step forward and reached out a tentative hand for him to shake in agreement. Brant eyed her hand before turning back to her eager expression. Throwing back his head, he laughed, unable to help himself. The sound echoed off the walls, loud and hard and crude even to his own ears. But what else could he do?

Her expression iced over at the sound. When he started to settle, his eyes tearing with merriment, she jerked her suspended hand away. Giving her a devilish grin, he was pleased when she stared at his mouth. He couldn't stop himself from licking his lips. She gasped, again turning her eyes away.

"It will not work, this plan. What if you are not pregnant after one time?" With deliberate slowness, Brant let his gaze caress her. A blush stained her cheeks and he knew she didn't understand his attentions. And, in not understanding, she had no defenses to fight them. He placed one palm on the wall and the other on the edge of the loom.

"Would you deny the facts? Is there to be no honesty in you to me, yet I am expected to speak only in truths? At least Stuart is man enough to tell me the truth about the marriage bed. That it only needs be done once and not the numerous times most husbands would have their wives believe." She closed her eyes briefly and softened her tone. "I will not tell the man secret to anyone. I will let you lie and say you had your fill of me. Tell your men I demanded too much of your attentions and you grew tired of me, for surely I'm not pleasing to your temperament. It's all right. You can get me with child that one time. Though I do request you drug me if you have the knowledge to do so. I would prefer to not remember it."

Brant laughed again. The woman was actually asking him to take her while she was lethargic. The thought of bedding a lifeless maiden gave him little pleasure. "It's not the truth your cousin speaks, lady wife."

"Stuart would not lie to me. He cares for me. He is my only family."

"Nay, I am now your only family." Brant moved his hand to gently cup her face, forcing himself to be patient. For a brief, tempting moment, he thought about taking her there in the sewing chamber, willing or no, as was his right. His body urged him to do so, painfully aware of all he denied it. Trying to ignore the insistence of his straining arousal, he took a deep breath. She tried to push his hand away, but he caught her wrist and forced it to the wall by her head. "Nay, I will touch you when and where I want. The sooner you learn to accept my handling, the better it will be for you. Of that I can promise."

DELLA'S IRE only hid the shameful tears that welled inside. Desire made its way into her and she hated the betrayal of her body. She couldn't believe Stuart would lie to her about the marriage bed. It was the one truth to which she had clung. Stuart had told her the marriage bed would not be pleasant, reluctantly confirming her worst childhood fears. He had no reason to lie.

Brant could never guess the pain she felt at his sexual promises. Why couldn't he leave her be? She didn't want to feel anything for him, didn't want the confusion of his nearness. Her eyes met his entrancing blue ones and her limbs tingled with the heat of his nearness.

"Why do you lie to me?" she whispered.

"Are you so misled, Della, that you think a man can control how a woman gets with child? Love-making is not an exact art. Oft times it takes many wonderful attempts to beget an heir and more so is done for pleasure with no thought of begetting heirs." Brant's words washed over her numbed brain and she was entranced by the movements of his lips. She jolted as his finger made a simmering trail down her arm to her wrist. "So you see, I cannot leave immediately after bedding you to travel the world thrice in comfort."

She didn't resist as he lifted her hand above her head to join her wrists together. All traces of anger seemed to fade from him to be replaced by something she didn't recognize. Her breasts swelled and her nipples hardened against the thin material of her dress, the peaks reaching out to him in deprivation. Heat worked its way over her and she tried unsuccessfully not to look at him.

The sewing chamber darkened as the torch on the wall sputtered. Light danced along his strong face. Relentless, his gaze pierced into her. She smelled the fresh scent of mint on his breath as he leaned closer.

"I have seen much of the world, Della, and it is tiresome to me. I long for a home to live in and a warm bed to go to each night. I'm weary of fighting and of wars. And when I have children, I wish to see them grow and play. I wish for peace, for I have seen much of death."

"Mayhap, you could reside at Blackwell. We could have it rebuilt any way you wished." The words were a last defense. His nearness confused her, until she ached to touch him. She would have if he hadn't trapped her arms over her head. "There is no reason why we must reside together. Blackwell is close enough that you could see your child when you wanted. All you will have to do is send for him and he will come to you. There will be no reason for you to see me, except, mayhap, once a year to go over the accounting of the land. You could keep a mistress there to warm your bed. I would not mind it. I would not care if people gossiped. It could work."

"Perchance, I should give you a small demonstration of how cold your misguided view is, lady wife. Mayhap then you will not be so eager to be rid of me." His breath whispered softly against her mouth as he looked at her breasts. The mounds ached to have his lips against them once more. Her breathing deepened, rivaling the beat of her heart. He adjusted his hold, pulling her arms higher. The gesture forced her more vulnerably forward and he groaned in approval.

Beginning at her captured wrist, he lightly caressed her through the thin material of her long tunic dress. She sighed and trembled, giving little resistance. He ran an uneven trail down the limb, under the curve of her elbow, over the pit of her arm, and down the side of her slim waist.

Leaning her head back against the wall, she bit her lips to suppress a moan. The heat of his gentle hand moved over the sensitive curve of her breast in a teasing press. She didn't think to fight him as he stirred the lustful fire inside her. The wave of pleasure she felt, as his breath fell hot against her throat, frightened her.

"Methinks my touch does not repulse you as much as you would like." Brant leaned close to her ear, but the words hardly registered. "You might have to lie with a man a hundred times before you carry his babe or only a dozen. When you finally do, there is no certain way to make sure it is a boy. You might have to carry several before you beget a male. That would mean even more time in the marriage bed. What think you of that, Ice Princess?"

"That is not possible." She could barely focus on what he said, or the responses she gave. An intense ache formed between her thighs and her hips begged her to lean more fully into him. He was all around her, yet he scarcely touched her. Closing her eyes, she offered him her mouth. "Stuart would not lie to me."

"Yea, he would. If he thought doing so would get him this keep and my title." Brant let his lips brush the side of her cheek. Della panted. Her breast pressed fully into his palm and he grabbed the soft mound of flesh, giving her the caress she unwittingly sought. He rubbed hard against her nipple until it slipped out of the top of her gown. She'd been so entranced by him that she hadn't felt him loosen the dress laces. Massaging the exposed bud with the tip of his finger until it was erect, he caused a soft moan to escape her.

"Nay, I cannot believe it. Stuart would not lie to me. He is not like you." Della tried desperately to remember why she must fight him, why she must hate him. She moved her head away. Like a faint beacon in the back of her mind, she recalled his unreason-able anger and deliberately said the only thing she could think of to protect herself. "Do you forget why you are here, m'lord? Do you still think I played you false?"

The words would anger him, but that anger was the only way she could drive him away from her. It took him a moment to understand what she asked, but the second he did, he stiffened and dropped her wrists. With a flick of his finger, he covered her nipple with her gown.

Della sensed an acute pain at his withdrawal and slowly moved her arms back down to her sides. Her sex was moist under her skirt and she wondered if she started her woman's time a sennight early. It would be unusual if she did.

That would explain the mysterious sensations in my body, she reasoned, needing to make sense of all she felt.

"Explain yourself. What were you doing here with Quinn, if not playing me false?" Brant's accusing gaze shot sparks of fire.

Della suddenly grew very tired of his assault on her character. His dizzying caresses left her weak and vulnerable and she didn't have the strength to keep fighting him. Defiant, she lifted her chin. "You are an unscrupulous man and you are overly jealous in nature. It's a wonder you let me out of your sight for more than a moment. Mayhap you should chain me to the bed by my leg, lest I try to go to the garderobes alone." She pushed violently past him and took several strides across the floor. Kneeling, she picked up the tunic Quinn had dropped in his haste to escape her husband's wrath. She was angrier at the betrayal she felt in her body than at him, but she blamed him anyway.

Damned pagan curse!

"Do not turn your back on me," Brant ordered. "You will leave when I say you can."

Della stood and turned, her mouth open in disbelief. "You lout. For your information, you are more to Quinn's taste in bed partner than I am. As for your mistrust of my virtue…" Brant pointed his finger in warning. Della raised her arm and launched the long tunic at his head. "Here! It was to be a surprise—a gift for helping me with my father's funeral." He caught it against his stomach. "But it would seem you are not deserving of the consideration. I should let you walk about the manor dressed as a pauper. As to the others I made you, I will have them burned immediately. I would never give them to you now. Go to Blackwell Manor and live there. Go anywhere, just leave here."

"Della," Brant interjected.

"Nay, I don't wish to hear another word from you!" Tears brimmed her eyes and pain poured from her heart. "I'm tired of being your wife. I hate you, I hate your friends, and I hate your heritage. I hate how I feel when you touch me. I hate everything about you. You repulse me, lord husband, and I wish to be rid of you always."

Della sniffed back any tears that might have fallen. Brant didn't move. Without another word, she spun on her heels and ran from the chamber.

BRANT WATCHED HER GO, at a loss for words. He shook with the force of his longing and could still smell the sweet scent of her neck, could still feel the ache caused by the innocent brush of her cheek. He wanted her and his member had been raised to the point of explosion. It had required all of his control not seize hold of her and take her on the floor like a rutting boar. But all desire had left his body at the blatant exclamation of her hatred for him.

The sound of her footfalls echoed farther away until disappearing altogether. When he could no longer hear her, he turned his stare to the black long tunic she had made for him. The fabric of the tunic was gripped in his palms and he could feel the fine quality of the linen.

During times of war, a knight had little use for finery, so he had never bothered to order it made. The tunic gift was perhaps the finest he'd ever owned. The stitching was small and precise and that she had made it especially for him he had no doubt, for the size was perfect and not many men would fill such a garment.

He felt like a fool as he ran his finger over the fine gold embroidery. Glancing near where she'd been working, he found five other finished tunics in a pile. Brant's pride in the garments welled in his throat. None were as fine as the black one he held, but all were of excellent quality. And all had been made for him. No one had ever taken such care in a gift for him before, let alone six gifts.

Gingerly, he picked up the tunics and laid them over his arm. Perusing them as he walked, he shook his head in shame. He had ruined his wife's surprise.

THE MAIN HALL smelled of lye as the maids hauled buckets of hot, soapy water from the kitchen's hearth to the bare stone of the hall floor. Several maids scoured the stone with coarse brushes made of animal fur, whereas others carted what was left of the dirty straw rushes to the bailey yard. The worst of the straw was taken out to a controlled fire Della had lit in a large outdoor pit. The rest of it would be stored as winter bedding for the animals.

Thoughtfully, Della waved an older servant to her. The plump woman walked with the ease of a girl half her age. Della ordered her to have the maids continue up the stairwell with their brushes. It had been months since the manor had been given a good cleaning and now was as good a time as any to do so. As an afterthought, she also ordered the tapestries shaken and the walls underneath scrubbed. The maid frowned at the order, not wanting to be the one to relay it to the already tiring servants.

Della stretched her hands over her head with a yawn. She watched in quiet satisfaction at the progress she had already made. After the failed encounter with Brant, she'd purposely not sought him out, choosing instead to have the maids begin cleaning the hall. The horrible chore had to be done and she refused to put it off another day. It would be too smelly in the keep if she continued to let the spilled wedding feast rot in the rushes.

Della hadn't seen Brant since his earlier tirade in the sewing chamber and was secretly glad for it. Although, she did look for him every time she helped cart a load of straw to the bailey. She hated to admit that she didn't trust herself around him. Until she found a way to counteract the pagan love spell he had woven over her senses, she would have to stay away from him. Or at least away from his magnetic touch.

"Riders are coming!" Rab's childish voice cracked as he ran into the great hall. Della glanced up and wiped her hands on her apron. The lad smiled boyishly when he saw her and waved to get her attention. "M'lady, riders are coming!"

"Rab, calm yourself and try to breathe." Della turned to the excitable child. Catching the eye of a nearby servant, she motioned to the bailey yard with a wave of her hand. "Cart that to the pit."

Rab bounced as he waited for Della to turn back to him. She gave a few more orders before giving her full attention to the boy.

"Now, what is it?" Della inquired of the noisy lad. Rab playfully bounded closer. Della reached out and rumpled his hair while pulling him to her waist with a hug.

"Riders, m'lady." Rab looked at his feet, tolerating her affection. Then, drawing away from her, he announced, "They are coming up to the main gate from the south. They are about a half of an hour ride from here."

Della furrowed her brows in concern. Who would be visiting the manor now? Had they not just gotten rid of a bunch of guests?

"Have you told Lord Blackwell?"

"Nay, m'lady." Rab gave her a guilty look. "I'm frightened of him."

Della tried not to smile at the boy's earnest answer. She felt relief that the lad still came to her. She'd feared that in locking herself away to grieve, the people's judgment of her authority might have wavered. Impishly, she could not help but encourage the lad's observations. "Yea, he is frightening, is he not?"

Rab chuckled. Della hid her guilty pleasure at the taunt.

"Shall we go tell him together?" She ignored the fact she'd been telling herself all day that she was not going to seek Brant out. "I believe he's in the exercise yard with the men. Mayhap they will let you watch."

Rab nodded.

"Keep working," Della ordered the maids, who'd stopped to watch them with interest. She moved her hand to the back of the lad's head and led him out the arch of the side door. When they were away from the listening ears of the servants, Della said, "I'm sorry that we have not had time for our lessons, Rab."

"Yea, m'lady." Rab gave a halfhearted smile. Della knew the boy was fond of her. Since she had taken an interest in him, none of the other children in the keep seemed to tease him as much. "I'm sorry about yer sire. We all knew you were abovestairs mourning fer the ealdorman. I would have visited you, but Isa caught me and said it was not fitting fer me to do so."

Della nodded as an unsuspected wave of grief overcame her at the boy's candid confession. Blinking fast so no one would see her tears, she sniffed and nodded.

"I want to see you tonight in the usual place after dinner. I hope you have practiced what I taught you last time. If you are going to be a clerk here, you need to know how to read." Della smiled fondly at Rab's overgrown hair. "And you are in need of a haircut."

"Nay, I do not want to be a clerk," Rab grumbled. The boy picked a stick off the ground and wielded it like a sword. "I want to grow me hair out like Lord Blackwell and his men. So I can be a warrior!"

"*My* hair," corrected Della. She gave him a stern look as she struggled not to smile. "And surely, Rab, you don't want to be a knight. You'd have to carry a sword and mayhap you would have a horse."

"Nay, a war steed!"

Della gave him a wry look as she thought about it. Nodding, she consented, "Yea, a war steed."

"I would have me own battalion of knights to

command!" The boy's green eyes lit up with delight as he imagined his grand future as a noble knight. "And I—"

"Wait," Della interrupted with a serious look. She studied the boy for a moment. The smile faded from Rab's lips as he awaited her words. The stick sword fell to his side unattended. "Would you be a good knight or a bad, black-hearted knight?"

"I would be a black knight," Rab said with little deliberation. "In the stories, the good knight always has to kiss the lady he saved. I would be the bad knight and scare all the ladies and make them tremble with terror, so none of 'em would e'er want to kiss me."

It took all of Della's willpower not to laugh. She rounded her eyes with pretend terror as she clutched her hands to her heart. "But would you storm my keep, black-hearted knight?"

"Yea!" Rab lifted his play sword high into the air. With a little show of thrusts, he hollered at Della, "Surrender yer castle, m'lady!"

"Oh, nay, it is the dreaded barbarian knight. Come to slay me and mine." Della put her hand to her cheek before reaching down to grab a small stick. "Hold, m'lord, lest you have me sword embedded in yer belly. I will not relinquish what is mine!"

Rab thrust his stick toward her. "I will not call back me men, m'lady, 'til yer keep be mine. No one can save you now."

"Nay, you will ne'er have my keep." Della screamed and ran several yards toward the exercise yard. Rab charged after her. With a swish of her skirts, she whirled back to him and moved to a fighting stance. She gave him a daring display of swordplay before yelling, "Help! Help! If no one will save me, I will fight to the death."

Rab brandished his stick sword above his head and let out a heathen scream. He charged at her, drawing the further attention of the servants milling about the yard.

Della planted her shoes firmly in the dirt and gritted her teeth. Snarling, she hunched her shoulders and got ready to fight off his advance. The attack never came. Suddenly, Rab skidded to a stop, his eyes wide. Her face fell in confusion and she started for the lad, intent on shielding him from whatever terrible thing frightened him. Before she had taken a step a strong arm wrapped around her waist from behind. Her captor jerked her off the ground keeping her from ever reaching the boy.

BRANT WIELDED his broadsword valiantly against Gunther in exercise. Several of the men stopped to see the mock battle between the two large men. Both combatants grunted as they defended the other one's blow. Their heavy swords thrust and clanged together in noisy affirmation of their strength. Gunther swept his sword forward, missing Brant's naked shoulder. Brant smiled and returned a thrust in kind. Sweat dripped freely down their naked chests as their muscles strained under the motions.

Several of the onlookers roared in masculine approval of the battle. A wager was called by a short, square-shouldered soldier and quickly took up by another. The delighted jeers could be heard over the bailey yard. By their expressions, each of the observing knights were glad the talented Vikings would be on their side in battle.

"Hold!" called Gunther suddenly, wiping the sweat from his eyes with his bare arm.

"What?" Brant automatically dropped his weapon to his side. "Have you got a difficulty?"

"Nay," Gunther smiled in delight as he nodded over Brant's shoulder. His eyes gleamed with mischief. "But methinks I might need to save a damsel in distress."

Brant turned. His heart skipped a beat as he recognized Della running toward the exercise yard. She looked scared. His urge to go to her subsided as he felt Gunther's hand on his arm, stopping him. Gunther jutted his chin boldly in the air in Della's direction. Brant watched. His wayward wife turned and she wielded a stick at a young boy. Her burgundy skirts whirled around her ankles in a wave of crimson splendor and the gold cord at her waist snapped through the air. She picked up a fistful of her gown and held it so she would not trip.

His first surge of concern soon faded as he heard her yell, "Nay, you will ne'er have my keep."

Brant could not help the smile that came to his face. He began to laugh, joined by the watching men whose attentions had been diverted from one battle to the other. The same square-shouldered knight called out a mock wager and the men guffawed in response. Brant ignored all of them, his attention held by the playful scene. His proper wife was making a spectacle of herself in front of everyone. Several servants had also stopped in their chores to watch the mock battle. He laughed at her technique as she swung her stick. It reminded him of their wedding day. She really didn't know how to use the weapon.

"Do you know that young boy, Gunther?" Brant studied the familiar lad carefully.

"Yea, it's only Rab. He's a foundling to whom Lady Blackwell has taken a liking. She lets him help about the manor," Gunther said. Della thrust the small stick sword in the air. "Methinks the lad wants to be a knight. I've seen him watching us from yonder tree."

"Yea, he's the boy from the other morn who told us about the raid." Brant nodded, the memory coming to him.

"The same." Gunther laughed louder. "Does yer wife know the scene she makes? Methinks Lady Blackwell is going to lose to the child. Look at how she holds her arm. If that was a real sword it would break her wrist. Mayhap you should teach her some technique, so that if the keep was e'er really in trouble she could defend herself."

Brant didn't answer. He wondered if teaching her to hold a weapon would be a mistake. It was possible his wife would turn the sword on him.

"This is not an extraordinary scene." Roldan, one

of the late Lord Strathfeld's soldiers, stepped forward. He rested his practice sword lazily on the ground, pushing his weight onto it to bow the thin blade. Snorting loudly, he spat onto the ground before continuing, "M'lady oft plays with the children of the keep. It's the only time her ice melts a bit and she seems human. She has some fondness fer children. Once she started a mud fight with them, took the servants damned near a fortnight to clean the muck from the castle walls. In the end, a heavy rain finally finished the task."

That surprised Brant. By her nature, he had assumed she was one of those women who didn't like children about them.

"Help! Help! If no one will save me, I will fight to the death," Della yelled. Her battle brought her closer to the exercise field.

"Shall I go?" Gunther asked, a mischievous smile lining his face. Brant stared possessively at his wife. The whole castle knew the couple didn't share chambers, and many speculated as to whether or not the lord and lady of the manor had even consummated the marriage. Since Della had been checked, there was no proof of a maidenhead to collect from the bridal sheets. Only Gunther knew the truth for sure. He read it well in his lordship's eyes and he wasn't saying a word. "M'lord?"

Brant scowled at Gunther before lifting his own sword as he stepped forward to be Della's champion. Gunther laughed harder. Brant ignored him. Within several strides, he was upon her. Ducking out of the way when she drew her arm back to thrust the stick, Brant shot forward and wrapped his arm around her waist. Lifting her slightly off the ground, he swung her to his side. Her feet dangled in the air. Not letting go of her, he said for her ears alone, "Death will not be necessary, m'lady. I will always save you."

DELLA GASPED as she felt a shiver work its way up her spine. Her hand opened and she dropped the stick from her trembling fingers. The unexpected touch took her by surprise. The soft whisper of his words fanned against her ear and tickled her flesh. She hadn't been expecting him. Brant's heat flooded her veins and instantly she was overcome by the same unfamiliar emotions that awoke in her every time he was near.

Oh, my.

In her play with the child, she had forgotten that she was supposed to hate him. Della looked at his naked arm, clamped about her waist like an iron brace. He lifted her as if she was no more than a feather and she placed her hands tentatively on his arm. The reminder of his strength overtook her senses.

Rab stopped his charge and stared at them in worry.

Brant lifted his sword and pointed it at the boy. "Do you dare to lay siege to what is mine, boy?"

Della shivered at his openly possessive claim to her. Brant lowered her feet to the ground, but kept her close. The words didn't irritate her as much as they should have. Rab's mouth dropped open. He looked at Della for confirmation and she nodded.

Adjusting herself so she could partially see her husband, she whispered, "He is playacting like he is a barbarian. He means no harm. It's just a child's game."

"It would appear that there are many of us barbarians here," Brant murmured against her throat.

Della shivered. "I—"

"Well, barbarian, it is a serious crime you have committed against me." Brant lowered his sword and looked sternly at the boy before winking at him. "Do you yield?"

"Never!" Rab visibly relaxed and again held up his wooden sword.

"You are brave, knight, but it is a mistake not to surrender. Now you will taste steel." Brant made a fake sweep toward Rab. Della jolted at the motion, but Brant held her safely within his embrace.

"You have conquered me, m'lord." The boy grabbed his gut and groaned viciously as he fell to the ground. Rolling about in the dirt, he clutched at his fake wound, dramatically dying. Then, making a quick recovery, he yelled up from where he'd fallen on his backside, "I yield!"

"Pledge your loyalty to me and my lady wife," Brant commanded, "and I shall make you my page."

Rab's eyes rounded in hope and he eagerly nodded. Della sighed as the boy kneeled before them.

Holding his stick like it was a sword, he swore his allegiance. She couldn't hear the entirety of what the boy said, but knew it to be as noble of a knight's pledge as ever spoken.

Brant tilted his jaw in satisfaction and loosened his hold on her, still not letting her go. "A wise decision, Rab. As my page, you will start training on the morrow. Perchance, someday, you will be knighted. Methinks you show much bravery and promise, but you must work hard. It will not be easy for you."

Rab looked at Lord Blackwell in wonder as the older man said his name. Della saw the hero worship in the boy's eyes and knew he was lost to the giant beside her. The loss didn't upset her as she thought it might. Feeling an overwhelming sense of appreciation and hope, Della turned to face her captor.

"My hero." Della sighed, caught up in the moment of the game. She didn't fight his embrace as she moved her hands to settle about his thick neck. She leaned her head against his muscular chest and felt the press of his naked skin against her. His arm flexed on her waist, his hand tightening on her hip. Hastily, she pulled back to look up at him.

It's only so Rab will see there is naught to fear in him. Della knew she was lying. Her eyes softened, as she breathed in the scent of his body. The hard, hot length of him molded into her, not leaving any space between them.

"Thank you." Her eyes held his.

"A kiss," Rab demanded, his voice cracking. Della

jolted at the noise. Brant froze. "A kiss fer the victor. The good knight always gets a kiss from the lady."

Della looked about in confusion as the onlookers cheered their encouragement. Their curious faces watched the noble couple with avid interest. Della blushed, but met Brant's eyes resolutely.

Brant whispered, "How about it, m'lady? A kiss for the victor?"

Della didn't know what was coming over her. The longing he stirred within her was turning into a familiar occurrence. The strong arm about her waist made her blood flow in a chaos of emotion. She looked to his parted lips and slowly moved her tongue to the corner of her mouth. Taking a deep, shattering breath, she nodded.

Brant lifted her up by his one arm and pressed his lips quickly to hers. Her hands tightened about his neck, but he released her. Della dropped to the ground in shock, confused by his swift kiss. It was as if he could not wait to be rid of her touch. Rab appeared at her side, distracting her.

"The riders, m'lady." The boy pulled on her sleeve. "Don't forget."

"Oh, yea." She cleared her throat. "M'lord, riders approach. We were just on our way to inform you."

Brant pointed to where he had been exercising and said to Rab, "Quick, page, get my tunic by the field."

Della walked numbly beside her husband to the main gate. Her lips still stung where he touched them. She wondered why he hadn't kissed her like last time.

At the memory, Della wrinkled her nose, remembering how sloppy it had been. "Thank you for what you did for the boy. It has always been his dream to become a page. Methinks he hoped one of my father's men would choose him, but they had no reason to. When a child is branded bastard, many do not find the time for him."

BRANT MADE A WEAK NOISE. Was Della actually thanking him? As he watched her, he waited for the moment her gentle amber eyes would turn cold. Part of him was afraid that if he looked away, he would realize her smile was not for him. But she was looking at him and he had never seen her eyes glint with such obvious tenderness.

He slowed his step, listening as the guards opened the front gate. Rab delivered the tunic. It was the dark blue one she had made for him. Waving the child away, he said, "Yea, it is of no matter. I needed a page. I have no kin with sons to lend to the task."

Della bit her lip and he felt her eyes stay on him as he pulled the tunic over his head. Instantly, her attention turned to the garment she'd sewn. It was long enough to hit just above the knees. She tugged the material at his side. "It's not quite right. I was unsure about the size. Mayhap I should have made it longer."

Concentrating, she grabbed his arm and began to lift it. Brant chuckled and instead moved his arm to settle over her shoulders, pulling her next to him. She didn't notice the familiar way he handled her or the stares their unofficial truce elicited from the yard. "It's fine, Della."

"Nay, I just want to see if you can lift your arm. Methinks I might need to take out the shoulder some and take in the waist, just a bit. I had thought your waist was bigger, what with the muscles." She bit her lip and tried to pull away to study it again. "I should just start over. This one is not right at all. Mayhap that is why you did not exercise in it? It doesn't fit properly?"

"Nay, Della." Brant stopped and stuck his knuckle under her chin, lifting her face to gain her full attention. "It's perfect. I thank you for it."

Della frowned, still concentrating on her craftsmanship. "It really would look better with the braccas I made for you and the new undertunics."

Brant stared at her in disbelief. He wondered how she spared enough time to make his six tunics in one sennight, let alone underclothing. Surely she'd had help from the servants.

He was still awed by her gift. Though he would never admit it to her, he had spent much of the morning trying all of them on in front of the mirror of polished silver in his chamber. "Della, it's fine and the fit could not be more perfect."

Della nodded, still examining the tunic for imperfections in the seam lines more than listening to him. Again she tried to lift his arm and again he resisted by placing it over her shoulders. The smell of her, the dancing innocence of her touch drove him mad with lust. He'd wanted to deepen the earlier victory kiss, but he'd been many months without a woman. If he would've held her too much longer, he would've lost control. His wife would not take kindly to him acting the barbarian. But her new compliance to his touch was overwhelming. It had been much easier to hold his passions at bay when she fought him. Even now, he wanted to throw her over his shoulder and drag her away to his bed.

"When did you have time to direct the servants to do them?" Brant tried to take his mind off her lips, as he glanced down at his tunic.

Della's head snapped up and she took a step away from him. "Servants?"

"Yea, to sew the clothing." He smiled, trying to bring the gentleness back to her eyes. It was too late. The look had faded.

"I didn't have the servants help. They had too much to do as it was with all the guests. I only had Quinn help with the embroidery, since he does it so much better than I." She gave a guilty laugh. "Methinks that mayhap it is because he is like a woman."

Amazed, Brant lifted a finger to briefly touch a wayward blonde curl. Then, dropping his hand, he asked, "How many did you sew?"

"Six complete outfits. Since you seem to change your clothes oft, methought it a good number. Why? Are you in need of more? It might take a few days, but I guess it would be my duty to sew more if you were in need. Methinks there is some fabric left in the storage chamber. The linen may be a bit coarse, but it would do for now."

"Nay, it's only that you must have gone without sleep to do it. Why?" He hoped to trap her into a confession of some kind. The fact that she'd paid close attention to his habits pleased him—not to mention her assessment of his muscled waist.

Even though she didn't move away from him, she withdrew herself quite effectively. Her face turned cold. "Nay, no more than usual. I don't sleep well at night. Not since I was a child. I needed something to keep my hands busy."

Brant watched with regret as her expression hardened. He had little time to wonder at it as the gate stopped creaking.

"It was embarrassing to see you looking like a pauper," she said. "It reflected badly on the manor."

Ah, there is the Ice Princess I know, Brant thought, refusing to be baited by her insult. He began to understand that she used it as a defense to keep him at bay. Mayhap she was that way to anyone who tried to get close to her. Instead he turned to the front gate. "Why would they open the castle without permission?"

"I have a standing order that Edwyn can make the decision in my absence. It must be a friend."

"It is no longer your decision to make when I am here," Brant decreed without thought. "Or do you forget who is in charge now?"

Any retort was lost as the sound of thundering hooves reverberated over the yard. A flag flew over their ranks, bearing a black dragon on red cloth. He instantly recognized the symbol.

"The standard is vaguely familiar. Who is it?" Della straightened her gown as the riders approached.

"It's the banner of the king's man." Brant frowned.

"Were you expecting them?" She seemed annoyed that he hadn't told her sooner.

"No."

"They must be here because of my father," Della concluded.

Brant wasn't so sure. "Get you quick to Isa. Tell her of our guests."

Brant didn't look to see if she obeyed, but he listened for the sound of her footfall. He sighed in relief when she gave him no argument, knowing the truce between them was fragile at best.

"Argh!" Della strode inside the manor without a backward glance. She wanted to tell him where he could shove his commands, but refrained, not wishing to argue with him in front of the king or his men.

She tripped with the urge to run, but forced her feet to glide with confidence. In truth, she was glad for any excuse that would take her far from her aggravating and highly confusing husband. Crossing over the threshold of the hall, she chanced a look back. He was already greeting their guests, motioning at the stable lads to tend to the horses. She studied him for a moment, watching the enigmatic way he commanded all those around him.

"Command all but me," Della vowed as she angrily went to inform Isa of their guests.

"Is it King Guthrum, m'lady?" Rab asked impatiently. He edged over to the open doorway leading to the hall from the kitchen. He tried to peek around the corner unnoticed.

"Nay." Della pulled him back into the kitchen, secretly wanting to do the same. "It's some of his men. They said they have a message from the king for Lord Blackwell."

"Do you think Lord Blackwell will let me read it? None o' the other pages know how to read. I could —"

"Nay, it's private," Della said, knowing he only wanted to brag about the skill to Brant. The nobleman's attention had boosted the boy's sense of self-worth and for that she was grateful. Rab had blossomed under her tutelage and now with the attention of her husband, he positively gleamed. She could easily guess how jealous the other boys would be of him once word of his new position spread.

Della finally gave into temptation and looked across the main hall to where her husband had entered with two very important-looking men. She was glad he wore the new tunic. Isa set out drinks at the high table, her large frame moving with a lumbering grace. No doubt the woman wanted to get first look at the newcomers for she rarely served the drinks.

Regretfully, the maids still scrubbed the hall floor. They were almost finished with their task, and had even started to place fresh rushes over parts of the stone. A maid passed with a bucket and Della reached out to stop her. The woman's nose was red and she rubbed it on her sleeve as she looked expectantly at her mistress. "Mary, have the others finish the stairs and the hall as quickly as possible, but leave off the walls until the guests leave."

The maid curtsied, but did not speak. Della turned her attention back to Rab.

"Get you to the stables. Help Boothe with the horses." She gave Rab a gentle shove. "Mayhap some of the king's knights will be out there and the other boys might want to meet the ealdorman's new page."

"Yea, m'lady." His face brightened.

"I promise to tell you what happens tonight."

Rab smiled and ran from the kitchen to do her bidding. Della watched him scurry off before turning to the men. She wondered if she should wait to be called, but curiosity got the better of her as she made her way across the hall to her husband.

"King Guthrum begs me to present you with this before we did so much as drink." An older gentleman with a lazy eye handed over a rolled missive to Brant. "He bid you to read it immediately and make your mark."

Della nodded in approval to several of the maids

working industrially as she passed. Then, turning her full attention to her husband, she forced a pleasant smile on her face. Brant frowned as he slowly unrolled the missive. Knitting his brows in concentration, he narrowed his eyes and scrutinized the document for a long moment.

The men shifted uncomfortably as her husband stared at the parchment. Della made her way closer, noting the grim set of determination on her husband's face. The man with the lazy eye looked at his dark friend in amusement.

He cannot read! Della realized with sudden insight. Though it was not unusual for Vikings to be illiterate, having no real written language of their own beyond a few scribbles, she found the revelation surprising. Brant had appeared educated and capable. He spoke like a gentleman, though his heathen accent thickened his words. And, although she had tried to find it otherwise, he appeared to be quite capable of making the decisions of his title.

Oh, nay. They are mocking him! Della frowned, instantly becoming protective as a jeering expression alighted on the little man's face.

Della rushed forward, mindless of her uninvited interruption, desperate to save Brant from the inevitable humiliation. Again, she forgot her displeasure over her marriage as she went to his aid. Her heart beat with a familiar ache as she tapped his arm gently.

"M'lord husband." Della smiled prettily as she looked at the two men. Threading her arm over

Brant's to draw his concentration away from the missive, she squeezed it insistently.

"Yea?" he said, clearly baffled by her attention. For a moment, the entirety of the hall faded into the clearness of his gaze. She found the slight curve of his smile and she couldn't keep the blush from heating her features as her lashes swept over her eyes.

"I don't believe I have been introduced." Della glanced expectantly at the two men. She gave them all a sweet smile.

Brant didn't answer at first and she worried that he wouldn't indulge her request. A man like him would probably think it was curiosity in their guests which caused her to ask. Della had to admit, that was part of her motivation, but mostly she wanted to save her husband from humiliation. As if finally deciding there was no harm in her meeting the king's ambassadors, he cleared his throat. Presenting her hand to the first man, he said, "M'lady, may I present Lord Aurick of Lester."

Lord Lester was the condescending man with the lazy eye. She gave him a simple smile, all the time cursing him in her mind. He might have looked like a noble in his new, padded green tunic with the gold stitching, but he smelled like rotted cream. Della suddenly appreciated all the bizarre morning rituals she'd witnessed from the Vikings. They cleaned themselves daily and changed their clothing often.

How could I have thought they were the smelly ones? She tried not to gag as the nobleman's breath hit her face.

She would wager that Lord Lester hadn't bathed in well over a fortnight.

"M'lady," Lord Lester squeaked in a high, nasally voice, as his cold fingers firmly grasped her hand. He rubbed his thumb inappropriately on her palm and she hid her revulsion as he kissed her hand. Opening his mouth, he pressed his greasy lips to her flesh. She shivered in disgust and Lester smiled at her reaction. Brant didn't notice as he looked over the missive.

Della waited for Lester to drop her hand. As he righted himself, the nobleman watched her through veiled eyes, but didn't let go. Jerking back from his lecherous grasp, she offered her hand to the second man. Lester frowned. Brant smiled in approval. Della ignored them both.

"And Sir Vladamir of Kessen." This time Brant rolled the missive and placed it under his arm. He watched carefully for her reaction to the younger, handsomer visitor. Della paid the man little heed.

"M'lady," Sir Vladamir acknowledged in a strange foreign accent. His low, soft voice was much more pleasant than his friend's had been. A shock of short black hair fell over his dark brooding eyes, as he quickly kissed her hand and released it.

"Gentlemen, this is my wife, the Countess of Strathfeld."

"My pleasure, gentlemen," Della said graciously as they bowed in acknowledgment of her title. To her it sounded strange. She always thought of the countess as her deceased mother. "M'lords, please forgive a foolish woman's interruption, but I must beg your forgiveness as I steal away my lord husband. It is a most urgent matter for which I need his assistance with, I assure you."

"M'lady." Sir Vladamir seemed bored as he glanced expectantly at his companion. When Lester didn't readily speak, he said, "Let me know if I can be of service."

"Thank you, but that will not be necessary. It's most urgent, though inane in nature." Della allowed a blush to creep over her cheeks. The redness wasn't completely fake. She could imagine what they thought she wanted with Brant.

"I must insist that you read the missive now, Lord Blackwell," interrupted Lord Lester rudely, shooting Della a look that said he didn't so easily forget her display of displeasure. "It's from King Guthrum, himself."

"M'lord." Della tried to be charming. "I don't think that even King Guthrum would mind me talking most urgently to my lord husband while you partake of the best ale in all of Northumbria. We have perfected the recipe in our brewery. Mayhap, you will have an opinion on it, being as you are so obviously well-traveled."

"Yea," Lord Lester assented unwillingly. It was clear he thought he faced an uphill battle with the simple woman. "But I must insist on quickness."

Self important pig! The man acts as if he is royalty.

"To be sure." She took Brant around the wrist that held the missive so he wouldn't be able to give it back. "The maids have set cups on the high table for you and I insist that you stay here to dine tonight. It will be roasted mutton."

"Self important pig!" Della muttered, dropping her hand from where it had been on Brant's arm. He didn't want to let her go, but she rushed ahead, viciously rubbing the back of her hand on her gown. Brant wondered whom she referred to with the comment. He rather thought Lord Lester was deserving of her scorn, but with the circumstances of their relationship, Brant was afraid the contempt was directed at him.

He had watched the whole interplay with amusement. If he didn't know his pretty little wife, he would have believed her act of innocence. His eyes strayed to where her hips moved, seductively swaying under the burgundy linen of her dress, and he wondered what *urgent matter* she spoke of.

The gold cord at her waist gave him a truly wicked idea as he wondered how it would look tied around her wrists in love play. He licked his lips. Involuntary lust pumped in his veins and he ached to grab her skirt and toss it over her backside so that he may have his way with her in the stairwell.

I doubt that is your urgent matter, Ice Princess. Brant sighed in disappointment. *Pity.*

"What was that, Lord Blackwell?" Della inquired as she reached the top. The mask of ice had once more frozen her features and her gaze revealed nothing as she directed it toward him.

"It's naught to be concerned with." He hated the way she insisted on using his formal title. The way she said it was so cold and distant.

When she turned, he realized his tone had been dejected. Seeing his eyes on her butt, she gasped and blushed. Brant smiled sheepishly at being caught, but didn't try to hide his brazen response.

"Lord Blackwell, please!" She was shaken and he saw her falter in her purpose.

Brant gave one last longing glance to the cord.

"Oh." Della grabbed her skirt in irritation, marching toward his bedchamber. Pushing open the door, she then turned and held out her hand, a heavy sigh escaping her lips.

A slow, amazed gleam sparked within him, surging from the depths of his tempered desire. Longing flooded him, coursing in his veins at the smallest hope she would offer herself to him. He stepped closer, his eyes straying toward the massive bed behind her and then to her hand. Could this be? He reached to take her fingers in his, hesitant yet eager for her touch.

"Nay." Della shooed his hand away like an annoying insect. "The missive. Give it to me and I will read it."

Brant wasn't surprised and still he waited for the words to take themselves back. At her insistence, he turned his attention to the rolled parchment. An acute pain assaulted him at her rejection. Frowning, he strode into the chamber, not handing it over.

"Give it to me. I will read it to you." Della followed him inside and quietly shut the door.

Was this a game? Could she truly not know what he would think her intent was, bringing him to his chamber in such a way? Did the woman mean to turn him around until he couldn't see straight, running him through with the dagger of her withheld affections?

Brant shot her a hard stare. "What do you mean to imply?"

"I saw that you were having trouble. Methought to save you the discomfort of admitting you don't understand what the missive says. It is naught to be ashamed of. Many nobles have not been taught. And, well, you *are* a Viking."

His frown darkened into a scowl. She took a step back as his body visibly stiffened. Brant didn't move and her attention seemed caught by the soft fur rug he'd ordered placed on the floor upon his arrival. Then, as if steeling herself, she swallowed any emotion she must have felt and looked up. Again, she held out her hand.

"If you like, I will teach you, and to write also," she said. "That way when you are about your travels, you will be able to read what I write to you and send direction. But, for now, hand me the missive and I will read it to you."

She hadn't given up on her idea of sending him away. Part of him wanted to laugh, but it was a small part. Then an idea formed in his head. His wife was trying to come to his rescue. He wasn't sure if he should be insulted by her presumption or flattered by her unsuspected loyalty.

He sat and put the missive next to him on the bed, beckoning her to join him with a tilt of his head. She came to him, her steps slow as if she didn't trust him. He remembered how good she felt against him and knew it was wise of her to be wary of his intensions. Though he tried, he couldn't keep the wicked smile from curving on his face.

Sitting, she stretched behind his body to pick up the message. Brant grabbed her arm, gently drawing it from behind his back to face him. She looked at him in surprise. "But—"

"I can read, Della." Brant took a deep breath, letting her scent settle around him. She carried the light aroma of wildflowers in her hair. The honeyed tresses were bound back to the nape of her neck, but fell freely from there. He could also smell the trace of soap from where she helped the servants to clean the hall.

"But I saw you struggling," she said, confused. "It's naught to be ashamed of, m'lord."

Brant heard the quiver in her words. Stroking his hand up her arm, he moved to touch her under her chin. He saw her eyes widen uncomfortably at his handling. He tilted her jaw back so he could look fully at her face. "It sometimes takes me awhile since this is not my natural language, but I can read it. My father insisted."

"So you were struggling? You did need my help?"

Why did I not see it earlier? Brant thought. *You, my*

little Ice Princess, like to take care of everyone. Whether an illegitimate child, a manor full of servants, or an illiterate husband. It seems this little trait even surpasses your unrelenting repulsion of my heritage.

Brant smiled suddenly. His wife was protecting a very soft heart underneath her glacial exterior.

"What was it?" she asked, once again trying to peek past him to the sheepskin parchment.

"It is but a formality from the king. It is not important." His smile broadened and he grew bolder when she didn't move away from him.

"You're finding amusement at my expense. I don't know why I even bother trying to do aught nice for you. You are an overbearing, dimwitted oaf. I should have expected such ingratitude from a Viking."

"Nay, enough, my Ice Princess." Brant liked the heat he saw curling in her gaze. It was a pleasant change from their icy coolness. It seemed her words were the only defense she had against him, so he ignored them. Brant had dealt with frightened people before.

"Quit calling me that," Della flustered. "I am not an Ice Princess, you barbarian!"

Brant shook his head and answered in a logical, even tone. "Then quit calling me a barbarian."

"I—" Della's words ground to a stop as she glared at him.

She didn't know how else to respond. He represented everything that she hated in the world, everything that had ruined her childhood and had taken her mother so violently away from her. But she still found herself oddly attracted to him. Unable to resist, she looked at his hands. They were strong, even in relaxation. Every time they were together in private, he found a reason to back her against the wall, and each time it became harder for her to fight his pagan spell.

He was so close. The heat of his body wove its magic around her. She detected the strong sinew of his muscular neck and the steady pulse that beat in a mesmerizing rhythm at the base of his throat. Tears stung her eyes as she looked at him. He pierced her with an uncontrollable fire and a longing that had more to do with her heart and less to do with physical aching. Turmoil invaded her entire being, but she could not draw away. Her voice soft, she said, "I want…"

"What Della? What do you want, princess?"

Della decided she liked the new version of his nickname much better. She was tired of being treated like she had no emotions, like she didn't feel anything. She was tired of living in the past, tired of the nightmares she was constantly fighting. But, most of all, she was tired of fighting him—of resisting him. "I want you to…"

His breath caught. He didn't move.

"Kiss me," she whispered. She studied her hands, refusing to look at him. Her lips quivered and she knew she might cry soon. He would never understand how hard it was for her to make the request.

"Do not be embarrassed," he said, like a rider trying to soothe a wild horse. "There is naught wrong with wanting when you are married."

Della still didn't look him in the eye. She felt exposed, defenseless. It had taken all of her energy to utter the words and she wondered why he hadn't honored the request. Did he not like how she kissed him? Did she not do it right? It wasn't surprising. What did she know of such things? A bitter, lonely pain unraveled in her chest and she knew she was unworthy of having asked it of him. Some people were not made for these things and she was one of them. Why did she let her guard down? Why did he have to look at her? She yelled at him to push him away, to keep herself safe from the pain being with a man caused. Why didn't he go when she told him to leave?

"I'm sorry. It's a stupid request." Her hands shook violently and she clutched them together. "You have to get back to your guests. I will not interrupt again."

Della stood, trying to retain as much dignity as she could. She swallowed over a lump in her throat, but it only moved to settle in her stomach. It was hard to breathe, and still she knew she must put on a brave face. She started to move away when she felt Brant's hand on her elbow, stopping her. It didn't take much to keep her from going.

She heard him stand, the near silent whisper of his clothes as he moved. He forced her to turn, but she couldn't meet his gaze as she stared at the floor, twisting the toe of her shoe into the fur. Her heart ached painfully in her chest. She was so confused. The past waged a horrible war with the present and she was weary from a lifetime of fighting it.

"I have to see to the preparation of the eve's meal. I did promise roasted mutton," she said by way of an excuse. Della tugged halfheartedly at the pull on her elbow, willing him to let her go. "I have to inform Isa."

"Look at me." He tried to lift her chin. A wet tear slid over his finger before she could stop it. She'd kept her voice calm. If he wouldn't have touched her, he wouldn't have known she was crying. "Della?"

"Must be my woman's time that's making me weepy." Della dashed the tears, knowing it was yet too early. She waited, but when he didn't answer, she pulled her elbow from his grasp. Turning from him she went to the door, not making a sound.

8

"ASK ME AGAIN," Brant commanded before she could leave him.

"Why? Would you like to refuse me again? I told you it was a stupid request." Della gingerly fingered the door latch, before turning to glare at him. The expression failed and she looked to the floor, avoiding his eyes. "I don't really want you to kiss me."

"Ask me again."

"Why? I already know that I must be lacking, otherwise you would have. So please, stop trying to humiliate me and go attend to your guests." Even as she spoke, she moved closer to him. "You have made your point. I will not bother you again."

"Ask," he persisted.

"Fine!" She took a deep, quivering breath, but her irritated tone quickly turned into an insecure whisper. "Will you teach me how to kiss you?"

"With much pleasure." Brant drew closer.

Della took a deep breath, her throat working violently. Not backing away as his hand cupped her jaw, she let him lift her chin. She closed her eyes, waiting.

"Nay, I want you to look at me and know who you are kissing," Brant murmured, an inch away from her mouth. "I will not have you pretending I'm someone else."

Della doubted that was even possible, but did as he commanded. Every fiber in her being pulled toward him, and she felt both vulnerable and afraid—emotions that were as unfamiliar as their cause. However, she had to admit she was also oddly intrigued by the request. She licked her lips, pursing them as she leaned forward once more.

"Not yet," he said. "Put your hands on my neck."

Della again did as he commanded. Her shaking hands encircled his broad shoulders. Firm muscles flexed beneath her, solid and warm. Tiny shivers of pleasure radiated from her fingertips, moving along her arms, making her aware of how close his body was to hers. Soft hair brushed over the backs of her hands. The increasingly familiar scent of him, the sweet smell of earth and mint, wove through her senses, enrapturing her, keeping her completely under his spell. Slowly, he wrapped his arms around her waist, pulling her so close that only a hairsbreadth of space separated them.

"Now, I will show you the first kind of kiss." His words were soft as he moved his lips to brush up against hers.

Her knees weakened as his closed mouth rubbed along hers. She held him tighter for support, breathing deeply through her nose. His lips were warm and dry, and she could feel the texture of them massaging her sensitive mouth in a soft but insistent press. Della bit back a moan of surprise.

Brant watched her carefully, not taking his eyes off her, even as her own vision grew cloudy. He pulled away after a moment and she felt as if she couldn't catch her breath. Her heart beat hard and fast. Heat gathered in her stomach, almost as if radiating from outside herself from him.

His accent grew thicker, as he instructed, "Now for the second, open your mouth to me."

Confused, she could not deny his persuasive tone. Licking her lips again, she parted them slightly. Brant moved his head forward and gently took her bottom lip in between his own. He bit down lightly with his teeth and she clutched at his neck. Her breasts pressed fully to his chest for support, her nipples rubbing against the hardness of his muscular form. His heat overtook her completely.

Della moved to do the same to his bottom lip, eliciting a moan from him. The sound was tortured and she started to pull back, but Brant held her fast, urging her with his mouth to try it again. She did and once more he moaned in tortured delight. All the time, she kept her eyes steadily on him, although her vision grew hazy and her eyes threatened to roll back in her head with the unexpected pleasure of his touch.

"And now," Brant continued his instruction. His words came out on ragged pants of air. The span of his widespread fingers explored her back in slow, agonizing circles. "Now for the final lesson on the mouth. Keep your lips parted."

Della obeyed. She wouldn't have been able to close her lips due to the rush of her breath as his mouth came once more to her. Gently, he crushed her mouth with his tender passion, drawing his tongue over the edge of her lips, testing her resolve. Then, finding she didn't resist, he moved his hand to her hair and forced her more fully against him. With each pass, he pushed harder, exploring deeper with his tongue. The beginning tenderness soon turned to fervent desire as he moaned, trapping her tightly to his length.

Della lost all feeling in her legs and leaned against him for support. Her eyes fluttered closed. She was unable to keep the lids open against the wave of pleasure that flooded her weakened limbs. Brant was an excellent teacher and soon she matched his rhythm with her own. A timid sound escaped her and she dropped her hands to his shoulders to help support her weight.

"The torture," he whispered, coming up for a deep breath, only to crush his lips to hers once more.

His heart thumped against her, matching the hurried beat inside her chest. She tried not to, but soft, little moans sounded in the back of her throat. His fingers managed to find flesh, their texture rough against her softer skin as they caressed her face and neck, delved into her hair, traced her ears. Then, moving to her bodice, he struggled with the ties that held her dress together. His kiss became harder, demanding, and his moans became louder. Teeth bit into her lips, stinging the tender flesh in an increasingly savage passion.

It was too much. Too hard. Too fast. Too violent. Unbidden, images of her mother's death came to mind, flooding her with their horror.

"Nay," Della gasped, prying away in fright. Her wide eyes watched him in panic. His fierce ardor scared her.

"What?" Brant moved blindly to pull her back into his arms.

"Nay, take it off," Della demanded, nervously holding up her hand to form a shield between them. Her lips burned with his taste and inside her stomach the confusing sensations swirled, becoming almost painful at her withdrawal.

"As m'lady wishes." Brant smiled. Without the slightest hesitation, he started to lift his own tunic over his head.

"Nay!" Della felt the blood draining from her face. "Not your tunic."

"Then?" Reason slowly took control of his desire and his eyes began to clear.

"Take off your pagan curse. Take it off me. I don't wish to have these feelings. Take them away now. I don't want this. I cannot want this," Della said in shame. She couldn't believe what she had asked him to teach her. Almost stunned by her own actions, she added softly, "I hate you."

A cruel laugh answered and she stumbled back, tears blurring her gaze. He loomed toward her, his eyes hot with anger. "Yea, I will take the curse off of us, but not the way you might mean."

"It will be by force." It was her only line of defense. She continued to back away. Her wet eyes darted frantically to the door and she wondered if she could push past him.

Brant glared at her for so long she thought he would incinerate her with the heat of his gaze. When he didn't answer, she was afraid the words wouldn't be enough. Finally, he turned and picked up the missive. Keeping his back to her, he said, "The next time you start something, you best be prepared to finish it. For this is the last time I will control myself. Next time, be assured I will have you—willing or nay."

Della wondered at the look of intense pain on his face as he stalked from the chamber. The door slammed only to swing open behind him. She watched to make sure he would not return to finish what had been started. Part of her ached to stop him, but she could not force herself to call out.

By All the Saints! Della sunk to her knees and cried. Her body was not her own, she didn't understand what it felt. *What have I begun?*

BRANT WALKED AWAY from the high table, not bothering to look back. He wasn't sure where he was going, only that he didn't feel like entertaining. King Guthrum's ambassadors were in his hall, drinking his mead and eating his food. The missive they carried was merely a formality sent by the king, securing Brant's pledge of loyalty before his majesty's arrival in two fortnights. The ambassadors were going to all of the manors in the kingdom.

Brant wasn't sure why the king would have use of such a document, but left his mark on it nonetheless. With his recent addition of a title, and because he was a well-respected knight known for his levelheaded resolve, Brant had been their first stop.

Brant also informed the men of Lord Strathfeld's death. They promised to get word to the king, if his majesty hadn't received the message that had already been sent.

If he'd been a gracious host, he'd have stayed with the men to entertain them. Brant wasn't feeling very gracious. There was only so much of Lord Lester's excessive self-serving gossip a man could stomach. Besides, the king already knew where his loyalty stood and he didn't need to prove it to his majesty's lackeys.

Brant ordered Ebba to prepare chambers for the ambassadors, insisting she draw baths so their every comfort could be met, with extra strong soap sent to the odious Lord Lester's chamber. He really hoped the nobleman took advantage of the generosity.

Making his way to the outer bailey, he turned

toward the steady thumps of the workers. Brant had ordered Edwyn to improve the surrounding walls, and from what he'd seen, the man was doing a fine job of overseeing it. The castle's stonemason was replacing the wood with stone to prevent any attackers from setting fire to the walls. Already the project was nearing quick completion. Strathfeld was quite self-sufficient in that regard.

Quite like its mistress, Brant thought with a scornful curse.

When Della asked for a kiss, he'd seen her uncertainty and had felt like a fool for not giving in to her right away. Only, he'd been basking in the pleasure of her request. It was the closest she'd ever come to admitting her attraction to him. He'd seen her insecurity and knew she'd never asked such a personal thing from anyone before. His little ice maiden was so self-reliant. He doubted she ever asked anyone for anything.

When he'd kissed her, it was sweet torture. Even now his body raged with wanton hunger. Still in a foul mood, his blood boiled as he thought of his wife's teasing kisses and standoffish desires. With a grim expression of discontent, he glared along the wall, hands on hips as he stood. He didn't see the new stone in his anger.

"Lord Blackwell." Edwyn nodded at Brant as he approached. It was clear by his look that he still hadn't sized up his new overlord. Though, in light of Lord Strathfeld's death, the man should've been grateful that Brant let him stay on at all. It was no secret that Lord Blackwell had his own seneschal to attend to the matter of repairing the manor. Many thought Gunther an odd choice for the job, being that he was a fighting man. Brant didn't care. He wanted his friend close.

"Edwyn," Brant returned with a distracted nod. The servant turned back to the laborers.

"This section should be done about two days hence," Edwyn said.

Brant stared blankly along the stone. Behind him, a woman laughed. It was undoubtedly a servant, but the gaiety of the sound sent chills over his spine. It was sweet and light, as a woman's laugh should be. His body jolted with unfulfilled desire and he considered taking his wife up on her offer. Mayhap it was time he took a mistress. If his wife was not going to fulfill her duties, there were many lovely maids in the keep who would. More than one had shyly shown their interest in him. Before Brant could seek out his new companion, Edwyn stopped him.

"Have you seen m'lady's plans fer the fortifications?" Edwyn inquired tentatively. "I wondered if you were to be continuing with 'em."

"What?" A dark storm rumbled in his words. "What would a woman know of such things?"

Taken aback, the man didn't hide his surprise. "Did they not tell you?"

"Tell me what?" Brant took a menacing step forward. He was very tired of all the secrets floating about the keep. Cleaning spirits, dead mothers, a woman who loved children but loathed the idea of having any of her own, pains in hearts caused by Vikings. And all of them centered around his darling wife.

"Lady Della laid the plans fer the castle herself." The man's face beamed with pride. It was the look of a father talking of his favorite child. Though Della was not Edwyn's kin, Brant saw the two were close and ignored his use of her old title. Not many referred to her as Countess or Lady Blackwell anyway. The seneschal had no children of his own. According to Lord Strathfeld, Della and Edwyn had spent many years together while her father was off fighting wars. Continuing, the man said, "These walls were her design. She had 'em constructed first of wood to make sure they would work properly and she has been slowly replacing 'em with stone. She took many of her ideas from the south, writing to nobles under her father's seal to secure the plans to the old Roman fortresses and then combining the best parts together. She can be quite persuasive when she puts quill to parchment. The result of her efforts is what you see here, Strathfeld Castle." Edwyn waved the broad sweep of his hand over the home with pride. "She is responsible fer almost everything."

Brant forgot his desire. "But she is so young. It is not possible."

"She started when she was eight. Though, at first, the servants had a hard time listening to her. That is why she has become so distant in nature. She had to be if she wanted to be taken seriously." Edwyn shook his head, looking uncomfortable. "Methought you knew."

"Come, let me see these plans." Brant assumed the older man gave too much credit to his lady wife.

Edwyn nodded, motioning him into one of the chambers built into the wall. A single torch lit the area, glowing over a small bed in one corner next to a wooden table with a few personal belongings. By the bed were rolls of old parchment.

"What is this place?" Brant asked.

"My chamber," Edwyn answered. "M'lady was kind enough to build it fer me, so that I may work in private."

Edwyn grabbed a torch off the wall and opened a small door that Brant hadn't noticed in his first inspection of the place. It led to a hidden chamber. Inside there were several long wooden tables with papers thrown haphazardly on top. On the floor there were a few writing quills, wax seals, and blank parchments neatly stacked.

Edwyn moved to light several torches, throwing the room into light. The smoke from them drifted up and out of a small crack in the top of the domed ceiling. Bricks were laid in a circular pattern on the floor, spiraling from the middle. It was an odd room, but impressive.

"It's m'lady's design. It has to do with the flow of the air. It took several years fer her to perfect the system. That is why the seam in the rafters isn't centered." Edwyn pointed at the dome. "It will take me but a moment to find the plans. We've had 'em memorized fer so long that we ne'er use 'em."

Brant slowly walked around the peculiar room. On one table several parchments looked like the practice sentences of a beginner writer. Brant's own writing wasn't so neat. Next to them was a master copy of the same sentences written perfectly. Continuing along the table, he found his wife's name girlishly carved into the wood next to a flower. He ran the tip of his finger over it.

Edwyn saw him and chuckled. "M'lady did that one night. She was thinking of carving images in all the wood of the manor, like giant, permanent tapestries. She must have been about fifteen then."

Brant stared in wonderment.

The seneschal turned back to the pile he'd been digging in. Still chuckling, he admitted, "It was glad we were when she decided it would be too much unnecessary labor."

Brant shook his head. He got the impression that his wife had spent many hours in the hidden sanctuary. In some serene way, the place felt of her. He ran his hand lightly over the table as he made his way along it. Spotting a pile of old children toys by the wall, he kneeled to pick up a tattered doll. "What is this?"

Edwyn walked over and took the doll fondly in his wrinkled hands. "I had forgotten about these. M'lady made 'em one year fer the cotter's children. These were left over. Methought she'd gotten rid of 'em."

Brant studied him in disbelief. "It seems my wife has many talents. Did she ever just play as a child?"

Edwyn gave Brant a pained look. The old man cleared his throat and tenderly laid the doll back in the corner as if it were a real child and turned back to his papers. "Surely you know of her sleeping habits. There are many hours in the day fer her."

"Has she always had trouble sleeping?" Brant refused to let the subject drop. He tried to sound like he knew what the man was talking about. In truth, he had never spent a night with his wife. How could he know her sleeping habits?

"It's not my place to say." Edwyn didn't look at him. "I have no wish to be disloyal to m'lady."

"What if I command you?"

"M'lady has been through much pain in her life. I will not add my betrayal to the list."

"You say pain. Like what?" Brant wondered what the man was not telling him.

"I am sure the plans are here somewhere," Edwyn tried to change the subject.

"You never answered. Did she ever just play as a child?" Brant watched the man's face carefully. Why didn't he just answer the question? It was simple enough.

Edwyn gave Brant another pained look and chose his answer carefully. "Nay. There was a time she was like other children, but m'lady is smart. She spent most of her time teaching herself many things. I suppose, in a way, that is how she played, by learning all she could."

"What changed, Edwyn? Children do not just stop playing one day because they are smart." Brant stepped to the old man, not giving him a chance to avoid answering. He was growing uneasy about what was deliberately being kept from him. "What am I not being told?"

"Perchance you should speak with Lady Della." Edwyn tried to turn away, but Brant put a restraining hand on him to stop the retreat. The old man sighed, unsure.

"I am speaking with you," Brant insisted.

"Mayhap you should ask yer wife." Edwyn risked much in naysaying his lord.

"Edwyn, it is obvious you care for m'lady." Brant let go of his arm. "So you must know her."

Edwyn nodded, giving up any pretense of looking for the papers. "Well, m'lord. I know her well."

"Then you know she will never tell me." Brant hated to admit it. "Why does she dislike me? Because I am a Viking?"

"You cannot blame her fer the prejudice. She was very young when it happened." Edwyn pulled a stool from under the table and sat. He gestured for Brant to do the same. He thoughtfully scraped his nail against a splinter in the old wood. Digging the offending piece up, he swiped it away with the back of his hand, pondering his words for a long moment. "I only tell you because I believe it best you hear it from someone who knows and not a bit of distorted servant's gossip."

"I understand." Brant sat.

"M'lady's mother, Lady Strathfeld, was a caring woman and she was extremely close to her daughter. She took the child everywhere with her. A kinder or more devoted mother I have ne'er seen. When Lady Strathfeld was very much pregnant with her second babe, Lord Strathfeld took the family to the coastal villages. A boat had just arrived in one of the towns bearing goods from faraway lands—silks, exotic spices, fragrances, jewelry. You know the like."

Brant nodded, willing the man to get on with the tale. Already his stomach tightened in dread. He kept his face blank and listened intently to every detail.

"Lord Strathfeld left his wife and child to look at the wares, telling young Della to make sure she looked after her pregnant mother. Back then, Strathfeld was a younger man, anxious to expand his fortunes. He met up with some traders and wanted to make arrangements to invest in their ship's next voyage. The men got drunk on foreign mead and before they knew it, they'd passed out.

"M'lady was about four years old when it happened. The family had been staying in a home owned by Sir Stuart's father, Lord Grayson. Lady Strathfeld must have gotten tired of waiting fer her husband and she and Della made their way back home." Edwyn took a deep breath. "The attackers were waiting there fer 'em. It's like they knew the women would be alone."

"Who?" Brant asked, though he was afraid he already knew the answer. *Viking mercenaries.*

"Vikings. Lord Strathfeld found his daughter the

next afternoon, tied to a bedpost and drenched in her mother's blood. Lady Della's hair was chopped off and thrown all about the chamber along with the hair of her mother." Edwyn swallowed in disgust, turning his eyes away. "And not just the hair from Lady Strathfeld's head."

Brant was sick to his stomach. He'd heard many stories of a similar nature, but the Viking's who performed such cruel acts were mercenaries for hire and not representative of the whole race. In truth, all races had mercenaries.

"Lord Strathfeld left fer the wars soon after, leaving m'lady in my care," Edwyn's words droned on in grim determination. "He loved his wife. Methinks Lady Della was a reminder of all that happened. As she grew older, she began to idolize her sire until he was a legend to her. No one could speak ill of the ealdorman. She wouldn't have it. By the time he came back three years later, it was ne'er mentioned between 'em again."

"What happened that night?" Brant was afraid of the answer, but he needed to know.

"No one knows fer sure, but one could well imagine. Lady Della, at least physically, was left unharmed. She'd been tied to the bedpost with a piece of leather strapped to her head so she could not look away from the bed. It was evident she had been forced to watch what they did, and they had all night to do it. Her mother had been raped, repeatedly, and tortured. The late countess's unborn child was cut out of her womb, the body ne'er found. The men left a torch burning the whole night. It was estimated Della had been there fer nigh on sixteen hours before she was found." Edwyn scraped the table harder with his thumbnail, the motion frantic as if trying to erase the past with the action. His eyes glistened with unshed tears and his voice cracked in pain. "She sat alone, gazing at the body of her dead mother the entire time. We ne'er understood why she was left alive and untouched. Methinks because living is a much worse torture than death. But we are glad she is with us."

"God's Bones!" Brant exclaimed, horrified. His heart went out to his wife and the poor child she'd been. How could he have guessed she'd been through such horrors?

"Yea." The old man cleared his throat and stood, rubbing thoughtfully at his forehead. "By the time Della was discovered, she had gone way inside herself. As far as I know, she hasn't told anyone what happened that night. I don't believe she has talked about it at all, but the nightmares have plagued her ever since. That is why she doesn't sleep, m'lord. Methinks she forces herself to stay busy so she doesn't have to face it. At least that was the way of it at first. Now, methinks, she stays awake because she doesn't know what else to do."

"They were never caught." The statement was more of an acknowledgment than a question.

"Nay." Edwyn again busied himself with the stack of papers. "Ah, here it is."

Brant slowly stood. Edwyn laid the plans on the

table. Taking his finger to them, Brant slid the parchment closer. It blurred within his vision.

It all made sense. His wife's unreasonable hatred of him was because of his Viking descent, and her uncanny ability to sew six outfits in a single sennight was because of her sleepless nights. It also explained her fear of bearing children and also her love for them, especially the foundling boy, Rab. She was trying to make sure he didn't feel pain as she had.

Brant felt awful at the way he'd treated her. She wasn't trying to be cruel and play games with him. She hadn't been trying to frustrate him sexually. She had honestly been trying to reach out to him and be a wife, despite what had happened to her, despite the idiotic lies her cousin had told her. Only he'd terrified her with his rough passion. Brant smiled grimly, sick with himself for his actions. He'd acted the boor, trying to rip her clothing from her, when she needed him to be slow and gentle and reassuring.

Brant saw well the passion in her for him. He should have also seen her fear. Her great passion would come in time, but first she had to trust him. She had to know that all Vikings, that all men, were not like the savage barbarians who attacked her mother. And, when coupling was done right, it was not a horrible experience.

His heart beat hollowly in his chest. Resting his hand solemnly on the castle blueprints, he stopped Edwyn from talking. He hadn't been listening anyway.

The seneschal looked up in surprise as Brant

shook his head. His expression said more than words ever could have. The old man nodded in silent understanding. Brant left, his shoulders hunched in anguish over that which he could not change.

EDWYN SAT QUIETLY, long after Lord Blackwell walked from the chamber, staring at the castle plans and not seeing them but for a vague impression they gave of the past.

9

"Countess, might I have a word with you?"

Della tried to smile pleasantly at the odious Lord Lester. The maids had just finished with the last of the rushes, so the hall smelled sweet with the fragrance of wild flowers and mint. The mint was a new addition to the usual scented mixture she blended for the stone floor. She hated to admit it was because she'd grown fond of smelling it on her husband's breath.

However, now it wasn't mint that filled her nostrils. The freshness of the hall was punctured by Lord Lester's unpleasant odor as he approached. Della hoped that if she ignored him, he would go away. She wasn't so fortunate.

"Yea, m'lord," she answered, not trying very hard to keep the exasperation from her voice.

Lord Lester smiled. His eyelids dipped low over his disturbingly shallow gaze.

"Do you look for my lord husband?" Della inquired when the man said nothing else to her.

Lester licked his lips with no ready answer. Touching the tip of his forefinger to his chin, he tapped lightly. The motion only drew attention to the red pockmark that scarred his face, which in turn led her gaze to his little upturned nose.

"Methinks Lord Blackwell is in the exercise yard." She nodded, turning to dismiss him. How had her husband formed such a friendship? The man was simply repulsive.

Politics, Della assumed with a distasteful grimace. She kicked at the rushes needlessly. *For surely Blackwell would not form such an alliance out of pleasure.*

"Nay, m'lady." Lord Lester reached a possessive hand forward to stop her from edging farther away from him. His fingers twisted about her arm in a presuming caress as he forced her around to face him. Della didn't even attempt to smile as her eyes alighted hauntingly on him.

The nobleman didn't notice. He was too busy ogling her breasts. "It's not your husband's company I seek. I'm in search of a more genteel partner to spend the eve with."

Della's mouth fell open in displeasure at his forward advance. Lord Lester's lazy eye stared eerily past her shoulder as the good one grazed over her body in sleazy perusal. He still wore the green tunic he'd arrived in that morning and she cursed the servants for not insisting he bathe. Though she was loath to send any of the maids to his chamber to help him. Even the most obstinate of them didn't deserve that unpleasant task.

"M'lord, methinks you forget yourself." Della yanked her elbow from his hand, worried she'd have to burn her burgundy dress now that he'd touched it. The material would undoubtedly reek of him and the strongest lye couldn't take such a filthy odor out. Not wanting to insult a guest of her husband, she eased her tone. "My lord husband could arrive any moment. I'm sure he would take offense to you saying such things to me."

Lord Lester glanced around the room, a secretive smile on his lips. "Of course, m'lady."

You odious pig, do you think I enjoy your inspection?

Trying to stay poised, Della shot him an icy look. To her amazement the man didn't back away. Her disdain only seemed to encourage him.

"It would not do for our affections to be made known." Lord Lester turned his back to the hall where people started to gather for the eve meal. He licked his lips as one eye continued to stare at her breasts. "It's said that your husband already sleeps in another chamber. It must be hard for you to be without his attentions."

No man had ever dared to address her in such a forward manner—no man but Brant. Was this what happened when one was married? Did men think since a bride had just lost her maidenhead she would gladly accept any invitation of bedsport? Della shivered at the prospect. If Lord Lester touched her again she would vomit all over him.

"It is naught to be ashamed of, for it is well-known Blackwell keeps two mistresses in Jorvik. Mayhap he brings them here to be with him. You should not have to be without a man because your husband is busy spreading his seed elsewhere." The vulgar man leaned uncomfortably close, pursing his thin lips as his beady eyes narrowed. "It's not your fault your husband cannot appreciate your body the way I could. And, when I am done teaching you all I know, he will never naysay you again."

"M'lord," Della warned in a heated whisper. Her cheeks stained with rage. "Mind your words."

"You must not be used to being spoken to in such a bold manner. I daresay after tonight you will not feel the same way." Lord Lester winked, as his eye again drifted down her chest. "That excites you, does it not?"

"Oh!" Della didn't know what to say to the repulsive proposition. She took a deep breath, her eyes dashing about, automatically searching for Brant to come to her aid. Not seeing him anywhere in the hall, she decided it would be best if she left his friend until she could better deal with the insults. She skirted abruptly past Lester to make her way to the head table.

Just wait until I tell my husband, you lewd son of a pig. Methinks you will not be so smug then! But even as she thought it, she wasn't sure what her husband would do about Lord Lester's offense.

Brant heard a maid giggle as he approached. Her shiny, short curls bobbed as she lowered her chin, but her eyes stayed on his face. He returned her smile with the benevolence of a leader and though she blushed prettily, her look was lost on him as he continued past.

Intent on finding his wife, there was much Brant wanted to say to her. First being an apology for his actions. Edwyn's tale had lit a flame of rage in his chest. He knew all too well that the world was filled with many people willing to perform those kinds of atrocities. There was much death in the land they lived in. Northumbria had been founded on death and wars. Brant himself had killed men in the heat of battle. But there was a big difference in the killing he did. He fought for his king. He fought for a way of life he believed in. And he always fought fair, while the men who had attacked Della's mother killed for either money or sport. Neither of which was a noble cause. Such acts disgusted him.

He smiled absentmindedly as he walked across the scented main hall floor. Soldiers filled the tables, helping themselves to mead. He nodded at those who addressed him, answering their greetings in kind. Many of Lord Strathfeld's men accepted his leadership with little dispute. The few who had problems with the arrangement had already left the keep. In total, there were mayhap three dozen of Lord Strathfeld's men still residing at the manor. The rest of the knights were his fellow Vikings. Beyond their numbers were those nobles and their own separate households whom he lorded over.

Already, he knew most of the late ealdorman's men and they knew him by his reputation. Brant laughed at some of the ridiculous names he'd been called. Brant the Flame was his personal favorite. Or what had Della called him on their wedding night? *Brant the Thorn in My Arse?* He smiled, remembering her heated blush as she said it. He wondered if she thought that of him still.

Seeing his wife step up to the high table, he sighed. She'd tied her hair back along the nape of her neck, binding the flaxen waves in a coiffure. Brant felt his stomach harden, as it did whenever he was about to go into battle. She was indeed beautiful, though her face was frozen with chagrin. He saw the hard set of her lips, pressing together as if not to yell, and her amber eyes stared coldly before her.

Could she still be angry with him? He frowned. Intentionally, he hadn't gone to her, even after speaking with Edwyn. He thought the time apart would have lessened her ire from that afternoon. It didn't appear to be so.

Deciding it best to speak to her as soon as possible so as not to let her anger boil any longer, he moved behind her to gently touch her elbow. It would be best if he escorted her to a private chamber where they might talk away from the ears of the hall. His lips parted to quietly say her name, but before the word could escape, she jerked her arm from his gentle grasp. The heated display took him by surprise and a twinge of irritation rose forth in his chest. He didn't have to wait long for her to speak.

"M'lord, leave me be," Della yelled, keeping her back to him. Her shoulders shook violently. "I will not sleep with you tonight or ever. So get your hands off me before I have you beaten bloody by the knights of this hall. You whining, stinking girl-child!"

Those gathered gasped in shock, their voices stuttering to a halt. A few of the men snickered behind the backs of their hands—the Vikings to see how their lord would punish the countess's wayward tongue, and the Anglo-Saxons with a bit of pride in their mistress, though none showed any intention of trying to overtake the new ealdorman. Brant ignored the men. His eyes narrowed in anger and he clenched his fists as she spun around.

"My husband…" Her words trailed off as she saw his face. Her eyes rounded in alarm and her skin became deathly pale.

Yea, you should be scared, Ice Princess. He forced a deep breath, the sound harsh over the stillness of the hall. It took all his might not to strike her. She looked over his shoulder in confusion and Brant heard Lord Lester's high-pitched cackle behind him. The sound inspired his anger to go from close to exploding to a full-blown rage. He forgot Edwyn's tale.

He fought the numbing anger that bubbled inside him, stemming from his chest, and curling out over his body like a wicked poison. Brant knew that if he was to take Della into private chambers to punish her, he would more than likely end up beating her for her public insults. It was bad enough she yelled, but to call him a girl in front of his men. It was a most unforgivable insult to his manhood—for who to better judge his prowess as a man than his wife?

DELLA BACKED away from her husband, her mouth working in horror as she shook her head. No sound escaped her lips as she struggled for words.

"This time you have gone too far, lady wife." The dark sound of Brant's words fell ominously over them. A few of the soldiers whispered fervently and a servant dropped a pitcher of mead. The crash on stone created a foreboding resonance and hushed the men to silence.

Grabbing a fistful of her dress, Della looked to the hall for help. None of the men moved, not even those who had been loyal to her in the time of her father. She knew she'd made a grave mistake. She came up hard against the dining table, knocking over a pitcher of ale. The dark liquid flowed over her hand onto her gown. Ignoring the mess, she held out her clean hand to stop her husband's advance. "M'lord, I—"

"I would put my wife in the stocks for a sennight for such a thing. A man who cannot control his wife —" Lester said.

"A man should not have to put up with your continuous insults," Brant interrupted. She leaned farther back over the table trying to escape him. His expression hardened as he looked at her. "Leave my table." Grabbing her extended arm by the wrist before she could pull it back, he jerked her away him, urging her down the stone steps of the raised platform toward the cold stone floor.

Della's body pitched forward and her feet caught awkwardly as she descended. He didn't throw her so hard as to do her great harm, but her foot caught on a stone and she tripped. Her limbs flailed as she stumbled. Reaching out, she grasped at the air for support, but could not stop her fall.

The straw rushes inefficiently padded her landing and her face bumped against the stone. Pain radiated throughout her body. For a long moment of breathless silence, she laid there until feeling came back to her limbs. Her palms throbbed angrily as she pushed to kneeling. When finally she turned to look at him, Brant stood high above her on the platform. Shock at her fall shone in his eyes. For the briefest of moments, he looked as if he might come to her aid.

"Well played, m'lord!" Lester decreed, stopping Brant's hand mid-action. "You cannot let her insolence go unchecked or else the whole country would think you weak and lacking in your manhood. I daresay the king would then regret giving you this title and land."

Brant blinked heavily, drawing his gaze away from her to look over the gathered crowd. His hands fisted in a tight ball, even as a blank mask covered his expression as if to challenge any to dispute his honor. None so dared.

Giving her a blistering glare, Lester said to Della, "By my authority of the king, you will eat there on the floor, lady, like a mongrel dog. Only feeding on the scraps your husband throws you until he decides how best to punish you."

Brant took his seat at the head table amongst his peers, keeping his eyes on those around him. Very quietly, he said, "So be it."

Never in her adult life had she been treated so callously. She touched her throbbing cheek where her face hit the stone. When she pulled her hand back, her fingertips were lightly dotted with blood. With a deep breath, she moved to stand, hoping to plead her case.

Brant saw her. The emotion hadn't died from his eyes.

"Do you dare to disobey the king's authority so quickly?" Lester challenged.

Della quickly sat back down and fought for composure. Her limbs shook and her insides crumbled with the sense of defeat. She had never seen him this angry before, not even when she was denying him his husband rights. Well aware of the soldiers watching her every move, she brushed the loose straw off her hair and gown in an attempt to save a bit of her dignity. Drawing her knees to her chest, she hugged them with her arms.

BRANT SAW what had happened to Della's face and despite his frustration, he was sorry for it. She lightly fingered the wound and winced in pain. Then, catching his eyes on her, she jerked her hand away and stared defiantly forward. Her words echoed in his mind and he wished she would just recant so he could forgive her.

Brant didn't know whether he was angrier at her outburst or at the idea that she would never grow fond of him. It was a very unhappy marriage he saw before them, just as she first warned him it would be. Taking a long drink of mead, he tried hard to swallow over the lump of despair in his throat. He wanted to go to her, but to do so would be to show weakness to his men and undercut his authority before the king's ambassadors. Not to mention, Lord Lester's decree in the name of the king that she should stay on the floor. To go to her now would mean to insult the royal name.

Brant motioned stiffly to the servants directing them to continue serving the meal. They had stumbled to a stop at Della's outburst. Those gathered in the hall were unusually quiet as the maids carried in trays laden with hot food. The men waited patiently for the servants to place the meal on the table before moving to take what they wanted. They made no secret about watching to see what their lord and lady would do next.

Gayla came to the high table. The maid's hands shook as she set a dish of roasted mutton before Lord Blackwell. She glanced to Gunther who motioned her away. The man-at-arm's face pulled into a grim line.

"It's wise to keep your lady wife in line, m'lord," Lester said.

Brant hadn't noticed that Lord Lester took the

seat beside him. Now as he directed his attention to the man, he wondered how he could've been so distracted as to not smell the overwhelming stench. Brant ignored him and took a bite of lamb. Inside, his heart pounded wildly as he forced himself not to look at his wife. Already the look of her wounded face emblazoned on his mind.

"It would not do for her to play you false," Lord Lester continued, leaning to block Brant's view of Della. "I have no respect for wives who cuckold their husbands."

Who said aught about cuckold? Brant bristled at the man's smug tone. He didn't like the offensive, gossiping noble commenting on his marriage.

Lord Lester chuckled, prompting some of the men to do the same, most of whom belonged to Lester and Sir Vladamir's traveling party. The knights of Strathfeld stayed woodenly silent, eyes shining in disapproval, though which of the nobles they were disappointed in was not clear.

Feeling sorry for his wife, he glanced over at her trembling form as she bravely sat before him. Her amber eyes watched him warily through a lash-shaded gaze. He detected the tears she refused to let fall. His wife was a proud one, mayhap as proud as he was. A piece of his heart broke away with the agony of what he was allowing to happen, but his stubborn self-respect refused to forgive her. She insulted his manhood in front of his men, in front of the king's men—men who were to ride all over the kingdom with little more to occupy their time than to spread the tale of this event to all who would listen. And for what? Because she was mad at him for desiring her? Would she even take his help if he offered it? Or would she scream at him again, insulting him more? Would the king regret giving him land and power if Brant allowed his Saxon bride to humiliate him so early in their marriage? With so much gained, he had even more to lose. It wasn't as if he were a pauper in the king's realm. With his new title, land, and pure Viking heritage, he was one of the most powerful men under Guthrum's rule.

Lord Lester laughed harder and slapped his knee. The sound soon turned into a cough. The pockmark on his chin noticeably darkened and he took a drink of mead to calm himself.

Brant chose to disregard him, not caring what Lord Lester thought. He took another bite of the roasted mutton, but did not taste it. Hearing Gunther grunt in disapproval, Brant turned a questioning look to him. He could have sworn Gunther shook his head in displeasure. When had that happened? When had Gunther found a soft spot in his heart for any woman, let alone Brant's shrew of a wife?

Brant ignored Gunther and the men, ignored the eerie silence which settled over the keep. Even the night air brought in no familiar sounds of insects or of animals in their pens. Brant forced himself to eat, trying to act as if nothing was amiss, willing the meal to end as quickly as possible. Secretly he prayed Della would find a way to redeem herself, though he had no idea what such a thing would be. He willed her to storm from the hall so he could chase her and end this in the privacy of their chambers. She did not move.

Roldan entered the hall from the side door, the smile of greeting dying on his face. Quickly, he took a seat next to one of his fellow knights. After a few whispers, the man frowned in Della's direction with an unhappy shake of his head.

"Methinks the dog needs a drink, m'lord!" Lord Lester's sudden words were abnormally loud.

Before Brant knew what the man was about, Lester stood and lifted his cup of mead into the air, throwing the drink onto Della. Amber liquid flew from the goblet. A burst of surprised laughter sounded as Lester's men pounded their fists.

DELLA KNEW Lord Lester's intent long before he tossed the liquid at her. Daring him with her eyes, she waited for him to stand. Part of her hoped Brant would stop his attack, but he sat watching in moody silence. As the liquid came toward her, she refused to move except to turn her head proudly away. She shut her eyes as mead doused her hair and trickled down the front of her dress. It soaked her face with its warm stickiness, burning the raw scrape of her wound. As the last of the contents soaked into her gown, she rubbed her eyes clean with her sleeve before redirecting her gaze to the table.

Brant didn't move, didn't stop Lester's evil laugh. She heard the soldiers' merriment—mocking her, disrespecting her, all except Gunther, who looked about in open disgust at the whole scene.

What had happened in the short time since she had been married? In just over a sennight, the men's loyalty had been won by Lord Blackwell. She'd fought for many years to earn their respect and in a few short weeks it was all gone—taken away by her barbarian husband. And there was nothing she could do about it. Suddenly she stood, having taken the humiliation long enough.

The liquor dried on her flesh, pasting thin strands of her blonde hair to her neck in misshapen trails. Her thin shoulders shook with anguish. Anguish at the betrayal of her manor. Anguish at the disrespect she was forced to endure.

Her voice was clear and sure as she announced, "I have had enough! Now, you *will* let me explain myself. After I have spoken my peace, you may judge as you see fit."

The hall went quiet amid a myriad of hushes. The onlookers craned their necks to get a good view of the front, wanting to see what Lord Blackwell would do next to his unruly wife. Brant tilted his head, stiffly giving her leave to speak. Her chin jutted defiantly in the air and she gripped the material at her waist to keep her hands from trembling. The braided gold cord tangled in her fingers.

"Methought you were that detestable piece of refuse, Lord Lester." She shot Lester a nasty scowl. The man had the audacity to look offended. Brant watched her through veiled eyes, stroking his bottom lip, but said nothing.

"A moment before, over there." Della flung her arm behind her, her chest heaving with gasps of air. Inside, she shook with the effort it took to face her menacing husband. Outside, she did her best to remain calm. "A moment before you came in, he dared to touch me and say that I was to spend this night with him. He said he would talk seductively to me, implying you didn't know how to treat me in the marriage bed. It was him methought I was shouting at, not you."

A tear slipped from her eye and she bit her lip as the salty moisture stung her raw cheek. No one dared to speak so she turned to Lord Lester and continued, "You, Lord Lester, are a lewd, foul-smelling pig. Get you quick to a bath lest my nose rots off from the offensive lingerings of your smell. Yea, and before I have to burn aught else you touch."

The soldiers suddenly slapped their fists on the table, shouting encouragement to her words. She turned a hard look on them until they quieted. Bitterly she frowned at them, shaking her head slowly. Not one of them had come to her defense before. A few in the front looked sheepishly away from her icy gaze.

"I would not say those things of you, my lord husband." Della's voice quieted. Brant had every right to be angry, though it was a misunderstanding. "I could not, for you are more man than this hall combined. I would fight to the death anyone who claims otherwise. I am sorry I yelled." Della sniffed. Her words trailed off into a mere whisper. "I beg your forgiveness."

She'd meant only to say the words to assuage his anger and restore some of his pride. But, as she spoke, she found part of her believed the words. She kept her head high and proud, though she'd humbled herself greatly.

Brant said nothing, his eyes searching her, looking her up and down, as if he weighed her words. Could she really blame him if he didn't believe her? Didn't trust her? Theirs wasn't a marriage built on trust. Slowly, his face reddened. His fist tightened in front of his mouth into a hard ball.

Believing his continued wrath was her doing, she knew she'd better take the chance to make it up to him. His reputation had been threatened. For a moment, she closed her eyes to the pain her words were going to cause her. A memory, brief and potent, of her mother came to her. She opened her eyes with determination.

"M'lord." Della took a step toward Brant and held out her hand. The men in the back shushed to better hear her. Resolute, she continued in an even tone, "I am sorry. The words were not meant for you and to prove it, I announce to all that I will lie with you this night and every night after, as you so please, for there is not a man in my eyes greater than you are. You shall have me until you tire of me."

Brant eyed her in astonishment, unsuccessfully hiding the beginning of a smile behind his fist. The men gaped at each other in wonderment, the Saxon men especially having a hard time believing their ears.

Della dropped her shaking hand when he didn't take it. She turned amidst the disbelief, feeling so very alone. "I will be in our chamber waiting for you."

None of the people of Strathfeld had seen their mistress so openly humbled. In stunned epiphany, they all turned eyes of great respect to their overlord. Some even looked at him as if he were immortal.

Della lifted her chin haughtily into the air. Her thin shoulders stiffened bravely in mock confidence. For once, the men had no crude comments to make. There were no words of encouragement for their lord, most even looked away when she met their eyes with her regal calm.

Della made her way with as much dignity as she could muster to the stairwell. When she ducked around the corner, she heard the hall explode with conversation. Her heart pounded. Hurrying abovestairs, she was careful that her footfalls would not be heard. And, as she reached the top of the stairwell, she ran the rest of the way to her bedchamber, sobbing in wretched disbelief.

Brant watched his wife leave, not heeding the commotion below him. It was not lost on him how her words affected the people of Strathfeld. Her public acceptance of him would do much in securing his role as lord. That was if any still had doubts to his claim. He also knew how much of her precious control she'd just relinquished in her open acknowledgment of his authority. Though the men would never have admitted to it, they valued her opinion. In accepting him, she had taken some of the power away from herself and turned it over to him. He knew how hard it had to have been for her. Strathfeld Castle was her entire life.

Suddenly, remembering her heated words, he turned his attention to Lord Lester. He read well the truth on his wife's face. She would not have been able to humble herself otherwise.

At the ealdorman's glare, Lester shot up in his chair and backed away from the high table. His complexion was flushed with outrage.

"M'lord, surely you do not take the word of a slanderous woman over an ambassador to the king?" Lester puffed his chest in the air. "I'm certain she only makes those accusations to secure your pardon for her previous behavior. I will not stand for an attack on my character. I demand public satisfaction. She should be flogged."

"That is not your decision to make." Brant stood and took a step toward the reprehensible man. A well of satisfaction flowed in him as he stalked his new prey. He lowered his head, anticipating the hunt. A smile tugged his lips.

"Lady Blackwell's word is not to be questioned," one of the Saxon knights shouted from below, eliciting a round of agreement from the others.

"Yea," came another. "You do not question the honor of our countess!"

"What do you think you are doing?" Lord Lester demanded with bravado, eyeing the shouting knights of Strathfeld.

Brant let the measured, cruel smile curve his lips until it shone mercilessly on his hardened face. He took another menacing step.

"I am an ambassador to the king. You would not dare to put a hand on me." Lester looked about for help. "Vladamir, where are you, man?"

Sir Vladamir shook his head before taking another drink of his mead. His low, accented voice was quiet, as he answered, "Nay, I told you she did not want you. Now you must suffer the consequences. Lord Blackwell has every right to exact punishment."

Brant reached forward, grabbed Lester by the cuff of his neck and dragged the stumbling, weaker man out into the bailey. The soldiers followed with loud jeers of encouragement. Sir Vladamir stayed quietly in the back, choosing not to interfere. He lifted his hand to stay the king's knights, keeping them from starting a brawl.

"I demand you let me go," Lord Lester yelled.

"My pleasure." Brant threw him to the dirt, stalking him as the man crawled along the ground like an infant. Kicking his backside, he sent Lester skidding across the earth. The onlookers cheered at the attack.

"Vladamir? Where are you man? Help me," Lord Lester screamed. When he received no help from that corner, he blustered, "I will put in a good word to King Guthrum to any man who would defend me against this injustice."

The Vikings laughed at the request. All of them were loyal to Lord Blackwell first.

"She begged me to make advances toward her. She bewitched me with her wanton ways. It's not my fault," Lord Lester persisted in desperation. "She's a witch."

That brought an angry growl from the crowd and they began shouting for blood.

Brant leaned down and grabbed the man. Hauling him to his feet, he laughed before announcing, "Methinks my wife was right. You are a whining, stinking girl and it would be most unfortunate to have you at my side in battle. Your stink would give away our position."

"Yea!" the men yelled in approval.

"How dare you!" Lord Lester swaggered as he tried to slap Brant's hand away.

"Open the gate," Brant ordered, staring the man squarely in the eye. The men readily obeyed. "You are lucky I do not kill you for your insults. The Countess of Strathfeld is no witch. Say so again and I will not be able to keep my men from violence."

"You will unhand me, Lord Blackwell," Lester whined in a shrill voice. His feet dangled in the air, his toes only grazing the dirt as Brant carried him across the yard. A large crowd followed behind.

Brant stopped as he neared the small moat

outside the castle. "Methinks my wife was right about another thing. You are in need of a bath!"

Lester screamed as Brant launched him into the moat. He landed in the shallow water, hissing and sputtering curses.

"Gunther, get Lord Lester's horse and lead it out. He is no longer to be welcomed here." Seeing Sir Vladamir approach, Brant gave him a hard stare.

"Nay, m'lord, you have no quarrel with me." Sir Vladamir laughed as he looked down at his traveling companion. He patted Brant heartily on the shoulder. "I will tell the king what has happened here. He will think it amusing."

Brant nodded, joining the laughter as Lester tried to make his way up the ditch only to end up sliding back down into the rancid water. His padded green tunic was caked with mud.

"To tell the truth, King Guthrum sent him on this mission to get him away from his camp." Sir Vladamir grinned, wiping his eye. "He also grew tired of the stench."

"And what crime did you commit, my friend, to get sent with him?" Gunther asked as he led a horse over the stone bridge. Letting go of the reins, he gave the horse a light pat to get it jogging. The mount made his way unescorted into the field before starting to graze.

"I wish to marry one of the king's daughters—a very dark and bewitching maiden." Sir Vladamir shrugged. "He said if I played nursemaid to this blundering oaf I could have her. So here I am."

Gunther shook his head. "Methinks no maid would be worth such a task."

"Ah, my friend, you have not found the one yet." Sir Vladamir sighed. "When you do, we will talk on it again."

Brant thought instantly of Della awaiting him in her bedchamber. He looked back to his castle.

Sir Vladamir sighed as he held his hand to Brant. "My apologies, but I must also leave. It is many more stops we have before I am free to go home."

Brant nodded and grasped the man's hand. "Gunther, help him with whatever he needs. Have Isa prepare a satchel of food for their travels."

Gunther laughed, "Yea, whatever he needs, so long as I do not have to fish his friend out of the moat."

Grinning arrogantly, Brant was unable to move fast enough as he went back to the manor. Della would finally be his.

"Yea, hurry m'lord. She be waiting fer you abovestairs!" a man yelled behind him.

"Yea, if it is help you need—"

"Enough! She is the countess." Brant didn't bother to turn, as he sliced his hand through the air for silence. He'd been waiting too long for this night and could only hope his wife didn't change her mind once again, for he doubted the fire in his belly could stand it if she did.

THE STEAM from the hot bath surrounded Della in a cloud as she stood from the tub. Her skin was heated red from the water and she hurriedly wiped the moisture from her flesh with the linen Ebba had left her. As she dried her hair, she froze when the chamber door opened. It was only Ebba bringing in the last of her clothing. A few maids followed behind to remove her bath water.

Della huddled in the linen as they went by. Several more came in and replaced the bath with fresh, hot water for her lord husband. Della knew he liked to bathe often, so she thought to take advantage of the habit and give herself more time. She only put off the inevitable, but she couldn't help it.

She'd had her possessions moved to the main bedchamber where Brant had been sleeping. He had said he wished for someone to warm his bed each night. It could only mean it was his desire for her to sleep there.

Della's limbs shook with nervous excitement. She hastily donned her nightclothes and, with unsteady hands, she tried to tie the laces of the conservative gown. Unable to reach the laces in back, she turned and Ebba did them for her. Digging her toes absently into the soft fur rug, Della shivered and looked around the room. The chamber was the largest in the manor and took longer to heat. She moved by the fire and added more wood. Holding her shaking hands to the flames, she rubbed her palms together.

"Ebba, quick, help me with my hair." Della

pointed at the silver comb the handmaid already carried in her hand.

Ebba went to her mistress, taking the comb to her long tresses, pulling the wet strands back, away from her face. "M'lady, it is fairly anxious you are."

Della didn't answer as a serving girl dumped more water into the tub. Ebba held the comb between her teeth and tousled Della's hair so it would curl as it dried. Then, hitting a knot, she took the comb to untangle it.

"Ebba, do you think he is still angry at me?" Della asked when the other maids had gone. "Do you think he will take me to bed in anger?"

"Hold still, m'lady. I do not wish to pull yer hair." Ebba sighed loudly. "And nay, it's likely he is not upset with you. Besides, you have been a wife now, you should be learning how to best cool his anger."

"What if I haven't?" Della bit her lip as she tried to keep from moving.

Ebba giggled. "There is nothing to pleasing a man. Just remember they think with their sword most times. If you tame that dragon, then you tame the beast that controls him."

"Tame a dragon?" Della inquired, puzzled. She wrinkled her nose.

"Yea, it's when the dragon spouts his fire that he is tamed." Ebba nodded, confident.

Sword? Dragon? By all the saints! Does Ebba actually believe she makes sense? Della tried to smile at the advice, though she didn't understand what Ebba was talking about. What came to mind was some of the drawings she'd seen of the sea. Her father had given her some when she was younger. Drawn at the edge of the world were depictions of horrible sea creatures. Della often wondered why anyone would sail if dragons swam in the water.

The handmaiden tugged at a tangle, trying to free it. Della flinched, but didn't move as a hard pull finally loosened the knot. She supposed that if a dragon came out of her husband, she would have to tame it. She only hoped she didn't have to get burned by the fire. Brant was usually very hot when she touched him.

"Lord Blackwell has turned his anger elsewhere." Ebba giggled in assurance.

"What do you mean?" Della froze, trying to make sense of everything and failing. Surely, Brant was not with a mistress tonight. She couldn't help but wonder at the acute disappointment she felt. If Brant chose a mistress, she should welcome him to it.

"I mean that after you left, he kicked Lord Lester in his arse. M'lord threw him in the moat, saying you were right, he was in need of a bath." Ebba giggled again, this time louder. "It was quite funny to see him sputtering about."

"Did he really do—?"

"Leave us."

Della's words trailed to a stop as a deep, familiar voice echoed the chamber. The sound was soft and sent her to shivering anew. It was the sound she had been both anticipating and dreading. It was a sound she would never forget.

Della didn't move, too afraid to turn around, so instead she stared into the fire. From the direction of his voice, Brant stood near the doorway. Her heart beat fast, racing uncontrollably. She took deep breaths, becoming more scared with each passing second.

"Just remember, tame the dragon," Ebba whispered with an audacious wink. She handed her mistress the comb, giggling as she scurried out of the chamber.

10

BRANT CLOSED the door behind the maid and walked slowly toward his wife. He had just been to her chamber only to be informed by Gayla that Lady Blackwell moved into his bed. He tripped over his own feet in his anxiousness to get to her and was a little disappointed not to find her naked and waiting, though he wasn't really surprised.

He took in the illuminated curves of her body as she stood outlined by firelight. Moving closer, Brant discovered it was too hard to see her figure under the conservative nightgown she wore. There were several layers to it, causing every feminine curve she had to be hidden beneath the material, except that which had been revealed to him by firelight.

Della didn't look at him as she fingered the comb Ebba had left with her, tracing the tip of her finger delicately over the metal tines. Shivers racked her slender form. Brant brushed his hand over the back of her neck, pushing aside her wet, heavy locks. She gasped, stiffening but not running way. He caressed her again, keeping his touch soft. This time she sighed, shivering. Gradually, he turned her around, watching the fire dance on her beautiful skin. The comb fell soundlessly to the fur rug. Her eyes widened as she directed her gaze past him, refusing to look.

"Does this hurt?" Lightly, he touched her sore cheek with his finger. The scrape was still an angry red, but looked much better after being cleaned.

"Nay." Della winced as his finger ran over the sorest-looking part.

"I am sorry," he whispered unhappily. "I did not mean to make you fall. Had I known that you were trying to fend off that obnoxious toad, I would have come to your aide. As it was, I was not sure you would have taken my help."

Della nodded again, appearing wary of his kindness. Brant realized this was one of the only times he'd touched her in neither anger nor excessive passion. It was hard, but he forced himself to go slow.

"You shiver." Brant's words were low. "Are you cold?"

"I had your bath," Della answered, instantly following the comment with a weak moan. Brant smiled. Flustered, she motioned her hand to the tub. She still hadn't looked at him directly. "I—I mean I had a bath drawn for you, naturally I did not have your bath. It would be impossible, would it not? Methought you..."

Della snapped her mouth shut with a groan. Brant smiled as she bit her lip. Obviously, she stalled for time. He studied the fine line of her neck, aching to touch her more but knowing he must hold back. It was a bittersweet torment, but one his body took willingly. For he knew if he denied his passions now, he would surely reap the benefit of the waiting later.

"Thank you," he whispered.

"Should I leave?" Della finally moved to face him. "I could send you a maid if you prefer, as I have never attended to…bath…never…ah."

He smiled as a thought formed in his head. Mayhap his wife's attempt to stall his advances would work to his advantage. It would give her a chance to get used to his body and it would be sweet torture to be bathed by her.

"I want you to help me, Della," he said. "No other."

"Oh." Della brought the corner of her lip once more between her teeth and swayed back. His hand moved to her throat, delicately rubbing behind her ear as he kept her near him. Her whole body focused on that one soft touch. She leaned into his palm for a brief moment, trying to get used to his gentleness. His tender caress did more to chip away at her icy defenses than his fiery passions ever could.

She met his eyes, no longer able to fight the pull he had on her. The blue orbs looked mythical, glowing with traces of firelight. Brant withdrew his hand, keeping his eyes steadily on her. His hair glimmered, except for the streak of fire that trailed down the one side.

He shrugged off his tunic, revealing his naked chest. Her cheeks flamed in embarrassment and she turned her back to him. Wringing her hands nervously, she plied her mind for anything to break the silence. "Did Lord Lester leave?"

"Yea," Brant said in a most attractive tone. "I tossed him in the moat."

"I'm sorry you had to remove your friend." Della heard the hush of his clothes falling to the stone floor. Curling her toes in the rug, she forced herself to stay where she was. Her apprehension outweighed her curiosity to see what he looked like naked.

"He isn't my friend. I just met him today." Brant sounded amused. "Is that who you think I would befriend? An odious man with a bad temperament?"

"I'm sorry. I didn't mean to imply—" Laughter cut her off. Della started to turn and then caught herself. She tapped her heel in agitation.

"Try to relax, Della. It is just a bath."

She wondered if he stood naked, waiting for her to look at him. Is that what he wanted? She'd heard his clothing fall, but no other sound. Her eyes searched the stone wall, as if to see a reflection there to assuage her curiosity. There was nothing, not even a shadow.

"Methought mayhap you wanted privacy," she said when silence became deafening. She hoped to hear where he was. Did he slither into the bath, silent as a dropping feather? Or did he still stand, naked and waiting? "I always do."

She took a deep breath and forced her hands to her side. Hearing a splash of water, she waited.

Brant cleared his throat to get her attention. Della jolted, startled by the sound. Little by little, she turned, her eyes finding him easily. He was in the tub, his back to her as he leaned his head against the rim. The strong muscles of his neck and shoulders shifted with every subtle movement. Taking his arms from the edge, he settled them into the water where she couldn't see. His long hair floated about his shoulders as he sank deeper into the steaming liquid. Staring in wonder, she watched his naked knees creep up and out of the water. They were covered with soft, dark hair, and very unlike her smoother legs. His limbs bulged with muscles, just like his chest, making her curious to see the rest of him.

She inched forward, trying to be quiet. Stopping a few yards behind him, she wondered what she should do. Inquisitiveness got the better of her and she rose onto her toes. Knees tapered off to large thighs submerged under the water. She wished she could cast a spell to make him fall asleep, so she could explore with her hands where her eyes strayed. Craning her neck, she tried to see deeper beneath the surface, to where his serpent was hidden by dark shadows. An arm moved to relax along the edge of the tub. She followed the trail of wet flesh, only to meet his eyes. Brant silently watched her.

"I was just seeing if you had soap," she lied. Della instantly came down off her toes.

"Come here, Della." The words were throaty and raw. When he looked her over, she felt exposed like he could see every inch of her form beneath the gown.

"Wash me." His command was soft and he held out a wet cloth for her to take.

Della hesitated, feeling lightheaded at the prospect of exploring him. The fireplace had finally begun to flood the chamber with its heat. His fingers purposely went out of their way to stroke the back of her hand. He was warm from the water and the heat spread itself in to her limbs.

"So-ap." Her voice cracked and she cleared her throat. "I need soap if I am to bathe you."

Brant brought it out of the water, handing it to her as he had the cloth. "Here."

Della took it from him and gently lathered the washcloth. Her hands shook with such force the soap slid from her fingers into the water with a splash. She jumped at the noise and looked to where the water rippled softly on the surface.

"Go ahead." Brant's look was now strained, his throat working. Leaning his head back, he closed his eyes. "Pick it up."

His voice was so calm compared to her shaking insides. Della reached into the water where the soap had disappeared in between his thighs. Her wrist brushed the inside of his solid leg. The soft, wet hairs tickled as she moved against his tight flesh. Finding the soap instantly, she didn't remove her hand right away. She liked the feel of him. Brant's head was still back, his eyes still closed, and his firm lips set in a long, harsh line.

Della moved her wrist along his thigh, soap in hand. The rub of his flesh sent a fire shooting though her body until all she could do was imagine how she wanted to touch more of him. She licked her lips, carefully watching his face for changes. His eyes tightened, holding closed. She ran her hand higher, noting how the water grew hotter as she did. Then she bumped against his hardened shaft. The smooth texture of it was the source of his fire. Brant groaned. She quickly pulled her hand from the water, not daring to touch his dragon again.

Anxious, she re-lathered the cloth. His member had been so hard, so unyielding. It wasn't at all like she'd imagined. And it was so hot. Was that the fire she had to put out? Mayhap during love play it grew so hot as to spout fire from his body. From what she'd felt, it hadn't been far from flaming. Unnerved by the idea, she set the soap aside and pushed the cloth onto his flesh. Della moved his hair from his shoulders as she began to scrub. He leaned forward to allow her access to his back as the soapy cloth glided over his bronzed skin. Her movements were rushed, but Brant didn't seem to notice.

"Uhh," he groaned as her hand pushed hard against a stiff muscle.

"Did I hurt you?" Della instantly drew her hand away. "I'm sorry, I never did this before. Mayhap I should send someone else to finish."

"Nay," he said, sounding anxious. "I don't want anyone else to finish what you've started." He paused, uncomfortably clearing his throat. Pleasure began to ripple inside her, but then he added, "Besides, the servants are probably busy cleaning the hall and you are already here."

"I see. I will try to be careful." She rubbed him lighter. "What happened to your back?"

"It's just an old injury that pains me sometimes."

"From battle?" Della asked, glad for a chance to break the silence of before with conversation. Many scars littered her husband's body, but she'd never paid them much mind, for they only added to his appeal. Her eyes became mesmerized by the soapy flesh, trails of white against the alluring texture of his sun-bronzed skin.

"I was hit with a club." Brant motioned dismissively, as if to say it happened to him all the time.

"Where does it hurt?" Della pushed on his back. "Here?"

"Yea." Brant grunted.

"Wait here." Suddenly, Della smiled. She dropped the cloth into the water and dried her hands on the skirt of her nightgown. Going to her personal trunk, she lifted the lid and dug through the small jars she had organized within it. Finding the one she was looking for, she picked it up. As an afterthought, she grabbed another before returning to the tub.

"Rub this on your back twice a day. It is a mixture of wild yams and peppers made for muscles and will make you feel better. I use it after I work too hard scrubbing the floors and the maids swear by it." She handed him the jar. "It might burn at first, but that is good."

Brant took the jar and set it next to the bath. He nodded his silent thanks.

"Now, dip your head under," she ordered. He gave her a charming half smile. Della's heart skipped and he did as she commanded. The head of his serpent peeked briefly from beneath the dark water. When he resurfaced, she said, "I got this recipe for soap from an alchemist traveling from Eblana. It's very good for the hair, if one does not use it too oft."

Brant eyed her suspiciously as she dipped her fingers into the gummy substance. "What kind of soap looks like curdled cream?"

"It is soap, truly," she said, defensively. "It's special for the head. As much as you wash yourself, you must have tight skin on your head, do you not?"

"Yea, mayhap sometimes." Reaching up, he scratched his short beard. He kept an eye on her hand as she lifted it to his head.

Without further comment, Della slapped the substance on his scalp and began to lather his long locks. Gliding her hands over his head, she untied the leather strap that bound the lock of his hair and ran her fingers to take the braid out of the red streak. Without thought of her words, she asked, "Were you really born with this red? Or do you bleach your hair?"

Brant groaned in enjoyment of her administering hands. She massaged her way down his temples and over his short beard. Her hair was beginning to dry and curl about her face. Through the veil of her locks, she saw Brant lick his lips. He was staring at her chest. Della followed his eyes. One of her long, damp locks adhered itself to the curve of her breast. At such a close proximity, the outline of her nipple could be seen through the thick fabric. She shifted her weight, causing her hair to fall over the globe to hide it. Finally, he answered, "I was born that way."

"It's also true then that you came from your mother in a blaze of fire?" Della questioned, recalling Gunther's comment. Suspicious, she scrubbed harder.

"Yea, it has been said." By the look on his face, he wasn't paying attention to what he answered. His eyes rolled lightly in his head as she pushed along his scalp. Again, he licked his lips.

"It's also true then that you have gone to many women that same way since?" She pushed harder, scratching her nails against his head, unmindful that her breasts bobbed closer to his face.

"Yea, it has been said." Brant again moaned.

"Oh! You hideous…" Della shoved his head under the water.

Brant came up sputtering. He reached for her before she could pull away.

"Let me go," Della yelled. "You are a miserable, perverted man!"

Brant lifted her into the air and onto his lap. Water sloshed over the sides of the bath to run along the stone floor toward the fur rug. Alone he filled most of the tub, so when she landed on top of him there was hardly a place she could go that wasn't next to his body. The moment his own words donned on him, he started to laugh. "Could it be you are jealous, little wife?"

Water soaked into her clothing and her gown became uncomfortably heavy as she struggled against his naked chest. Furious, she swore, "I am not jealous. I care not that you have two mistresses in Jorvik alone!"

Brant laughed harder, holding her firm against his length.

"Why don't you go there and torment them?" She faltered in her movements. "I do not need you here. I already said you could have them. I care not."

"Nay, Della. You will not be rid of me so easily," Brant said. "Gunther should not have told you that."

She gave one last, valiant shove against his chest before letting his strong arms pull her forward. Her lips were inches away from his neck and she didn't protest as much as she should have. "Then tell me how I will be rid of you?"

"Princess, I don't think you ever will." Brant sighed in heavy contentment.

Since she'd stopped struggling, Della settled hard against his flesh. Her knees straddled his left thigh and her hands pressed into his chest. When he looked at her, her heart actually ached. Insecurity filled her.

"Besides," he continued, "those other women were before our betrothment."

Della slowly warmed to the idea of having someone around to share her life, even if it was a

Viking barbarian. But Brant wasn't like the others. He was kind to Rab. He was amusing at times. And, except for earlier in the hall, he had never laid a violent hand on her and even that could be seen as an accident. She rested her head on his chest, feeling the steady beat of his heart under her palm. He drew her closer.

"How long before?" She was unable to hide her interest, as she pouted her lower lip, awaiting his answer.

"Nigh on a fortnight before I arrived here." Then, his tone light and teasing, he said, "Methought you wanted me to have mistresses."

"I do." Even to her own ears, her words were unconvincing. The idea of him in such a position with another woman bothered her greatly. "Just not right now. What I mean to say is, will you be moving to Blackwell with them?"

"Nay." Brant nuzzled her, placing a kiss on the top of her head. "Nay, I will be living here."

"With them?"

"Nay, Della." Brant swallowed hard.

"You would not lie?" Della nudged him under the chin with her head. He stroked her hair and she was very aware of his heartbeat against her hand. It was strong and sure, just like the rest of him.

"Nay, I will never lie to you, Della."

She placed a soft, shy kiss next to his collarbone and he didn't move to stop her. The feel of his arousal grew larger beneath her, tangling in the wet folds of her nightclothes. The water had cooled, or mayhap it was because he was so hot that the water felt colder in comparison.

Her breasts strained against the confines of her gown, her nipples hard. Again, she became frightened. Suddenly she drew away and he didn't stop her. Della pulled at her wet gown to better hide the shape of her breasts. As she looked into his blue gaze, she knew they'd strayed into strange emotional territory for both of them.

"I should get out." Nervous, Della tried to stand. Pushing against the rim of the tub, she straightened her legs to rise precariously over him. Brant angled his head to better see down her nightgown and grinned. A hot glow flamed her face at his interest.

Ducking his head under water to rinse off the remaining soap, Brant resurfaced with a gasp. He pushed his hair out of his face. Droplets trickled over his chest in captivating rivulets.

Della straightened fully, teetering as he moved in the water, uncertain if the heaviness in her limbs was from the wet gown or his nearness. She'd been so close to him, had felt his firm body pressed intimately against her, and yet he didn't touch her as he had before. Where was his barbaric passion? Mayhap she talked too much, demanded too much with her questions. Mayhap he decided he didn't want her anymore.

She began to lift her foot to climb out of the bath, but before she could move, his large hands clasped her bare feet to stop her from leaving. His fingers stroked her toes, only to work slowly over her ankles and up her calves. She panted, her breath quivering as pleasure rippled over her. His hands dipped down only to glide back up over her skin with the aid of the water. When he leaned forward to reach farther up her gown, her knees weakened, her whole being focused on his touch.

Brant's eyes stared piercingly at her, holding her captive in their powerful trance. His will overtook hers and she knew she would do anything he asked of her. She didn't care if he cast a spell over her. How could she, if it felt like this? The whole world faded away—the knights belowstairs, the servants, Strathfeld Castle, and the Vikings. She was just a woman and he was just a man, alone in their chambers.

Della welcomed the myriad of sensations that his touch brought to her body. Her breathing deepened, becoming ragged gasps of air. His hands passed the intimate curve of her knees and slid their way to the back of her thighs. Brant's head was only a hairsbreadth away from her midsection. He focused on her stomach and his nose came very close to nuzzling between her thighs. She grew hot and moist at the close attention. He kneeled, a pleasant smile on his face as he rubbed her legs under the wet gown. Each movement was slow and easy.

She gazed past the top of his head and saw the tip of his hardened serpent peeking out of the water. It peered at her like a sea dragon. Della took a deep breath, fearfully thinking of Ebba's counsel.

"Why do you wear so many layers to bed?" Brant groaned as the heavy folds of her gown inhibited his roaming. He dipped his hands back into the water, only to move them once more over her legs. Nestling his face intimately against the apex of her thighs, he inhaled through the wet material, shamelessly reveling in her scent. She trembled.

Della watched him in wide-eyed wonder. As he leaned his head nearer her center, her body weakened. She could feel the press of his chin pushing intimately against her sex. His mouth opened wide where her hip met her thigh and he gave her an opened-mouth kiss through the cooling fabric, heating it and her. She moaned lightly, unable to move, unsure what to do. His lips closed and he pulled the wet material into his mouth, biting it with his teeth, enflaming it with his breath. Her strength gave out and she was forced to put her hands on his shoulders for support.

Brant rose to his feet in one smooth motion, intent on capturing her in his arms. He seized her mouth with his own in a tenderly passionate kiss. Fingers grazed lightly over her cheeks, slow and gentle. He molded his body hard against her. The more he kissed her, the less she could resist him.

"Stop." Della pulled away to breathe. He was naked, with only her wet gown keeping their bodies apart.

"Nay, not again," he begged, his tone ragged and soft. He rocked his hips, pressing his hard arousal along her stomach. "Don't deny me. My body could not take it if you did. I need to feel you. I need to be inside you."

"Just for a moment, I cannot think when you kiss me like that." As if to attest to the truth of her words, her dazed eyes threatened to clear.

Brant's animalistic groan reclaimed her mouth in a slanting assault. She pitched fully against him, unable to support herself. When he broke away, he said, "Nay. Do not think tonight, Della—only feel. I can give you so much pleasure, if you but let me. I can show you things you never thought possible. I want to give you pleasure."

Della shivered at the promise in his husky words and for once she found herself believing them. Brant's hands wandered the length of her back, her sides and her hair. He grew frustrated as her clothes stopped his exploration.

"Take off your gown. I want to see you."

They were still standing in the bath water. Della pushed against his chest until her own feet once again supported her.

"I cannot." She bit her lip and looked away. A blush stained her cheeks.

"Yea, you can." Brant touched the back of her neck. "You are most beautiful, Della. You have naught to be ashamed of."

"That is not what I meant." Della flushed, shyly enjoying his compliment. "The tie is in back. I cannot reach it."

Brant smiled as his fingers found the tie hidden in the gown the same moment she said the words. He pulled at the string and the heavy linen immediately slid to her shoulders. His fingers moved over the wet, naked skin he found there. Pulling her arms from his chest, he angled them down so the gown slid completely from her to pool around her feet in the tub.

The chilled air of the bedchamber hit her naked flesh. Before she could react, Brant lifted her into his arms, one hand wrapping intimately around her naked thigh and the other winding behind her back, his fingers grazing the side of her breast to skim close to her nipple. Their bodies were still wet from the tub. His feet splashed in the spilled water as he carried her to the bed. As he walked, he kissed her jaw just below her scraped cheek. Della hid her face in his neck, but she didn't fight him, didn't tell him to stop.

Placing her on the warm fur coverlet, Brant crawled onto the bed and leaned over her. His eyes swept her body in a wondrous caress, devouring her hungrily. An unfamiliar pride overwhelmed her senses at his approval. Unable to keep his bold gaze, her eyes dipped underneath her lashes.

"You are so lovely, princess." Brant cupped her breast briefly before sliding his hand down her flat stomach. She didn't touch him in return, only lay still, letting his hand move where it will. "Your skin is so soft."

He touched her pelvic bone, drawing leisured circles down her thigh. She saw that her body excited him and knew she should be embarrassed to be so exposed to his view. But she couldn't be, not when he looked so approvingly at her.

"Do I look as other women do?" she whispered, hesitant. "You have seen many."

"What an odd question." Brant chuckled and the sound rumbled in his chest, but his laughter died when he met her eyes. Her words hadn't been accusing or bitter, but they were serious nonetheless. "Yea, Della. Only you are the most beautiful."

"You promised never to lie to me." Della stiffened at his words. A slight frown marred her face. "I don't expect you to say those things to me. I will not command any such sentiments from you. I know what I am."

Brant looked at her intensely, but didn't answer. He moved his hand over her stomach. The ache returned to her midsection as the fire inside her grew into an inferno beneath his touch. She wanted to grab him to her, but she didn't know if it was allowed so she held back. His fingers lightly brushed over the soft curls intimately guarding her slick folds and she jolted in surprise as an uncontrollable shiver shot through her at the private handling.

"You like that, don't you?" He inched his body lower, settling next to her hip to kiss below her navel.

Della arched toward his mouth. Moaning, she instinctively wanted his lips to move lower, wanted to force him more fully against her, but his kisses stayed light and teasing, dancing over her flesh. She wanted to touch him, as he did her, and she wanted something deep inside her belly.

"Please," she implored, not knowing what she was begging for. "I cannot think like myself, but methinks you must stop. I'm sure you shouldn't be there."

Brant chuckled again as he crawled over her, straddling her with his legs. He brushed his nose against her nipple until it became erect. Before taking the hard peak into his mouth, he said, "You are not to think."

"But, oh." Della gasped, shaking her head. "I want…to ask you…something."

"What?" His word vibrated on the soft mound between his lips like a hungry growl.

"I want…" Della's words trailed off. She shook her head, trying to concentrate past the gentle movements of his lapping tongue. She grabbed a fistful of fur to keep her hands off him. The urge to touch him became unbearable. "You have to stop that for a moment."

Brant grunted his refusal, taking her nipple more forcefully between his teeth. His arousal rubbed lightly along her soft inner thigh.

"Wait. Do not stop that just yet. Just let me think." Her back arched against his mouth.

Brant grinned as he gave her right breast the same treatment. His shaft continued to stroke her, the touch like kindling to fire as it flamed her wet center.

"I want to touch you," Della gasped, recalling what she wanted to say. "I mean…can I?"

"If you do, I might explode," he said softly, so soft she wondered if she'd heard him at all. But louder, he answered, "Yea."

Della's hands instantly went to his head, pushing

him more firmly to her chest trying in vain to end the sweet torture that coursed in her blood. A loud, gratifying moan escaped her lips. His tongue moved more fervently against her. She moaned louder.

"May I touch you anywhere? I'm afraid I do not know what it is I'm expected to do." Della raised her knee along the inside of his thighs. His smooth, thick member pushed into her tender flesh. The sound of her heart beat in her ears.

"Yea, touch me however you like, there is no rule on how to do it. Later I will lie still for you and let you explore to your heart's content."

"I do not," Della gasped, "want to get burned."

"What?" He maneuvered his legs inside of hers.

"Ebba said I had to put out the dragon's fire." Della answered him honestly, not able to do anything else.

Brant laughed. She moved instinctively in her passions. "My darling little wife, you really know nothing about the art of lovemaking. It's only an expression, princess, not a real fire."

"Yea, it is, m'lord." Her hips sought his touch and he spread her willing thighs, putting his legs between them. "I can already feel it starting to burn."

"It will not hurt badly, Della." He brought his lips to her mouth, moving slow so she felt every single moment in painstaking detail. "Mayhap only a little at first, but there will be no real fire, lest you refer to the flames you now feel within you. I will be as gentle as I can."

"Oh." Della would've been embarrassed if she

could have concentrated long enough on one thought.

Braced on an elbow, Brant reached between them. His hand brushed over her soft curls, back and forth, back and forth, pressing deeper into her folds with each pass. She opened her mouth wide. Wet with her cream, he slid his fingertip along her opening with precision. Wiggling her hips, she tried to anticipate his movements, forcing him more firmly against her. His finger encircled the tight bud between her thighs and she weakly cried out, the sound swallowed by his hovering mouth. He breathed into her, harsh and loud. Before she knew what he was about, he thrust a finger inside. She stared at him, stunned by the feel of pressure within her body.

"Oh," he breathed, biting his lip. Firelight illuminated his handsome face, glinting off his trim beard, giving heavy contours to his chiseled features. "Ah, such a wet, tight sheathe for my sword."

With a groan, he finally kissed her mouth, taking it hard as his tongue delved deep only to pull back. The movement mimicked the finger inside her, moving in and out, in and out, faster, deeper. The thickness of his finger grew, as if suddenly there were two stroking her intimately. Pressure built and he pulled his mouth back with a loud growl.

"Della, I'm sorry. I cannot slow. I need to feel myself inside you before I burst. I have waited too long to possess you." Brant pulled his fingers from her and moved his shaft to her opening. "I know you do not, cannot understand, but it is taking all of my control not to ride you like a wild mare that needs to be broken."

Brant rubbed the tip of his erection along her wet folds, following the path his fingers had traveled moments before. She groaned as he pushed her legs open, widening her passage, causing her to tense in a strange mix of nervousness and anticipation.

"Don't be frightened, Della. I'm meant to be inside of you." The words sounded tormented.

Della began to speak, but he swiftly thrust into her, cutting off her words as he imbedded himself fully. She yelped in surprise as her muscles were stretched around his thick arousal. The penetration was deep. Brant made a strange, animalistic noise. Her eyes widened in bewilderment and she felt claimed, conquered. For a moment, he held still, frozen with a look of ecstasy on his face.

"Finally," he whispered.

Brant pulled his hips back, rocking in short, deep thrusts, as if to test the fit of their bodies. Della didn't move, just let him take control. The ache lessened and she was left with the beginning sensations of pleasure. His movements became bolder. The pressure eased as his shaft glided to her entrance.

Thinking he meant to stop, Della leaped into action. She moaned in protest as she wrapped her legs around the backs of his. Using all of her strength she forced him to thrust into her again, this time even deeper. The eager motion brought with it throbbing gratification. She loosened her legs to intuitively do it again. She could not have stopped if she wanted to.

The force within her was so innate, so natural that she was helpless against it.

Driven by the primal need for release, her head turned back and forth on the bed in sweet torment. Brant grabbed her under her knees and forced her legs farther apart. He pushed her legs as up and open as they would physically allow, tossing one of her knees over his shoulder. As he showed her how deep this new position allowed him to delve, his finger moved to her sex, rubbing along the hard bud. Sensation after astonishing sensation washed over her.

Della stiffened, the tension building with each of his thrusts. She panted and moaned in encouragement, mindless of anything but the man on top of her. His hips slammed against her, almost violent in their need. She wasn't afraid of him as she returned his savage motions thrust for thrust. He moved faster within her, pushing her toward an unknown destination. Without warning he tensed between her thighs, pressing one last, hard time into her. Della felt her body quake with an inner force that was so great she swore she fell off the edge of the earth.

Brant's primeval yell reverberated off the chamber walls. She was beyond sound as her mouth opened in wonderment. He jerked his release, staying deep as he staked his claim to her. She would never be the same again.

BRANT DIDN'T MOVE. Something unfamiliar stirred within him as his heart slowed and his blood calmed.

For so long, he could think of nothing else but bedding his beautiful wife. At first, as he bathed, he'd been taken aback by the small shows of affection she'd given him, and the torture of her innocence had almost been too much for his straining body. But, as her resistance faded, so did her fear. The entire time he'd been with her, all his wife had needed was a gentle hand. He smiled at the thought, savoring the stillness of her body against his.

He'd waited so long to hold her against him and now here she was, all his. Brant shifted his weight, pulling out of her so he could rest on his side. Words welled within him, but he wasn't sure he liked where his thoughts traveled. He treaded on unfamiliar territory. His stomach tightened, unsure as to what to say to her, but he knew he was not about to get trapped into a sentiment of love just because his body felt more sated than it ever had.

Once he was inside her, deep and sure, he'd been hard pressed to allow her time to adjust. Never had he resisted the natural urges of his loins for quick penetration, but before he never had a reason to go slow. The wanton maids he'd been with sought as selfish of a release as he. And though he treated them gently enough, they were nothing compared to the woman at his side.

He propped himself up on his elbow and ran his index finger down the valley of her breasts. Della shivered and tried weakly to pull the fur to cover her body. Her cheeks colored and she hid her face from him.

"Nay, princess." Brant moved his hand more possessively around her waist. "Do not hide yourself from me. I am your husband and I get much pleasure from looking at you. There's no shame in it."

Nuzzling her neck, he was careful not to scratch her with his beard. Her lids were lazy over her eyes, as she said, "I'm cold."

Brant sighed and sat up. He tugged the fur from underneath them and tenderly wrapped it around their bodies. Then, pulling her into the crook of his arm to lay tightly next to him, he rolled onto his back. The movement forced her to turn so that her head rested on his shoulder. A soft breast molded itself against his side and, though he couldn't be sure, the nipple felt as if it might still be hard. It was almost as seductive as the wet curls tickling his thigh.

"M'lord?" Della sounded as if she were reluctant to break the silence.

"Brant. My name is Brant. Do you think you could use it?"

"Yea, Brant." The word was a soft whimper. "Did I hurt your back?"

He chuckled quietly before yawning. His eyes drifted shut in contentment. "The things you say, lady wife. Nay, you did not hurt me."

"Do you think we should get dressed?"

"Nay." He yawned again and scratched his stomach. "Methinks that you will never wear clothes to bed again."

.   .   .

DELLA'S BODY hummed with pleasure and she sighed as she laid her hand tentatively on his chest. She felt warm and safe in his arms. The sensation warred with the guilt that slowly threatened to seep back into her mind. As she watched his eyes close, she didn't feel at all tired. It was still too early for her to fall asleep.

Unsure if the weakened state of her limbs was normal or if her stomach should feel so turbulently calm, she thought to ask him about it. But his breathing had deepened into a soft snore and his bare chest rose and fell in easy breaths. Touching his bearded cheek for the briefest moment, she tried to roll out of his embrace. His slumbering body seemed reluctant to let her leave, but she finally wiggled her way loose. Slipping from the bed, she grabbed a nightgown from her trunk and walked over to the fire.

Sweet Lord, what have I done?

11

"IT WOULD SEEM the ice has melted a little."

Brant shot Gunther an amused smile and refused to answer. All day his eyes had carried a self-satisfied glint and at the slightest provocation he would grin. The news of Della's announcement the eve before quickly spread throughout the manor until every one of his men made a point to comment on his good fortune.

"It's coming along nicely." Brant nodded in approval of the bailey wall. Edwyn and Gunther both directed the workers and they'd almost completed another section. Within a fortnight, the wall and gate-house would be finished. Gunther oversaw the section they were now by and Edwyn was farther down the wall.

A cool breeze picked up, giving a pleasant relief to the warmer evening hours. He couldn't help another smile as he looked at the magenta streaked sky. Evening fast approached and Brant had yet to see his wife. When he awoke that morning, she was not there, much to the disappointment of his erection. He'd gone to the exercise field, searching for her in the twilighted bailey yard, but she was not there. Then, after his morning drills with the men, he looked for her in hall as he broke his fast. She wasn't there either. Those in the hall had been elated with their lord's good humor and the meal tarried overlong.

Brant turned his attention back to Gunther, seeing that the man's eyes were on the distance where Edwyn worked. "Have you seen my wife, Gunther? Methinks she has been missing all day."

"Yea, she was with the foundling child again." Gunther gave Brant a knowing look. "Did she not satisfy you enough last night, m'lord, that you are forced to seek her again so early in the eve?"

He didn't answer, much to Gunther's obvious amusement. However, the man's smile faded with Brant's next words. "Mayhap you can find something better to do than repair this wall. Edwyn seems to have it well in hand. I don't know if your time is best spent standing here, staring at rocks."

"Yea," Gunther agreed.

Brant knew he merely delayed his decision to replace Edwyn. Gunther knew it as well. Leading toward the main hall, he said, "Methinks the chapel should be rebuilt."

"And methinks you are trying to find work fer two men. Patching the chapel stone will work just fine." Gunther kicked at the ground. Originally he hadn't wanted the duties of seneschal but, being without property and high title, he had agreed. Now, he would be reluctant to give the arrangement up.

Not knowing how to answer, Brant didn't. Again, he changed the course of their conversation. "Did you see the way the Saxons practiced? Perchance you can show them how to be more effective."

Gunther's face lightened. Soldiering was one domain where he was more skilled than Edwyn. "Yea, Roldan and I have already spoken on it."

"Stuart!"

Brant stopped as the sound of his wife's voice rang joyfully over the bailey. For a moment, his heart soared to hear her, but when her words penetrated his mind, he frowned. His eyes narrowed and he turned to see Della running toward the main gate. Anger instantly welled in his chest and he swore a string of dark Nordic curses under his breath. Without thought, he stormed across the yard to stop her reunion with her cousin.

Those milling about the bailey turned their attention to the front gate. A few of them joined Della in her rush forward to greet the visitor. Gunther followed behind in silence.

The soft linen of Della's dark blue gown swayed enticingly as she moved, clinging to her form. Beneath the dress, she wore a lighter blue undertunic, which was exposed at her arms and sides. The honeyed locks of her hair shone in the sun and were neatly pulled into a braided coiffure at the nape of her neck. Dirt stained her apron, indicating she'd been tending her garden.

Liquid hot desire filled his blood at the sight of her, causing him to curse once more. He'd kept his passions tempered back during the day and had thought their night together would've sated him some. But his appetite for her raged, fueling his already blazing ardor.

Edwyn had already given the command for the gate to be opened. Brant should've dismissed his wife's standing order to let the seneschal control the gate, but it was too late, for Sir Stuart was already being let inside. If he were to turn the man out now, he would look like a jealous fool. And he could not be certain his wife would hide her icy displeasure in the decision.

"Stuart!" Della hopped in excitement, clapping her hands as the sound of horse's hooves. Her face lit up in girlish pleasure as her cousin's gray stallion came into view. The man traveled with only a few servants at his side, but acted as if he led a whole army of knights. He paused in his ride, waving graciously at the gathered peasants before continuing forward.

Della moved as if to go to the man, but Brant gripped her shoulder, squeezing to get her attention. Into her ear, he hissed, "You forget yourself, lady wife."

He felt his arm twitch with the need to shake her, but he refrained. The scent of wildflowers over-whelmed him and he took a deep breath. Jealousy, swift and sure, consumed him as his eyes bored into her. Yet even now, he wanted her.

"M'lord," she gasped, looking at him.

Brant bristled at her distant use of his title. She'd yelled familiarly to Stuart for all to hear and yet she could not bring herself to simply call him Brant. It was always *m'lord* or *Lord Blackwell*.

"You will mind yourself, wife," he warned, "lest I must remind you that you are wed to me."

DELLA SHIVERED at the darkness in his tone. It sent chills of both fear and excitement through her. Startled by the angry threat in his voice, she nodded. The happiness she felt at seeing her cousin drained in light of her husband's anger. She turned her head, straining her neck to look up into his piercing blue eyes. Disappointed, she found his expression hard. His hold did not loosen and she forced a nonchalant expression to her face, one she didn't feel. Her heart raced with nervous fear, but there was another emotion as well. She didn't wish to give it a name.

Della hadn't thought it possible, but her husband looked more handsome than she'd ever seen him. Beautifully dressed in the black and gold tunic she'd made for him, he also wore a new undertunic and braccas. She'd laid the clothes out for him early that morning when she left the bedchamber. It only seemed natural to do so, and she'd wanted to see how the black tunic fit since she worked the hardest on it. She wasn't disappointed. He was ravishing.

"M'lord…" The full knowledge of what they'd done kept her from finishing the thought. All day she'd hidden from him, unable to face him, too unsure of herself, unsure of him, of their marriage, of what had happened. She was afraid he'd look at her with tenderness or love, and afraid he wouldn't. His manners gave nothing away as she studied him. How was she to act after such a night? Was she the only one spellbound by it? Was she just another woman he'd conquered?

And why should I care? I don't love him. Cannot. Will never.

"Did you hear me?" he said when she didn't speak. "I said you will mind yourself."

Della's mouth fell open at the veiled threat and her gaze shot at him in icy displeasure. "I don't so easily forget who my husband is, even if it's you. I will not apologize for my excitement over my cousin's arrival, m'lord, because Stuart is the only family left to me."

"Nay, Della, I'm your only family." Brant leaned down, pressing his face into hers. Instantly, his gaze fell to her lips. Della shivered at the intensity in him, the quick burning anger that turned to passion and back again within a flickering moment. The bailey yard fell away until they were the only two left in the world. For a moment, she thought he might kiss her. There was no doubting Brant came from fire. His moods burned hot and bright for all to see.

The idea brought her back to what was happening. Through the corner of her eye, she saw Stuart swing down from his horse. Della started to answer Brant, but her cousin wrapped his arms around her waist and flung her through the air like a child. The motion tore her from her husband's hold. Brant thankfully let her go, otherwise the battle over her limbs would've hurt. Stuart dropped her to the ground, spun her around, and lifted her once more so she faced him as he danced about in circles while holding her in the air.

"Ah, my little cousin, how you have grown to be a fine woman!" Stuart finally lowered her to the ground. His handsome, dark face smiled gaily at her as he looked her over, and his hands lingered at her waist as if disinclined to let her go. "It has been too many years since I have last seen you. We have much to talk about."

"Ah, Stuart." Della tried to smile for him, but her cheeks were hot with embarrassment at his enthusiastic greeting. Well aware of the quiet stares of the others and of her husband's darkening rage, she put her hands over Stuart's and gently pushed them from her. Before letting go, she gave him a light squeeze. It was all the affection she would dare. "There is much to speak of, my cousin."

"What has happened to your face, Della?" Stuart's expression dropped into one of concern. A frown creased between his eyes as he studied the bruise on her cheek. Lifting his hand as if to touch her, he let it hover, only to draw his fingers back to his side.

"It's naught to be concerned over. I fell yestereve,

tripped on the dining platform stairs." Della refused to look at Brant. "I was careless."

"Yea," Stuart acknowledged, dropping a familiar arm over her shoulder. He didn't question her explanation. It had always been thus between them. Stuart ignored Brant as he tried to escort her to the castle. "Where is my uncle? I should like to greet him."

"Ah, Stuart." Della ducked from his friendly gesture. Stuart looked hurt, but let his arm fall to his side. He cocked his head, his eyes wondering why she shied away from him. Growing up, they'd always had an easy friendship. Stuart seemed to be in as much pain as she in childhood. But they were no longer children and Della was all too aware of her husband's watchful, disapproving gaze. Her father's warnings to Brant didn't help her cousin's reputation. "My father died, nigh on a fortnight past. We would have written you, but we didn't know where to find you."

Stuart mulled the information over. He didn't look too surprised by the news. "Are you well, Della? I know you were close to him."

"Yea, I'm fine." Tears tried to come at the still painful memory, but she fought them, blinking hard. She took a step toward him, not wanting the servants to overhear her anguish. "It has been hard, but I am surviving."

"Yea, sweet Della." Stuart spoke as if they were the only two in the bailey. He touched her lightly on the chin. "You have always done that well. Survive, I mean. But fear no longer. I'm here to help you. We will get through the formalities of the inheritance together. You have had too large a burden these many years."

Della smiled at his kind offer. In her heart she knew he meant well, but didn't think her husband would feel the same. Glancing over Stuart's shoulder at Brant, it was as she suspected. Her husband's hands were on his hips and he glared at them. Even in anger he captivated her, leaving her breathless.

In light of what had transpired the night before, she saw Stuart differently. He wasn't the fine figure of a man she'd once believed him to be. She used to think him the bravest, most handsome man alive, but now he just looked like a man—handsome, yea, but handsome in the way that was so common. He was nothing compared to the rolling fire of her virile husband who burned her with his presence every time he was near.

Brant cleared his throat in irritation and Della realized she'd failed to introduce him. Stuart frowned at the rude interruption. There was no way her cousin could know of her marriage.

Stuart put his hands on his hips as he studied Brant. "I am Sir Stuart, Della's cousin. I trust you are here on behalf of King Guthrum to attend the funeral and to see to the inheritance? You can deal with me as freely as you do Della. She will tell you, I am Lord Strathfeld's closest male heir."

Della glanced helplessly back and forth between the two men. A slow, triumphant smile curled Brant's mouth as he answered, "I am Lord Blackwell, Ealdorman of Strathfeld."

"Yea, Stuart," Della interjected, trying to shelter her cousin from the sting of Brant's words. She didn't want to see them fight. Stuart's back was to her and she couldn't see his face, but she saw the stiffening of his body. "I don't believe you have heard of my marriage to Lord Blackwell. It happened right before my father's death. We didn't know where to reach you else we would've told you of it also. Like you said, so much has happened."

Slowly, Stuart turned. When he looked at her, he was smiling. "Congratulations, Della." He kissed her cheek.

Della felt like she was between two snarling wolves in search of a meal and she was the hapless rabbit who crossed their paths.

"Thank you, Stuart." Della took a step away from both men. "With your permission, Lord Blackwell, I will tell Isa of our guests."

Brant stiffly nodded, but didn't take his gaze off Stuart.

STRATHFELD'S KITCHEN was quiet as Isa cleaned the cutting table with a brush and bucket of hot water. The servant had sent the maids to other chores, as was her custom, preferring to be alone right before the hassle of the eve meal. Going to the spit that hung over the blazing fire, she turned the last of the roasted chickens. Then, wiping her hands on her apron, she checked the baking bread.

"Isa, we have more guests." Della's heart pounded wildly as she looked at the servant.

Isa's round face turned red. The cook poked her finger at Della. "I daresay that is thrice this last fortnight I have been called upon to cook fer guests. Before yer husband got here, we ne'er had guests more than once a year. It was fine by me like that. Now, I'm expected to cook fer the king's whole army."

"It is my cousin, Sir Stuart, Isa," Della knew what the cook meant. They'd been plagued with many guests. "Please see that the best mead is brought to the tables."

Isa shook her head in warning. "Yer brewing trouble, m'lady, and I well know when things are brewing."

"What do you mean?" Della asked in surprise. Isa was one of the oldest fixtures in the castle and had grown to believe that gave her the right to freely voice her opinion to anyone. Usually Della found she didn't mind, but today the woman's words grated against her nerves.

"Do not think Lord Blackwell doesn't know of yer desire to marry yer cousin instead of him. The whole castle knows of how you two have been fighting since the day you met." Isa turned back to the fire. Lifting her apron, she grabbed a hot loaf and tossed it on the newly cleaned table. Continuing this way until all the loaves were out, she spoke, "It's not well done of you to treat yer cousin so royally in front of yer husband. M'lord is not likely to approve."

"I'm not treating Stuart like royalty. All I said is to put the best mead out." Taken aback, she ran her fingers over one of the loaves. Was the whole manor really talking about them?

"Yea, first it's the best mead. Next you will be saying to put out the best meat and to use the best herbs from the garden." Isa shook her head. "Then you will find yerself catering more to Stuart than you do yer own husband. You are brewing trouble is all I am saying."

Della bit her lip. She'd been about to request the best herbs for the chicken Isa was preparing. Removing her hand from where it hovered over the hot bread, she studied her fingernails thoughtfully. "Nay. Just the mead, Isa."

Della quickly left the intuitive old cook. Brant and she had been prone to their fights, but mostly they kept them private. Then, touching her cheek, she fingered the slight scrape that was still there.

Well, perchance, we have not been as discreet as we should've been, Della admitted to herself. Did the manor really know about her first deception? Did they know that she had been checked for that deception? She shivered in embarrassment. Foolishly, she'd convinced herself no one would find out.

As she walked into the hall, a maid passed by her with the mead she'd ordered. Her husband and cousin had already found their way to the high table, accompanied by Roldan and Gunther. Roldan had sat at the high table with her father only to be moved down when her husband arrived. She was glad to see him back at his old place of honor.

Recoiling inwardly at the sight of their strained faces, she stopped. Even Roldan frowned disapprovingly at Stuart and she'd thought the knight liked her cousin. The maid stepped up to the table, setting goblets before the men. Brant's face was stiff as he watched Stuart in unveiled mistrust. Deciding she didn't want to face them in an empty hall, she turned to go back into the kitchen. She ignored Isa's knowing chuckle as she scurried through the side door into the garden.

Taking a deep breath once outside, her chest heaving with apprehension, she smelled the potent herbs of the garden. She hurried around the castle, ducking into a secluded corner along the outside wall. No one would be able to tell she was there unless they specifically looked.

Della needed time to sort her thoughts. She saw how well Stuart had taken the news of her marriage. Had he not told her often when they were children that he didn't want the title of ealdorman? He'd only been willing to marry her because she hadn't wanted to marry at all and neither had he. In fact, Della was sure it had been she who had first mentioned the idea to Stuart.

Della looked at the ring Brant had given her. The brass gleamed in the evening sunlight, as did the polished amber. It was not so bad being married to Brant, not like she'd first imagined. Sure, he was stubborn and hardheaded and he made her angry more often than not. But he could be so sweet to her, too. Like when he held her in his arms and made her body tremble. He was kind. In fact, he had done nothing to prove he deserved her condemnation.

Aside from the misunderstanding with Lord Lester when he'd flung her to the floor, he didn't beat her when she was insolent, which was often encouraged of a husband. Della shuddered as she thought of the insane notions of the Anglo-Saxon priests. They thought you had to beat a wife to keep her in line. Did they not realize that you could do so more effectively with kindness and a gentle touch? Did they not realize that most women only wanted to be listened to, respected, and protected?

Della held up her hand and studied the polished amber more closely. She remembered how odd a choice the ring was for a wedding band. Slipping the thin metal off her finger for the first time, she held it up to the light and smiled as the sun glinted through the perfect oval of brownish amber. The jewel was held into place with delicate brass tongs. The fine craftsmanship was quite old if the smoothed brass was any indication.

Seeing a smudge of black dirt on the inner band, she took her thumbnail and absently scraped at it. Her nail snagged against the metal and she lifted the ring closer to study the dirt. It wasn't dirt at all but a tiny engraving. Della had never seen such tiny carvings before. She examined it closer, turning it in the sunlight.

My love was etched in Latin. Della gasped in

surprise as she read the words. Had Brant engraved the ring especially for her? Her heart beat erratically at the thought and her lungs filled with pants of air. Had he loved her from the first moment? Tears came to her eyes and she closed them to the unsure pleasure that welled in her chest. She hadn't really thought of there being actual love between them. She'd never dreamed she would want such a thing to happen. Could he truly love her? She knew they would be compatible if she tried harder, and she was growing very fond of him.

But love? Did she love him? Could what she felt when he'd held her be considered anything but?

The answer rushed over her in a sweep of emotion. *Yea, I do love him. I love my husband. I love Brant. Oh, how did it happen? I don't care. I love him and he loves me and the past no longer matters.*

Della opened her tear-stung eyes, awed at the sweet emotion pouring from her. She'd never thought she was meant for love, never dared to dream she would find it. None of the rest mattered. Not that he was a Viking. Not that her mother's death had been at a Viking's hand. It wasn't of Brant's doing. She wanted to tell him how wrong she'd been. She lifted the ring to make sure the words were real, that she'd really seen them.

My love she read again, overflowing with joy. Then, as she turned the ring in the sunlight, she saw there was more. Leaning closer, love surging from her heart, she read the rest. *My love, My Lynnea.*

Della gasped and dropped the ring to the ground

as if it suddenly caught fire. She stared in disbelief at the metal, as if it were a poisonous serpent. The ring hadn't been meant for her at all. Her husband insulted her by putting the ring meant for another woman on her hand. A woman named Lynnea. Bitter anger and betrayal overtook her and she gasped for breath through the pain in her chest. The anguish of the moment choked her and she knew if she didn't die in the pain of this moment, she surely never would.

***

"SIR STUART IS A SLIMY CHARACTER." Gunther glared to where the man had disappeared out of the main hall door. "I wouldn't trust him about the manor unescorted."

"Lord Strathfeld thought as much," Roldan interjected. "E'en as a child, that one gave me chills. He used to drown small animals in the moat fer pleasure when he thought no one watched. We ne'er told Lady Blackwell of it though. It would've crushed her."

"Yea." Brant thoughtfully scratched his whiskers. He didn't see what his wife found so appealing about the man. It was obvious Stuart spoke with a forked tongue. "Have some of the men watch him, but be subtle. I don't want him alone with my wife. We don't know what he is about, but it cannot be good."

"I'll warrant it's this keep he's after." Gunther frowned.

Brant stood. Gunther and Roldan moved with

him, following him to the bailey yard. When they reached the door, Stuart had already disappeared.

"Find him," Brant ordered quietly.

The knights nodded and left to do as they were told.

Brant took a lungful of evening air. He hadn't seen Della since she'd disappeared earlier, but it was just as well. The less time she spent near Stuart, the better he'd feel about it.

Was the nagging suspicion mostly due to his jealousy? Brant shook his head at the thought. Nay, there was more to it than that. Brant was jealous, but that didn't affect his gut instinct. Lord Strathfeld had sensed it too and had warned against letting Stuart into the manor and near Della. Sadly, his wife had no clue as to her cousin's true nature. He saw the way Della looked at the man, the way she didn't cringe from Stuart's touch. But he also saw how Stuart looked at her.

Brant wasn't fooled by Stuart's easy smile. The man had been well aware of Lord Strathfeld's death. Could it be he had also known of the marriage? Did he already seek to outdo Brant in his wife's eyes? Was this his game? The man thought to take what was rightfully his?

Brant scowled, moving toward Edwyn's chamber, intent on finding his wife. He would keep her by his side until he could persuade Stuart there was nothing for him at Strathfeld—nothing but the end of a sword if the man tried to take what didn't belong to him.

12

"THERE YOU ARE, cousin. I was worried when you didn't join us at the high table."

Della glanced up from her hiding place and slipped the ring back onto her finger. The sun had almost disappeared along the edge of the earth, yet there was enough light for her to see Stuart clearly. "Yea, here I am."

Stuart smiled as he joined her in hiding. "I had a feeling this is where I would find you. See how well we still know each other?"

Della chuckled, but the laugh was halfhearted. "It is a wonder you remember after so long. But I'm always here when avoiding something, so it's not too hard to figure out."

"Has your husband figured it out yet?" His eyes probed her for her answer.

Della shook her head. *Nay, Brant could not know.*

Stuart sat beside her and leaned his back against

the wall. "I hope it's not me you wish to avoid. I will leave immediately, if you so command it."

"Oh, nay, not you. It's the battle between you and my husband I seek to avoid. As far as I am concerned, you will always be welcome here." Della laid her hand gently on his forearm. She'd been trying to compose herself and was glad she'd stopped crying long before Stuart found her. She wasn't sure what her cousin would do if he discovered she was unhappy.

"Ah, sweet Della." Stuart held her hand to his arm. "Then it's your husband causing you discomfort. There is no battle on my side, lest you commanded it of me or if I had reason to believe you were in danger."

"Why are you here? Why now after so long?" Della wondered, though not upset by his visit. She missed their friendship and, even though she now understood it was only friendship, she still felt the familiar connection she'd always had with him. They knew each other and had shared so much. Time could not diminish her affection for him.

"You will laugh at me if I tell you." He refused to let go of her hand, choosing instead to rub gently at her fingers.

"Nay, I have never laughed at you."

"All right, I will tell you, but remember what you just said." Finally letting go, he turned to face her, his head leaning against the stone wall. "I had a feeling you needed me. I was in southern Mercia, fulfilling my political obligations to King Guthrum, when one night, right out of a deep sleep, I shot up in bed and saw your face. I swear I saw you crying, calling to me as if in a dream that was real. '*Nay!*' you screamed to me. The next morn I completed my obligations early. It took me a fortnight to get here."

"That is when my father died," Della said in awe. Stuart had always claimed to have a strange connection to her. In childhood he often sensed things about her that she'd told no one else. He would even know things about her mother's death. Just one look at her and somehow he knew some little detail she'd never told anyone. He'd been a child when he came to her home, only ten years to her tender age of five. It was amazing he still felt so connected to her after all the time that had passed.

"Was it not also the day of your wedding?" Stuart prodded. His lashes dipped low to hide the expression in his eyes as he lifted her hand to finger her wedding band. He twisted it thoughtfully around on her finger. "It would've been your wedding night, I believe."

"Yea, it was," Della acknowledged. His attention to the band only reminded her of its message. Her heart beat dully and she pulled it from his grasp. "But that's not what you felt."

"Then you enjoyed the marriage bed that night." Stuart's face turned dark as he gritted the words. His hands tightened into fists.

"Nay," Della allowed. Stuart had twisted the band on her finger so it faced the wrong direction. Unconscious of the action, she righted it. Not thinking to say anything but the truth, she explained, "We didn't share the marriage bed that night. Lord Blackwell let me out of the duty for grieving."

"Ah, so you have not yet gone through that misfortune." Stuart brightened once more as he reached an arm to nudge her in childish play. "I was afraid it might have been too late for you. That barbarian no doubt will try to tell you lies about what must be done during that time."

Della blushed and avoided looking at him directly. "Last night."

Stuart stiffened and his eye began to twitch. "Last...?" He didn't finish.

Della wondered at his reaction and then realized he probably felt sorry for her.

"It wasn't so bad," she said, needing to explain herself better. "Truly."

"But he is a Viking." Stuart swore under his breath. "Do you so easily forget what his kind did? How could your father have forced you to marry such a detestable man? How could he, after what you had been through at their hands, do that to you?"

Della had never seen Stuart angry. Until that moment, she would have guessed he didn't know how to rage. And, unlike Brant's, she felt unsafe around her cousin's anger. He lacked the steely control of her husband. His eyes moved back and forth in his head, as if the mind behind them raced with thoughts.

"Mayhap the wedding was not completed? There was a lot happening that night. Mayhap the ceremony is not legal." Stuart turned a knowing glance to her. "Think, Della! Is there aught that was not finished?"

"Yea, it's legal," Della assured him. "We have about two hundred witnesses, both Norse and Saxon, to attest to the fact. My father didn't pass until after every detail was done."

Stuart cursed again.

Della laid a gentle hand on his arm. "Stuart, please. Don't carry on so for me. I know what happened to my mother and I also know that my father sought only to protect me. So don't hate him in his death. He thought to please King Guthrum so I would have the protection of his armies behind me if there was to be another war."

"But I could have provided you with protection. I, too, have the ear of King Guthrum." Stuart lowered his tone to a more pleasing pitch. His expression was veiled. "I would've protected you with my life. And I would've been the kind of husband I have always promised to be. I wouldn't have forced you into my bed."

"It wasn't force." She didn't want to tell her cousin about her father's last comments about him. Stuart didn't need to know that her father didn't like him. "I went willingly to his bed, as was my duty."

"Then he used his pagan magic," he concluded. "Which is worse, Della? Taking a woman against her will or taking the will away from the woman?"

Della swallowed hard. She'd suspected Brant had put a pagan curse on her. Was that what happened? Had she become so blind by his magical spell that she had forgotten her own mind completely? Mayhap it was the curse of the ring. Mayhap Lynnea was a pagan goddess or a witch. Mayhap the engraving was not an endearment but a spell. Mayhap that was his power over her. But could she dare to take the ring off? Be seen without it? Could she dare to openly defy her husband? And how could she test her feelings without doing so?

"I'm so sorry, Della. I have failed you." Stuart pulled his knees into his chest and rested his head on them. "I should've known to come to you sooner. I was busy campaigning for King Guthrum and now I'm too late. How you must despise me."

In the past, Della had always been moved when Stuart showed such open feeling in front of her. It was not masculine for a man to cry, but somehow, when Stuart became close to tears, she felt herself experiencing the same emotion. He only showed this side of himself to her.

She wrapped an arm around his shoulders. "Nay, don't say such things. You cannot control the world. You cannot control the minds of other men. My father did what he thought he had to. Mayhap he didn't know that you were so close to the king."

"Nay, Della. I should've been here for you. I shouldn't have stayed away so long. Methought that if I worked hard, as I have these past years, and got into good stead with King Guthrum, you would be proud of me. Methought I…" His shoulders shook. "I have failed you and I'm sorry. But I will find a way to make it up to you, even if it takes the rest of my life."

He lifted his head. No tears spilled forth from his eyes, but she could well see the pain in them. Della trembled.

"Oh, Stuart, don't carry on so. I don't blame you for any of it and I'm proud of you. It's done and there is naught we can do to change it. I wish it could have been different, truly. But I'm married, and I will have to live with Brant." Della rubbed her hand soothingly over his back. "We are not children anymore. As an adult, you realize that life doesn't turn out the way one plans."

"You call him Brant? So familiar." Stuart groaned. "Nay, it's not fair, Della. I have given up many proposals of marriage, to many beautiful women over the years in waiting for you. And now you call him Brant and do not love me anymore, when I have done naught but stay faithfully attached to you."

"Nay, don't say such things." Della hugged him to her. "I do love you. I always have, and I will always love you. You, my dear faithful Stuart, are the brother I never had. But I am married now. I'm sorry you gave up happiness to be with me. I'm sorry if your plans were ruined out of faithfulness to me. I wish I could take the pain of childhood from your heart. I wish you could find true love. I should never have made you promise to wait for me. I should have never said we would be married. It was selfish of me to trap you from love. Given the right woman, your heart will heal. It's my fault you are alone and so hurt. I am a selfish woman and a bad friend. Stuart, could you ever forgive me?"

"*Della.*" Stuart hugged her to his chest. "Nay, it's not your fault. I wanted to be married to you, too. You know how cruel my mother was to my father. She tormented him. I wish to be away from the pain a woman can inflict. And I realize this must be a sign I am to always be alone."

Tears spilled from her eyes as she cried against his shoulder. Guilt at what she had done to him choked her. He felt so familiar, was her oldest friend, and was in so much pain. And she was so confused. Had Brant cast a spell over her? Did she love her husband? Or did she truly love Stuart?

But when she held Stuart, she felt none of the turbulent emotions she had with her husband. There was none of the pain or joy that came from loving Brant. All she felt was kinship and the well-versed pain they'd both clung to in childhood.

Pulling back, she searched his eyes. Before she had time to react, Stuart's lips came up against hers in a kiss. His lips parted, obviously expecting more of a response from her. Della gasped and pushed against his chest.

"Nay, Stuart!" Della struggled out of his embrace. Frightened, she stumbled to her feet. His warm lips created none of the feelings Brant's gave her.

"Oh, Della, I'm sorry. I don't know what came over me." He turned his face from her. Quietly he stood, his shoulders hunched. "I am so humiliated."

"Nay, it's not your fault." Della was discomforted

by his actions, but believed to understand them. "You are upset with the news of my father and my nuptials. With all the work you have been doing for King Guthrum, it's no wonder you are under much strain."

"Now you will tell him and he will surely kill me." Stuart stared coldly at her. "He has taken you away from me."

Della wondered if Stuart had always been so possessive of her. She didn't remember him being so emotional when they were children. Guiltily, she suppressed her revulsion his dramatic display caused. "Nay, I will not tell him."

Stuart watched her, tilting his chin proudly in the air. His expression hardened as her eyes slid from his face.

Nay, how could I tell him? He would likely blame me, Della thought as she pressed her lips together. Walking slowly toward the yard, she knew Stuart would not follow too closely behind.

BRANT GLANCED AT HIS COUNTESS. She sat quietly next to him during the eve meal. In fact, the entire high table was unusually devoid of conversation. Della's face was pale, her eyes swollen as if she'd been crying. He wanted to pull her into his arms and wipe away the pain he saw etched in her expression. Her cheek was still red and bruised—a reminder of his harsh treatment. It wouldn't leave a scar on her flesh, but her heart was another matter, and that muscle had been ill-treated as it was.

Sir Stuart sat on Della's other side, eating quietly. The man met his stare dead on and a small smile formed on the corner of his smug mouth. Brant clutched his fist, resisting the urge to reach across the table and hit him.

Did Della cry for her cousin? Or did she cry because of some other inane female reason? Brant was afraid there could only be one answer and he didn't like it.

While they dined, set high before the eyes of the great hall, wasn't the time to study Stuart and Della together. If he wanted any real answers, he would have to find an excuse to get all of them alone.

"Sir Stuart, it is said you have admirable skill at *hnefa-tafl*. I have been known to take a few games myself and am in possession of a fine *tann-tafl* if you are willing to play after we dine." Brant kept his tone formal, not giving the man a chance to gloat. An arrogant expression crossed Stuart's face as he looked at the ealdorman. Brant's stomach tightened in animosity as the man's eyes glinted in mischief.

Della turned to him in surprise, a warm look of gratitude shining on her face at his request. Her voice carried in it a persistent encouragement, as she said to her cousin, "Yea, Stuart. Perchance you could play one game."

Stuart nodded his head, smiling kindly at his cousin. His eyes seemed to say, *all right, but only because you wish it, Della.* Brant gritted his teeth. Della smiled prettily, looking back and forth between the two men.

"Yea, Lord Blackwell. I would be most honored to teach you what I know." Stuart turned to his mead. Swirling it thoughtfully in his goblet, he didn't look back up.

Gunther grunted at Brant's side in disapproval, but he ignored it. Brant didn't mean to get a lesson from the obnoxious man and Stuart knew it also. How dare the man try to make him look foolish in his own home? *Hnefa-tafl* was a game of much skill and political maneuvering. To suggest one was not well-suited to the game was to suggest one lacked brains on the field of battle.

When her back was to him, Brant glared past Della's shoulder. She whispered something to her cousin. He couldn't hear her words, but knew it didn't matter. He would have the answers he sought soon enough.

As he turned to his trencher, his appetite was not as hearty as it should've been. None at the head table broke the silence through the rest of the meal. After receiving Brant's permission to start evening games to entertain the men, Gunther and Roldan quickly finished their food and departed. Brant even had mead brought out to the grounds to keep the men there and offered a prize of five gold pieces to the night's winner. He wanted to be free of prying eyes when he probed Stuart and Della for their reactions.

Roldan would stay at the exercise field in charge of the men and Gunther would come back to the hall to witness Brant's private tournament. He didn't even have to tell his old friend what he was up to. The man instinctively knew. They'd fought together for many years.

Tonight, *hnefa-tafl* was more than a game of intellect played on a table. It was a game of wits played over his wife.

DELLA KEPT her eyes cast down during the meal, ignoring both her husband and cousin equally. She felt the heat of Brant's gaze as he kept close watch on Stuart, who in turn studied him. Each man weighed the other's measure in a silent war over her bowed head. She hated it.

After the meal, the *tann-tafl*, tooth table, was set up on one of the lower tables in the main hall. Many of the soldiers were encouraged to go out to the exercise field to participate in the games of strength. Torches burned high and bright over the great hall and serving maids carried the last of the food trays to the kitchen. One left a pitcher of mead at the game table. Gunther spoke to the woman while she poured him a goblet. She blushed and scurried away.

Peeking out from the stairwell, she finally saw Brant step over the threshold to the hall. She'd been waiting for him. Hesitant, she touched his arm. "There you are, m'lord. I've been looking for you."

Brant stopped walking and turned to her. His steeled face showed no emotion as he glanced dispassionately at the nervous hand on his forearm. Flustered by his stare, she let go.

"I wanted to thank you for your kindness in letting Stuart stay. He and I are all that is left of our families. It's a true and noble thing you do, especially after all I said the day we met, even though I was punished quite thoroughly for it. It proves you are a great man."

Brant nodded, as if not sure what to make of her praise.

"Come, husband, they are waiting for you." Della tried again to pat his arm. She wanted to feel the fleeting touch of his skin. Breathless, she waited for a tender word or gesture, only to be sorely disappointed. Swallowing over a hard lump forming in her throat, she glanced at her ring, wondering, yet again, if what she was feeling was the cause of a pagan curse. "Do you wish for me to leave?"

"Nay. Stay and watch."

Della nodded, glad he at least spoke to her. He didn't seem too angry, not like before. Mayhap he realized she didn't love Stuart in the way he'd suspected and didn't want to lay intimately with him. In fact, the only man she wanted to be with was the attractive, virile man she'd married. A blush crept to her cheeks, as she wondered if Brant would want to do it again this night. She hoped he did. He had promised to let her explore his body.

Della slowly sat beside her husband. She hadn't seen Stuart enter the hall and was surprised to see him. Her cousin looked confidently, almost arrogantly, at Brant.

"Are you familiar with how the game is played, Lord Blackwell, or do you need my instruction in that as well?" Stuart's smile was angelically intact, with only a slight bite to his words.

"Nay, I didn't mean to imply I needed any lessons from you. It has been said in some lower circles that you are an adequate player—for one new to the game. I wished to see if I could trounce you." Brant also kept his smile intact. "Merely as a diversion, naught else."

Della looked from one man to the other in opened mouth awe, dumbfounded with the knowledge of their intent. They were having an ego contest over a table game. She shook her head, not wanting to bear witness to their male stupidity. However, as strong as the urge was for her to stand and leave, the urge for her to stay was twice as powerful.

Gunther stood at the end of the table and watched the opening move with much seriousness. Della followed his gaze to the board, observing in quiet as the men tested the other's skills. Occasionally, they would exchange a manly jibe at the expense of the other's judgment. Both were competent players and, after an hour, Della thought surely one of them could have thwarted the other. She witnessed several opportunities to win the men kept missing.

"It would appear that I'm not so much an amateur, am I?" Stuart laughed as he stole a vital game piece from Brant. "Mayhap it's not I who is less of a man."

She felt the anger emitting from her husband. The insults were becoming more blatant with each exchange. She shot Stuart a hard look, willing him to stay quiet. Both men ignored her. Unconscious of the action, she rested a hand on Brant's thigh under the table. His leg tensed, but didn't pull away.

"Nay, I'm plenty man. Just ask Della," Brant returned with a victorious smile.

Della gasped at the bold implication and quickly removed her hand. Her cheeks became hot with embarrassment.

"Yea, it's an easy thing to take a woman with pagan charms. But to earn her trust, that is the real test of manhood. I have done that long ago. Is that not right, Della?"

Stuart's bold response made her color more. They were heading into dangerously personal territory. She glanced at Gunther for help. He tapped his fingers lightly and turned his attention back to the game. Della refused to answer either of them, furious as she glared at the board.

"You can be a child and earn the trust of a woman. It doesn't make you a true man. Many young maids have foolishly given their trust to the wrong person." Brant dismissed the claim with a small gesture of the hand.

Now I'm foolish? Della fumed at the unintentional insult. Neither man dared to look at her.

"It's more than her trust I have," Stuart rebutted.

Brant's fist clenched around a discarded game piece. He studied the small, carved figure for a moment, digging his nail into a wooden crease. "Nay, don't confuse pity as being aught more."

Della again glanced in disbelief from one man to the other. Both had stopped the pretense of playing. Their eyes met and locked in a battle of wills.

Leaning back in his chair, a baiting smile curving his lips, Stuart said, "Della, do you remember when we were younger? Do you remember what we did out by the old apple tree?"

Della clamped her mouth shut. The men weren't talking to her. Stuart had promised to never tell the tale. She'd been twelve and had let Stuart kiss her quickly on the cheek. But it had only been to seal a pact of friendship between them. At the time, she'd been embarrassed by it. Now, in light of how her husband kissed, she knew it had been nothing more than a meaningless touch.

"Della, do you remember last night?" returned Brant with a smug smile of satisfaction. Stuart glowered and Gunther hid his amusement under a cough.

Della stood, shocked and disappointed in the both of them. They turned to her in surprise, as if they'd forgotten she sat there listening.

"Enough," she demanded. "I will listen to no more."

"But, Della, it is only a game." Stuart gave her an angelic look. Della knew better.

"A game?" Della leaned forward and moved the men's pieces quickly over the squares of the *tann-tafl*.

Making the winning move for Brant's side, she laid Stuart's last piece over in defeat. Both men gaped in awe at her swift skill. "Then it's just a *game* you have lost. Now, tell Lord Blackwell that naught happened in the apple orchard. It's not as you suggest."

Stuart refused to speak. Brant began to laugh heartily as his opponent's face turned red with outrage.

"I don't see why you laugh." Della turned her icy thorns to her husband. The amusement faded from his eyes. "You are just as low as him at this moment, discussing private matters for all to hear. It's shameful and it's most disrespectful to me."

Brant met her gaze boldly and Stuart looked sheepishly away. She couldn't tolerate either one of them at that moment, so she did the only thing she could think of. She ran out of the hall and into the kitchen.

"Methinks you have your answer." Brant stood, intent on following his wife as soon as he was able. He set the game piece he clutched on the board. It hadn't been his intention to humiliate her, but he'd been so angry at Stuart's implications. "Methinks it's time you left Strathfeld—permanently."

Stuart stood. "Nay, it has only begun between us, Blackwell."

"Do not threaten me, little man. I would think naught of beating you within an inch of your life." Brant turned to Gunther. "See him out."

Gunther nodded, clearly intent on forcing the smaller man if he had to. He reached for Stuart's arm, who jerked his elbow away.

"It's not a threat, but a warning." Stuart glared at Brant and then Gunther before storming out of the hall. As Gunther followed him into the bailey yard, he heard the irate man swear, "I will have back what is rightfully mine!"

13

THE SOFT BLUE glow of the moonlit sky bathed the ground in its splendor, feeding the isolation of Della's soul. She shivered uncontrollably. In the distance, she heard the sound of laughter from the soldiers as they played games in the exercise field. Their excited cheers rose and fell in the merriment. Della had no desire to join their sports, choosing instead to be alone. However, knowing they were nearby was oddly comforting.

She couldn't believe Brant and Stuart's excessive competition over her. Though flattered by the attention, she hated to see the two men she cared for at war. She wondered if she should have left them alone together. It was very likely they would kill each other before the night was through.

Della walked by her garden in silence, enjoying the privacy afforded by the night. She kicked at a weed that dared to poke through the rich soil. Tired of the fighting, she wished for once the land could be at peace with no wars, no bloodshed, and no family members dying. Even more, she wished her heart could be at peace with no pain, no sleepless nights, no all-consuming loneliness.

The squeak of the front gate caught her attention. It could only mean Stuart was leaving. Part of her wanted to go after him to say she was sorry for her harsh words, the other part was still too angry. Her poor, dear cousin had been through so much. His mother had been a cruel woman who used to beat him. Once, she'd locked him in a chamber for three days, without food or water, because she claimed he was too attached to her.

Della's pain had been intense and lasted only one dreadful night. Stuart's pain hadn't been as concentrated, but had been drawn out over many years. Often, they'd found solace only in each other's company. Stuart had lived at Strathfeld for a short time after the death of his mother, about the same time as her own mother's demise.

She detested herself for not showing Stuart more consideration, but how could she? He'd been so unreasonable during the game. And to imply she'd done something improper with him was inexcusable. He'd been treading on very dangerous ground and could have done her great harm with his carelessness.

Brant was no better, all but saying in detail what had gone on between them. She was mortified by the very thought of speaking aloud of what had transpired. It was somewhat of a double standard, for she had told Stuart that they consummated the marriage.

The difference was she had told him as a loyal friend. Brant had used it as a taunt.

She felt awful. Why were they doing this? It wasn't as if Stuart was madly in love with her and he'd always said he didn't want the title given to her husband.

"What are you thinking, just now?"

Della felt Brant's voice drift over her like the heat of a warm flame. She'd sensed he was near before he spoke. Looking down, the weed she poked was shredded into several pieces, but was still rooted into the ground.

"I wasn't pining for Stuart if that's what you're suggesting," she snapped, unable to help her wayward tongue.

"I didn't say that." Brant took a step toward her.

Della turned to study him in the moonlight. His hair flashed silver, except for the streak that was bound as usual in a braid. Whiskers along his jaw glimmered in the luminescence of the moon. He was a striking figure and she wondered, if they were to grow old together, if he would still take her breath away every time she saw him. Somehow, she thought he just might.

If all she felt was a pagan spell, she wasn't sure she wanted him to take it off. She fingered her ring briefly, turning it around on her finger. God help her, she was in love with him and she didn't know if she wanted it to go away. But with the love came a bittersweet pain—a pain that he might not feel the same way, that he might never come to care for her more than a prize awarded him for loyal service to a king.

"Do you regret that you married me?" Brant didn't move.

"It's too late to ask that," Della replied evasively. How could she answer without giving her emotions away? Her face iced over to hide her feelings. "We are joined."

"Nay, that is not an answer." Brant searched her face, as if trying in vain to read her. "I regret you thought I meant to disrespect you. I didn't."

Della nodded. Really, she already knew. Watching the moon for a moment, she enjoyed its peacefulness. It was so big and full in the velvety sky, as if the earth had pulled it closer for the night. Then, turning back to Brant, she waited patiently for him to proceed.

"Where did you learn to play *hnefa-tafl* so masterfully?" he asked.

"I taught myself, playing out different strategies until I mastered a plan for each one. The game is really not that difficult once studied."

"Yea, I forget sometimes there are many hours in a day for you."

"Did you cast a pagan spell over me?" Della didn't mean to say the words aloud, but didn't try to take them back. She eyed him thoughtfully. A now-familiar sense of longing washed over her when she looked at him. His piercing blue gaze met hers steadily. Every pore reached out to feel him. "Tell me the truth."

"Nay." Brant chuckled. "I would not know how.

You ascribe too much to a pagan's abilities. Besides, it is not really a following I practice."

Della was saddened by the admission, for it meant that the ring had truly been meant for another woman. "Who is Lynnea? Was she a great love to you? Do you miss her?"

"Lynnea?" Brant's eyebrows rose high on his forehead before his face darkened a bit. "Who told you of her?"

"Just answer the question." Della tried to harden herself to his handsome face. She felt tears threaten and her vision blurred, but she kept her face hauntingly still. "Did you love her?"

"Yea." His expression confirmed the truth. "I suppose I did, as much as any man can admit such emotions."

It felt as if her heart had been ripped from her chest. She kept her body as still as a stone. "She is dead?"

"Yea," he said again. "She is."

Intense longing and jealousy began in her stomach. Her heart lurched and her nose burned with the unshed tears. Loving a man who didn't return her feelings was worse than the fear she had lived with her entire life. "I'm sorry for your loss."

"Della, what are you going on about?" He eyed her wearily. "She died a long time ago, when I was young."

"How?"

Why do I torture myself?

Because I have to know the truth.

"She took her own life." Brant's face hardened and she imagined it wasn't something he liked talking about. "She didn't like my father's mistresses."

"I don't understand. Why would she care if your father had mistresses?"

"I believe it was because she truly loved him. Not everyone is like you, Della. Some women care if their men take other women to their beds."

"Wait." She held up her hands, stopping him. "Then why is her name inscribed in the ring that you gave to me? Did you love her? And she loved your father?"

"Della, Lynnea was my mother. That was her ring." His face softened. "It's all I have that was hers. She gave it to me the day before she took her life and bid me to give it to my bride. She hoped it would bring my marriage more luck then it did hers. It was her blessing, in a sense."

"Your mother?" Della choked, suddenly overwhelmed by the thought he'd put into the gift. "Methought she was your love, your woman. Methought mayhap you pine for her still."

"Nay, silly female." Brant took a step closer and cupped her jaw. He was but a hairsbreadth away from her. "You are my woman now. My only one."

She tried to smile and shook her head. The gentle pressure of his hand turned her until she faced him. In essence he was right. He'd claimed her soul, but he didn't say he loved her.

"I ask you again," he said when she met his steady gaze. "Do you regret our marriage?"

The wind blew gently at her back, pushing loosened bits of her hair toward him. The thin strands hit his chest, caressing him, as she wanted to do. Della refused to reply. Her body ached with uncertainty. If she answered, she would only succeed in embarrassing herself. Her love would have to remain her own secret.

Lifting her hand to his chin, she rubbed her palm against the coarse hair on his jaw. He was so large, her husband. His shoulders blocked the moon from her view. The moon's glow made a halo around his hair and the silvery white strands floated in the breeze.

She lifted her other hand, knowing he waited for an answer she couldn't give. Pulling his lips to her, she lightly kissed him. It was the first time she'd willingly instigated a kiss and she was happy Brant didn't refuse her. His firm mouth moved steadily, giving her what she sought. His heat drew her to him until she melted against his form. Now she knew what to expect from his handling, she wasn't scared.

Brant moved his arms to encircle her back in a loose embrace. Della tried to get him to deepen the kiss by nudging his lips with her tongue. He groaned, opening his mouth to hers. A mutual flame coursed through their bodies in shared desire. Her tongue traced the line of his mouth, while her hands pulled at the back of his head to urge him closer.

Finally, she broke away to gaze up at him. Her gaze traveled to his swollen lips. Her chest heaved for want of air. "Teach me more."

Brant pulled her back to his slanted kiss and lifted her by the waist. He carried her dangling body to the small orchard, not taking his lips away until they were hidden within the bend of the trees.

"Can we please go inside? I'm through talking." Della blushed at the admission and was glad he couldn't see her face in the darkness of their small sanctuary. All thoughts of the past fell from her mind, along with all the insecurities of her heart. For this night, Brant would be only hers. "I want you to keep your promise."

"What promise?" he asked in a husky whisper against her throat. His hands searched her in the darkness. "I don't remember a promise and you never really ask me for anything."

"You said you would lie still while I explored you." Della tilted her head shyly to the side, but she didn't back away. "You said it would be all right if I touched you."

"Nay, there is no reason to go abovestairs for that." Brant kissed her again. His fingers ran passionately over her upper body to find a home on the soft curve of her breasts. He massaged the globes gently, peaking the nipples through her gown. "I can show you pleasure right here and you can explore me whenever you like. It's not a promise that needs granting. My body is yours. Use me how you will, princess."

To prove his point, Brant shrugged off his two tunics at the same time, dropping them both on a patch of grass. Della shivered at his declaration. Her hands glided over the firm length of his tightly drawn flesh, needing to feel him. She caressed the deep folds of his muscles, finding the buds of his nipples. Brant growled as she boldly licked his skin.

He grabbed her waist and lifted her up until she was face to face with him. With a barbaric growl, he leaned to give a quick kiss the top curve of her lush breast. His mouth ravished her throat in hot oscillations of desire. Setting her on the ground, he commanded, "Take off your undergarments so that I may show you how easily we fit together."

Della quivered at the heated promise in his words, her cavern wet and warm. Squinting to better see his face in the dim light, she heard his anxious breathing. Quickly, she wiggled out of her underclothes, which consisted only of a light pair of linen braccas, leaving on her undertunic and gown. Going back into Brant's arms, she kissed him passionately. She ran her hands over the muscles of his chest and down his waist.

"I love the feel of your skin," she admitted shyly. "Are you always this hot?"

"Only around you." His tone was husky and he gave a slow shake of his head. She knew he had to see the uncertainty she tried to hide. His body was tight, as if he forced himself to hold still while she stroked him.

Running her hands to his waist, she teased along the waistband of his braccas. She leaned forward and licked his nipple as he had done to her the night before. "Does it feel the same for you as it does for me?"

Brant nodded. He closed his eyes as she licked him again. His body shivered in response.

"Is it wrong of me to say such things? Does it make me too wanton or unattractive?" She pulled back. Her hands stayed their movements on his chest.

"Nay, not when you say them to me. I want you always to be honest with me, to say what you feel. I want you to tell me what feels good to you and methinks it's very attractive when the bold words come from your mouth." He leaned to kiss the long line of her exposed neck, scorching her flesh, proving his point. His hands sought the curves of her hips, forcing her hard against his rising member. He groaned and rotated his covered erection into the softness of her tunic gown. "It makes me burn for you. Your words set my blood on fire. You make me want to plunge myself deep inside you."

Della pushed his arms off her to free her hips. Brant groaned his protest. His words hummed delightfully in her veins.

Eagerly, she moved to draw kisses along his chest to his back. She circled him, exploring his body with her hands and tongue. Conquering the sinewy length of back, she moved her hands over his shoulders and down his sensitive spine. She hid her face from him, trying to get used to the bold ways he claimed to enjoy.

"I like it when you kiss me and I cannot breathe. I like the way you felt last night. I liked it when your finger…" Her voice trailed off shyly. She was unable to force the words.

"You liked it when I dipped my finger inside of you to test your softness," he continued for her in a low, sexual voice. His head rolled back on his shoulders at the words. "I liked it also. Should I tell you how you felt to me?"

Her heart pound wildly. Della felt empowered by the nearness of him. He was so strong, yet so gentle. Loosening her gown so the front fell forward, she then pressed the exposed curve of her breasts to the heat of his back. She enjoyed the way his breathing quickened when she rubbed sensually against him. Her fingers slid along his waistband, pulling at the ties she found in the front. The material loosened, but did not fall from his hips.

She stepped away from him just enough to explore his firm buttocks with her eyes. The moonlight hit him just right, allowing her to see the tight, hard mounds of flesh. He was like a healing draught one could get addicted to and she reveled in that addiction. Running her hands over his lower back and onto his firm cheeks, she felt the strong muscles flex in her grasp. She moved her fingers over his hip and around to his front. Her groan joined his as she found the length of his erection. The material of his braccas was hooked over the thick tip. She lifted them and they fell silently to the ground around his ankles. Touching him, the smooth, hard length pulsated in her hands.

Brant moved his hips to thrust his arousal into her hands. She stroked him several times from behind, amazed at the strength she discovered. Then, letting go, she went around to study his serpent from the front.

"Do all men look as you do?" She peered at his erection as it stood tall and proud against the moonlit night—just like its arrogant master. It was longer than she'd imagined and appeared a thick, solid limb of scalding flesh. She touched the tip of it with her finger.

"Yea, more or less." His body jerked almost painfully. "Ah, your touch is such sweet torture. I would gladly endure it for an eternity."

He grunted and a droplet of moisture came from the tip. She glanced up in surprise, but the surprise quickly turned to passion as he growled ravenously and lifted her by the waist. In long, demanding strides he brought her deeper into the trees.

"I lied. No more," he moaned. "I can take no more of your tormenting caresses."

"Tell me how I feel to you." Della breathed shyly against his ear, not forgetting his words. He pressed her into the seclusion, not pausing as he pulled her bodice. The delicate blue gown ripped and fell forward, fully exposing her hardened nipples. Then he brought her up against the large trunk and kneeled to lift her skirts.

"Your center feels like warmed cream." Brant bunched her dress around her waist. His fingers moved with a deft precision born of sudden urgency, cupping her mound as he ran his middle finger to separate her folds. He stroked her gently, testing her softness. Then, bracing his weight against the limb of the tree to trap her, his mouth sought the valley between her breasts. Kissing passionately up her throat, he confessed to her as his finger continued to stroke, "Your sex is like hot silk, so moist and slick against my finger."

His lips devoured her neck, pushing her harder against the tree. His chest grazed hers and she arched her back in pleasure. A sweet, low moan escaped her lips as she gasped for breath. He held the back of her head captive by her hair. Forcing her chin into the air, he bit lightly at her ear. The hand between her thighs continued to stroke her—a mindlessly precise rhythm.

"The taste of your skin excites me. It drives me mad with lust and all I can think of is embedding my sword within you." His words fanned scorchingly across her exposed skin. "I long to feel the warmth of your sex caressing me, accepting me into your depths. I want to conquer you."

Della thought she would swoon at his sinfully delectable words. If it was a sin to enjoy such things, she knew she was forever damned. She would never have the will to refuse him.

"Then do it," she urged, engulfing him with the strength of her desire. "I cannot stop you. I cannot stop myself."

Brant groaned at her throaty confession. Della grabbed onto his shoulders in anticipation and parted her thighs to him. When he pulled his finger out of her and lifted her up, she was forced to reach into the branches for support. Brant sucked a ripened nipple into his mouth, sucking, biting, licking, kissing. A hand kneaded the flesh of her butt as he took himself in hand to guide his arousal to her wet folds, teasing as he rubbed the tip back and forth over her swollen nub.

Arching her back, she thrust forward in the rhythm he'd taught her. He slid into her with ease. Della let out a loud moan of satisfaction, propelling him forward with a mighty thrust of her hips. She was so hot and her liquid caused his shaft to glide freely. Brant grunted his animalistic demands into her heaving breast as he continually sheathed himself within her.

Della seized another tree branch above her head for support as his movements became more fervent. His lips grazed the opposite breast, giving it as much attention as he had its twin.

"Yea, Della," Brant encouraged with another violent thrust. "That's it, accept me within you. Let me ride you."

He plunged in and out of her softness, his shaft possessing her very core with its thick length. She treasured the potency of her husband as he claimed her. He was so strong, so powerful. His size dominated her. His strength commanded and controlled her. She gripped the branches as his hands supported her backside under the heavy gown she wore, squeezing and spreading the mounds. The rhythm of his hips quickened, urging her to her release.

Della screamed as she neared the trembling end of her agony and the beginning of her zenith. His hips attacked with the unrelenting persistence of a conquering army, pumping deeper and faster inside her. Suddenly, his barbarous yell joined hers as he released his seed, their joined flesh trembling in perfect unison.

As the quaking subsided, Della's limbs weakened and dropped from the tree onto the support of his shoulders. Her heavy breath mingled with his.

"It's a good thing one is only allowed to do that once a night, lest it might get addicting." Della sighed against his shoulder, completely sated. She was too weak to be self-conscious. "It might be I who shackles you to a bed. Methinks I may make you my prisoner."

"Ah, my poor misguided wife." Brant chucked as he kissed her brow. "We shall see how many times a night one can do that."

"You mean?" She leaned back as he set her on the ground. He nodded as he fastened his braccas at his waist. A heated flush came to her features, but her eyes flashed with excitement. "How many times?"

He leaned over and picked up the rest of their discarded clothing. Looking up through the long strands of his blond hair, he shot her a devilish smile. "Come, wife, let us go abovestairs. We shall find out together."

"M'lord?" The midwife looked up in mild surprise. "How did you get in here?"

"Never you mind how." Stuart slipped off his wet

undertunic and threw it on the floor near the small fire. The full moon had outlined the hard lines of the castle and he had seen the lax castle guards easily in the pale blue light. They didn't expect intruders, instead watching the distant competitions in the exercise yard, jesting and wagering at their posts. He'd swum the freezing waters of the moat and scaled the rough stone of the newly constructed wall to get back inside Strathfeld. The stonemason had yet to completely smooth the stone, making it easier to climb.

Stuart shook the water from his short hair and gave the woman an irate look. She crushed herbs and paused to scrape at the powder she prepared with her long fingernail to test its consistency and dig out a few unwanted specks. "I wasn't about to sleep on the ground without the benefit of my servants, who even now slumber soundly within the keep."

Serilda nodded and motioned to the bed. "Then sleep if it's why yer here, m'lord."

Even her flattery in using the title that was not his didn't cheer him.

"Why did you not send word sooner, Serilda? Do you know how much harder things are now?" Stuart pouted in anguish, ignoring her invitation for sleep as he scowled.

"No, why don't you tell me how hard things are?" Serilda glanced to where his shaft lay between his thighs and gave him a catlike smile. She busied herself grinding another handful of herbs into powder, crushing them onto a slight piece of marble with a flat stone.

"This isn't amusing," Stuart fumed. "I have spent my entire life catering to her fears, becoming her friend, so much so that five years ago I could take it no more and disappeared. I trusted you to keep me informed."

"You soon forget," Serilda said bitterly. "You also left me five years ago."

"Nay, I have been back since then. Do you forget our nights together so easily?"

"Nay." Serilda hid her emotions from her eyes, instead choosing to flash him a relaxed smile. "Though one can hardly claim that once or twice a year is being attentive, m'lord."

"I never stopped you from finding pleasure elsewhere." Stuart said with a lustful smirk. "In fact, I remember watching you get it elsewhere on occasion."

Serilda chuckled. "I ne'er claimed I waited alone."

"Is that why you didn't tell me sooner? Because of your stupid woman's jealousy?" Stuart walked to her table and leaned his palms on the wood. "I have already told you, if I was allowed to marry you I would have, but then we would be poor. Where would we live? In a cottage while you sold your poisons?"

"I did send you word," Serilda shot back in irritation. "It was I who told you of the proposed marriage."

"But you were to make sure it never happened.

You knew well what I would have wanted. If I couldn't make it back in time, you were supposed to take care of him."

"Have you seen him? He is as healthy as they come. He ne'er has need of my services. Mayhap if he needed a soothing ointment fer his muscles or a sleeping potion I could have done something. But I could not poison his food without killing everyone in the manor." Serilda waved a dismissing hand. "Besides, who was to know the betrothal announcement would come so quickly? And the wedding so soon after that?"

"You were supposed to make sure Lord Strathfeld died from his wounds." He pounded the table. "Della would have never allowed the marriage if not for her father!"

"You didn't get back in time, m'lord. Mayhap she isn't as taken with you as you think. Five years is a long time in the heart of a woman," Serilda defended, bitterness touching her words. A solid mask fell over her dark beauty. "Don't blame me."

"How could I have gotten here on time? I only found out about it a sennight ago."

"It's not my fault." Serilda scooped up the powder with her little fingernail and tasted it. Lowering her voice, she said thoughtfully, "Almost ready."

"You were to stop Lord Strathfeld from making the betrothal announcement." Stuart rubbed his wet hair in frustration. "You were supposed to kill him!"

"Yea, and I did, too. Have you seen him up and about of late?" Calmly, Serilda lifted her hand and held out a fistful of grainy powder. Motioning her fist to a goblet at the end of the table, she commanded, "Mix it in that ale there."

Stuart took the goblet and held it under her hand. The grains fell silently into the liquid as her finger's loosened. Eagerly, he watched her stir the concoction with her long nail. He licked his lips in anticipation.

"Now, drink it," she ordered, turning back to her grinding stone and licking her wet finger slowly while watching him.

Stuart did as she commanded, drinking the mixture in several gulps. He wiped his mouth on his arm. Setting down the goblet, he moved to her small bed.

"Now, we can talk." Serilda smiled as she set down the grinding stone. She dipped her finger into the bitter powder only to place the herb into her mouth, swallowing it with her spit. Turning to him, she unfastened her simple dress. "Soon, you will not be so aggravated."

Stuart watched her as he sat on the bed. He licked his lips, jealous and aroused by the idea that she had taken other lovers. "How many have you taken since I was last here?"

"Men or women?"

He groaned, his shaft so hard it felt as if it might break.

"I seem to remember watching you get yer pleasure elsewhere." Serilda let her dress fall from her shoulders. "Would you like me to drug a maid for you, my lord?"

He didn't answer.

"How did you do it?" Stuart fell on his back in her bed, calmed drastically by the drink. "How did you kill him?"

"Lord Strathfeld was wounded at Martin. I made sure the wound ne'er healed and when he did not die fast enough, I rubbed poison into it." Serilda came to him on the bed. "He would not have lasted much longer. I just helped him along."

"You didn't do it soon enough." He grabbed her, pulling himself up so he could press his face between her plentiful breasts.

Serilda rubbed his short, dark hair, scratching her fingernails into his head. "It's true, but you said she would ne'er marry the barbarian. Mayhap it's you who misjudged her."

"He took her maidenhead," he whined. "It was to be mine."

"Nay, I took it from her." She shot him a naughty grin as she lifted two fingers to show him her shortened nails. "He ordered her 'checked'. Methinks he feared she carried yer babe."

Stuart laughed. His arms tingled with the potion she had given him.

"I have a present fer you, which might make you feel better." Serilda let go of him and opened a small trunk by the bed. She picked out a bundle and handed it to him.

"I know naught of presents, but come back and I will show you how to make me feel better." He scratched his naked stomach as he fell back onto the bed.

Serilda laughed as he dropped the unopened package and pulled her to his chest. Strange and colorful lights began to dance around them. "Do not worry. Soon, there will be no one to stop you. I have seen the future."

"Yea, witch." Stuart let the drug take him over completely. "I have seen it, too."

14

DELLA LANGUIDLY STRETCHED her arms above her head, sliding against the soft fur coverlet. A contended sigh whispered dreamily from her parted lips. She refused to open her eyes, satisfied to lie in the soft cloud of the bed. Her body still stung with pleasure from the night of lovemaking. Brant's stamina had been tireless and Della swore she could still feel the brand of his touch over the whole length of her body.

By the end of their fourth joining, Brant had explored every inch of her. She in turn learned the workings of his desire. His lips, his skin, his appetite, everything had been so new to her. He'd shown her repeated pleasure until her body refused to move, and he'd shown her positions from which her limbs would surely never recover. When he was sated and finally let her rest, she'd drifted into a deep, peaceful sleep at his side.

She felt him breathing next to her naked body.

His knee came between her legs from behind and his arm wrapped around her so that his hand rested possessively on her breast. He flexed his fingers gently against her nipple. A wave of longing shot through her.

Again? She smiled, liking the idea. She wondered if he still slept.

Opening her eyes, she saw it was indeed late in the day. She couldn't remember when she'd lazed about so long in bed—probably because she never had.

"Brant?" Della's eyes sparked with naughty pleasure. "Lord Blackwell, are you awake?"

When she received no answer, she disentangled her legs from his and turned in his arms. He slept quietly, his chest rising and falling in a deep, even sleep. She took her finger and ran it down the center of his chest, watching his eyes to see if he stirred. Her sex grew moist as she thought of him inside of her.

Leaning back, she peeked at his member. It lay limp and soft on the bed. Della frowned in puzzlement. It had looked much bigger at night and had been very hard.

I've broken it! Della gasped.

She watched his face to see if he showed any signs of pain as she flicked it with the tip of her finger. He didn't move and he didn't seem to be hurt. Growing adventurous she touched it more fully. It was silky and pliable and the skin moved peculiarly when she rubbed it. Della tried not to laugh as she glanced back up. Brant's chest still rose and fell in sleep.

Mayhap it only works at night, Della concluded. Her heart dropped a bit in disappointment. But then she felt his shaft twitch in her hands and quickly looked down to see what had happened.

Before her eyes, it started to grow and form in her palm. The more it grew, the firmer it became. Della moved her hand to the base of his shaft. She wrapped her fingers about the width and squeezed gently while running her hand to the tip. Almost instantly it sprung to capacity. Her breathing deepened as she recalled the delight he had been able to give her. Grabbing his butt, she pulled him toward her hips.

"Methinks you are up to no good this morn, wife," Brant grumbled sleepily. He'd felt her turn in his arms. It had been part of his war training to be able to wake quickly and look as if he still slept. When his mind had determined there was no need for him to be too on alert, he'd relaxed enough to let his wife explore his body. It had taken all of his might to hold still and let her touch him. Lifting one eyelid to study her, he asked, "Are you not sated, wench?"

Della blushed prettily, but didn't stop her bold advances. "It's your pagan curse, m'lord. If you have complaints, take it off me."

Most women of little experience were too self-conscious to make such bold confessions. He was amazed, though greatly pleased, by her assertiveness and by the quick change in her temperament toward him. She'd softened dramatically. Brant moved his hand over her smooth hip. In one deft motion, he lifted her leg with his hand and rolled so he could enter her. "Nay, wife, if you are cursed, I will you to remain so."

Della shifted her hips to accept him.

"Nay, not yet." Brant gave her a purposeful growl. He still wanted her, but after the night of love play he was finally able to control his lust. During the night, every time she'd moved to accept him, he had been unable to resist. "Let us play a little game."

"But—" Della's hips searched again.

"Nay, I will ask you a question and if you answer, I will let you have a little." Brant smiled, proud of the idea. "Yea, and if you choose not to answer, which is your right, I will take a little away."

"But—" Della moved her hands to his hips and tried to pull at him.

"Nay, you cannot touch me. You have to keep your hands above your head."

Della grumbled, but did as he said.

"Do you understand the rules?"

"Yea." She pretended to pout.

"All right, my first question."

"Nay, I answered the first! Where is my reward?"

"Greedy wench." Brant liked her eagerness. He rubbed the tip of his shaft against her. "Now, who is the cleaning spirit?"

Della cleared her throat. "I don't know what you mean."

"Hmm." Brant frowned.

"She is a spirit that cleans," she offered weakly.

"If you don't want to tell me, fine." Brant made a move to roll off her.

"Nay, I'll tell you!" Then, her voice a small whimper, she said, "It is I."

Brant laughed. "Methought as much. Why?"

"The servants were being lazy. It was the only way I could get them to listen to me and clean. At first I would just do some of the chores myself while they slept, but then one night I got angry at all the work that needed to be done. It was as if they stopped working on purpose to let the spirit do it. So I tore the manor apart. A few discreetly placed hints and the servants were working for fear of the spirit." Della blushed. "I was seventeen years and I could think of nothing else."

"All right," Brant allowed with a thoughtful nod. He narrowed his eyes to examine her closely. "How many years are you?"

"Two and twenty." Della rolled her eyes.

"Methought you were a bit aged," he teased. In the opinion of society, she was past her prime. Girls usually got married as early as thirteen and then it was to old men.

"Nay, methinks you are the elder one, *Brant the fiery thorn!*" Della hit him in the shoulder. He swayed off her in mock pain.

Della straddled him and held him by his wrists. If he really wanted to, he could throw her off him with little effort. He didn't struggle too hard.

"What will you do to me, m'lady?" Brant pretended to be scared, but it didn't hold for he was soon eyeing her breasts as they bobbed before his gaze.

"I don't know yet," Della pondered. "Mayhap, if you are behaved, I will let you stay here as a slave."

"Bed slave?" Brant questioned hopefully.

Della laughed at the eagerness in his tone. "Nay, I have too many of those at the moment. But I do need someone to clean the garderobes."

Brant growled, bucking her naked body off him.

Della landed on her backside and Brant quickly rolled to trap her with his leg.

"That isn't amusing, lady wife." Brant nuzzled her throat, tickling her with his whiskers, causing her to shiver. Even in jest, the idea filled him with jealousy.

"Fine, then if not a slave…" Della sighed. "I have a question."

"Yea?" The sound was muffled into her throat as Brant forgot his game.

"Where did you get all the scars on your body?"

"In battle."

"That much is apparent." Della inched away to look at his face. "How?"

"You don't wish to hear such things."

She gave him an odd look. "Don't think you know me so well. If I didn't want to know, I wouldn't have asked."

He breathed deeply as he saw her icy temperament returning. "Which one do you wish to know about?"

"All," she answered with a firm nod. Then, when he lifted an eyebrow in amusement as if to say, *that would be impossible*, she pointed to his chest. "This one."

Brant looked briefly at the thin scar that ran across the right side of his upper chest. "Sword in battle."

"And this?" She pointed to a small mark right under it.

"I don't remember getting it." Brant grew apprehensive. Wars and battles were not exactly something he wished to discuss with his wife, especially in light of the horrible atrocities she'd witnessed as a child. The things he'd seen were not stories for delicate women.

"This?" She touched a thin scar on his forearm.

"Blade."

"This?" A strange puckering on his leg.

"Mace."

"This?" A healed gash at his side.

"Spear."

"And this?" A cut on his firm stomach.

"Sword in practice."

"Hmm, and this?" She moved her hand to his hip.

"Lance."

"Is there a weapon with which you have not been hit?" she queried with a dubious shake of her head. "It would seem your body should have fallen apart by now."

"Yea, methinks it has at times."

"Do they still pain you?"

"Only some—like the club to my back." He lifted

his leg and touched his inner thigh. "And here, where a lance hit."

Della leaned closer to his hand and narrowed her eyes. "I see naught."

"Look closer," he chuckled.

Della's mouth fell open as she realized what he was doing and she hit his chest. "I don't think you have a wound there, m'lord."

"Then why does it hurt so?"

"You complain much." Della wrapped her arms around his neck and pulled him toward her.

"Mayhap the wound is internal," he persisted. "Will you check?"

Della reached to touch him. Stroking him boldly, she said, "I don't feel a thing wrong with you."

"Then put your hands above your head. I have a few more questions." Brant smiled, remembering where he'd left off.

"Well?" She lifted her hands over her head, quirking a brow.

"Do you regret marrying me?" he asked in all seriousness. He hadn't forgotten her refusal to answer him the night before. His heart held quiet, waiting an eternity for her to speak. He didn't know why the answer was so important to him, but he needed to know.

"Don't." Della shook her head. The smile faded quickly from her eyes to be replaced by her frozen resolve, but the ice again melted as he rubbed his member against her.

Why do you refuse to answer me?

Brant decided to leave the question alone for the time being. "Have you a scar, m'lady?"

"Only one that I can think of."

Brant moved himself to her opening. "Where?"

"My leg." She arched into him.

"How?" With each question, he inched deeper and deeper into her depths.

"Stuart and I were racing horses. I tried to jump a low branch and fell." Her eyes remained closed.

Brant frowned, but didn't move from her. Her cousin was not someone he wished to discuss at the moment, but her words only reminded him how she kept referring to Stuart as her only family. Mayhap it wasn't meant as a slight to him, but an affirmation of all she had lost. He thought of Edwyn's tale of her mother. And again, mayhap it was meant as a slight against him. "Do you love Stuart?"

"Yea." Her answer tore at him. "But only as a brother. We grew up together."

His desires diminished some at her answers. She lightly moaned, blindly urging him forward with her hips.

"Do you ever think you will come to love me?" The words were spoken before he had a chance to stop them. But, having said then, he could not take them back.

Della's eyes shot open, her mouth tightened in a scowl. "Don't ask those things. Why can you not leave well enough alone?"

"Are you refusing to answer?" He kept his face blank, forgetting what they had been doing.

She chose her response carefully. "Nay, I am not refusing. But I don't like the question."

Still, Brant didn't move, feeling as if his entire being descended into hell. Her hesitation could only mean one thing. She didn't think she ever could.

"Methinks that," she hesitated. "Methinks there might be some tender feeling in time. We are married and I believe we should make the best of it, for it is a long time we may be together."

Brant nodded. At least she didn't spout curses at his head and denounce their marriage as a sham. He knew he should respect her for her honesty, but he didn't find himself liking it.

"Brant?" Della inquired, uncertain.

"Yea?" He realized he was still in her, though the pleasure had lessened from the lovemaking. Thrusting fully in her, he stopped the game. He didn't want to hear any more of her honesty.

WHY DID he have to ask her about love?

Why did she answer him?

Even as Della thought it, she knew the reason. If she didn't answer, he would know the truth. He would know she thought to be in love with him. So, instead, she'd given him a small version of the truth.

Della felt her body accept him, though she'd lost most of her passion. Her heart ached for that which she could not have. She watched his face as he moved inside of her. And, as they silently found release, neither of them acknowledged the barrier that had built up between them.

ALMOST A SENNIGHT PASSED and Brant didn't make love to her again. Having never been with a man before, Della didn't know if it was normal. Could it be that a man's desires were exaggerated? And, if they were, why did she still want to touch him? She'd always heard men were the ones who demanded their marital rights, never the wife.

He didn't seem to be sleeping with any mistresses and each night he came back to her bed, kissing her on the cheek like a stranger and then turning from her to sleep. When he said goodnight to her, she was sure it was the most he'd said to her all day. And when he slept and she could not, she sat in bed and studied him.

Della tried to busy herself with chores, but her heart was not in them. She was distracted and ended up being more of a hindrance than a help. Many of the servants grew exasperated with her efforts and encouraged her, none too gently, to find work elsewhere. In the last sennight, she'd weeded her garden until there was no more soil to churn. She'd overseen the shearing of the sheep, which if truth were told, the chore was done too early. She'd ordered the manor deeply cleaned, until every surface shimmered. She'd instructed the dying of cloths and the weaving of new bed linens. And she'd set some of the maids to brewing more mead when it was not needed. The stables, the workshops, the chapel, all of them were attended to. There was not much else with which she could busy herself.

Della had even schooled Rab until the boy revolted and hid from her teachings—not that he was available much these days. Brant stayed true to his word and let the boy help the men on the exercise field. It was a task Rab would much rather do.

This was why she now found herself walking aimlessly about the castle grounds searching for something to occupy the time. Restless, she began to curse her highly efficient home. Why had she made things run so smoothly? Why had she made it so she wasn't needed anywhere, for anything?

Even Edwyn, having all but finished the stone wall, was busy instructing the seasonal dredging of the moat and could not be bothered. Roldan, Gunther, and the other knights were on the practice field exercising—as was her husband, as far as she could tell.

The sun shone bright over the bailey, the day warm. She thought of Brant and her feet turned toward the loud shouts of the soldiers. Passing close to the exercise field, she saw her husband supervising some of the men who sparred without weapons. His tunic was off, his exposed chest sweaty. Next to him was Rab, his face beaming at Lord Blackwell in boyish awe.

Brant noticed her and nodded politely before turning back to bark an instruction at the men.

Getting into the fray, he showed one of them a fighting technique. He didn't look at her again. His cold indifference was an effective dismissal and she didn't continue toward him.

Argh! If I don't get out of here, I will scream.

Suddenly the walls of the bailey were too confining. Brant would not talk to her. The servants shooed her from every corner. Della felt unwanted in her own home.

If no one wants me about, who would notice if I was to leave?

Della made her way to the private chamber in the bailey wall, slipping easily past Edwyn's room. No one in the manor, except for Edwyn and herself, knew of the secret entrance she had built into the castle. For some reason, she'd never even told Stuart of it.

At first, she hadn't thought building a tunnel under the moat would actually work, but it had. The builders had been contracted from far away to complete it and, when they were done, she hadn't thought to tell anyone. That was years ago and the workers, honest ones the whole lot, had been paid well for their silence. She liked having it as her own secret tunnel. It made her feel more secure knowing there was a way to escape the castle that didn't include swimming, since she didn't know how.

It had been a long time since she'd used the passageway. Often she had escaped outside the castle walls just to look at her home from a distance. At sunset, the castle was marvelous—its towering form reaching into the blue and purple heavens.

Making sure she was not followed, which didn't seem to be a problem since she was not sought after, Della pulled up a secret latch. It was cleverly hidden in the stone wall. The opening shifted slightly as a mock panel fell back. Grabbing a torch, she pushed the panel all the way open.

The underground corridor was narrow and damp. The tapping of the servants sounded as they dredged over the stone ceiling. She closed the panel. The door didn't secure as well as on the inside of the walkway, but after careful consideration it had been determined that no one would notice the flaw unless they knew to look for it.

Della briskly made her way down the passage, ignoring the cobwebs that hung from the ceiling. She always worried that if she tarried too long, the torch would dim and eventually would burn out. For that reason, the walls had been marked with various grooves so one could find their way if trapped.

The corridor turned, marking that she was almost to the end. Her lonely steps echoed dismally and she tried to quiet them so the servants above would not hear. They had never been able to test the passage to see if it was soundproof.

Coming to the end, Della pushed at the ceiling. The wooden boards fell away with a gentle shove and light streamed in from above to puncture the dimness. She snuffed the torch and laid it on the passageway floor. Bracing a foot against a stone that jutted out from the wall, she lifted herself to peek out into the surrounding forest. Birds and insects chirped. All was serene.

Della hoisted herself out, smiling as she saw the castle. Strathfeld, the old Roman fortress she'd built into a home. Not allowing herself the pleasure of staring too long, she covered the entrance with leaves. She was free.

BRANT STRETCHED his arms above his head. The sun began to set in the distance and by the men's tired grumbling, he knew it was time to dine. He hadn't seen Della since she'd walked past the exercise field several hours earlier. It wasn't unusual, though, for Strathfeld was a large place. She could be anywhere in the keep.

"Enough, Blackwell," Roldan grouched.

"Yea, enough exercise this day. Let us rest." Gunther's tired yawn joined the rest of the men's. "You have worked us all hard this last sennight. What says you we leave off on the morrow for a day of leisure?"

"Fine," Brant agreed unwillingly. His assent cheered the men as they made their way quickly to the main hall. He'd been pushing them all rather hard, but it was only to exhaust himself before going to bed. Though he found that no matter how hard he pushed his body, at night when he rested beside Della, it was all he could do not to touch her.

Every time he thought about reaching for her, the memory of her face during their last coupling made him stop and keep away. Although he waited, she never reached out for him. He didn't wish to bed an ice maiden and he didn't know how to thaw her heart.

"They fear you will change yer mind and make them stay longer." Gunther laughed halfheartedly when they were alone. He leaned over and picked up a discarded practice shield.

"Yea."

"What is ailing you, Blackwell?" Gunther probed. "You have been pushing all of us hard these past days. If I didn't know better, I would say you are readying us fer battle."

"It's always wise to be ready for battle." Brant flashed a quick smile, one he didn't feel.

"Yea, but you have been pushing yerself most of all. I should think with a beautiful new home and a lovely bride to share yer bed, you would be avoiding the likes of us—mayhap lazing about in that bed."

Brant just grumbled, shooting the man an irritated scowl.

"Wedded bliss not like you pictured?" Gunther turned serious. "Are you thinking…?"

"Nay, not divorce. A man would have to be a fool to give this up." Brant threw his hand in the air to encompass the castle.

"Ah, then she is an unpleasant lover. Can't she be

taught? Methought she had melted toward you, but mayhap that is why she is called *Della the Cold*."

"Do not call her that." Brant's fist tightened in warning.

"Nay, not me, but others," Gunther said, unaffected. "You cannot quiet all the tongues."

Brant didn't answer.

"So is she unpleasant?"

Brant stopped walking and ran his fingers through his sweaty hair. "Nay, she is quite hot-blooded."

"Ah," Gunther laughed, suddenly realizing what was wrong. "You love her."

"Nay," Brant denied too quickly.

"Methinks you do."

"You do not believe in love." Brant swore under his breath.

"Nay, I have ne'er said that. I have oft said love is the ruination of a man. I have oft said I wish ne'er to find it. But I have ne'er said I do not believe in it." Gunther laughed harder. "Yea, I have e'en seen it oft enough. To me it would be like a bloody curse."

"Nonetheless, it is not love we are in. She thinks that she can mayhap come to care for me in time."

"Perchance she is mistaken. You are not the easiest person to whom one can confess. Just ask the many men we have taken in battle."

"Nay, I don't frighten her and she doesn't lie. I have seen the truth in her oft enough." Brant sighed, eyeing the entrance to the hall wearily. He didn't feel like going in, but he had no choice.

"Then you must win her heart, Brant," Gunther

said. "You are a knight after all. If anyone knows how to fight for what he wants, it's a knight."

"When did you become so sentimental?" Brant glared at his friend in irritation. But, even so, he thought Gunther might be right. Maybe all Della needed was more time. There was no reason to continue to punish his body when she came to lie willingly next to him each night. Gunther gave him an impertinent grin, his mouth opening to speak. Brant quickly stopped him. "Nay, Gunther, don't answer. I've had enough of your counsel this eve."

Gunther laughed heartily, swinging the shield from his shoulder and placing it by the entrance to the hall. The smile still lining his mischievous lips, Gunther began to sing a loud, bawdy tale as he left Brant alone.

THE MOON SHOWED in the distance, faint against the setting of the evening sun. A cool breeze drifted over the forest, carrying a bit of stickiness to the air. Della didn't mind it as she stretched her hands above her head. The grass beneath her was soft, as was the sounds of the forest. Insects hummed and she heard cattle mooing in a nearby field as they grazed. The wind picked up, causing the leaves to rustle overhead.

Sighing, she knew it was time to go back. She'd waited long enough to see the sun set over the castle. Inside the walls, they would be gathering together for the eve meal and it would be noticed if she were not there to attend them.

She stood and brushed the foliage from her hair and gown. Patting the coiffure at her neck, she tucked a few wayward strands back into place.

"Della?" The voice startled her as it came out of the darkness.

Della quickly turned, squinting to see who it was. "Stuart? Is that you?"

"Yea." Stuart stepped from the trees. It was hard to see him, except for the shadowed impression he made. "Methought you were a night apparition. What are you doing out of the castle? Are you alone?"

"Yea." Della suddenly felt uneasy.

"I have been camped outside the walls. I didn't see the main gate open. How did you escape?"

"I would not say I escaped." Della forced herself to relax. "I just came out for a walk."

"How did you get out of the castle?" His voice edged with an unnatural eagerness. "Did you fly?"

"Nay." She sighed heavily. It looked as if her secret was out. "Promise you will tell no one?"

"Yea."

"I have a secret passage that goes under the moat. I used it."

"Who knows of this passage?"

"Only three of us," she answered, ignoring the nagging urge to say nothing. "You, me, and Edwyn."

"So your *husband* doesn't know?"

"Nay." Della took a step toward him. "Stuart, please don't hate him. I so wish for you to become friends with him. You are both my family now."

"*He* will never be my friend," Stuart said vehemently with a toss of his head.

"Nay, don't harden your heart," Della pleaded. "I know he had you thrown out, but you kept pushing. What else could he do?"

"You care for him," he accused bitterly.

"Nay," Della denied, but her heart burned with the lie. "I care for Strathfeld and its people."

Stuart straightened his shoulders. "Then come away with me tonight. We will go to King Guthrum and get your marriage annulled. When we come back, we will rid this keep of the barbarian lord. We will do right by your people."

"You want that I should leave Strathfeld?" Della shook her head. "Nay, the marriage is of the king's doing, he would be reluctant to dissolve it now. My marriage is legal, there are no grounds."

"Then come with me anyway." He took a step toward her, but hesitated when she recoiled. "Leave this place until we may find a way to reclaim it."

"Nay, I cannot leave my home," she answered. "I am married. It's time you accepted it. I have."

Stuart said nothing.

"Stuart?"

"Yea?" he growled.

"Why have you been camping outside the walls for so long? Your servants left after you, didn't you see them?" She took a step back from him. He shifted his weight and she was finally able to see more of his face. His features were smudged with dirt and his eyes were wide, almost crazed in their intensity.

"Yea, I let them go. If I'd stopped them, I would've been discovered. I have no need of their services here."

"Stuart, why are you hiding in the forest?" Della searched the trees for a sign that they were not alone. She couldn't see anyone, but the thought gave her chills.

"Now you question my honor, Della?" Stuart shook his head. "Very well, I'm here to protect you. To make sure you are truly happy. I'm here to make sure he hasn't bewitched you and that your will is still your own."

"Don't worry for me, dear cousin." Della took another step back. Stuart was saying all the right things, but his eyes made her uneasy.

"But I do."

"I should get back inside. They will be waiting for me." She reached within a pouch hidden in the folds of her skirt for a flint to light the torch lying at the bottom of the passage. "Take care of yourself, Stuart. Mayhap come back in a few fortnights for a visit. I will speak with Blackwell on your behalf. Mayhap, after your tempers have cooled, a reasonable truce can be made. I should hate to never see you again."

"Nay, don't waste your breath on my behalf." Stuart stormed off into the trees. She could hear his voice in the distance as he yelled, "It would seem you have chosen your side."

Della waited a moment until she no longer heard him moving around. Turning, she made her way to the hidden entrance. She jumped down into the hole, found the torch, lit it and then hurriedly reached to latch the opening shut. Something in the way Stuart had looked at her scared her. He was no longer the boy she knew in childhood.

Taking a deep breath to calm the skipping of her heart, she made her way back through the passage. With a determined frown, Della decided she would have their wars no more. She would speak to Brant about Stuart, heedless of her cousin's passionate denial of wanting a truce.

"Where is she?" Brant grumbled under his breath. Fear for his wife's safety made his temper hot and short. He didn't like feeling helpless. He didn't like not knowing where she was. Reaching his warhorse, he jumped on the animal's back. He turned to Gunther who did the same. "They have searched everywhere for her. There is no sign."

"She has to be within the castle walls. The bridge has not been lowered," Gunther answered. "Do you think Stuart has kidnapped her? He did say he would take back what was his."

"I don't know, but it would seem likely." Brant

tried not to let his uneasiness show as he ordered a man to open the front gate.

"Nay, m'lord!" Edwyn ran to the men. Brant whipped around on his stallion. The seneschal eyed their drawn swords. "Do not!"

"Do you know where she is, Edwyn?" Brant asked.

The elderly man shook his head in denial.

"Then we have no time to waste. If she is within these walls, she is safe. However, if she is not, we must leave while there is still a trail to follow. Stuart could have crossed the moat with her." Brant began to rein his horse away, but the man stopped him again.

"If he did, it would be a mistake. Della cannot swim," Edwyn insisted. "She would scream if he even tried to take her into the water. Sir Stuart knows this. You must come with me, m'lord. I have something to show you."

Brant swung down from his horse and hurried to follow the seneschal, giving the order to leave the front gate closed. The man at the wall nodded, signaling the change in orders. As Brant strode after Edwyn, Gunther followed right behind.

The seneschal led him into his chamber. Taking a torch off his wall and lighting it, he moved to the small hidden door.

"Do not waste my time for this, Edwyn. I have looked in the secret chamber." Brant began to turn in exasperation. His heart pounded with dread and he felt Della was not within the walls of the keep. His head ached with all that could happen to her out of reach of his protection.

"Nay, it is the secret passage," Edwyn persisted when Brant would go.

"What?" Gunther asked, surprised. "There is a secret chamber?"

"Yea." Before Brant needed to explain further, Edwyn opened the door leading to it. The men followed the seneschal through the small door into the domed chamber. Gunther let loose a low whistle of appreciation. Brant scowled. Gunther shrugged.

"Where does the passage lead?" Brant looked around the room, not seeing an exit.

"Outside the bailey walls, m'lord," the old man answered. "If she was taken, then it would be best if they didn't know you came."

"Yea, he's right," Gunther added. "Sir Stuart would be listening for the bridge. All it would take is one good archer to knock you from your horse."

"Quiet," Brant ordered suddenly. He dashed his hand through the air. "What is that noise? Rats?"

The men turned to the sound of scraping stone. It came from the other side of the chamber. Unexpectedly a false wall fell forward and a snuffed torch was thrown onto the floor to land at their feet. The Vikings watched in amazement. Edwyn grimaced in foreboding. A delicate hand reached up, feeling around the ledge until it found hold on a stone.

Brant knew that hand. The ring he had placed on his wife's finger gleamed under the light of Edwyn's torch. He stormed forward and grabbed Della by the wrist, hauling her up and out of the passage in one swift motion. She screamed in surprise and he shoved her behind his body as he peered down into the hole. Satisfied she was alone, he turned his blazing eyes to her.

"Br-ant," Della stuttered in astonishment. She rubbed her wrist where he'd grabbed her, searching the other two men before turning back to her irate husband. Her words deceptively innocent, she asked, "What are you doing here?"

"I should ask you the same thing." Brant kicked her discarded torch aside as he loomed over her.

"Come, Edwyn, this is not our fight." Gunther ducked out of the secret chamber. The old seneschal quickly leaned over to shut the passageway entrance before following the soldier.

"I was walking," she answered as soon as the men left. Della stumbled away from him, maneuvering to put a table between their bodies for protection.

"With whom?" His tone deadly in its seriousness, he followed her. Shoving the table out of the way with one hard push, he felt small satisfaction as it screeched along the stone before crashing to a stop against the wall. Della jumped at the noise.

"I don't like the accusing tone in your voice, Lord Blackwell."

"You will like the beating I give you even less, lady wife," he snarled viciously at her. He'd been so scared, so worried, so jealous that she might be with Sir Stuart. "Who with?"

"No one." The words were breathless. He wanted

to believe them, but how could he? "I was walking alone."

"You dare to go outside the castle on your own? Unescorted?" Brant seized her about the shoulders and gave her a hard shake. "What were you about?"

"It's not as bad as all that," she protested weakly.

"Oh, yea?" Brant gave her another hard shake. He saw the fear in her and lessened his grip. Even now, he couldn't hurt her, not like the warrior in him wanted to. Gritting his teeth, he asked, "Then why was the manor turned upside down looking for you?"

"You were worried about me?" She tried to hide her smile, but failed. "You were worried I was gone?"

"Yea," he whispered, entranced by the way her smile dove into his chest to stop his heart. Her eyes twinkled just so, making him forget his suspicions.

"I didn't think you would notice." She bit her lip. "You really looked for me? You knew I was gone?"

"Naturally, I knew." He kept his fists at his side, uncomfortable with the turn of conversation. "You were not at the eve meal as you properly should be."

"Then you were only worried you would look bad in the main hall." Della nodded. Ice fell over her expression, hiding what he thought might be disappointment. It was too hard to be sure. He wanted so much for her to feel something for him that he didn't trust his judgment when reading her. How did he know any tenderness in her face wasn't his own mind grasping for a reason to hope?

"Where did you go?" Brant tried to ignore the rise

and fall of her chest. The soft globes of her breasts were just beyond his reach.

"I was outside the castle walls." Her shoulders relaxed, as if she realized he wasn't going to beat her. "Walking."

"Could you not walk within the bailey?" His hands loosened a bit more, unclenching at his sides.

"Yea, but I wanted to be alone. Have you ever just wanted to be alone? Away from the prying eyes of servants and knights?"

Brant studied her eyes. She looked so earnest that he found himself believing her.

When he didn't answer, she lifted her hand to his face, brushing her palm against his whiskered cheek. "I did naught that you would consider dishonorable. I promise."

Brant wanted desperately to trust her. Foolish as it might be, he did. The alternative was too painful. That she could be unfaithful hurt too much. "You are not to leave the castle again without my permission and I will inspect this exit later with Gunther. We may have it stoned in."

Della nodded, though she clearly wasn't happy with the decree. His flesh stung where her hand met his cheek. The familiar smell of her, mingling with the freshness of the forest, sent longing throughout his very being. He missed her touch, her attentions. He missed the way she felt against him. But he was a warrior, a soldier. Men like him didn't feel such deep emotional need, not for a woman, not for a wife. The emotion was too strong, too uncertain. Mayhap the spell was of her doing, for she ensorcelled him.

"M'lord, before you stone the passage in, please consider this first." When he lifted an eyebrow, ready to argue she rushed on, "Just consider how convenient another exit is in such a castle as this. It leads out into the woods and would be very useful if one was in need of an escape. Many within these walls cannot swim and they would drown in high moat waters if they were to try and escape during a battle."

"Yea, but have you considered we may also be attacked by means of such a weakness?" He frowned in thought. "Or do you mean you would be the one in need of an escape? For I hear it is you who cannot swim the moat."

"Nay." Della made a small choking noise. "It would be for times of war, which is why I designed it."

"Who all knows of it?"

"Edwyn and I. Outside builders were contracted and they are all dead or off in faraway lands." Della looked guiltily away and he wondered if she was lying. Did someone else know? "And now Gunther and you, m'lord."

"Lord Blackwell. M'lord." Brant scowled in displeasure. "Must you always be so formal with me? I am your husband, wife."

"What would you have me call you?" Her body swayed nearer.

"Call me what you wish," he responded hoarsely. "It was only an observation."

"Have I done aught to displease you, m'lord?" Della hesitated.

"Besides wandering about the countryside without a proper escort?"

"Yea, I mean before then. Is there a reason why you do not look to me this past sennight? Is there a reason you have not touched me more than in brief passing?" She dropped her hand from him, looking shyly away as a pretty blush spread over her features.

"Nay." He swallowed hard as he uttered the half-truth. "I have been busy training the men. It takes a lot of my energy and time. There is much I need to accomplish if the knights are to fight well together."

Della obviously didn't believe him, but he was glad when she did not question his answer. "Methought, perchance, I did not please you anymore. That you had grown tired of me."

Brant's hands turned caressing as he moved them to cup her cheeks. He liked the insecure way she was looking at him, as if weighing his answers very carefully. It meant she cared, at least a little. "Nay, Della. I'm not unhappy with you."

He dipped his mouth to lightly kiss her. She moaned, instinctively leaning into him, winding her arms around his neck to return the kiss. Della sighed and trembled. The sweetness of her embrace drew over him.

Brant growled and tore his mouth away. "Let us go abovestairs, lady wife. And I will show you how unhappy I am not."

DELLA BOLTED UPRIGHT IN BED. A loud knocking resounded on the chamber door. The early morning light shone through the narrow slit of a window. She tried to pull out of her husband's arms, squirming in his embrace, but he held her fast in their nakedness. Brant laughed and pulled her tight against him until she was once more along his side. Grabbing the fur coverlet, he pulled it over her.

"But, the door," Della said, horrified. Her eyes rounded in embarrassment as she motioned weakly to the thick oak. She'd been awaked by her husband's tender kisses on her neck, only to be jarred to her senses by the knock. Torn between the need to hurry and the feel of his taut length against her, she eyed him and then the door. His hardened arousal pressed suggestively against her thigh. Brant was winning.

"You are my wife and there is naught to be ashamed of." Brant chuckled as he ran his hand over her hip, lightly rubbing himself suggestively along her leg. "Do you think no one knows what goes on between us?"

A small sound of derision escaped her tight throat. Realizing he was not going to let her go, Della drew in her arms to bury herself in his chest. She turned her head to peek at the door.

"Yea?" Brant yelled when she settled.

The door creaked and Ebba poked her head around the side. Her face paled in shock at the scene on the bed.

Della groaned and hid her face in Brant's chest. Feeling his soft chuckle, she pinched him obstinately in the stomach. It didn't affect him. When she glanced up at him, she saw him grinning.

"Yea? What is it?" he inquired.

"Raiders, m'lord," Ebba stammered. "Along the west this time. Two o' the cotters just arrived. Gunther said to wake yer lazy arse… He said it is time you awoke and I was to tell you that he would meet you by the gate with yer horse."

"Thank you, Ebba," Della dismissed the girl. She pushed lightly at Brant's chest, trying to be free of his grasp. "His lordship will be right down."

Brant frowned. "Yea, Ebba, begone."

Ebba shut the door. Della pushed away from Brant, all desire having faded from her body at the news. Worry filled each breath as she hurried to her trunk to don a fresh undertunic. Her hands shook with her need to help as she pulled her hair back to the nape of her neck. More to herself than to him, she said, "I should never have stayed in bed so long. What was I thinking?"

Brant stood and grabbed his braccas, sighing in obvious disappointment as he slipped them over his hips.

"I should have been belowstairs." She hurriedly pulled on her dress. "Not in bed doing naught."

"Naught? I would not say we were doing naught, lady wife." Brant pulled on a new undertunic.

"I shall ride immediately," Della announced, barely looking at him. She swallowed hard, not daring to ask his permission. "I should have ordered Ebba to ready my horse."

"Della, you will not be going." Brant's tone made the finality of his decision unmistakable. She didn't intend to obey.

"Nay, I will. It's still my responsibility to care for these people. Just because you are my husband does not give you the right to forbid me from doing my duty." She placed her hands defiantly on her hips before looking up at him. Fire burned in his eyes, but she didn't back down.

"Because I am your husband, I do have that right. I will see to it, Della. It is a man's affair to be dealt with. You will handle only the womanly concerns of the keep."

"And what is a woman's concern?" Della preened with a false smile and bat of her eyelashes. Inside she fumed at his daring.

"Cooking, sewing, cleaning," Brant stated. He gave her figure a meaningful look. "And keeping your husband's bed warm."

"Nay," she insisted with a tight snap of her jaw. "A woman's concern is to care for and to nurture the people of her keep. Mayhap that sometimes means feeding and clothing them, but more likely it means a woman should ride to the site of a raid and help with the care of the survivors. It's likely I will be needed there more than you. You are a man and a man should stick to what he knows—fighting and leaving a mess for the woman to clean."

He didn't move and she was secretly glad.

"The services of your sword are most useful while fighting. I can handle the aftermath." With that, Della brushed a wayward strand of hair from her eyes.

"Della…" Brant began in warning.

"If you try to leave me behind, I will just follow you. So better you take me along. Better that than to have me traipsing along the countryside alone, *unescorted*." Della stood her ground. She'd been feeling sorry for herself long enough. Ever since he'd arrived at Strathfeld, she'd forgotten her responsibility to the people. She would wallow in self-pity no longer.

Brant moved to grab her. "You dare too much, lady wife."

"And you too little. It's my life to put at risk." She grabbed his tunic and threw it at his head, effectively stopping his advance. Brant ducked out of the garment's way and caught it with the swift reflexes of one hand. When he looked at her again, she was almost to the door. "So get dressed, lest *we* leave without *you*!"

"Is that a threat?"

"Nay, but this is," Della charged, not heeding her words. "Mayhap I will run into Stuart while you are gone. He could not have gotten far since last night."

"*What?*" Brant's eyes turned deadly. In a rising growl that echoed past her, he shot, "You said you walked alone!"

Della realized what she'd revealed and stopped right before ducking out the door. Trying to amend her rashly spoken words, she rushed, "I did walk alone, only I ran into Stuart on my way back. Naught happened that would shame you. Methought you would not understand and get angry." His look proved how right the assumption was. "I swear on my father's grave that naught dishonorable happened."

She quickly moved out of the chamber, slamming the door in her haste to get away from him. It was not wise of her to be alone with him after such an admission. She ran to the hall, deciding to let his anger cool before confronting him alone. Brant would not make a scene in front of the servants or his men.

Brant glared after his tigress of a wife. Her defiance stirred his blood and he took grim pride in the proud tilt of her head, the hard tone in her voice. She was a strong one, his Della. Even though her stubbornness grated against his very nature and they clashed heads more often than not, he could not help but feel a fire in his soul for her. He glanced longingly at the bed, wanting to toss her back onto the soft mattress to finish what had been started that morning.

It was not to be. Duty beckoned him and the reminder only soured his mood. He shook in fury as he jerked the rest of his clothing on. Rage clouded his judgment as he whispered, "Methinks you are about to find a beating, treacherous wench. I have stayed my hand with you long enough."

DELLA PATTED her mare on the neck to steady the animal. It had been too long since she'd ridden outside the walls of the castle. So much had changed since Brant's arrival. The men no longer quickly responded to her authority. Although she knew each one would keep their oath of loyalty, they turned naturally to accepting the leadership of a man. She resented them for it. Had she not spent many hours proving she was worthy to follow? So what if she didn't kill men gallantly on the field of battle like *Brant the Flame*?

Brant refused to talk to her from the moment he came down. She was already on her horse waiting with the men. Not one of the knights dared to question the claim that she was to come along until they saw Brant's fiery expression as he looked at her in disapproval. He glared her into silence when she'd started to say his name. Della knew her coming angered him, but she assured herself she didn't care.

Brant rode silently next to her, training his eyes forward in detachment. By the hard line of his jaw, it was difficult to remember the affection between them the night before. His disinterest somehow hurt her insecure ego. For, after the night they'd spent together, she was desperate for a kind gesture from him. It was not to be. Apparently, her husband was only kind to her when he wanted someone to warm his bed. Had he not spent the last sennight ignoring her, until yestereve when he wanted her?

Studying him through the corners of her eyes, she couldn't help but notice how incredibly handsome he was. Always confident, he sat bravely astride his giant steed. The tan destrier dwarfed her mare, just as Brant towered over her. He had yet to say anything about her meeting with Stuart. Could it be that he trusted her? Della doubted it. More likely, he was avoiding a conflict in front of the men.

"M'lady, are you well?" Gunther asked quietly from her other side.

Della jolted, clearing her throat as she turned to the knight. She'd forgotten he rode next to her.

"Yea," Della responded with a polite smile. Trying to shade her look with her lashes, she shot a last glance at her husband.

Well, if m'lord husband will not talk to me, mayhap someone else will.

Gunther followed her gaze briefly to his friend.

"It is lovely out, is it not? For such a dreadful day," Della said.

"Yea, m'lady," Gunther replied. "Did you know the cotters well?"

By the look on his face, he knew what she was doing and he didn't seem to mind. In fact, he seemed a bit anxious to help her stir up trouble. Not daring another glance in Brant's direction, she imagined she could feel his eyes burrowing into the side of her head. "Yea. They have worked the land for many generations. Helga's family often comes to the castle to help with the brewing in the fall."

"Helga?" inquired Gunther.

"Yea, she and her husband are the ones who reported the raid." Della swallowed hard as she studied her hands on the bridle. Her words were weak, as she admitted brokenly, "It's close to Blackwell Manor—closer than the others."

Gunther nodded.

"Will we be stopping at the manor, m'lord?" Della turned to ask her husband, curiosity to see his home getting the better of her. In the past, she'd never dared to venture to it. She wondered what kind of a manor he kept without the benefit of a woman's touch.

He glared at her for a long, hard moment before snapping, "I will."

Della swallowed past the lump forming in her throat. Stiffly, she clutched her horse's reins and stared at her trembling hands. She knew that meant he would be staying there alone. Did her defiance upset him so much that he was to abandon her? And why did she care? Is that not what she'd wanted since the beginning?

Gunther slowed his horse so he could edge his stallion between the warring couple. Shielding Della from Brant's dark scowl, Gunther turned his attention to his leader, asking what Della thought, but couldn't say. "Brant, do you mean to stay there alone?"

"Nay, there are servants and I will take two of the men with me. It's time I checked on the manor." Brant ignored Della, purposely rejecting her involvement in the discussion. "What better time than now, while I am so close?"

Della effectively felt excluded. She turned her attention forward, but kept her ear on their words.

"It will give me time to learn if any there know of the raiders," Brant continued in low tones. He quickened his stallion's pace.

"And I?" Gunther asked, keeping in stride. "Will I be going with you?"

"You will accompany Lady Blackwell back to Strathfeld and make sure she stays there. You are given permission to use any means necessary." Brant finally turned his eyes fully to her. "Even if you must lock her in her chamber with irons."

Della gasped and paled. Brant let a hard smile tilt his lips.

"Yea, m'lord," Gunther acknowledged. He looked helplessly at Della when Brant's back was turned to yell a fast order to the men.

When Brant finished, he continued speaking with his eyes forward. "She is not to be alone at any time except while in bed. I want a man posted at her door. Make sure he knows that she goes to sleep late and wakes early. I will not have him asleep at his post. And she is not, under any circumstances, to see Sir Stuart. I hear the man is in the area as of late."

"Yea," Gunther said. Della knew Brant's words were just a show. Gunther was his friend and would know that her cousin was not to be let in. The detailed orders were meant to scare her. It was working.

Della turned her eyes and ears away from him, not wanting to hear more. The humiliating punishment he planned was chastisement enough. She let her mare slow until she trailed the men. Without having to be told, two of the soldiers rode forward, giving her their silent protection as they built a shield of human and horse around her.

IT WAS late morning when they arrived on the west section of Strathfeld land. The party moved in relative silence, aware of the grimness that was awaiting them. The earth was charred black from the recent fire and the cotters' homes had been burned to the ground. Only a few cottages' frames stood amidst the destruction. The raiders had killed a half dozen families and the smell of their charred flesh floated on the breeze. Brant recognized the stench immediately.

His wife hadn't said a word regarding her impending imprisonment inside the walls of Strathfeld. In fact she had said little. Gone completely was the light mood of sport between them, to be replaced once again by the icy barrier of her countenance. Brant was sorry for it. He knew her reasons for hardening herself against him and also the reasons she felt compelled to naysay him at every turn. Knowing didn't make it easier to live with. He was her husband and it was his duty to protect her, but beyond that, he had given his word to Lord Strathfeld before his death. And if locking her away was the only means he had to keep her safe, then so be it.

"You dismount," Brant commanded a group of men to his right. Then, circling his horse, he pointed to another nearby group, and said, "You ride. Search the area."

The soldiers were well-trained and obeyed his orders immediately.

"Della, get back here!" he yelled. His wife had swung from her horse and was running full tilt to the nearby destruction. He quickly dismounted to fetch her.

DELLA SKIDDED to a stop in front of a burned cottage frame. Her mouth fell open in fright, trapping the silent scream that died in her throat. She heard the vicious howl of her husband through the fog in her head, but ignored it. Her heart beat wildly in her chest, so savage a rhythm she thought it might explode from the constraints of her skin. She shivered in dread.

Walking forward, she tripped over a metal lock covered in ashes. It was still bolted to a piece of charred doorframe. Inside, where the walls of the dwelling had once stood, the scorched figures of a mother holding her child sat amongst the ashes. They were burned into an eternal embrace. She again looked down at the lock, realization dawning on her. The family had been locked inside to burn. Brant caught her as she stumbled backward, her twitching hand on her throat as if the action could keep the bile from coming up. She looked at him in horror.

"Dead." Her breath came in great open-mouthed pants and her eyes widened in alarm as she took in more slain bodies that littered the nearby ground. "All…dead."

"I know, Della. Why do you think I didn't want you to come?" He moved forward and tried to hug her to his chest.

"Who would do such a thing?" Tears spilled over her cheeks, as she stepped away from Brant. The image of the mother and child would not leave her. The smell in the air had been oddly familiar and, seeing the bodies, the memory came back to her in a rush.

"They burned her," she whispered, backing away from Brant in dazed terror. "The Vikings burned my mother with a candle from her trunk. My mother had just bought it the night before from a poor beggar woman. She didn't even want the thing. It was so ugly and it smelled like rotted cream, but she bought it to help the peasant so her family might eat. And they laughed… They laughed at her when she screamed for help. I was tied to the bed so I could not make them stop what they were doing. And they just kept laughing."

"Yea, Della." Brant made a move for her. "It is a most monstrous thing. Let me take you back to your horse."

"Who?" she managed to ask when her eyes cleared of the memory. Della motioned despairingly to the burned cottage. "Who could do such a thing? That is just a child—an innocent!"

"M'lord, I found this by the edge of one of the cottages." The noble couple turned their attention from one another at the sound. One of the soldiers held up a leather waist bag. "It looks as if it was dropped as the raiders departed."

Della glanced pathetically at the man as he unintentionally answered her question. He was new to Strathfeld and she guessed he'd signed on after her father's death. Her eyes drifted from his ruddy red face to the satchel he held. An all too apparent yellow mark of two hammers glared at her.

"Vikings did this." She stared at Brant. "Your people. How could you? Does your kind have no soul? No conscience?"

"Nay, I had naught to do with this." The reasonable tone in his voice didn't affect her. "Della, do not judge me by the actions of others. I would never do such a thing. You should know this of me by now."

"Nay!" She held up her hand to stop his advance. Her wild eyes flashed in panic as he continued to move toward her. Pointing a finger, she said carefully, "I want no more of you or your pagan curses. How could I have thought I loved you? You are a *Viking*. Your kind did this. This is what they do. Your kind killed my mother. Your kind has no soul."

"Della," Brant persisted.

She shook her head, unable to reason. Tears froze eternally in her eyes. "Do not come near me. Go to your Blackwell Manor. Live out your days there. I want no more of you."

"But, Della—" Brant was cut off by her vicious glare.

She turned from him, her pain keeping her from staying to hear anything he might have to say.

"Della, wait," he tried anyway.

"Roldan!" Della yelled.

The man was instantly by her side. "Is all well, m'lady?"

"Nay. It was a mistake for me to come." Della turned and didn't take her eyes off Brant. His face was hardened to her, his blue eyes dark with an emotion she could not ascertain. She matched his deadly stare. "Take me home, Roldan. I am done here."

Brant felt his heart collapse into the pit of his stomach. When she'd looked inside the cottage at the bodies, he'd known she was punished enough for her defiance that morning. He'd seen the great fear in her eyes and was helpless to fight it.

Then, as she remembered the past, he recognized the crazed light that momentarily flickered within her. She didn't see him, but a painful memory. He'd lost many promising soldiers in the same terrifying way. It would happen after a fierce battle, when they'd witnessed more carnage than their minds could fathom. They went momentarily crazy, unable to take the mental anguish.

But the battle Della remembered was old and ingrained into her soul so deeply, he feared no one would ever pluck it out. What chance did he stand against the spirits of her past, the haunting memory of their cries? He was only a man and men did not fight spirits.

How could I have thought I loved you?

His heart would have filled with untold joy at her unintentional confession had her eyes not disputed the fact. But any droplets of happiness that flowed in his chest were bittersweet and didn't last. There was no reasoning with her. Not about this, never about this. And as she rode away, his pride didn't let him stop her.

A FORTNIGHT CAME and went since Della had last seen Brant standing outside the ruins of the burned cottages. He hadn't come home that night, not that she'd been expecting him to do so. Those long, lonely days brought both tremendous rain and unreasonable shine, and the castle worked on despite the rift left by the missing ealdorman.

Della had made how she felt about seeing him again very clear. In that first sennight, she'd told herself repeatedly that she didn't care if he rotted like the burned bodies of the peasants. But she thought of him constantly and her treacherous body ached for the feel of him.

Gunther returned to Strathfeld late the same night of the fires, briefly informing her through tight lips that Lord Blackwell was at Blackwell Manor and was not expected to come back anytime soon. He was to have her escorted during the day and confined to her chambers at night, protected by a guard, where she would remain until she notified her warden she was ready to come out in the morning.

"You are not a prisoner. Lord Blackwell does this fer yer safety," Gunther had explained grimily, though Della hadn't questioned the order.

The words still rankled. *Right, not a prisoner. Yet every time I wish to do so much as relieve myself, I have to do it with a guard outside my door.*

Della slept less than before. The smell of charred flesh brought with it a myriad of memories, all of Lady Strathfeld's death—images she'd long tried to silence. They rushed forth to torture her like the giant waves of a thunderous ocean mingling amongst the sailors of a sinking ship. They united with the new image of the dead child and its mother, a new torture with the old. Why had the Vikings let her live all those years ago? She would've rather died alongside her mother as a child than live the life of agony she'd come to know as an adult.

It had taken her only a few days to realize through the clouding fog of pain that Brant was not at fault for the raid. The knowledge did little to ease her suffering. Her hate was unreasonable, but she couldn't help it. The past was becoming too hard to fight.

Mayhap if her mother's killers had been brought to justice, mayhap if she had seen them dead, then she could have healed. But they were still out there. She could only imagine the number of crimes they had committed over the years.

What am I to do?

Della cried inwardly as she looked about the dejected manor. It was clear everyone felt the discord of the married couple. The servants were not as cheerful, the men not so boisterous, and her heart did not beat as much as it should.

"You might as well be of use again this morn, Cedric." Della gave a wry look to the young soldier ordered to follow her during the day. He was the same man who'd held up the leather satchel at the raid sight. Della was not pleased with the reminder his face brought, but said nothing when he had been assigned as her main guard. "I will teach you how to churn butter. No doubt your strong man-arms will be of some use to us."

The soldier groaned. "Nay, m'lady, I beg of you. These past sennights I have helped you to dust the manor, I have picked herbs in yer garden, and I have e'en helped you to sew yer blankets. Do not make me tend to more women's work. I beg it of you. It's degrading as a man and as a loyal soldier who has done no treachery."

"You can always leave your post." She smiled pleasantly, though her eyes dared him to go. "I'm sure I would not mind."

"Nay, m'lady, Lord Blackwell would have my head if he found out."

"Then quit whining like a girl and help churn butter. Prove yourself a man and churn more than the women." She stormed bitterly into the kitchen and the sullen soldier was quick behind her.

BRANT RAGED throughout the dingy halls of Blackwell Manor in a rampage. After living in the luxury of Strathfeld, he realized how deteriorated his home was in comparison. Over the years, the neglect of his father and then of himself had taken its toll on the once proud keep. What remained was the shadow of a once majestic home.

The rushes along the floor were filled with rotted food. The stench of them, which had never really bothered him before, now stuffed his nose and made his gut twinge with their foul mix of human sweat and decay.

Mayhap the smell was not this bad last I was here, he reasoned. *Yea, and mayhap I am too soft from Strathfeld's comforts.*

The tables in the main hall had been broken up into firewood. Tapestries rotted on the wooden walls where they hung neglected, their old designs hardly noticeable through the thick caking of dust that lay over every inch of the manor. Even the treated wood of the manor itself seemed to be infested with an unsightly green and black growth. Brant wrinkled his nose as he saw a nest of mice in the corner.

The servants had all but abandoned the care of the manor. Many of them slept on the cots meant for soldiers, their straw mattresses infested with lice. It was apparent they hadn't thought Lord Blackwell would be coming back home after his marriage, but the neglect itself had been going on for much longer.

Brant missed the clean keep of his wife—the way her scented rushes kicked up a pleasing smell when walked across. It was the next best thing to the clean scent of the outdoors. He missed the way the servants attended every need of the castle, even before being asked.

At Blackwell, Brant had to command to even eat. The food he was served and the ale he drank was not of the quality that came from Isa's pristine kitchen. He refused to look at Blackwell's kitchen, not wanting to know what rodents ate the food on his plate before it came to him.

He'd spent too little time at Blackwell Manor in the past and he wanted to spend little more. The sooner the place was burned to the ground the better. He now had the resources to rebuild it.

"You," Brant called to a servant leaning against a wall. "Clean something. Dispose of these rushes at once."

"Yea, m'lord." The servant yawned and pushed himself lazily from the wall. He kicked at the rushes in disinterest. To Brant he looked like a bored child.

Brant growled and stalked away from him. How did Della do it? He could command men to give their lives on the field of battle, yet he could not direct a lazy servant to clean a keep. He found a new respect for her spirit method and wondered if the cleaning spirit would consider traveling.

Brant had missed Della these past seventeen days. He missed the scent of her hair, the chilly scorn of her face, the warmth of her naked body against his.

Every night he lay in bed he thought of her, every day he walked through the filth of his manor he longed for her. But was it better to be in her scornful presence, unable to touch her through her icy façade? Or mayhap, was it better to be without her presence completely? He found it tormenting to be near her, unable to touch her heart. And he found it even more torturous to be without her.

But her face had been so full of fear the last he'd seen her and her eyes had hinted near hysteria. As she'd stalked away from him, his chest had tightened and as she'd ridden off at Roldan's side, she hadn't bothered to turn back. Though he'd pretended not to watch her leave, he had from the corner of his eye. Della had effectively banished him from her. She was afraid of him and not for any action of his own, but for the actions of mercenaries.

Brant studied the leather satchel. It was not Viking made, but a badly done imitation. The leather pouch was that of an Anglo-Saxon peasant, the clay symbol easily dissolvable in water. Who would want to frame the Vikings? He was afraid he didn't like the answer. *Stuart of Grayson.*

Stuart was the only one who had something to gain by his fall. It was clear the man wanted not only Strathfeld, but also Della. He'd seen well how the man looked at her.

Della had so readily accepted the satchel as an explanation. She had willingly thought the worst of him and his people. It wasn't fair. And had she really said she loved him?

Loved not love, Brant reminded himself. She'd said loved. He hadn't hoped for so much. How had he not seen it? If she'd said something sooner, communication would have been so much better between them. Brant knew nothing of a woman's love but that it kept them loyal and they would risk much for it.

He cared for her, but love? Nay, love was something best left to women. It was of their nature to care for others.

By the end of the seventeenth day, Brant had enough of his solitude. He decided if he couldn't touch Della, he would at least be near her. He wanted to go home, and if his wife didn't want him there, then so be it. She would just have to stay out of his way, for he would no longer stay out of hers.

DELLA SHIVERED, a chill working over her as she walked into the bailey yard. The sky was bleak, almost as dark as her mood had been. But now hope evaded that dim place in which she'd dwelled. Brant was back at Strathfeld.

Rab ran ahead of her. The boy had been standing guard on the wall since she'd arrived without Lord Blackwell. He waited for the nobleman to come and now he had.

Della couldn't speak as she moved toward the front gate, drawn to see Brant, desperate to look upon his face, to see he was well. At the same time, she was afraid.

Brant rode his horse through the gate, carrying himself as majestically as a king, even though weariness shone from his face like a pauper fighting the plague. He still wore the old tunic she'd last seen him in and she'd forgotten he didn't have a change of clothing with him at Blackwell. Della ignored the urge to order a bath drawn. He undoubtedly wouldn't appreciate the wifely gesture.

It had only been a fortnight and four days since she'd left him by the burned cottages, yet it felt as if she'd been without him for an eternity. Her first impulse was to run to him and be gathered into his arms, to press kisses against his mouth and demand he go abovestairs with her. Instead, she forced her heart back into her chest and she constrained the emotion from her eyes.

Straightening her shoulders, she lifted her chin, waiting to see his reaction before she gave hers. As she watched, he talked to some of the men who'd come forward to greet him. The moment his eyes found her, his smile faded and his face gave nothing away. When he acknowledged her with a slight nod, she tilted her head regally in return. Her heart fluttered as he took a step toward her. Della waited for him to come to her.

Brant looked wearier than she'd first thought. Dark circles marred the flesh beneath his eyes, his cheeks were sunken, and his beard was overgrown. He looked more beautiful than she remembered.

"M'lady." Brant's voice held no affection as he watched her through veiled eyes. Stopping before her, he vigorously scratched the back of his head. She felt like a stranger greeted her.

"M'lord," Della answered, her voice was frozen.

He searched her eyes for a long moment. Then, seeming to find what he looked for, he started to turn away.

Wait! Della trembled, but her voice was calm. "Was all well at Blackwell Manor?"

Brant turned back around. His eyes once again probed her face. "Yea."

"You were able to rest? They fed you well?" Della looked him over, resisting the urge to touch him. He looked starved.

"Yea."

"And the manor?"

"It still stands."

"Did you," Della began, only to close her mouth. There was really nothing else she could ask. *Did you miss me? Did you make use of a mistress? Did she please you?*

Brant squinted and waited for her to continue.

Della lifted her chin and motioned weakly to the side. She hid her tortured soul from him, finding the comfort of her icy mask more bearable. What else could she say?

Brant snorted and brushed past her, going to the main hall.

Della's body weakened and she swayed on her feet before catching herself. Aching deeply, she turned to watch him disappear inside.

Did you miss me, Brant? As I have missed you?

The freshness of Strathfeld was a blessing after the hell he'd lived in at Blackwell Manor. Swearing, he reached to scratch his head again. His scalp would not stop itching and he suspected Blackwell Manor had infested him with lice. With a morose laugh, he doubted his wife would appreciate him spreading the plague of little creatures into her cleanly home.

My wife.

He shook his head, a grim smile crossing his humorless lips. Upon seeing her lovely face, he'd hoped she came to greet him because she missed him as he did her. Brant hadn't realized how much he wanted to hold her until he saw her in the background. He'd actually walked away while Gunther was in mid-sentence.

But Della hadn't missed him. She only greeted him out of duty and to ask all the proper questions expected of a wife, leaving off in mid-inquiry. She didn't even care enough to continue the charade. It reminded him of the day he'd first met her—the way she looked icily down her nose at him with practiced perfection, her scorn barely concealed behind her beautiful amber eyes.

My beautiful Ice Princess, I should have heeded the warning and kept my flame far away from you. But, fool that I am, I kept trying to warm a heart that cannot be warmed. I am like a burning twig against one of the giant ice blocks floating in the northern-most waters. One might be able to melt off a few drops, but soon the cold will put out the flame and the droplets will quickly freeze again.

He wondered if he would have been better off staying away, but as he scratched his scalp again, he knew he would rather burn down Blackwell Manor than to spend another night inside the lice-infested walls.

Deciding it best he take care of the problem before it got much worse, he went to search out Serilda. She would have a healing draught for the itching on his head.

Yea, it's too bad she does not have a healing draught to melt my wife's icy heart or to mercifully kill the painful beating in mine.

Brant stepped into the scarcely lit chamber of the midwife. The fireplace burned low as a caldron bubbled within. It gave off an unpleasant, spicy odor. Like the rest of the servants' quarters, the chamber was humble, only Serilda stayed by herself, whereas many of the others shared theirs with at least one person. He guessed it was because none of the others would sleep with such a smell in the room.

"M'lord, what may I do fer you?" Serilda eyed him in mild surprise, but didn't stand to greet him.

Brant glanced at the long table where she sat. It had been fashioned in the middle of the room. Atop the wood were several piles of dried herbs and ground powders. When he again looked at her, Serilda smiled sweetly at him from the other side. Her dark hair hung loose about her shoulders in the fashion of a virgin, but the way her eyes glinted in playful invitation he guessed she was hardly innocent. Bringing her long nails to her lips, she licked them slowly.

Brant ignored her advances as he moved thoughtfully along the table, picking up a vial filled with a yellowish liquid. He frowned, recognizing the substance. It had been an old war practice to dip the end of arrows in poisonous venom, but it was found to be a deadly one to the careless soldier who pricked his finger fumbling for arrows in the heat of battle. "Venom?"

"Yea," Serilda answered. "I don't like it myself, but Lord Strathfeld ordered it kept. He thought he may have use of it someday."

Brant didn't like having poisons in the manor. They could easily fall into the wrong hands. "Get rid of it at once and any others like it."

"Yea, m'lord." Serilda smiled and batted her eyelashes. "A wise decision."

Brant studied the rest of the items. "What is this you are grinding? This powder?"

"Oh, this?" The midwife reached out her hand to stop him from touching it, quickly pulling the pile toward her into a bowl. "It's fer a man."

Brant raised an eyebrow.

"What I mean, it is fer a man's member, fer when he cannot raise his own sword in battle."

Brant grunted as he got her meaning. "You know of many cures?"

"Yea. Are you ailing, m'lord?"

"Nay." Brant scratched his beard and then his

hair. "Blackwell Manor is infested with lice. I seek to rid myself of them before I infest Strathfeld."

Serilda licked her lips as she shot him a mournful glance. "It's a sad circumstance we still have lice. It's easy enough to cure."

"Good, give me the draught." Brant held out his hand. "I wish to be rid of them immediately."

"Nay." Serilda shook her head. A small grin curled on her lips. "It's easy to cure, but one who knows the potency must apply the draught. I will apply it fer you if you wish—unless you trust someone who is skilled not to burn you with it?"

Brant thought of Della. *Nay, she would burn me on purpose.*

"Fine, get it done with." He sat in one of her chairs.

"Not here, m'lord. It is necessary to do it while you bathe."

Brant gave her a disbelieving grumble. He swung around in his chair to face her. She smiled innocently. "I have not heard such a thing."

"It is so you may rinse the draught instantly. Mayhap, we could go to yer chamber. No one would think aught was amiss if you ordered a bath there."

"Yea." Brant sighed as he scratched his head again. Standing up, he gruffly motioned her to follow him. "Bring what you need. Just be quick about it."

DELLA FELT AWFUL. Brant had left with little effort to speak to her. She hated the fact she'd walked the grounds in search of him, desperate to see him again, to know he'd really come home. He was nowhere to be found and that could only mean he was purposefully avoiding her. It was just as well. She didn't know what she'd say to him if she saw him.

With her husband's arrival, she'd hoped Cedric would be ordered to stop following her. The knight complained more than any man she'd ever met, until she was finally forced to order him to stay at least five paces from her at all times lest she be tempted to scream. Stopping in her progress across the hall, she suddenly turned to make her way abovestairs to her chamber. She glanced over her shoulder as she climbed and grimaced—there was her dutiful guard exactly five paces behind her.

"M'lady?" Cedric asked as she scowled at him. His voice held the natural whine she'd come to despise. "Are you to be sick again?"

"Nay." Della scowled, remembering that morning when she'd vomited in her chamber pot and the eve before when she'd almost vomited on Cedric's boot. In truth, her stomach did feel a little queasy. Nonetheless, she didn't want her guard knowing. His over-attentiveness was just as annoying as his complaining. "I'm going to lie down awhile."

"You appear a bit gaunt. Would you like me to fetch the midwife?" Cedric continued to follow her abovestairs.

"And leave me unattended?" Della gasped in mock alarm. "I might run off."

"I meant after you were locked in yer chamber," he gritted through clenched teeth.

"Oh." Della bristled at the reminder. "Nay, I don't wish for Serilda's attentions this day or any other."

Cedric chuckled under his breath and his insolent face gave away the fact he knew of her checking.

Della narrowed her eyes at the sound. "Do you have aught you would like to say to me?" She kept her glare merciless, as she placed her hands on her hips.

"Nay, m'lady." Cedric's expression became blank and he turned his gaze sheepishly away. "Naught."

Della cursed under her breath and pivoted around to continue angrily up the stairwell. When she reached the top, her abdomen tightened. Rushing toward her bedchamber, her stomach churned violently. She lifted a hand to her mouth and pushed her way inside. Running to the pot, she vomited the sparse contents of her morning meal into it. After a few heaves, she was left taking deep, gut-wrenching breaths until the sickness began to subside. The strange nausea left as briskly as it came. Suddenly, the sound of splashing penetrated her thoughts. Della froze, bent over on her knees above the chamber pot.

"Della?" She heard her husband's voice.

"M'lady?"

Serilda? What is the midwife doing here? Alone with my husband, no less?

Della was sure her heart stopped as she wiped her mouth on her sleeve. With as much dignity as she could muster, she stood and turned to the tub.

She swallowed hard against the awful taste in her mouth. Her beautifully naked husband stood in the bath next to the guilty countenance of the midwife. Serilda's hands dripped with soap, matching the suds that adorned her husband's body. They ran down from his hair, over his rippling muscles in little streams.

Cedric made a loud noise of surprise, gaping openly at the scene from the doorway. Della stared for a stunned moment before taking a fierce breath. Her vision swam red.

Before God, I swear I will kill him for this insult!

Nausea again rose in her throat. She shivered and it took all her energy to remain standing.

Brant took in his wife's pale expression as she looked from him to the midwife and then back again. He saw the awful conclusion she came to. Her hurt amber eyes closed and her body swayed uneasily on her wobbling feet. She started to speak, her mouth trembling in anger, but before the words left her mouth she was turned and puking once more into the basin.

Brant ordered Cedric from the room with a brusque nod. The young soldier watched Della with boyish impudence. He listened to the door shut before going to his wife.

"Della?" He touched her shoulders gently.

"Back off," she gasped. "Get your treacherous hands off me."

Brant did as she commanded, watching helplessly as she vomited yellow bile into the basin. Standing, he grabbed a linen towel from Serilda and wrapped it around his waist. Then, crossing once more to Della, he dropped a linen by her head.

"Serilda is there naught you can do for her?" Brant knew what Della suspected he was doing with the woman, but now was not the time to explain.

"Yea, m'lord." Serilda stepped forward. "M'lady, please."

Della glared at her from under the strands of dark blonde hair that had worked loose from the braided knot at her nape. Sweat beaded her forehead and she refused to stand. Instead, she picked up the dropped towel and wiped at her mouth.

"M'lady, if you would lie on the bed." Serilda's sugary-sweet tone was a contrast to her usually brusque nature. Brant didn't pay attention to the midwife as he concentrated on his wife.

"Yea, Della," Brant encouraged. "Rest."

"Get your whore out of our chamber," Della whispered. "How dare you bring her here? Take her to the pasture with the other livestock."

"Della." Brant couldn't help the warning in his voice.

"Nay. If you wish to bed the whore at least take her somewhere more appropriate. Perchance the stables would suit you more than the pasture. There will be some privacy." Della rose to her feet with the help of the straw mattress. "You will not take her in my bed."

"I'm not a whore," Serilda protested.

"Quiet!" Brant ordered her.

Della swayed and leaned against the poster of the

bed for support, as if it was taking all her energy to stand so proudly before him.

"But I'm not," Serilda pouted.

"I said be quiet," Brant ordered. He swiped the suds from his eyes as he turned to his wife. "It is not as you think. Serilda is applying healing draughts to me."

"Is that what you wish to call it?" Della laughed weakly and waved her hand listlessly through the air. "Fine, have her apply her *healing draughts* in the barn with the other animals. It is where you belong."

"I will ignore that since you are obviously ill and speaking out of your head," Brant reasoned with as much patience as he could manage. "Lie down so Serilda may inspect you."

"Nay." Della fell against the bed. "I will not have your woman's hands on me again. I have been checked by her and that is enough."

"Della, you are sick." Worried, he reached as if to touch her, but hesitated.

"Yea, I may be," Della jerked away, "but I will not be laughed at again."

"What are you talking about?" Brant asked, perplexed. Serilda shrugged her shoulders with unconvincing naiveté.

"Did she not tell you? Your little woman here told everyone what you had done to me." Della's face paled again and she took a long breath. "The whole of Northumbria knows of my checking and they are laughing at me."

"Nonsense, Della, they are not laughing. The

results were satisfactory. They would praise a maiden for that." Brant frowned as he turned to Serilda. Again the woman looked innocently at him. He sighed. This was not a conversation he wanted to be having in front of a servant. Going to the tub, he ducked his head under the water and rinsed out the remainder of the soap. When he finished, he said, "Enough of this."

Serilda moved to pick his braccas up off the floor, handing them over. Della frowned at the familiar action. Brant grumbled in irritation, but tugged on the clean wool, glad to finally be rid of the lice and filth of Blackwell. He saw how intimate the action looked to his wife and would have been pleased by her jealousy if she wasn't so sick. He wondered what was wrong with her when an idea finally struck him. Suddenly he smiled.

"What is wrong with you, barbarian?" Della hissed. Her voice was weak, but her words were poisonous nonetheless. "Methinks you have gone mad, *Brant the Thorn*."

Brant ignored her ire, too happy for the moment to pay it much heed. Hopeful, he asked, "Serilda, do you know what ails Lady Blackwell?"

The midwife understood his meaning and motioned her hand toward the bed.

"Della, methinks you should let Serilda tend to your illness," Brant said when Della began to speak. "We can discuss this misunderstanding later."

"Nay." Della's features were set, as if she tried not to sway on her feet. "I will not have that woman touch me again. I care not what you do with her, only leave me alone."

"Be still, Della." He motioned Serilda to the bed, hiding how Della's words stung him. "I will not leave until you do so."

Della frowned. "Fine, but only because I am too tired and too nauseated to argue with you any longer." She moved toward the bed, only to stop and grab Serilda's hand tightly in her own. Twisting the midwife's fingers back, she threatened, "Treat me as you did last time and I will have your fingers broken and your battered, naked body thrown into the moat for all the men to enjoy."

"Yea, m'lady," was Serilda's not-too-meek reply.

Brant smiled at that. His wife had a lot of fight to her, even when sick. It would also seem she was not going to be as silent as her last inspection.

"Turn away," Della told him. "I do not wish to see your face."

Brant nodded and did what she wanted, too excited not to comply. In his head he counted the days since their first lovemaking. It was not too soon to tell if she was with child. His child. His heir.

After a few moments, he heard Serilda stand from the bed and turned in excitement. The midwife bit her lip and gave a funny look to Della, who had closed her eyes and curled into a ball.

In a not-too-quiet hush, the woman said, "It is only a sickness of the stomach. It will pass within a sennight. Give her broth to eat and let her rest."

"Are you sure?" Disappointment unraveled inside him.

"Fairly sure, though it could be too early to tell." Serilda backed toward the door. "I am usually right, though. I don't think it's that."

"What?" Della asked without opening her eyes. "My head is spinning and I don't have time for this nonsense. What did you think it was? The plague? An outbreak? Has there been news of others? Is that why you seemed so happy? You thought I was to die on you?"

"M'lord thought you may be with child," Serilda answered unceremoniously.

Brant wanted to slap the impudent woman, but instead he ran his fingers through his wet hair. To his annoyance, he discovered there was still lice soap in his locks. Frowning at Serilda, he realized the soap didn't burn at all.

"I'm sorry, m'lady. You are not." Serilda left the chamber.

Brant watched the door close quietly behind the midwife.

"Go ahead. Go after her." Della eyed him wearily. She rolled away from him in disgust.

Brant didn't like the dejected tone of her voice. While he talked, he leaned over to once again rinse the soap from his hair. "Naught happened, Della. She *was* applying healing draughts."

"Nay, do not call it that. I saw you with my own eyes." Della refused to sit up. "Take your lies elsewhere, barbarian."

"Della—" Brant dried his wet hair with the discarded towel and moved to the bed.

"It's all right," she broke in. Brant stepped closer to hear her better. "I said you could leave for Blackwell and live there with your mistress. Serilda is a fine choice. She cannot bear a child of her own."

"I'm not leaving Strathfeld." Brant sat on edge of the bed. He reached to touch her hip in a light caress. She didn't move under his hand. He wondered if the jealousy he thought he'd seen was imagined. "I have reason to stay."

"Oh, yea, I know your reason. You wish for an heir." Della inched away from him. Her voice fell into a low murmur. "Would you really have me perform marital duties now? I'm likely to vomit on you."

"Della. That is not what I meant." Brant withdrew his hand and let out a long, frustrated sigh. *By Thor's Hammer, wench, you are most aggravating!*

"Fine, then leave me be." She pulled at the coverlet behind her back. After several hard jerks, Brant was forced to stand and let her have it. "Go to Serilda. I'm done talking to you."

"Della," Brant started, uncertain. He shook his head and again ran his fingers through his wet hair. He was pleased to discover that the itching was gone from his scalp. Serilda's potion had worked magnificently, even if she had lied about the administering. "Never mind, I'm done arguing with you."

His wife didn't answer him as he finished getting dressed and she didn't look at him as he sat on the bed to pull on his shoes. It was as if she didn't care that he was there and he imagined she wished he wasn't.

Fingering the gold thread on the brown tunic she'd made, he traced over the intricate design. He didn't understand his wife. Did she still blame him for the raids? Did she still blame him for her mother's death? It made no sense, her unreasonable anger. But it was there and it was very real. He no longer had the strength to fight it.

"I will not force marital duties on you, Della. I never have, never will. Serilda is not my mistress." Brant leaned closer to her prone body. Her side rose in even breaths as she refused to look at him. A light quiver worked over her. "I don't want anyone but you."

There, I have said it, Ice Princess. Now you know. I have no desire to take breath without you. Methinks I am in love with you. Nay, I am fairly sure I know it. I love you, wife.

"I love you," he whispered. He hadn't meant to, but now it was said and he didn't try to take it back. Brant waited for an answer to his shaky admission. He'd known the moment he'd seen her at the gate that morning. He loved her. He wanted to say more, but her silence forbade another word to whisper past his lips. She didn't answer, which to Brant could only mean she didn't care.

Silently he stood and turned from her. His heart fell against the walls of his chest in heavy thuds, the weight of his blood tingling painfully in his limbs. He felt a beginning choke form in his throat, but didn't let the moisture fall from his eyes. Soldiers didn't weep and he was one of the best.

Taking a deep breath, he opened the door and walked slowly from the room. Not once did he look back to see if she noticed and inside his heart went dead.

Della awoke to hunger pains twitching in her stomach. Slowly, she pushed herself up on the bed and she looked around the dimly lit chamber. She was alone. The fire had been allowed to burn out, which meant no one had been to check on her. Had no one noticed she was gone? How long had she slept? From the heaviness of her eyelids she would have easily guessed two days.

Lifting her arms, she stretched her sleep-tightened muscles. The nausea was gone and she felt well enough to get out of bed. As she swung her foot over, she frowned. The chamber pot hadn't been changed. Yawning, she looked out the narrow window and noticed it was indeed dark outside. She'd slept the day away and it both amazed and frightened her. How had she gotten so tired?

It took only a few moments to straighten her clothing before she was ready to leave the chamber. Her stomach growled. She was starving.

"Cedric?" Della called as she opened the door to the chamber. Her voice sounded odd from sleep. "I'm ready to go down."

There was no answer. She looked around the darkened hall. Her dutiful guard was not at his post. Had Brant called the man off?

"Lord Blackwell?" she whispered, but received no response. Shutting the door behind her, she walked down the stairwell. Then, like a slap to the face, she remembered catching Brant with the midwife. Della cursed as she realized that even now he was more than likely with his mistress. As she made her way to the hall, her mind focused on the sounds below. She heard a clamor of tumultuous laughter followed by fists pounding on wood.

Cheerful voices projected from of the main hall, growing louder with each step she took. It had been a long time since the hall had been so loud. It reminded her of the time of her father and she wondered in momentary confusion if she'd dreamed her marriage to *Brant the Barbarian*. The thought soon left her as she neared the main hall. The playful scream of a maid rang to the boisterous encouragement of the soldiers. Music filled the castle, something she vaguely remembered being at her wedding, but the celebration hadn't been as lively as it now sounded to be.

Della quickened her steps, curious to see who was now visiting to demand such attention. *Could it be the king? Why was I not told we had such an important guest? I should think I needed to be there. Brant the Fiery Thorn will not take kindly to me not making appearance at his table.*

She rounded the corner to the main hall, her mouth gaping open in surprise. A serving maid danced on top of a table, surrounded by several of the soldiers. Her young body flung around in undisciplined movements and she kicked food and drink onto the floor. The rowdy men pounded the wood in time with the music, cheering the woman on, screaming louder when she took off her apron and tossed it aside. Della gasped and ducked to avoid the flying garment. The maid continued to take off her clothes, much to the delight of all. Della couldn't watch.

The hall was a mess. Ale and mead flowed freely and, by the look of the drunken faces, the gaiety had been going on for quite some time. Traveling musicians played loudly near the center fireplace as couples danced around, kicking the rushes into messy piles on the floor. From where she stood in the crowd, the musicians were the only strangers to the hall she could see.

Another maid screamed frantically, running past Della in her haste to get away from a lustful suitor. She didn't try too hard, for he caught her easily and they both went tumbling to the floor in a fit of laughter. Della felt the blood draining from her face. Her limbs were weak and her stomach tight. Never has she laid witness to such debauchery at Strathfeld.

Cedric arm-wrestled with a burly-looking knight. Food littered the once tidy floor. A piece of roasted mutton flew past her head, hitting the clean tapestry behind her. It soiled the thick cloth with a greasy stain. Della watched in stunned silence. *This refuse-hall cannot be my home. I'm having a dream. Nay, a nightmare!*

As another playful scream drifted through the air,

Della moved into action. She skirted past the revelry and made her way to better see the high table. Surely Brant would not allow such indulgence in his presence—not in her orderly keep. The people defiled the main hall, they spoiled the carefully scented rushes and after she so recently had them replaced.

Finding no guests at the main table, she stiffened. The only occupants at the table were her husband, Gunther, and the two women sitting across their laps. On Gunther was Gayla. Della knew that out of all the women, that particular maid spent the most time there. Della didn't care about Gunther. Her gaze turned slowly to Brant. She didn't want to see it, but how could she avoid looking at him? At them?

There, on her husband's lap, sat Serilda. Brant had a goblet of mead in one hand and Serilda in the other. Della couldn't move. Sound faded as she stared at them, replaced by an intense pain. In anguish, she watched Brant lean over the woman with a mouth full of ale. He let the liquid fall from his lips so it ran over the woman's dark skin in trails of red. The midwife leaned her head back in lusty laughter, grabbing Brant by his hair. Della's insides burned.

No one seemed to notice her as she stood motionless in the middle of the hall. The loud shouts punctured her dull senses, but she ignored the obnoxious yells, ignored the loose-moraled maids. But she couldn't ignore the pain that wrapped her tight, squeezing at her heart.

That lascivious son of a whore! Della made her way to the table, letting anger settle over her body, unable to deal with the hurt Brant's actions caused. *How dare he disrespect me?*

Della stalked to the high table to where Serilda wantonly nuzzled Brant's throat. The woman's hands were on the ealdorman's thigh, very close to massaging his member. Unmindful of her actions, Della ferociously grabbed the woman by her hair and yanked her from Brant's body, throwing Serilda to the floor.

Brant's drunken eyes shot up in dismay. Seeing Della, his frowned deepened and he had the audacity not to look guilty at being caught.

The imbecile is drunk! Della stood before him, hands placed firmly on her hips. Her heart beat heavily in her chest and, though she tried to breathe, the air could not find her lungs. She wanted to yell, but her voice was lost. How could he? Here? With Serilda? Why Serilda? She stared at him, not wanting to believe what she'd seen with her own eyes.

Serilda screeched behind Della in outrage. Della turned to the midwife and growled. "Begone from my sight, whore! Before I have you kicked into the moat with the rest of the excrement."

"How dare you!" Serilda yelled back. The usually controlled woman looked fit to kill. Her eyes wildly dashed about in her head and she raised her fingers like pointed claws as if she were about to attack.

"You dare to raise your voice to a lady?" Della scolded. Never before had she used the power of her station to make her point. Usually she was above such paltry things, but now, in front of the midwife, she would say anything she could to get the better of the woman. For in light of her husband's attraction to Serilda, she needed all the assistance she could get. "Must I remind you that the penalty for such an act is death?"

"Nay, m'lady." Serilda's angry brown eyes shot hot flames, but the woman bit her tongue as she looked past Della to Brant. He sat lazily in his chair, but said nothing. "I didn't mean to raise my voice."

"Begone from this manor by morn. If you are still here on the morrow, you will be hanged for your insults to me." Della smiled at the sour victory, knowing she had every right by law to banish her from the manor.

"Yea." Serilda gathered her dress over her exposed chest and stumbled from the hall. The few men who'd heard the interchange were laughing merrily at the noblewoman fighting with a servant over their lord. The rest of the hall was too drunk to pay much heed, but would no doubt learn of it later.

"Why did you go and do that?" Brant slurred from behind her, drawing her attention back to him.

Della turned to glare at her husband. Her chest heaved with the effort it took to control her rage and she didn't dare to answer him immediately.

"She did naught wrong," Brant continued unabashed. "In fact, she was fulfilling your request.

"How?" Della shook as her fury started to find the words. Gunther had quieted at Brant's side and both he and Gayla watched avidly. "How could you, m'lord, in front of everyone? In the main hall, at my place at the high table?"

"I'm sorry, *wife*. I had no idea you wanted my lap. Here, come." Brant swayed toward her and pulled her onto his lap. Gayla giggled. Gunther held her fast, turning her head to give the ealdorman and his wife what privacy he could in a crowded hall. "You shall replace her, though I doubt your cold lips can compare to the warmth of hers."

"Let go...of me," she hissed as she fell against the warmth of his chest. "I will not be treated as such!"

"Such as what? Such as a woman? Such as a wife? Such as desired? Wanted? Loved? Lusted for? Favored? Adored?" Brant returned in a heated whisper of his own. His ale-laden breath hit hot upon her ear. "Or mayhap you mean such as a lover? Or whore? Or mistress? Or wife? Tell me, how will you not be treated, lady wife?"

"You make no sense. You are too far into your cups." Della struggled against him. The smell of the liquor made her stomach curl with nausea. She'd thought the sickness had passed, but apparently it hadn't. "Let...me...go!"

"Nay. Answer me. How shall I not treat you?" Brant successfully pinned her arms at her sides. Her feeble strength was no match for his war-hardened build. She ignored the encouraging cheers of the drunken crowd of knights who still watched the show, unable to feel anything past her husband's nearness.

"Nay, you're drunk." Della strained against him. His power over her excited her and she tried to push the pleasure of his nearness away. He'd been away so long. How could he go to Serilda? Shivering, she saw the fine texture of his lips as they loomed near. When he was gone, she'd imagined his kisses, his mouth on hers, but now shuddered at the pain they caused her.

"Yea, that I am, but all the more reason for you to listen to me," he warned. "I cannot control myself so well when I drink to excess. Mayhap, it's the Viking in me wanting to come out. Is that not what you say of me? That I am a Viking barbarian? A thorn? A ravisher? A lewd boor?"

Brant leaned in to nuzzle the pulse in her neck. The short hairs of his freshly trimmed beard brushed along her skin and he licked her throat in a surprisingly expert caress. It had been so long since she'd felt the embrace of his arms, the heat between his thighs, large and wanting. She fought the desire, desperate to stay mad at him.

"I will not be treated with such disrespect." Her argument lacked conviction. "You treat me like a whore in your hall."

"Come, wife, what do you think of me?" he inquired of her neck, ignoring her protest. His hands turned caressing as he held her tight against him. The onlookers cheered, some inspired to grab maids of their own.

"Let go," she demanded weakly against his strength. Inside she ached for him. It had been so long since she'd felt his hands, heard his seductive voice. She imagined his touch every night in bed. But she didn't want him like this. Not drunk and using her as visual pleasure for his men. To add to her pain, she couldn't forget that he had been doing the same thing with his hands to another woman a minute ago.

Nay, not just another woman—Serilda!

Della didn't know what fact bothered her more. That he had been acting wanton with another woman. Or that the other woman had been Serilda. Or that she was so enjoying his attention at the moment that she wanted to forget her reasoning and let him continue.

"Don't feel like talking, wife?" Brant slurred against her silence. "I have never seen you lacking poisonous barbs. Come, where is my Ice Princess?"

"I told you once not to call me that," she whispered, hurt by the deliberately rude nickname.

"Why not? Is it not the truth? Have you not hardened yourself to me?" Brant laughed humorlessly as he leaned back. His arms loosened only slightly to allow room between their bodies. "Isn't it true, *Ice Princess*, that you do not feel?"

"I'm not an Ice Princess. I have feelings, feelings that you should respect. But instead, I find you fornicating in the front hall with a whore. You disrespect me and most of all you disrespect Strathfeld. And you let your men dirty my hall!" Della pushed away from his chest, her heated whisper not appearing to affect him in the slightest. Unable to break his embrace, she knew she only extended as far as she did because he chose to let her, just as he could choose to pull her back. His strength both frightened and excited her.

"You could have fooled me," Brant snorted. "Methinks you do not feel at all."

"Stop it!" Della tried to hide the tears that brimmed in her eyes. "You're being cruel and for naught."

"But is that not my nature? The nature of my people? We are naught but Viking barbarians. Murderers. Ravishers. Savage pillagers." Brant suddenly stood, drawing her up with him so she was trapped against his chest. With each word his voice got lower and harder to resist. "What says you wife? Care for a dance?"

"What? You drunken lout! You speak nonsense and then wish to dance? You make no sense." Della tried again to pull away from him. She'd missed him, but not like this, not being intentionally cruel.

Brant laughed and pulled her toward the dancing couples. They twirled in circles to the fast paced beat of the music. Tilting his head to the musicians, he laughed again. The beat stopped, only to immediately begin once more at a slower tempo. The hall cheered their approval as Brant lifted his arm to Della in the first position of the dance.

"Methinks we didn't have time for this the eve we were wed. What say you we dance in celebration of that day now?" Brant asked in low, mocking tones.

Della had no choice but to lift her arm to join his at the wrist. Couples linked around them to do the same. Slowly, Brant circled her in one direction, his movements like a stalking beast, before turning to walk around her the opposite way. They touched only by their wrists, but Della felt his fire through her entire length.

The warmth of his hand moved to close over hers in a hard grasp. "This is the first time I have danced with you. As I remember, you were too anxious to get to the marriage bed at our wedding celebration."

"That isn't how it happened and you know it. My father was dying."

"Yea, and methinks all kind thoughts you had for men died with him." He turned her in the other direction, releasing her only long enough to switch.

"Nay, I like Rab."

"He is a child. I speak of men." Brant said. "Ice Princess."

"Stop." Tears threatened her eyes at his intentional barbarity.

Brant bowed mockingly toward her in time with the dance steps. "As you wish, lady wife."

They danced in silence for a moment, joined at not only the wrist, but also the eyes. A silent battle brewed between them.

"Why?" Della asked, thinking of Serilda. She lifted her chin proudly, as if the gesture might help. It didn't.

"Why not?" He knew instantly to what she referred. "Did you not say I had your blessing to take a mistress?"

"But why her?" Della whispered, disappointed in his choice. It was true that at one time she'd have welcomed him to find another, but now…? Now was different. "Why Serilda?"

"Why, are you keeping Serilda for yourself? Are you upset that I didn't ask you to join us? Is that what you like lady wife? You wish to have another woman in our bed? Why did you not say so? Leastways, you both could ravish me at the same time." Brant's smile widened. "Who should I ask?"

"I-I-ah," Della stuttered, not knowing how to respond. The idea that one could do the marital act with more than one person at a time confounded her. It wasn't a prospect she'd thought of before and she found she didn't like the idea of sharing her husband.

"I had no idea you were so unconventional in your lovemaking tastes. You should have told me. I'm your husband. I'm well experienced and could teach you things you never dreamed possible." Brant's expression was serious, but Della thought to detect a teasing light to his eyes.

"What do you mean?" Della didn't like his first idea at all, but was intrigued that there could be more.

"I don't think you are ready. Mayhap, I will show you someday. More than likely, I will not."

Remembering herself, she stiffened, angered by his comments, angered by what he hinted and would not tell her more about. What he had done with others and now claimed she was not capable of trying? Had he been with several women at once? Had he enjoyed it? Did he truly want her to be one of the women?

I will not do it!

. . .

"Nay, Della?" Brant lifted a brow when she didn't speak, purposefully confusing and taunting her. It was an easy mark, hitting her with her innocence, but he was drunk and he was mad. He'd begun to sober during their dance, though his words still carried a slight slur to them.

"Nay, I will not be privy to your sinful ways." Even angry, she was beautiful. "It is enough that I have been expected to share your bed in the past."

At that Brant frowned, seething in irritation at the slight. The dance ended and he dropped his arm to bow to her. What else could he really say? Della curtsied properly to him and bowed her head in half-hearted acknowledgement of those around her. Unable to help himself, Brant pulled her into his arms and kissed her. Della made a weak noise.

He couldn't continue, or he wouldn't be able to stop. Her felt her heart beating hard and fast against him. As soon as his lips left hers he whispered, "Get you abovestairs and interrupt my festivities no more. Lest the next time I see you tarrying, I will suspect you wish to be shown what you claim to want no part of. Repeatedly."

Della jerked away from him. Fear swam in her gaze as she looked at him. Without another word, she turned and ran abovestairs. Brant stared for a long moment before moving toward the high table. He ignored all who spoke as he grabbed a goblet of ale. It should only take a few more drinks before he could feel nothing at all.

BRANT DIDN'T COME to her bed that night, as she lay awake, her heart pounding in her throat, in her chest, even in her thighs. She'd seen the distant anger in his blue eyes when he looked at her. Those eyes belonged to a man she had never seen before and, for the first time, she truly feared him.

Though she lay awake night after night, he didn't come to her bed. The feasting and gaming continued on belowstairs, much to Della's dismay. She hadn't seen Serilda in the hall again and had been informed that the midwife had indeed left the keep. In that she could take some bleak pleasure. However any happiness was short lived.

Her sickness held on, making her rest more than usual, but sleep was not peaceful and she almost preferred to stay awake. She missed Brant, missed the smell of him. The nightmares she had of her mother were gradually replaced by nightmares of Brant in the arms of other women. Often times they were faceless images sent to torment her, sent to remind her that she could not have the one thing she wanted —her husband.

Della believed her depression somehow kept the sickness in her. After the fifth night of hiding away from the main hall, she'd had enough. The few glimpses she'd been afforded of the dining area were enough to make her stomach churn.

On the sixth morning of exile, she dressed in one of her best gowns and took special care plaiting back her clean hair. She smiled pleasantly as she made her way belowstairs, preparing herself for what awaited her. Della was not disappointed as the fresh scent of rushes washed over her. They were being applied to the floor and were a great relief after the spilled food from Lord Blackwell's festivities.

"What goes on here, Ebba?" Della questioned the maidservant in forced surprise. "Has Lord Blackwell stopped the gaiety so soon?"

"Nay, m'lady. It's the cleaning spirit again. She appeared to Gayla last eve." Ebba pulled at her short black hair in agitation. "She said the spirit was angered greatly by the mess the men made in her hall and that we had to clean it at once!"

Della gasped, trying her best to look awed. She'd said no such thing to Gayla in the night. "The spirit, she talked?"

"Yea, m'lady, and not just to Gayla. Many of the others swore that they saw her too. She told Isa that if the kitchen was not scrubbed, she would cook us black in the caldron and then the spirit threw Isa into a wall. And e'en Edwyn said she told him if we didn't remove the stench from the rushes, she would make us part o' it! She'd make us part o' the stench!"

My spirit has gotten most violent.

Della tried not to laugh as she nodded. In truth, Gayla was the only one she'd run across in the hall during the darkened hours of the night. Everyone else had been passed out in a drunken slumber. And she hadn't talked to Gayla.

"And what did my lord husband say to this?" Della wondered aloud.

"M'lady, it's most like he doesn't know of it," Ebba admitted.

"Why?" Della's stomach fluttered as she awaited the maid's answer. "Has he left Strathfeld?"

"Nay. He has spent many nights away from the rest of us. No one knows where he sleeps." Ebba looked away as she blushed. "Or with whom he sleeps."

Della frowned at the blatant statement. "It is not your concern, Ebba. Mayhap you should get back to work before the cleaning spirit hears of your harsh gossiping tongue. I should hate to see her foul temper taken out on you."

"Yea, m'lady." Ebba curtsied. Her eyes darted around the hall only to close with relief when she saw no spirit.

The idea that Brant had more than likely found another to warm his bed hadn't escaped her. Serilda was gone, but that didn't mean one of the other servants wouldn't want to be under the prized protection of the Ealdorman of Strathfeld—and if the ealdorman just happened to be an excellent lover and a virile specimen of masculine health, so much the better. Any serving maid would be foolish not to want to be his mistress.

Della made her way to the kitchen. She'd purposely missed the morning meal, not wanting to risk seeing Brant. His last warning had been clear.

"Isa, some bread if you would," Della said as she entered the kitchen. "And do not serve me any of the maids who have blackened your cauldron. It's unlikely they will sit well upon my belly."

Isa chuckled. "You will not be the only one here who gets a bit o' fun."

"I have no idea what you are speaking of." Della sighed in feigned innocence. "Did the spirit fling you about until your arse was bruised from the fallings?"

"Oh, yea, m'lady." Isa winked as she handed her a crust of bread. "Just remember, I was once in charge of washing the dirty laundry. There are many a white nightgowns that get scrubbed in a sennight's time."

Della coughed. "Interesting, Isa, though hardly relevant, I am sure."

"Oh, yea, it's most interesting. The cleaning spirit, she'll not e'en do her own wash." Isa's cackling laugh echoed off the hard walls of the kitchen.

"Isa, I can take no more of you this morn." Della gave the cook a playful wink. How many people suspected that she was the spirit? "I shall walk about the grounds."

"Be sure not to step on yer husband while you walk, m'lady," Isa teased.

Della shook her head, no longer amused by the woman's jesting.

By all the gods! What is that horrible stench?

Brant wrinkled his nose in disgust. The sun streaked heavily through the stable's rafters to shine uninvited on his face. He turned his head to avoid the accusing glare of the afternoon rays, but as he moved away from the sun, the smell only grew more distinct. Opening his eyes, he stared straight into a warm, steaming pile of…

Dung!

Brant shot up, ignoring the now constant pain in the back of his skull. He coughed heavily, his movements having stirred up dust. Next to him, his horse fussed and pawed at the ground. The stallion's neigh sounded quite mocking considering the circumstances. Brant eyed the fresh manure and then his stallion.

"Do you think to defy me as well?" Brant growled at the horse. He shook his fist in the animal's insolent face. The stallion tilted his head back in protest. "Has my loving wife been to whisper her deceits into your ears as well?"

"M'lord?"

Brant jolted at the sound. He looked hastily behind his back only to see Rab near the stall opening. The boy crouched behind the wood frame, his round, green eyes moving from the horse to the ealdorman.

"Begone, Rab." Brant didn't want to be the cause of the child's amusement.

"M'lord," Rab said quietly before clearing his throat. "M'lady wished me to find you."

"Which lady?" Brant growled in outrage. The sound rang in his head until it started to ache. Surely his wife would not send a little boy to spy on him.

"Lady Del…Blackwell." The boy took a brave step forward. Brant's scowl deepened by menacing degrees. Rab lifted his head proudly. "She wishes fer you to come and greet yer guests."

"Guests? Do you speak of the musicians?"

Why was the boy still talking? Had he not told him to leave? Brant grabbed his head and pressed his palms into his temples to get it to stop pounding.

Rab frowned. "Nay, m'lord, the musicians left two nights ago. You banished them fer playing too many disheartening ballads."

Brant grimaced through the fog of his memory. Vaguely he recalled doing just that. The songs had reminded him of Della. He once again waved at the boy in agitation. "Yea, I am awake, Rab. Begone! Tell your mistress to bother me no more."

"M'lord?" The boy bounced back and forth on his feet.

"Yea, go relieve yourself then, Rab."

"M'lord, shall I tell you the rest of the message?"

"Pray tell." Brant waved his hand in the air before

dusting the straw from his clothing. "If it will get you gone any faster."

"M'lady, that is Lady Blackwell, wishes fer me to tell you to get cleaned up and proper smelling before you come to the great hall. And these are her words, m'lord, not mine. She bid me to tell you not to dare disgrace yerself just 'cause yer too proud and pigheaded not to listen to her this once—"

Brant punched his fist through the side of the stall. The stallion lifted his head in protest. Rab flinched, jumping back. Brant grimly examined the hole he made.

"M'lord," Rab continued, his voice faint. "She bid me to tell only you and not to repeat the command to anyone else."

"Command?" Brant repeated, his tone harsh. He was pleased to have an outlet for his wrath.

"Nay, not command," Rab corrected. "Request. That is what she said m'lord—request. Humbly request."

"Nay, do not protect her. I know m'lady better than that." Brant took a deep breath. Della had sent a boy to wake him? And she dared to enter the hall after he ordered her not to? For that she would pay.

"M'lord, wait. I have not told you who is in the hall." Rab chased after him.

Brant ignored the child. Intent on finding his wife, he stormed angrily toward the castle. The sun shone bright over the yard. Servants and peasants watched him, stunned. A few recoiled in horror at his stern expression and beastly appearance. Brant didn't care.

Most of them had been avoiding him and his foul temper anyway. He preferred it that way, choosing to spend his solitude away from their prying eyes and gossiping tongues.

Stopping as he entered the hall, his eyes took a moment to focus in the dimmer light. His nostrils were assaulted with the smell of lye. With a grimace, he noticed the floors had been cleaned. What had his meddling wife done? Why did she disobey him so openly at every turn?

He disregarded the pleasure the clean hall gave him, intent on the pretense of hating her. Rudely making his way to the high table to face his wife, he stopped below her. It took a moment for her to notice him, but by that time Brant recognized their guest.

"Your majesty." Brant bowed. His anger faded as he witnessed the distress on his wife's face. No doubt he embarrassed her. That was punishment enough for now. Brant genuinely smiled for the first time in a long time.

"Lord Blackwell." King Guthrum stood and reached his hand out. "Your lovely wife has been entertaining us. Delightful creature."

Brant nodded, not knowing what to say. His wife did indeed appear lovely. Her hair was plaited neatly at her nape and, though her skin looked overly pale, it was flawless. She wore his favorite burgundy dress with the gold cord. Looking at it, he couldn't tell that it had been stained and torn. Her flushed cheeks turned a darker red at his perusal, or was it the king's pretty compliment? It didn't matter. She looked like an angel compared to the drunken hell he had been living in.

An Angel of Ice. Brant snorted.

The king cleared his throat. "Brant, it has been too long. Your lady wife told me you were currently bathing."

Brant let an easy expression settle over his face as he shook his head to clear the image of Della's naked body from it.

"Yea, your majesty. I did say that. Methought he was, but it would seem I was mistaken. M'lord?" Della turned to her husband and gave him a look of desperation. "Was it so terrible, the break in the wall?"

Brant just nodded, having no idea of what she was speaking. What was wrong with the wall? He raised an amused brow at her. She reminded him of the time Lord Lester and Sir Vladamir visited. She'd tried to save him from the embarrassment of not being able to read. How had he forgotten that kindness in his anger toward her? How had he forgotten her many kind acts?

"I was telling the king that you were awakened early this morning to fix a wall that tragically fell last night—behind the chapel." Della narrowed her eyes. The amber gaze begged him to pay attention.

"Yea. It's done." Brant smiled at her relieved sigh.

"Wonderful," Della proclaimed in relief as she looked at the king. "So you see your majesty, it's not necessary to send your stonemason to assist us. My lord husband has all of Strathfeld well under his control."

Since when do you acknowledge my control, lady wife? Brant smirked.

Della moved from her seat to make room for Brant beside the king. She directed her dazzling smile at him and his heart clenched in his chest. He knew her concern was only an act, but nonetheless it poured over him like droplets of refreshing rain.

"Majesty, what brings you here? I wasn't expecting you for at least another fortnight." Brant took his seat at the table. His sore back twinged in protest, the muscles having been aggravated by the many nights in the stables. Ignoring the pains and aches of his body, he saw Della motion to a maid to bring him a trencher.

Brant couldn't help but wonder at the change in the hall. By the looks of his home, no one would suspect that the lord and lady of the manor were estranged, and just the night before, the hall had been littered with rotting food and drunken, fornicating knights. Or that the ealdorman had been bingeing himself into a stupor alone in the stables.

"Sir Vladamir reported the death of Lord Strathfeld. I came to pay my respects to his daughter and to congratulate you both on the success of your union." Guthrum took a sip of his mead, obviously proud of his part in deciding the match.

Brant gave a soft laugh as he thought of Lord Lester sputtering in the moat.

"Yea, I heard of that as well." Guthrum

suppressed a grin and Brant wasn't surprised the man read his expression so easily. "You were quite right to throw that obstinate man out on his arse. Though, in the future, please be more hospitable to my ambassadors."

"Yea, your majesty." Brant took a drink to hide his smile in his goblet, trying his best to look properly chastised.

A maid brought forward a trencher filled with cold meat, cheese, and slices of bread. She set it before them. Guthrum leaned forward to take a piece of cheese, chewing it thoughtfully. Brant ignored the food. His stomach protested its very smell.

DELLA WAS AMAZED at the familiar way her husband addressed the king. Occasionally, she pretended to sip her drink as the men quietly discussed matters of politics. Surely she hadn't known Brant was a man of such import, to be trusted so readily by royalty.

When Rab had informed her of their guests, she'd panicked. The king's banner could be seen long before they could make out the king within the traveling party. For royalty, it was a small entourage that accompanied King Guthrum into the keep. Nevertheless, Della suspected that more of his men camped in the forest just beyond the sight of the castle. No one had seen Lord Blackwell and the king insisted he be produced. Distraught, she'd said the first thing she could think of—that he was overseeing repairs—then she'd sent Rab to find Brant.

"Della, would you see a bedchamber readied for his majesty and cots for his men?" Brant looked as if he had been hesitant to make the request. She could not blame him. They had done nothing but fight as of late. She'd been sitting quietly for so long that it took her a moment to realize he addressed her.

"M'lord, I have already taken the liberty." Della smiled, lost in her own thoughts. She turned back to her mead, content to watch the liquid swirl in her cup.

"M'lady, mayhap you should check on the preparations," Brant insisted.

"Nay, I trust Ebba to see to them." Della smiled again with a vague nod.

Brant cleared his throat. "Della?"

"Yea, m'lord?" She turned to look more fully at him. He was filthy and smelled of the stables. By the straw in his hair, she guessed that is where he'd slept the night before. She unconsciously lifted her hand to remove a piece of straw from his beard. The whiskers were overlong and needed to be clipped. Nervous, she fingered the straw between her thumb and forefinger, rolling and crushing it.

Brant looked at her in surprise, one brow arching like she'd often seen him do. It amazed her how familiar he really was.

Next, his lip will curl slightly in the right corner, she thought, dazed by his attractiveness. A blush heated her cheeks when it did.

"I see the match is well made!" King Guthrum slapped Brant hard on the back, knocking them out of the trance.

Brant's half smile turned to a laugh. He glanced over to acknowledge the king and then turned back to her.

"M'lady, would you see to my bath?" Brant asked, polite.

"But I already have," she answered, not really paying heed to Brant's words.

"M'lady, are you feeling ill? Shall you go lie down?" Kindness shone in his gaze.

"Nay…" Suddenly, she realized that not only her husband, but the king, was giving her an expectant look. The men wished to talk privately. "Yea, m'lord. Perchance I am ill and must lie down, but right after I see to your bath and the king's chambers."

She smiled as sweetly as she could, save the circumstance, and made her way from the head table. Her heart thudded and she felt as if she floated on a sea of trembling emotion. Now she thought of it, she was feeling quite ill again.

19

BRANT'S EYES narrowed as he watched Della walk away. His expression gave away none of his thoughts, but inside he worried. She looked pale and she was overly thin. The slenderness worried him. She'd always been a slight maiden, but now her gown hung on her frame a bit too freely. Mayhap the stress of late was starting to wear on her as it did him. Mayhap she was ready to call a truce.

King Guthrum took a sip of his mead as he watched Brant in silence. They'd known each other for a long time. Setting down his goblet, the king waited until Della reached the stairwell before clearing his throat to get Brant's attention.

"Delightful lady." King Guthrum interrupted his thoughts, slipping into their shared native tongue. "I wager you are not so upset about this match as you once were."

Brant grunted and said nothing. He didn't have to. Shooting a bemused glance at the king, he then directed his atention back to the empty stairwell entrance.

"Methought so," King Guthrum chuckled. "So where were you, really? The poor dear cannot lie to save her life, but the way she tried to cover for you was charming."

"Who said she lied?" Brant sniffed, not giving anything away with his expression. Picking up his goblet, he took a deep drink. Then, leaning over, he grabbed a slice of fresh bread to keep his hands busy as he spoke. "It is as she said. I was mending a wall that mysteriously fell in the night hours."

"From the stables?" The king laughed heartily.

Brant lightly waved his hand, not answering.

"And may I see this wall?" The king shot him an innocent smile. Brant didn't trust the mischief in it.

"The wall would not interest you. It is only a wall, much like any other. I doubt even I could find it again."

The king shook his head, amused. "Fine. I will allow you your secret, Lord Blackwell, but only this once."

Tearing off a crust of bread, Brant bit into it and slowly chewed. The morsel sat heavily on his empty stomach, but he forced himself to take another bite.

"Where is Gunther?" The king thoughtfully traced the royal crest emblazoned on his ring. "I have yet to see him about."

"I sent him to Blackwell Manor. I'm having a great section of it burned down." Brant grimaced at the reminder of his lice-infested home. "Damned place is infested with lice, rats, lazy servants."

"All hard to be rid of," the king said. "I noticed your wife keeps a very clean keep. Mayhap I should move in here with you, for this keep puts all five of my properties to shame."

"Nay, it is too much to expect a man to bow every day before he breaks his fast." Brant leaned back in his chair and crossed his arms. His own smell was beginning to offend even him. "Besides, I should hate to see what happens if the king also decided to take a liking to my lovely wife. I am not a man who shares my things well."

"Fair enough," the king laughed, not at all offended by the deliberate words. "Lady Blackwell is indeed beautiful, but I respect you too much to cuckold you."

"So, what is so urgent that you must ride all the way here? And do not tell me you came to see me content in my marriage. I should think you have more to consider than my happiness with a Saxon bride," Brant stated. "I already signed your document."

"Alfred wants a peace treaty," King Guthrum stated unceremoniously, not at all stunned by Brant's swift perception of his visit. "Methinks he just wants to get me alone so he can have my head and take my lands."

"Nay, not even the impertinent King Alfred would be so bold. He knows we would revolt against his rule. The Vikings would never live under his tyranny."

Brant knew well what the king was going to ask of him.

"Yet you are so willing to live under mine." Guthrum shook his head in amusement. "Nay, Alfred has the impudence of youth in him. He may try to be overbold. You are well respected by him, *Brant the Flame*. I want you at my side for fear that we may need to fight our way back."

The king was not asking, but demanding, and it was Brant's duty to obey. He didn't want to leave Della, or Strathfeld. He was tired of wars, tired of campaigning, of bloodshed. "When do we leave?"

"Good man." Guthrum nodded. "Send word to Gunther, he can stay here in your stead and protect what I have given you. And, although I will miss his sword, I fear he will not get here before the dawn."

"Dawn?" Brant asked with a sense of dread. Again his eyes moved to the stairwell.

"Yea, we will leave on the first light of morrow." Guthrum coughed and raised his goblet to his lips. After drinking, he said, "Go get you to a bath and take leave of your new wife properly. I shall understand if I see you no more this day."

DELLA STARED BLINDLY at the ceiling of her quiet bedchamber. The lonely strands of an abandoned spider web fluttered in the slight draft coming from the narrow window. A fire burned in the fireplace giving the room a soft, orange glow. Curling into a ball on the bed, she rolled on her side. She'd taken her hair down and now pushed the long length out of her eyes.

When she closed her eyes, she thought of Brant. Then, as if bidden by her longing, she heard his heavy steps on the stairwell long before he reached the door. The noise stopped and she sensed him outside the chamber. When he didn't open the door, she turned her head on her pillow to stare at the wooden entryway.

Come in, she beckoned silently. Della pushed herself up, never taking her eyes from the door. Her heart beat wildly as she waited in breathless anticipation. She could not force herself to call out to him.

Della waited for a long moment. Still he didn't come in. She knew it was her husband, knew the familiar sound of his footfall as he'd approached, and felt him as sure as she felt the mattress beneath her. As quietly as possible, she moved to the edge of the bed, gingerly placed her feet on the floor, and soundlessly walked over the hard stone.

Resting her forehead against the smooth oak barrier, she willed him to come to her. With her eyes closed, she could imagine him standing on the other side, disheveled from his nights of drinking and yet most handsome. Finally gaining courage, she reached for the latch. Her hand shook in nervous excitement. Would they fight? Would he still be mad? As she pulled, she felt him push gently from the other side.

Della's insides melted with expectation and her gaze instantly sought his blue one. She froze, not seeing the gaunt expression lining his tired features, not noticing the awful smell coming from his unwashed clothes. Her eyes could only see the man she loved—the man she'd missed desperately.

Brant hesitated outside the door. His eyes dipped over her form before finding their way back to her gaze. They both stood with their hands on opposite sides of the door latch, staring at the other. Both expected anger or ridicule from the other and didn't find it.

Coming to her senses, Della took a quick step back, moving so as to not block his entry into their chamber. It had been a long time since they'd shared the same space without fighting. She swallowed, unable to speak. He invaded her with his forceful presence.

Sweeping his gaze over the chamber, his attention paused near the fireplace on the bath she'd ordered drawn for him. When he again looked at her, he watched her intently. Brant took a single step in, holding his free hand out to her as the other fell from the door. "M'lady, you dropped this in the hall."

She stood before him as he held out a crushed piece of straw. It was the same piece she'd taken from his beard. He angled it to her like a tentative offering of peace.

"Thank you, m'lord." Della didn't dare take the straw and risk touching him. If she touched even his smallest finger, she would be swept away into his magnetic embrace. Only she didn't know if she would be accepted there and didn't wish make a fool of herself yet again. "Please, come in."

Brant nodded, coming inside he closed the door behind him. The straw fluttered to the ground as he moved past her. His shoes crushed softly into the fur rug, muffling his movements. Without comment, he shrugged off his overtunic.

"Did Rab not find you?" Della asked, curious. She had wondered.

"Yea, he did." Brant slipped his undertunic from over his head and turned his back to her as he dropped the dirty clothing on top of the discarded overtunic to make a pile.

Della shivered, staring at the strong lines of his naked back. "I would never have sent him after you, only there was no time. I could not look for you myself and I was not sure who you were with."

Brant stiffened. Della bit her lip and suppressed a moan. Her fingers shook and she grabbed a fistful of gown at her waist to hide it. She hadn't meant to reveal so much. Watching him apprehensively, she waited for his reply.

"Would you have really cared, Della?" His tone matter-of-fact, he didn't turn to look at her. He pushed his breeches off. They too landed on the floor in the pile. With his hands on his naked hips, he stretched his back, standing frozen in glorious perfection as if not caring that she watched. Her blood stirred and her breathing deepened. She wanted to touch him, to explore the long lost folds of his tight muscles.

Della's body filled with an intense fire only he could tame. Longing and desire swam in her head until she thought she might faint from the torture of his nearness. She wanted to hold him, but didn't dare try.

Brant moved to the tub. Stepping into the water, he sank into the bath, resting his head on the hard metal edge. Only then did he look at her, his eyes searching hers, but she didn't know for what. Insecure, she looked away, naturally making her expression icily calm.

She picked up his discarded clothing, careful to keep her eyes from straying to his perfect form. His unanswered question still hung in the air, but she could not find the right words. Would she care if he were with other women? How could she not? The thought burned her with the jealousy it caused. She could not answer him for the truth was too painful and she would not lie.

Della held the material to her chest and finally managed to meet his piercing gaze. "I will see that these get to the wash. There are fresh clothes in your trunk. If you like, I will set them out for you when I get back." She started to go, only to stop. "Oh, and there is some soap on the far side of the tub, on top of the linens."

Della didn't want to leave him and stood for a long moment, thinking of something she could say. She was tired of fighting. The unbearable nearness of his naked body wreaked havoc on her already swirling emotions. Lust burned a trail through her soul, leaving hot, tingling sensations all over her flesh. She wanted him to look at her as he once had, with a roguish smile curling his firm masculine lips. But that was before her anger had taken her too far—before her heart had realized how harsh its hatred of him was and how misguided.

"About Rab, I asked him to tell you that I humbly requested you bathe and change. Did he not say that?" Della kept her face blank. "I did not wish to anger you."

"It's fine, Della. Fret no more about it."

THE BOY HAD BEEN TELLING the truth. Brant closed his eyes, not moving in the warm water. She'd avoided responding to his question, just as she avoided touching his hand when he entered the room. A well of hopeless despair deepened within him, swallowing his heart. What did he care? His heart was dead anyway.

Brant heard his wife moving about the chamber behind him. He rotated his head against the rim of the tub to stare aimlessly into the fire, knowing when she left with his dirty clothes and the moment she returned. She was quiet and he didn't know what to say to her. Finally making himself move, he washed with the strong soap that had been laid out. He tried to pretend she wasn't there, but he was always aware of her.

He heard his trunk open and guessed she laid out his clothing. He splashed unintentionally and her breath caught. Brant glanced at her to see her bent over her own trunk, pulling out some of her jars. Her long hair spilled over her shoulders, slightly disheveled. He quickly turned away before she saw him looking.

"Let me help you with your hair," she said.

The fleeting touch of her fingers glanced over his shoulder as she kneeled beside him. In her hand was a pair of shears. Hesitant, she lifted her hand to his bearded face. Her eyes stayed steadily on his. Brant didn't move as her fingers glided near his lip. The caress was small and unintentional, but it caused his gut to tighten as lust centered between his thighs. He wondered if she detected the reaction because she hurriedly turned his jaw to the side and his eyes away from her. Lifting the shears to his face, she began to trim his beard. Brant tensed, waiting for the blades to slice through him, not sure if he'd be surprised if she stabbed him in the chest.

He felt the subtle shift of her fingers, as she angled his head to trim the other side. Her beautifully pale face was set in concentration and her scent lingered in the air, embracing him in wildflowers. Her lips parted, forcing him to suppress a groan of agony. The slightest movement would meet her mouth with his, but he held fast, refusing to kiss her. She leaned closer and her breath whispered over his skin, tickling his shoulder. Brant closed his eyes and forced himself to relax.

"Go under."

Was he mistaken or did her voice seem a bit

husky? He did as she commanded, too weary not to comply. Resurfacing, he wiped the water from his face.

"Would you like me to trim your hair as well?" she asked.

"Nay, it's fine as is."

Della began to stand. Brant grabbed her arm, wetting her sleeve as he kept her next to him. Her eyes rounded and she settled once more beside him.

"If you would not mind, I would like it if you washed my hair for me." Brant almost hadn't made the request. He eyed her thoughtfully.

Della nodded, reaching to the side to pick up a jar. She dipped a finger inside and rubbed her palms together, lathering the soap before moving to massage his scalp. Scrubbing his hair and beard clean, she ordered him to rinse the suds from his head. When he surfaced, she applied another cream to him. Brant instantly recognized the smell. It was the same concoction she'd used the first night they made love. Did she remember it also?

"Della," Brant turned to her and grabbed her wrist lightly. He massaged the wet, sudsy pulse he found there. "Della?"

"Please." A tear slipped over her cheek. His caress became bolder, working in slow circles to glide farther up her arm beneath her dress, testing to see her reaction. "Please, may we call a truce? Just for now. I'm too tired to fight with you."

"Yea, Della." Brant wondered at her sadness as he

gently wiped at the tear. The moisture slid across her cheek under his thumb. "Are you still ill?"

"Nay, yea," she mumbled with a dainty shrug. Suddenly, she leaned forward and her lips pressed firmly against his. His hand trembled as it was forced into the warmth of her hair. His palm cupped her cheek and he felt her hand glide onto his shoulder, her fingers wrapped around his neck keeping him to her. Della moaned as she traced her tongue between his lips.

Brant gasped in surprise at the bold move and she took advantage by kissing him more fiercely. A low groan escaped him. Her mouth slanted eagerly against his, delving her tongue into the warm depths. His body lurched to full attention, his muscles tightening, his arousal hard and full. She kissed him like a woman starved of his affections. Mayhap she felt as desperate as he did.

Brant moaned, finding her arms to pull her back. Della's eyes widened, as if panicking at his withdrawal. But he only broke the kiss to quickly rinse the soap from his hair. Before she could move, he hurriedly rose from the tub. Water trailed his flesh, tiny caresses against his sensitive body. Della stood to join him. Without words, he scooped her into his arms and carried her with a gentle urgency to the bed. The moisture from his body soaked into her gown, but she didn't seem to care as she clung to him. Afraid she'd change her mind and push him away, his movements became frantic.

He set her down on the bed, gentle despite his

passion, and went to her. He touched her hair, the golden cord at her waist, the ties of her gown. She returned the kisses as fervently as she received them. She touched his wet back, her hands gliding easily over him.

Brant groaned as the familiar sensations of her caress overwhelmed him. This is where he wanted to be. Here, with her, touching her, kissing her. Nothing else mattered.

Della moaned, unable to stop herself as Brant touched her. She wanted him so badly, had waited for him to make the first move as she washed his hair, but in the end, she couldn't hold herself back. She needed him like she needed to breathe.

His beard tickled as their mouths moved in a steady, powerful rhythm. She hadn't realized how much she missed him and in the instant their lips met, none of the other things mattered—not the rumors of other women, not the fighting, not his heritage. She could not refuse him. She could not refuse herself.

Brant's mouth took over the tempo of their kiss, slowing her mouth so he could explore inside. Restless and needy, her legs moved against him. Her skirt slowly edged up to expose the long line of her calves. The first rub of his naked, warm skin along her legs made her groan. He maneuvered himself between her thighs, his stiff erection pressing hard into the folds of her gown as it blocked him from her hips.

She thrust against him, rubbing through her clothing.

Brant pulled at her gown, freeing a breast. Instantly, his warm hand was on the flesh, massaging it as he moved his hips in slow, agonizingly perfect circles. Her sex was wet and tingling and she needed more.

"Look at me, Della," Brant commanded, staring down at her. Her eyes remained closed as she rubbed sensually along his frame. In a gentler tone, he urged, "Look."

"Brant," she moaned as she opened her eyes. His gaze shone brightly with an emotion she could not understand. He was so beautiful it made her heart ache with bittersweet joy. So many questions floated between them. None of them were answered as they silently drank in the comfort of the other's presence.

"I want you to be sure this is what you want," he said.

Della didn't know what she would do if he were to try to deny her. She wasn't sure her body would let her stop. She ached for him too badly.

Brant's hips pulled back. Della breathed hard, panting as she reached for her skirt. Grabbing it, she urged the material up to expose her upper thighs. He looked down between their bodies and made a weak noise. Her dress rode even higher, showing him how ready she was, how wet and willing. Unable to say the words in her heart, she said the only thing she could, "Make love to me, Brant. I want you to."

Brant's eyes shone passionately at her. His lips

curled with the familiar sultry smile. He touched her shoulder, slowly drawing his fingers over the tender flesh there. Della moaned and arched a breast toward his lips. He grinned, kissing her collarbone instead.

"Ah, sit up." Brant pulled her arms, quickly undressing her. Once naked, she lay back down and his hands instantly found the length of her body. She was just as eager to explore him, touching him in every way she could—legs to legs, hands to arms and chest, lips to lips. He moved his hand down and parted the slick folds between her thighs. He stroked her, encircling her clit, sinking a finger into her depths. "You are so soft."

Della's legs parted wide, silently begging him for more. Brant grinned, though the look was pained. With a controlled thrust, he gradually entered her. Della moaned as the muscles of her sex accepted him, stretching and hugging him tight. In awe over his gentle strokes, she ran her fingers over his chest. Brant rose up on his arms, his hot eyes watching her as he moved. Della shivered. Her body craved completion and he brought it to her with deliberate caresses. She stiffened, letting the pleasure wash over her as she finally met with perfect release. His groan soon joined hers as he jerked violently. And, as they came down, trembling and spent, there was no room for words.

20

BRANT LEFT before dawn with the king, without saying a word to her, not even to tell her he was going. They'd made love twice with agonizing tenderness and had slept in each other's arms. Or so she'd thought. She'd been sleeping when he left, waking alone as the sun peeked over the horizon. Somehow, she knew he was gone before even opening her eyes. Hitting her pillow in frustration, the softness stifled the sound of her heartache.

Then, finding strength, she dressed and made her way belowstairs. Doing so only confirmed her fear and Della spent the morning hours strolling gloomily about the castle grounds.

The sun shone bright over her head as she kicked her feet in the drying morning dew. Looking to the sky, she stood motionless in the bailey yard. Puffy clouds lined the blue heavens. She felt sorry for herself, was so confused by what had happened, but the clouds held none of the answers she sought.

"M'lady."

Della jolted at the sound of Edwyn's voice. Shaking her thoughts back to reality, she watched the old seneschal jog across the bailey, waiting patiently for him to join her.

"Gunther approaches," he said.

The cold winds of fall were beginning to blow across the land, turning everything a golden brown. Della made herself halfheartedly smile at her old friend, shivering in the cool breeze. But inside a gentle sadness swam within her and not even she could hide the emotion with her icy demeanor. Edwyn looked at her, his expression holding pity. She didn't want to see it, not from the man who'd raised her.

"Did you let him in?" Della asked. "He comes from Blackwell."

"Nay, m'lady. Lord Blackwell bid me not to make the decision." Edwyn didn't try to hide his amusement. "It's yers to order whether or not we let Gunther inside."

"Oh, yea," Della rolled her eyes. "Let him in, then!"

"Yea, m'lady," Edwyn bowed gallantly. "It will be as you wish it."

Della shook her head and could not help but chuckle. Some of her husband's policies were getting a little out of hand. A few of the maids had asked her permission before cleaning the dreaded garderobes and Isa, in her usual taunting manner, asked if she should cook the chicken before she served it, or if she should just set it out raw and still clucking.

Actually, the more she thought of Brant, the more hurt she felt, and with the hurt came her irritation. He hadn't bothered to tell her the night before that he was leaving with the king. If he had, she wouldn't have succumbed to him so readily. She would have demanded the conversation she'd thought they would have that morning. The partial truce they'd made had to mean something. Was he lonely? Did he think he could have her whenever he wanted?

With each thought, her irritation grew into anger.

I will not stand to be treated like this. I will show Brant the Flame who is in charge of Strathfeld. It's time I stop playing the meek and mild housemaiden and live up to my name, Della the Cold!

She let the irritation overtake her as she strode over the yard to tend her garden. Gunther rode his horse over the lowered bridge, spotting her as she stormed past. The man-at-arms looked at her in surprise. Della ignored him and, as she found the sanctuary of her herb garden, she turned her rage to the hapless weeds.

"I KNOW well why my mood is black, but why do you stare at yer plate as though it were about to attack you." Gunther leaned toward Della to whisper in her ear. He was still mad at having missed the king and the action the traveling party would undoubtedly see.

"I am not!" Della denied, but she still didn't raise her hand to eat. The smell of meat made her stomach curl. She pushed the trencher aside and leaned back into her chair. The hall was moderately quiet. After the stint of drinking, the men just wanted to sit in silence. Already many of them had gone off to find their beds.

"You are still at odds with him, then?" Gunther sighed in obvious disappointment. "Methought as soon as he stopped his mock celebration and you came down from yer prison tower, the two of you would reconcile."

"Methinks you should mind to your own, Gunther." Della sank into her chair in dejection, trying to edge away from him.

"Yea, m'lady, you and Brant are my own. Yer the only family I have and you look as if you could use a friend to talk to." Gunther shook his head. "So, little sister, I will see yer wars waged no longer. Tell me what goes on that you cannot find peace in yer marriage."

"Gunther," Della began harshly, sitting up to face him. She softened her tone when she saw the caring in his expression. "I cannot. It's too humiliating. Besides, you have sworn your loyalty to Brant."

"Yea, that I have," he admitted. "But I would also swear it to you. Tell me, should I kneel before you with my oath?"

When Della didn't readily answer, Gunther shot her a mischievous smile. Standing, he moved as if to go before her. She shot her hand out to stop him.

"Nay, Sir Gunther." She could not stop the grin that threatened her features. Giggling despite her sorrowful mood, she said, "Sit down. I have no wish to see you kneel before me. I will take your silent oath."

Gunther sat back down at her side, absently waving the attention of a few of the men away. "So, what is it then?"

"I already told you it's too humiliating." A blush stained her cheeks. She refused to look at him and instead trained her eyes forward. When he didn't speak, she peeked at him.

"Yea, that is it? He is no good between the linens?" Gunther tried to look concerned and failed.

"Nay!" Her blush deepened and Gunther winked at her. "Do not make your pleasantries with me."

"I'm glad to hear the ealdorman's performance is not in question, fer there is naught I can do about that."

"Nay, it is that it is in too much question," she answered, disheartened.

"What is this?" Gunther was apparently shocked. His smile faded as his eyes rounded in surprise.

"Gunther, he is too virile and not in my bedchamber," Della stressed her words carefully. She didn't know what made her confess such a private thing to Gunther, but she needed a friend and he was the closest one she had. He wasn't like the gossiping servants. He would be loyal to her, he'd sworn to be.

"Yea?" Gunther took a thoughtful sip of mead. "Who?"

"I know not—Serilda, one of the maids, several of the maids." She shook her head as she pushed the tray further from her. The smell was still getting to her. Nausea waved up in her chest to war with the lonely despair.

Mayhap, I have been poisoned, she thought, dispirited.

"Serilda?" Gunther shook his head and laughed. He pounded his fist on the wooden tabletop until those in the great hall stopped and turned at the commotion. As he threw himself back, his drink spilled onto the floor.

"M'lady, would you like to share the jest with all of us?" Roldan leaned past Gunther with a hopeful smile, eyeing her from the other side of the table.

"Nay, Roldan. Turn back to yer mead," Gunther denied for her. A maid righted the fallen goblet and set it on the table. Then, filling it quickly, she retreated back down the platform. Gunther lifted his goblet to Roldan and announced for all to hear, "Let not m'lady repeat her poisonous barbs. They are likely to make e'en you blush."

Roldan laughed, believing to understand. The man turned back to his meal and the soldier with whom he conversed.

"I am glad you find my husband's bedsport with Serilda amusing." Della glared at him once they were again free to speak. She stiffened, about to stand.

"Nay, Della, stay. I did not mean to imply methought it amusing." He tapped her arm lightly to keep her beside him. "I cannot believe Brant did not tell you. It was a mean jest, truly."

"What?"

"Serilda on his lap. He saw you belowstairs and pulled the closest maid into his embrace. Methinks it was to make you jealous. I see it has worked." Gunther nodded in personal satisfaction.

"But, then, he didn't bed her?" Her breath quickened at the thought. She trembled, hardly able to believe it true. Carefully, she watched Gunther's face for a lie.

"Nay, and he would have told me if he had, of that you can be assured."

"But that does not excuse the others. Who was he with in the stables?"

"Nay, there are no others, not since he wed with you, m'lady." Gunther met her eyes.

"You speak the truth." Della saw his honesty. A smile came unbidden to her face. Relief, so sweet, washed over her and for a moment she could again forget her anger. Taking Gunther's hand in hers, she whispered, "But he let me believe. The servants said…"

"Servants oft gossip about things they know naught about. Of m'lord's reasons I know naught. Brant is a proud man and proud men do not explain themselves." Gunther patted her hand, before lifting it from his own and placing it away from him. "Mayhap he likes a jealous wife."

"Please, Gunther, you must excuse me. I-I…" She paled and her words trailed off. Darting to her feet, she moved hastily down the platform stairs, almost knocking a maid's tray to the ground as she made her way through the door to the kitchen. She mumbled a quick apology to the stunned servant before continuing on.

Falling to her knees on the kitchen floor, she vomited into the first empty pot she came to. Several of the maids tried to watch her in curiosity, but Isa shooed them from the kitchen. The cook silently rolled her dough, waiting for Della to stand.

"M'lady." Isa glanced up from her rolling to give the noblewoman a matronly smile. "Be there aught wrong with the meal?"

"Isa, do we have a crust of bread? My stomach cannot handle the meat tonight." Della tried to smile. When Isa frowned, she amended, "The meal is wonderful. My stomach is weak. Methinks I'm ill."

"Hmm." Isa grabbed a fresh loaf and tore off a piece. As she handed the dry morsel over, she asked, "Have you told his lordship, m'lady?"

"What?" Della was confused as she took the bread. Tearing off a piece, she stuck it in her mouth and chewed slowly, not too eager to swallow.

"About the babe." Isa continued her rolling. Then forming a loaf with deftly precise hands, she placed it aside on the table.

"Whose babe?" Della took another bite of bread. "I did not see a babe. Was it one of the cotters?"

"M'lady, are you not with child?" Isa asked in pointed amusement. She nodded toward Della's stomach. Isa formed another loaf and placed it with the other. "You have the sickness."

"Oh, Isa, nay. It's only a weak stomach, though I

do wish it would go away." Della reached down and touched her narrow waist. "I am afraid I have lost weight. When you are with child, you gain it."

"Who told you that nonsense?" Isa laughed so that her plump body shook with the force of it. She reached down under her cutting table for a bucket of water. Lifting it, she said, "Fer it is nonsense."

"My eyes tell me women gain weight and, well, Serilda told me it was a stomach sickness." Della watched Isa wipe the dough crumbs into a pile and sighed. She fingered the bread, but didn't take another bite.

"That one!" Isa shook her head in disapproval. "You did right in throwing her from the manor. I know not what she would have to gain by lying to you about a babe, but she did lie."

"She had naught to gain. That is how I know I am not with child." The idea of carrying a babe rolled over her curiously. She didn't know what to feel. If what Isa said was true, would Brant leave for good? Would he feel the extent of his 'duty' had been accomplished? Della swayed and leaned against the table.

"Nay, m'lady, I would wager my kitchen on it. You carry his lordship's babe in yer belly." Isa smiled kindly. Ignoring her bucket of water, she moved around the table as she dusted off her hands. In a rare moment of seriousness, she touched Della tenderly on the shoulder. "It's no stomach illness, child."

"How can you tell? Do I look different?" Della

inquired through her shock. She gazed intently down at her waist and smoothed the blue tunic she wore over her flat stomach. Spreading her fingers wide, she pressed them into her midsection. She felt the same.

"Nay, but soon you will." The cook gave her a delighted smile. "You have not had yer woman's time since before yer marriage and you are sick in the morn and at night. Am I right?"

"Yea, and sometimes in the oddest hours of the day."

"And the sickness, it comes as suddenly as it leaves?" Isa persisted logically. "And you are overtired?"

"Yea," Della whispered as the reality of what Isa was saying started to make sense. Her hand fluttered nervously over her stomach. Swallowing over the dryness in her throat, she asked softly, "But how? It is not possible."

Isa chuckled as she patted Della on the arm. "If you have to be asking that, you best bring it up with yer husband. It's my guess he would be the one to tell you about the how of it."

Della's hand shook and she dropped the crust of bread, letting it fall forgotten to the floor. Isa sighed as she leaned over to pick it up. Della wordlessly made her way to the kitchen door. Isa whistled a tune softly behind her, but Della kept walking, needing to be alone.

BRANT SPURRED his horse onward as King Guthrum motioned for the ealdorman to join him at the front of the traveling party. Along the sides of the trail was nothing but forest. Brant knew the outriders would be nearby, hidden well within the trees. They had ridden hard since dawn through Mercia toward the northern border of Wessex to meet King Alfred on hallowed ground, where it was believed no blood would be shed by either side for fear of angering the Christian God. Brant thought the idea foolish since Guthrum didn't believe in that God.

"Your majesty," Brant allowed as he slowed his stallion to an easy trot beside the king. Guthrum held up his hand, motioning the guards on either side to fall back.

"Lord Blackwell." The king kept his gaze trained forward as he spoke. "It is a strange journey, is it not?"

"Strange?" Brant stiffened and looked around. Always the loyal knight, his hand went to the hilt of his sword to rest. No birds flew in the sky, the insects of the forest hummed lively. Nothing seemed amiss. He relaxed his guard as he turned to the king. "I detect naught in the forest."

"Your men, do they doubt our mission?" The king busied himself, straightening the frippery on his horse's mane. The ribbons of purple velvet matched the king's cloak. Brant looked at his own horse, decorated in only the barest leather straps. He didn't feel the need to dress the animal in finery.

"Nay. They are all loyal, as am I." Brant managed

a polite smile. The king's words were true though. His heart hadn't been in the mission. It was left back at Strathfeld in Della's infallible keeping, although she didn't know it.

"Then why are the men in such disheartened spirits? I have never seen such downtrodden knights, even in the face of tremendous battle." The king stopped his horse and motioned to one of his guards. "Here. We camp here. I would not stay too close to the border."

The soldier nodded and passed the orders down the line of men. Two riders were dispatched on either side to tell the outriders the plan. The sky had just begun to turn a purplish red and the cool autumn breeze picked up. It whipped Brant's hair into his eyes. He tucked the strands behind his ears, not bothering to give an answer.

"Lord Blackwell, methinks it is because their leader is dispirited," King Guthrum continued as if they hadn't stopped talking. He was content to sit astride his horse as he watched his orders being carried out. Several of the men headed toward the trees to set up a small camp.

Brant still didn't answer for he could not deny it. It was true. He had been a little sharp with the men. He missed Della. Thoughts of his wife only caused his mood to fade into extreme sadness. She didn't care for him and at every turn she made sure to let him know. But she did desire him, and in that he took a little hope. Mayhap in time she would grow to love him.

Brant remembered the soft line of her sleeping face as the combination of morning and firelight caressed the softness of her flushed, naked flesh. She'd slept on her stomach, her back completely exposed to him, and he'd stared at her in wonder as he quietly dressed. He'd wanted to wake her before he left, but thought it best not to, since she had been so sick as of late. Her illness worried him. Thinking of it only made him ache to turn around, but he would never forsake his duty for his own personal whims.

"So, it is as methought," the king declared with a knowing grin. Brant was not sure if Guthrum's eyes held pity or joy. "The legendary *Brant the Flame* is in love—and with his wife, no less."

21

DELLA GRADUALLY BECAME accustomed to the idea of her pregnancy. Now that she accepted what was awry with her body, she didn't seem to be as ill, or mayhap it was she didn't care because she knew the cause. The last several days without Brant had cooled her anger toward him, and she had to admit Gunther's words helped a great deal in lessening her animosity. They left her longing to see him and deathly afraid of what he would say when she did. At times she wondered if he would come back at all. Mayhap he would leave her like she had often urged him to do.

At night, the image of his body haunted her. She woke up in the early dawn hours dripping with sweat, her heart pounding in apprehension. She worried for him. King Guthrum would not have ordered him away unless there was to be danger. During the day, she wondered if her child would have the same red streak in his hair, or the same mischievous glint to his eyes. Or mayhap it would be a girl who looked like her. She smiled to think of it and again ran her hand possessively over her stomach. Already she felt a hardening bump where her child would grow. Nothing else mattered, not so long as Brant was delivered safely back to her. Once he was, she would make sure he never left again. And, no matter how hard it was for her, she was determined to tell him how she really felt.

"M'lady!" Rab's yell echoed over the bailey as he flew around the side of the castle.

Della looked up from where she leaned against the wall and smiled at the foundling boy as he skidded to a stop. His red cheeks puffed with each breath and his hair was tousled about his head.

"Yea, Rab, calm yourself. I am here." Della motioned the boy to her side, stepping away from the wall and into the sunlight to see him better. The boy's face paled dramatically to see her.

Blessed Saints, Brant's hurt.

"What is it?" She asked when the boy didn't speak.

Rab looked hesitantly at the ground then back to Della. "Another raid, m'lady. They burned the crops and slaughtered the cattle."

Della's heart leapt in bitter relief that it was not bad news about Brant, but that was before Rab's words sunk in completely. Her limbs weakened. "And the cotters?"

"Killed. About twenty o' them."

Unsure as to what she should do, Della began to walk toward the gate only to stop in disbelief. Turning back to the boy, she said, "Nay. It cannot be. Not with Lord Blackwell gone. Did you inform Gunther and Roldan? Do they ride out?"

"Yea. Roldan bid me to find you. He and the other men ride at once. He is leaving Cedric to watch over you and a few of the other knights to man the walls until he is back. He said it should only be a day and a night at most." Rab stepped forward as Della swayed uneasily on her feet. "*M'lady?!*"

"I'm all right, Rab," Della protested as the young boy made her sit on the ground next to the castle. He fanned his hands frantically in her face as she took deep breaths. She lifted her hand, bidding him to stop.

"M'lady, should I get someone. Yer face is as white as the fresh linens." Rab made a move to leave. She reached out her hand to stop him, but he was already running.

"Nay, Rab. Hold!" Della yelled. When he turned to look at her, she motioned him back. "I do not need you to fetch anyone. Just come sit with me a moment."

"M'lady." Rab bounced anxiously on his feet as he looked over his shoulder. "Not a lesson now. The men are about to ride out and I must watch if I am to be a knight. Gunther said I must help to man the wall while he is gone."

"Nay, not a lesson." Della smiled and patted the ground insistently. "A secret."

"Secret?" The boy came back, intrigued. "Between only us?"

"Yea, between only us for now." Della already knew Isa would tell no one.

"What?" Rab seemed to realize he was being overanxious and leaned against the stone wall. He tried to act disinterested, but his excitement showed in the jittery movements of his body.

"First, I must secure your promise to tell no one. Not until I tell you it's fine." Della shaded her eyes and looked up at him. He had thinned out in the face, no doubt a benefit of Brant's training and attention. She pulled a weed and wove the stem through her fingers. "I shall keep you to this promise."

"Yea, I will tell no one. Not e'en under torture." Rab leaned closer. "Not e'en if they pull out my fingernails and—"

"I shall hold you to that," Della broke in before the boy could go on. "I carry Lord Blackwell's babe."

Rab's eyes rounded and he giggled. Della grabbed his hand and pulled him down to sit by her. Wrapping her arm around his shoulders, she tousled his hair. He tolerated her affections with an impish smirk before fighting the embrace.

"I will expect you to be a good example for this child, Rab." Della pinched his cheek playfully and released him. "I depend upon you to help me."

The boy nodded. "I will guard him with me—*my* —life."

"And if it's a girl?"

He thought about it for a moment. "I'll teach her how to hold a sword and climb trees. That way she'll be fun to play with."

Della chuckled. "You best go if you are to see the men off."

Rab gave her an impulsive hug before jumping to his feet. With a jaunty wave, he ran toward the main gate. She watched him until he disappeared, feeling too lazy to get up. Twisting the weed in her fingers, she picked a few more and plaited them into a braid. A frown marred her face as she thought of the poor cotters.

Horse hooves sounded like distant thunder as the men left. Gunther and Roldan undoubtedly took many of the soldiers to investigate the raid and even more had left with Brant. Aside from the peasants and servants who lived within the walls, the castle was almost empty. Della yawned and tossed the weed to the ground. She heard the front gate close.

"At least Edwyn does not have to seek my permission before he lets people out of the castle, lest I might think I lived in a prison." Della gave a short laugh.

"Is it not a prison, Della? Has your heart changed so quickly?"

"Stuart?" Della jolted in surprise, pushing up from the ground. Straightening to her full height, she dusted off her tunic gown as she glanced in the direction of the gate. From what she could see, the bailey was empty. She was alone with him. "You frightened me."

"I did not mean to. You must have been lost in your thoughts not to have heard my approach." Stuart took a leisurely step forward. A deliberate smile lingered on his face. Della wondered how long he'd watched her before making his presence known. Lowering his chin, he tilted his head thoughtfully, studying her. She shivered, but held her ground.

"How did you get in here? Gunther would not have let you pass. Lord Blackwell has forbidden it. Methinks he is still angry from your last visit." Unable to take his intense gaze, she took an uneasy step back.

Stuart's eyes were rimmed with dark circles and he looked like he hadn't slept for some time. His chin held two day's worth of whiskers, where he normally was clean-shaven and well kept. When he laughed, the sound was mocking. "Oh, yea, Lord Blackwell." Stuart looked to the heavens as his laughter slowly died. He seemed unconcerned that any would hear him. When he turned back to her, his face appeared solemn. It was as if he decided the effort to smile was not worth it. "Your black-hearted husband."

"Do not say such harsh things, cousin." Della lifted her chin. He took a step toward her only to suddenly stop and laugh again. The sound twisted unevenly in the air until she was forced to back away from him in fear, inching along the ground.

"Nay? And why is that, pray tell?"

"Lord Blackwell is my husband and I have told you there is naught to be done about it." The hairs on the back of her neck stood tall. Looking over his shoulder, she tried to find help. The yard was still empty. She took a deep breath and willed her heart to still. Keeping her voice calm, she asked, "How did you get in here?"

"You showed me. Remember?" Stuart snickered as his eyes traveled over her body. He licked his lips.

"Your moods change too quickly. It is odd, Stuart." She continued to inch past him. "I did not show you the way, you merely saw me. I trusted you to know better than to use it. If you are caught within these walls, they will take you prisoner. You will be locked away until Lord Blackwell decides to set you free. It may be months—years even. Did anyone see you? If you hurry you can leave the way you came."

"Nay." He waved his hand in dismissal of the suggestion. "You think me odd, dear cousin? Surely that is of *his* influence. He has poisoned your mind against me."

"Stuart—"

"And your body," he snarled.

From their position, no one would be able to see her as well as if she were closer to the main gate—not that anyone knew to look for her. Cedric was left to tend to her and he would not search her out unless summoned. He was still angry with her for making him churn butter.

Stuart appeared to read her thoughts. "Nay, they are gone. Be assured. We will not be interrupted."

"I don't know what you mean." Della let the lie slip quietly from her lips. "Mayhap, if we get you out of the sun. Come, let us go inside for a draught of mead. Methinks it might help to cheer you. You look thin, cousin. Come, let me feed you before the men get back."

"Do not play games, Della! I know how he has

poisoned your mind. You don't have to be afraid of him any longer. I know how you got that scrape on your face the first day I came back. I know he beat you in the hall for all to see. I know how he has humiliated you, disrespected you. I know of the whores he has slept with right under your nose. I am your friend, Della. I am here to help you. I have come to take you away from the heathen Vikings." He held out his hand and motioned her to go with him. Glaring at her expectantly, he willed her to come to him. "I have come to claim your hand."

"Nay, I stay with Strathfeld. It's my home and my life." She turned, intent on walking away. His words of Brant planted a small seed of doubt. If Stuart had heard tales of other women, did it mean it was true? Had Gunther lied to protect his friend? It would not be the first time a knight lied for his lord. Either way, this was a matter between her and her husband. It was not a reason to abandon her home or her people. She walked faster.

"Do you forget your own mother so soon?" Stuart sputtered in fury when she didn't join him. "And for what? The lascivious touch of a godless barbarian?"

Della froze in mid-stride. She hadn't forgotten her mother, but it was time to stop the hatred. The men she sought would never be punished for what they had done. Revenge and justice were not hers to have. And yet Stuart's words still plucked at her heart, causing it to ache dully with longing. "It was too many years past. The men who did that will never be found. It's time to let the pain die. I need the pain to die. I cannot live with it any longer. I need peace. If you love me, cousin, you will leave me be. You will let me make my own happiness here, and if happiness is not mine to have, then at least I will have some peace in my time."

"Nay!" Stuart disagreed with a mighty growl. He pointed his finger at her in both accusation and absolution. Della watched him from the corner of her eye. "I bring you the peace you so seek. It is revenge I have come to offer you. Justice! That and your freedom."

"Freedom?" Della said the one word in wonder. Her eyes swept over the yard. She heard him take a step toward her and could not move. Trembling, she remembered her mother's face. The memory was as clear as it had ever been. Time hadn't faded a single line or a single tortured scream.

"Yea, freedom from the tyranny of the *Viking barbarian*. Freedom from those endless nights filled with demons. Freedom from Lord Blackwell, black-hearted knight." Stuart's words grew softer by degrees until they were a gentle whisper. "True freedom, as only revenge can bring you."

His breath fell hot against her neck. Her limbs would not move and her mind forced her to listen to what he had to say. Revenge. It was what she'd prayed for since that night long ago. Was it possible after all the years of waiting and praying? Could she avenge her mother?

"Come with me, Della. Remember what they did to her." His breath fanned her cheek. He smelled of stale liquor and sweat. She barely noticed. "Remember her cries. The same cries you have heard every night since, at least before that heathen wove his spell about you."

"I have not forgotten," she whimpered. She wanted to move, but couldn't. It was like that night, when she was a child—helpless, scared, weak. His hand hovered just above her hair to land hesitantly on her shoulder. She stiffened. Stuart frowned.

"Close your eyes. Remember," he urged her. Della obeyed. "Remember the acrid smell of burning flesh, how they cut her nether hair. Remember how they raped her, one after another, until she bled their heathen seed from her body. Remember what they did to your brother. He was alive when they cut him out, was he not? Did he cry for you to save him? Does he cry still?"

"Enough," she begged, opening her eyes.

Della didn't want to hear anymore, as air filled her lungs in great heaves. Her eyes blurred and her vision swarmed until blackness threatened to overtake her. The images were too close to her heart and she began to weep. Stuart grabbed her shoulders and gave her a hard shake to force her mind back to reality.

"You are too cruel," she whispered.

"Nay, not me. The cruelty you speak of belongs to another. Avenge your mother. Avenge your slaughtered brother. Remember them. Honor them. Remember how the babe cried as they sliced his throat." Stuart had her undivided attention. He smiled as he loosened his hold on her shoulder. Della didn't move. "How long did he live, Della? How many hell-filled moments?"

Della did remember, all too clearly. Her hand fluttered to her stomach, protectively covering her own baby. She felt her mother's pain—more real to her now that she was to bear her own child. She didn't remember telling Stuart of her brother's death, but she had been young when they were together. Who knew the details she'd confessed all those nights they sat alone, whispering in the moonlight? Her limbs were numb with the pain of the past and a detached fear came over her. Her tears dried on her cheeks and she absently wiped her runny nose on her sleeve.

"I offer revenge for what they did to your mother and to your brother. I offer revenge for what they did to you, for what they took from you." His voice was harsh.

"You...know who?" Her throat tightened in horrible anticipation and her heart squeezed in her chest, until it felt as if it caved in on itself. Gooseflesh covered her arms. She was unsure if to believe his claim, but part of her wanted it to be true so badly. "How?"

Della could not ignore him. She wanted revenge. She wanted their blood to spill as her mother's and brother's had.

"I have been looking for them since our childhood. I have not told you for fear you would get your hopes up, but it has been my life's mission to make you happy and to avenge your mother. Finally, after all these years, I have discovered the truth." Stuart nuzzled his stubbly cheek against hers. Della flinched at the sudden, intimate touch, but didn't pull away, not really feeling him. "Where do you think I was all those years? Working for the king? Nay! I was working for you. My life's work has been to make you happy."

"Tell me," she commanded, paralyzed.

"I came as soon as I discovered the truth, for I feared you were in danger." The smile was back fully on his face when she pulled away to look at him. Della could no longer smell the stink of his breath. Her body could no longer feel. Her eyes could no longer see.

"Tell me who they were? One of Lord Blackwell's men?" Della mentally ran their faces through her mind. Most seemed too young to have been there.

"Nay. It was Lord Blackwell," Stuart growled victoriously. He grabbed her arms and pulled her back against his body. Squeezing her painfully, he kept her from running.

"Stuart, Brant is too young. I remember the men being his age now when it happened." The acute disappointment threatened to choke her. She wanted to vomit.

"Nay, not Brant. His father," Stuart affirmed. "It was Blackwell's father. That is why you knew not to trust him at first. You must have felt the blood connection between them. That was before his pagan spells wove over your senses and blinded you to the truth."

"But how? Why?" She shook her head. Nausea continued to rise chokingly in her throat. Della shut her eyes. "I cannot believe—"

"Think on it Della. Blackwell Manor borders your own land. Mayhap he thought to take your land for his own. Mayhap he was a sadistic barbarian. Your mother was a very comely woman." Stuart let his hand drop from her shoulder, as if he knew she was not going to leave him. He was right. Her will had drained from her limbs.

Della turned to him, tears streaming freely down her face. She swayed on her feet. "But how—"

"How did he know you would be on the coast?" Stuart broke in with confidence. "Think, Della. His land is not far from here. He would have had spies in your father's house. A servant would hardly be noticed as she cleans. A small page could have easily been bought. Blackwell would have known exactly where to find you and your mother. Yea, it was even a captain who lured your father to drink that night, was it not? Captains. Ships. *Vikings*. It all makes sense."

Della could not deny that his words did indeed make sense. What Lord would not be jealous of Strathfeld land? It was envied, wealthy property with rich soils.

"She died for land?" Della asked in bewilderment. It didn't seem fair. It couldn't be true. "For petty greed?"

"Yea. And now, because of your marriage, the heathen's blood finally possesses that land she died for. If you stay with Blackwell, they will have won. So, it is Blackwell who must pay for the death in place of his godless father." Stuart clearly thought she couldn't deny him any longer.

"Nay." Della shook her head, proving him wrong. As the initial shock wore off, her sanity returned. "I will not punish the child for the sins of the parents. Give me the whole of your knowledge and I will ask Brant to seek out the truth. I am sure he will bring swift justice to the responsible parties."

"The sins of the parents flow through the blood of their children. It is in his blood, Della." Stuart paced back and forth, pulling at his short hair until it stood wildly on end.

"Nay. To believe that would be to say Rab deserved to be ill-treated for the adultery of his mother. I cannot give credence to such judgments and I know deep inside, you cannot either. Would you be judged for your father? Would you judge me by mine?"

Stuart stopped pacing and turned his cold, narrowed eyes to her—hating her logic, as it didn't fall in with his. As he spoke, his words increased in volume until he was screeching at her. "You are coming with me. This is my land. You will be my wife. You will be loyal to me. You will *love* me. That is the way it should have been, if not for your father's meddling. I am the rightful heir to the title of ealdor-man. I am the true lord of Strathfeld!"

"Nay, Stuart. You are mad." Della backed away from him in fright. The man before her was a stranger. The boy she had grown up with was gone.

Part of her wondered if he'd ever existed. His eyes rolled in his head as he raged more to himself than to her. He flung his hands frantically.

Ready to run from his ranting, she began to turn. Instead, she bumped into an iron clad chest and fell to the ground. Looking up in surprise, she saw Cedric.

"M'lady?" he asked, as he made no move to help her. His arms were folded over his chest. He glanced questioningly at Stuart and then back to her. The knight frowned, his red eyebrows furrowing as he studied her.

Della reached for him, knowing how bad it must look, her talking to a man who was forbidden from entering the castle. When Cedric didn't help her to her feet, she pushed herself to standing and dusted herself off before looking up at the young soldier.

"Cedric. Thank goodness it's you. Please, you must help me. My cousin, Sir Stuart, has gone quite mad. He thinks to be the Ealdorman of Strathfeld." Della rested her hand on Cedric's arm as she motioned to Stuart. As she turned, she froze at the smirk on her cousin's delighted face. Her heart sank from her chest.

"And so shall he be," Cedric gloated behind her in merriment. "So shall he be."

***

"I DON'T SEE any signs of a raid," Gunther said to Roldan. He reined in his horse as he motioned his hand along the evening sky. Their band of knights had ridden hard all afternoon. "There is no smoke, no signs of trouble, and I have yet to see a slaughtered cow."

As if to prove his point, a nearby heifer mooed loudly in the pasture. The sound caused the herd to move further away from the mounted men. Gunther's scowl deepened.

"Yea, it is odd. We passed the area it was supposed to be nigh on an hour ago. Methought perchance they had been mistaken in the location, but none of Strathfeld's people live beyond yonder ridge." Roldan shook his head. "This is not as it should be."

"I agree," Gunther said. Both men looked steadily at each other. His stomach tightened, as they turned to the men behind them. "Who reported the raid? Let the man come forward."

"It was Cedric," one of the knights hollered from the back. "He was left behind to guard Lady Blackwell."

"Yea, the coward volunteered to be a nursemaid," another knight offered. The soldiers laughed.

Gunther frowned at Roldan, who in turn nodded. Swallowing visibly, he looked around one more time. He gripped his reins and spurred his horse in a tight circle. Clearing a path through the men with his steed, he galloped toward the keep. Roldan was directly behind him.

"Back to Strathfeld, with much speed. There is

trouble at the castle," Gunther yelled, spurring his horse faster to race forth to Strathfeld.

The men's faces sobered and soon they beat a trail back toward the castle. Gunther feared they might be too late.

BLESSED SAINTS!

Della moaned as she fought for consciousness. Her heavy eyelids fluttered and she forced them open. All around her was ominous darkness and she could make out a faint humming, low and cheerless, coursing through her ears. Soon the humming turned to crackling and the darkness began to fade into an orange glow. She blinked several times, trying to focus her vision.

The strong odor of musty animal skins penetrated her nostrils. Even fainter, but not any less repugnant, was the smell of stale air and rotting wood. Shivering, she closed her eyes, willing the stench to go away. It only grew stronger with her concentration and she was forced to once again open her eyes.

The eerie orange light that radiated around her grew as her eyes shifted around in her head. Her temples throbbed as if someone had driven wooden spikes into her skull and she pressed her palms over her eyelids. When the pain lessened, she pulled her hands away and was able to focus on a decaying piece of timber. It leaned against a wood and earth wall. She was in an old cotter's hut.

Jolting fully awake, she realized she couldn't be at Strathfeld. There were no old dwellings like this on her land. Then she remembered Stuart and his declaration. Nausea rose in her throat, making it hard to concentrate. Her body ached terribly. She pushed up from the cot she was on, feeling the rub of dirty, matted fur under her hands. A matching fur had been thrown over her body for warmth. Though she tried to remember more, the last thing she recalled was Cedric's cruel laughter before her world had gone black.

"Yer awake."

Gripping the fur coverlet in terror, she spun around on the bed to face the bearer of the loud voice. Instantly she was sorry. White lights shot through her eyes with a searing pain. The pitiful, sullied chamber dimmed for a moment. "Cedric?"

"Yea." All formality was gone from his tone.

Della blinked several times. Cedric sat on the only chair in the chamber, one leg lifted to rest atop a roughly hewn wood table. The chair was tipped back on two legs and he chewed absently on a piece of leather that hung from his thick lips. Taking the strip from his mouth, he snorted and spat disrespectfully on the floor in her direction before putting the leather back between his yellowed teeth.

"Cedric, where have you taken me?" Della asked

as calmly as she could. The cottage had clearly been abandoned long ago and she doubted anyone would be left in the area to hear her cry out. "You know your lord will not take kindly to your kidnapping me."

"Now, the way I see it, his lordship might not care at all that you are gone." He didn't take the leather from his mouth as he spoke. "He didn't seem to care that you were there."

The venomous barb was calculatingly delivered. Trying to ignore his laughter, she lifted her shaking fingers to the welt on the back of her head. She winced to feel the wound covered in dry blood. "What did you do to me, Cedric?"

"Oh, that. It would seem m'lady fainted and fell upon my fist." He laughed harder and the piece of leather jiggled from side to side at the movement.

"You dared to lay a hand on me?" Della bristled in disgust. Her voice sounded weak, even to her own ears. She mentally checked her insides for any feelings of violation. Satisfied the welt was the only injury done to her, she sighed in relief. His insistent chomping turned her stomach and she looked at the crumbling fireplace instead. The low fire crackled, but didn't drown out the sound of his mouth. "You dare to lay hand on a lady?"

"You deserved it, making me churn butter." Sulking at her reprimand, he didn't meet her eyes. "It is woman's work."

"Why, Cedric? Do the codes of honor mean naught to you? You swore allegiance to Lord Blackwell. Your name will be forever scarred by this folly.

You will be blackened for eternity." Della focused her attention haughtily on him. She had years of practice behind her and knew how to handle fighting men. In her most commanding tone, she ordered, "Take me back and I will ask Blackwell to be lenient with you."

"You dare to question *my* honor? You, a faithless woman?" The leather dropped from his mouth, falling to the floor as he stood. Towering over her until she cowered on the bed, he sneered. "Where was yer honor when you took Blackwell to yer bed? Where was yer loyalty to my Lord Grayson?"

"Lord Grayson? What does my dead uncle have to do with this?"

"I have sworn my loyalty to the living Lord Grayson, rightful Ealdorman of Strathfeld."

Della frowned. He was calling Stuart, Lord Grayson? Stuart was only a knight.

"I didn't come to the manor with Blackwell, nor did I reside there under yer sire, but you would little notice a single soldier. The Vikings thought I hailed from the keep and yer sire's men thought I was with the Vikings. No one questioned my presence. Why would they? What with the commotion of the raids."

Della saw the truth reflected in the man's eyes. He was responsible for the raids, if not in whole, at least in part. And he'd shown her the Viking pouch. She refused to reveal her fear. "You killed those people? They were innocent."

"They were peasants. They had more use in death than they ever did in life." Cedric chuckled, pleased with his actions. Spit flew from his mouth and landed on her face. Della grimaced, wiping her cheek with the back of her hand. "You should have seen yer face when I held up my satchel. It was most amusing. We didn't expect you to come along that morn, but methinks I handled matters. And you believed the lie so readily."

"Where is my cousin? Send him to me at once!" Della straightened her spine, yelling up at him. "When he finds out what you have done—"

Cedric slapped her with the back of his hand, effectively spinning her words into silence. She touched her cheek in shock. When he lifted his hand again, she flinched. The man laughed.

"You would do well to remember that you don't command me, m'lady," Cedric broke in to her would-be protest as he withdrew his hand. He eyed her face and she knew a red handprint probably marred her flesh. It would turn into a bruise. His gaze traveled down to her breasts, ogling them as he lewdly continued. "Nor can you control what I do to you."

"You would not dare to lay another hand on me. If you do not fear my husband's wrath, then fear my cousin's. Do you think he will take kindly to your mishandlings?" Della tucked the furs under her chin. Pointing to the chamber door, she yelled, "Begone from my sight at once."

Again Cedric laughed maliciously. His whole body shook as he left without saying another word. Della's gaze fell on the discarded piece of wet leather on the floor.

What am I going to do? I don't even know where I am.

Cedric's blow caused the throbbing in her head to worsen. Nevertheless, she gave herself little time to dwell on her sorry state. Forcing herself into action, she edged to the side of the bed and made sure her gown didn't overly expose her body. She placed her feet on the floor and regally lifted her chin. When the door opened, she was ready to face Stuart.

"Stuart." She tilted her head in acknowledgement, watching him through cold, hard eyes. Balling her hand into a fist, she suddenly wished she knew how to fight with her hands.

"Della." He smiled his old, familiar smile and strolled into the chamber as if nothing was amiss. The look reminded her of the boy he'd been. His face was clean-shaven, his clothes laundered and pressed. When he smiled, the dimple in his cheek appeared to add an impish charm to his face. His eyes no longer brimmed with an insane red, but were clear and rested.

"Stuart, you must help me," Della beseeched him. For a moment, hope welled within her. Had she imagined the crazed Stuart? The one who had pronounced she was to love him and be his wife? This man standing before her could not have said those things. "Cedric is responsible for the raids. He killed all those people. You must—"

"Cedric informed me you knew the truth of it," Stuart interrupted with an understanding nod. When she tried to speak again, he hushed her like a child and she closed her mouth. "We did not expect that you would have gone to the site with the men. You had never ridden out before. You were never meant to see those things, only hear of it from Roldan. If I had known you would go, I would have found a way to detain you. I am sorry, Della. I never meant to hurt you. I love you."

"You knew?" Della refused to acknowledge his declaration of love. She had often told him the same when they were young, but not the way he said the word *love*. It was like a sleazy caress against her skin. His eyes were not the eyes of a friend. He was gazing at her as a lover would, like he knew her most intimate secrets. She wondered if his eyes had always been so daring. "Stuart, how could you? They were innocent people. They meant no harm to anyone, least of all you."

"Nay. They were peasants. Merely expendable peasants." Stuart glowered when she didn't return his sentiment. He moved as if to touch her, his fingers reaching for her sore cheek with a confused frown. Della flinched as he neared, jerking slightly. He lowered his hand and studied his dirty fingernails.

"But they were women and children," Della insisted, mindless of the warning echoes in her brain telling her to be silent. "They were innocent."

"I never imagined you would go out there, but it worked out nicely. It persuaded you to cast Lord Blackwell from your bed swiftly enough." Though his tone was regretful, he chuckled at his own private joke. His voice was no longer soft and kind, as he continued, "Peasants breed like rodents. A few will not be missed from my land. They will always be there to serve us, the strong. Do not worry so, Della. You will be looked after. Those who died served me more in their deaths than they ever could in life."

"Stuart," Della began again, gentler than before. Cedric had said the same thing and it was clear the traitorous knight had been fed the lies of her cousin. For a moment there was silence and Della thought she heard the soft pattering of rain against the thatched cottage roof. "They are not your peasants to command. They were people—Strathfeld's people. They were not meant to serve you."

Stuart frowned. "I am the true master of Strathfeld, Della."

"This is insanity. I told you already. The marriage *will* stand. The king himself was at the castle to bless the union. It was Guthrum's wish that Strathfeld and Blackwell Manor be joined and so they have. There is nothing to be done for it. You must go and find your own life. You must bring me home at once. Take me back to my castle."

"Soon, cousin, but first you must rid him from your heart. I hoped by bringing you away from him, it would be enough to release you from his pagan spell." He sat on the chair that had so recently held Cedric, pondering her through thought-veiled eyes. "I can see that it will take more time. Mayhap when you see his severed head before you, you will be free of him."

"Nay!" Della lurched forward. As her weight settled on her legs, the limbs did not hold. She fell back on the bed. It was as if a thousand sewing needles pricked her skin at the same time. Rubbing them in confusion, she glared at her cousin.

"Strange sensation, is it not?" Stuart laughed, unmoved by her emotion. "Serilda is indeed a talented woman. A bit of powder pierced into the legs at just the right spots and the muscles will be too tired to support you."

"Witchcraft," Della swore, terrified.

Stuart frowned, but did not answer. He bit at his lip, sucking air through his teeth to make a strange hissing noise before continuing with his insanity. "I see you still wear the barbarian's ring."

Della looked at her finger and touched the bronze band lightly. Remembering Brant's face as he'd told her the ring belonged to his mother, she was reluctant to part with it. She shook her head in denial, knowing what was to come. Grunting in frustration, her cousin stood and held out his hand.

"Give it to me." Not waiting for her to comply, he instead leaned over and jerked it roughly from her finger. Without looking at it, he dropped it into the small satchel at his waist. "I will give you a jewel as large as you wish—not some silly heathen's ring of bronze and amber."

Eyeing the satchel helplessly, her heart pounded in a painful rhythm. There was nothing she could do, nothing she could say. This man was not the cousin she loved. This man was a stranger. The Stuart she knew was dead.

"Serilda is outside. She will see to your head." Stuart turned to go, only to stop at the door. "And to your cheek. You really must be more careful in the future. I'm sure that bruise was not there earlier."

"Nay," Della answered, vehemently. "I don't want that whore touching me."

"So be it for now." He gestured with a sigh of indifference. "But, sooner or later, she will have to attend you."

Her flesh crawled as his gaze moved to her stomach and then back to her face. Della read the meaning in his expression, but she couldn't believe it. "Just what do you mean? I do not need her help."

His amused laughter echoed so terrifyingly loud that Della imagined the rafters shook with the force of it. She edged away from him, no longer able to feign bravery. When he finished, he shook his head and refused to answer. With a gallant bow, he left her alone in the chamber, locking the door behind him.

Terrified, she tried her legs. They failed her and she fell back into the small cot with a heartbroken sob. What was she going to do?

Della hit the wall, trying to break through the rotted wood. It was stronger than she'd imagined. Her knuckles scraped along the rough surface. The wounds were superficial, though some did bleed. It didn't matter. Even if she could break through the walls, she couldn't crawl to safety before being discovered. She wouldn't even know which direction to go.

Lying back in the bed, she rested her hand over her eyes to block out the firelight. Despair welled within her and a tear trickled from beneath her fingers. Silently, she prayed for the protection of her child and the safe deliverance of her husband. But, as she thought the words, she wasn't sure anyone heard them.

BRANT SHOOK HIS HEAD, leaning back so his hair fell away from his face. A relentless rain pelted him and his troops. The knights huddled on their mounts, trying to stay warm beneath the thin cloaks they carried. Their horses' hooves dragged sluggishly through the muck in steady thuds. The foul weather notwithstanding, it was good to be going home.

Brant hated the politics he had been forced to endure, and no peace would be met between King Alfred and King Guthrum, though neither party admitted as much. The entire evening they were together had been filled with drinking and the silent measuring of each other's resolve. The kings talked of many noble things and agreed on none of them.

After the long meeting, King Guthrum gave Brant and his men leave to ride ahead. Guthrum's political campaigning would take him away from Strathfeld. Although no war had been declared, Brant feared that soon one might be—if not a war with King Alfred, then a battle with his beautiful Della. He was not sure whom he feared most—a great army or his wife.

They approached the isolated wall of Strathfeld and he reined his destrier on the stone path before the main gate. It stayed closed, shutting him out of his own home. The horse's hooves pawed restlessly beneath him, sensing his displeasure. He motioned to a knight to hold up a banner. The man obeyed, waving the blue cloth before the wall.

Frowning, he briefly wondered if Della locked him out. He'd known she would be angry at his hasty departure, but he didn't fathom that she would be so bold as to openly defy him in front of his men. Even if she did, Gunther would not stand for it.

He looked over the long line of drenched men-at-arms. With a grim sense of foreboding, he slashed his hand toward the knight, ordering him to drop the banner. The manor was eerily quiet. He studied the wall, but saw no guards, no signs of attack. Taking his stallion by the reins, he galloped along the edge of the moat, around the side of the outer bailey wall, trying to gain a watchman's attention with the sound of pounding hooves.

"Edwyn!" Brant yelled into the wind several times. The man probably couldn't hear him in the stormy weather. Spurring his horse back to his men, he sat astride his steed and pondered the length of the wall. Instantly, he thought of Della's secret entrance, but knew that it would be a shame to have to make its presence known to the men if it were not necessary.

After several baffled minutes of staring along the dreary stone not knowing what to do, he heard the bridge begin to lower. The wood creaked slow and steady as it neared the ground. The sound was unnervingly loud in light of the abandoned wall. His gut clenched with apprehension, as he led his knights forward. Straightening his shoulders, he bravely faced whatever was ahead. He almost hoped it was an army and not an angry wife. An army he could well handle.

Brant laid his hand on his sword and several of his men did the same. Through the mist of the heavy, gray droplets, he recognized Roldan's form shadowed on the other side of the bridge. The man waved him forward.

Brant urged his horse forward carefully, scanning the manor for any sign of life. The bailey yard was empty of both people and animals. When finally the ealdorman pulled his horse to a stop and dismounted with no incident, he let his body relax and released the hilt of his sword.

"M'lord." Roldan rushed to Brant's side. His wan expression apologized for the delay. "Please, quickly come inside."

"Is aught amiss?" Brant held the horse's reins, not moving to go indoors. His chain mail clanked quietly. The rain was breaking, making it just clear enough to be bearable. "Where are the guards? Why are they not at their posts? Where is Gunther? What has happened here?"

"It's Lady Blackwell," Roldan said bluntly, when it was obvious his lord was not to follow him in.

"What is it?" He tensed, glancing around the yard in vain, as if he could will her to appear. "Has she gone ill?"

"She is gone," Roldan said. "Cedric reported a raid to some of the men, who in turn reported to

Gunther. When we went to check it out, there was naught there. We rode back as fast as we dared, but Della and Cedric were missing when we got here."

"When?" Brant again searched the inner bailey, eager for any sign of his wife, for any hint that Roldan was mistaken.

"Yestereve." Roldan motioned the riders toward the stables and started to grab the reins from Brant's hand. "Gunther is out searching e'en now."

"Nay." Brant refused to give up the horse. He gripped the leather straps tight.

"I was about to send riders to search fer you. Edwyn is writing missives e'en now, for we did not know where you were or when you would be back. Methought it best to send most of the men with Gunther—hence the empty wall." Roldan motioned to a passing soldier and ordered, "Bring my horse at once. I ride with the ealdorman."

Brant lifted his face to the darkening sky. Searching for his wife would be hard in the black rain of night. Any tracks would've melted away and no doubt Cedric would be long gone. His heart beat erratically in his chest and he, who was generally not afraid of anything, felt his hand tremble in fear.

Afraid of naught except the idea of losing my Della.

Brant swore under his breath, waving the knights who had ridden with him inside to rest. Then, swinging his tired body back onto his horse, he didn't wait for Roldan to mount. Brant tore from the castle as if pursued by demons with Roldan trailing quickly behind him.

DELLA SCOWLED AT SERILDA, who in turn glared back at her maliciously. Their eyes waged a silent war until the midwife finally turned away first to wipe her fingers on her dirty apron. Huddling underneath the matted fur coverlet, Della's body still quaked from where the woman had touched her. Stuart hadn't even left during Serilda's forced examination, choosing instead to hold down her arms. Her cousin's eyes roamed freely over her exposed thighs and stomach and when she'd tried to kick Serilda, he had threatened to call Cedric to hold her legs. Della had let the woman examine her.

Stuart followed Serilda's silent beckoning and they retreated to the far corner of the chamber. Della tried to hear their fervent whispers, but could only make out the tones of their voices, not the words.

"It is true then, Della?" Stuart glared at her. "You carry his bastard in your belly?"

"It is not a bastard. We are wed." Della protectively cradled her stomach. "So you see this is pointless. Even if you kill the father, the child will live and he will be the heir to Strathfeld. You cannot kill us all and still be ealdorman."

Stuart chuckled, though his eyes were filled with disgust as he looked at her protective hand. "Foolish cousin, to believe there are not ways to rid a woman of a child. You just cannot see the greater scope of things. You were always foolish though, cousin."

Della had begun to see what others did in him.

She'd spent much of her life feeling sorry for him, when he was indeed the animal people had called him. He'd murdered innocent people and now planned to murder her unborn child. He was no better than the men who had attacked her mother. He was right in calling her foolish. She had been a fool—a fool for believing in him, in defending him, in wanting to have married him.

"As was your sire," he continued in a contemptuous whisper.

"My father was a great man." Della gritted her teeth. "How dare you speak ill of him. He was thrice the man you could ever wish to be."

"Yer sire was a fool," Serilda chimed in with a sneer. "Why else would he trust me to tend his wounds with poison?"

"Serilda!" Stuart sliced his hand through the air for silence, stepping in front of Serilda to hide her from Della's view.

"You knew of this, Stuart?" A wave of queasiness drifted over Della. "How could you? My father took you in, raised you as his own son."

"His own?" Stuart spat. "If I were his own, he would have given me the title I deserve. Instead, he gives it to that barbarian Viking. Your sire had to take me in. It was his duty to do so. He had no love for me."

"Yea, he knew. We would plan it while in my bed," Serilda gloated, ignoring Stuart's hiss for silence. She skirted around her lover to face Della. "As soon as you wed with him and produce his heir, you will come to yer tragic end. I will be Lady Strathfeld and you will be a corpse."

"Serilda, silence!" Stuart warned before looking properly apologetic.

"You will never be a lady, Serilda. Murderous whores can never be ladies," Della proclaimed. "You are a fool to believe he would marry you. The best you can hope for is to be his mistress."

"Yea, it would seem I am surrounded by a company of fools." Stuart laughed, clearly liking the idea that the women argued over him. Giving Serilda a gentle push toward the door, he ordered, "Serilda, go attend Cedric. I promised him you'd see to his pains. Then ready yourself to depart."

The midwife left, pouting, "His pains are hardly worth lifting my skirts fer."

Stuart waited a long moment in silence. He paced the room thoughtfully before coming to sit on the edge of the bed. When another door slammed, he said, "You are quite right to believe that I will not marry her. She was merely a necessity. I don't care for her."

"You had my father killed." Della balled her hands into fists, wanting to punch the smirk off his face and the self-satisfied gleam out of his eyes.

"Also a necessity," Stuart admitted. "I did it for you, for us. Everything I have ever done has been for you. Your father sold you to a barbarian. I sought to free you from that bondage. You needed a friend. I was your only friend. You needed a husband who would not harm you. I offered to be that husband. I waited for you, but you had little faith to wait for me. I find the murderer of your mother and you spurn me for it. I have done everything in my power to make you happy. I loved you and you betrayed me by bearing the brat of that Viking inside you!"

Her blood ran cold until a numbing pain made its way over her limbs. "You kidnapped me. You murdered innocent people. Do not say you did that for me. I never asked it of you."

"You did ask me to marry you, to be your husband. You begged me to save you from the marriage bed."

"I was a child."

"You still are a child, foolish cousin."

"I never asked you to kill for me."

"I did what I had to."

"You kidnapped me."

"Nay, I rescued you! Why must you insist on seeing everything as it is not?" Stuart's pacing turned frantic and he started mumbling to himself as he shook his head. "Nay, you will see soon enough. Serilda will deliver my message for Brant and he will come alone. When I present his head to you, you will see that he is dead to you and that you do not care. Then after Serilda cuts the child from your body, we will wed. And you will see. You will…"

Della slowly nodded her head, but Stuart's words rambled on. She realized yelling at Stuart would not aid her cause against him. Angering him would not see her and her child safely home. She did her best to hide her distaste as she said, "You may be right. I feel as if my head is beginning to clear with the logic of your words. He has woven a spell around me. He has poisoned me with his pagan ways. At the wedding feast, he gave me this drink. Methinks there might have been blood in it."

Stuart brought his head up sharply to stare at her, looking as if completely unaware that he had been speaking aloud. "You mock me."

"Nay." Della widened her eyes with what she hoped was innocence, lowering her face so she looked at him from beneath the thick of her lashes. She'd never been one to play the docile maid, but she gave the performance all she had. Pouting, she said, "If only I could stand to comfort you, sweet cousin, but my legs still do not work. I have been selfish, have I not? You have been through so much and I have done naught but live in the comfort of Strathfeld. I should have waited, but it had been five years. Methought you had forgotten me. It's your fault for not sending word to me that you still cared. I was jealous. And then I see you with that woman, Serilda. It makes my blood run cold to think you—"

"Yea." Stuart gave her a hesitant smile. She knew part of him desperately wanted to believe her, but there was uncertainty in his gaze, as if part of him still mistrusted her. "You will stand sooner than you think. But, if this is a trick, I will cut the legs out from under you."

"Nay, it is no trick." She paused before suddenly lifting a finger in the air, as if struck by a sudden idea. "Quick, what note do you send? A ransom? Nay, it will not work. He is too smart to come alone to such a demand. Methinks you would want him to come alone. It would be pointless to kill your future knights, and you would not want them to witness your victory for they are stupid and would not understand. Nay, it would not do at all to have the others there. And just ask Cedric. Lord Blackwell would not part easily with money. He would not pay a ransom for me."

"Nay, he will come." Stuart shook his head. "He knows of the child—"

"Nay, he knows nothing of the child. The king took him away before I discovered it. If Serilda would have told me the truth, the ransom would work for then he would know I carry his heir. Nay, don't ask for ransom." Della narrowed her eyes in deep thought. Stroking her lips to hide their trembling, she said, "Bring me a quill and some parchment. He knows the look of my hand and Edwyn can confirm it. I will send him word to meet me—alone. He believes himself to be in love with me. He will come. His pride will make him. Besides, he thinks I am his property and he will want his property back."

"But you just said that he would not part with the money to ransom you." Stuart furrowed his brow in doubt.

"Stuart, you know as well as I that *his* love is naught more than male vanity. I would wager male vanity is quickly put aside for a gold piece." Della saw Stuart desperately wanted to believe she'd changed. "And if not his love, then his anger will bring him to collect me. He will not think kindly of his property disappearing."

Stuart pondered the logic of her answer. Suddenly, he smiled at her cunning. "Yea, cousin. It would seem you are indeed free from his spell. Write your missive."

Della nodded, grateful that he hadn't seen through her lies. Stuart hurried from the room to gather a quill and paper. Already she composed in her head what must be carefully worded. For, unless she warned him, both Brant and her unborn child would be lost.

23

MY LORD HUSBAND,

If those words of love you have whispered to me bear any truth, then meet me where the large oak bends to the east. Roldan will point you in the direction. Prove your love and come alone, I will explain everything then. Until dusk this eve, my love.

Della

Brant's hand trembled as he grasped the missive in a clenched fist. The crumpled parchment weighed heavily, like a sword he could barely lift. Forcing his hand to relax, he watched a maid walk by with a bundle of clean linens draped over her arm. He recognized the woman, but didn't know her name. The pug-nose servant eyed him curiously as she passed, but didn't stop in her duties.

The parchment had been tacked onto the head table of the main hall and had only his name on the outside fold in the tight, feminine script of his wife. Along the crease was a dried blot of candle wax and a faint impression that Brant knew to be his wife's wedding ring. He looked about the manor for sign of anyone watching. There was no one, save Isa, in the hall.

"Isa, did you see who placed this here before you found it? Did you see anyone unusual?" Brant swallowed hard, as he again read the ominous message. He tried to find hidden meaning within the words and could not. His hand trembled and he crushed the missive once more in his fist.

"Nay, m'lord, there was only the missive and since I cannot read, methought only to get you." Isa craned her neck to look at the parchment. Her eyes were lined in worry, but they did not follow the words. "Is it about m'lady?"

"Nay, it's from m'lady," Brant mumbled. He thought back to the night he whispered his love to an unresponsive wife. She hadn't acknowledged it until now.

But, why now? Why after disappearing for days with no word?

Brant blinked heavily to hide his anguish. Had she truly only run away to escape him? To mayhap think of what she wanted? And why would she involve Cedric, she had no connection to the man. Brant shook his head. The questions were no different than the ones he'd asked himself since learning of her disappearance. The eve before he'd searched endlessly with Roldan, unable to find a trace of her.

Brant had even examined the tunnel closely. There was no indication of her having gone through, however there was no proof she hadn't. Edwyn knew nothing. The servants knew nothing. Even the guards, who had been left while Gunther, Roldan, and the others investigated the raid, knew nothing. She had disappeared and now he cursed himself for not caving in her secret tunnel.

Della had said one might need the passage to escape. Had she meant to escape him? Were the clues all there, just waiting for him to figure them out? He wasn't sure he liked where the facts pointed.

"Isa, find Gunther and Roldan. Have them meet me by the gate." Brant didn't wait for a reply as he made his way to the stables. He hadn't slept for nearly a sennight and the exhaustion only fueled him on. His heart pounded in low, hard thuds and his gut hurt terribly. A cold breeze whipped his long tunic about his legs, but he barely felt it.

"M'lord!" Rab ran toward him. "M'lord!"

"Nay, Rab, not now." Brant held up his hand to stop the boy from coming closer. "I have no time for childish games."

"Nay, m'lord. It is not a game," Rab insisted. He jogged next to Brant, trying to keep up with the larger man's gait. "Please, m'lord."

Brant stopped at the entrance to the stables. Yelling into the darkness, he barked, "Boothe, my horse!"

"M'lord," Rab pleaded, his voice cracking in near hysteria as he pulled at Brant's sleeve.

"Begone, Rab," Brant said, as he had for the last several days when the boy tried to approach him. He knew the boy was close to Della, but did not have time to coddle him like a babe.

Rab flinched and began to walk away. Suddenly he turned, mustering up his courage. "Nay, I must speak with you."

Brant lifted a brow. If he hadn't been so tired, he would've found much amusement in the lad's show of strength. "All right. Be quick."

"It's about Serilda. She was here." Rab took a brave step forward and stopped. "I saw her sneak through the manor. Methinks Edwyn hides her in his chambers, fer she is still in there."

"Edwyn? And Serilda?" Brant inquired skeptically.

"Yea." Rab nodded. "I didn't want to believe it, but I stood guard and watched the door until just now when I saw you. She is still there. She ne'er came out."

"Boy, I have no time for this." Brant turned to go. What did he care about the midwife?

"But, m'lord, Serilda is in love with Sir Stuart. He visits her. I have seen him swim across the moat. When I tried to tell Edwyn, he laughed at me and said I imagined it, but now Serilda hides in his chamber. And Sir Stuart, when you played that game, he said that he would take what was his. Was not Lady Blackwell his?"

Brant hardened at the reminder. "Who told you that?"

"I was hiding under a table. No one ever notices me." He kicked at the dirt. "I meant no harm. I just wanted to watch. Methought you would fight Sir Stuart over m'lady."

"Go on." Brant turned the full force of his attention to Rab.

"And Lady Della told me a secret the day she left. I was the last one with her." He kicked the dirt again. "I promised not to tell what it was."

Brant froze and suddenly wondered why he hadn't thought to talk more in-depth to the boy. Every time the child had tried to approach, Brant shooed him back.

"But I know, m'lord, that she was not thinking of leaving Strathfeld. She told me there could be a plague between these walls, but if e'en one person remained within them, she would not leave. She said she would ne'er leave here, leastways, not without me." Tears came to his eyes. "She ne'er lies, m'lord. Not to me. She would ne'er leave me behind."

"That was her secret?" Brant asked, confused. A small flame of bittersweet hope kindled in his heart despite the hollow pain that resided there. Although everything pointed against it, mayhap she hadn't left him willingly.

"Nay, the secret I promised not to tell." Rab clenched his lips tightly together, as if the secret might slip out.

"Rab, I'm your lord and your leader. You swore your allegiance to me. Do you remember what we said about the field of battle? When you are fighting, there can be no secrets between the men and their leader. If there are, people die." Brant shook. It took all his strength to keep from grabbing the boy and shaking the secret out of him.

After deliberating, for what felt like an eternity to Brant, Rab nodded. "Yea, I remember."

"Lady Blackwell is a smart woman. She knows this also, and right now we are in battle over her. She knows you must tell me and will not be angry. If she does get upset, I will take the blame. I will tell her I tortured it out of you." Brant took a deep breath. Boothe came from behind with his horse.

After some considering, Rab agreed, "Yea, m'lord. You are right."

Brant took the reins and motioned Boothe away. Gunther and Roldan approached in the distance. "Tell me, Rab."

"She carries a babe. Yer babe."

Brant wasn't sure if it was joy or fear that took hold of him. *A child? My child? Della carries my heir within her belly? Why would she not tell me?*

"We ride?" Gunther asked.

Brant stared blindly at the child. Rab paled and took a step back. When Brant turned to Gunter and Roldan, he noted their weary but willing expressions. "Yea, we leave at once."

"Do I ready the men, m'lord?" Roldan asked.

"Nay, we ride alone." Brant swung onto his stallion, nodding at Rab before urging his horse toward the front gate.

"Bring her back, m'lord!" Rab yelled.

Brant stopped outside the castle only long enough to gain Roldan's directions to the oak tree. None of them wore armor, not having taken the time to put it on. The only weapons they carried were the swords hanging in fleece-lined scabbards, their daggers, and their grim determination to see the countess back safely. Overhead, lightening burst, streaking across the sky to light their way, followed by the booming sound of thunder.

***

TIME WORE on until Della had no idea how long she stayed in the cottage. Hours felt like days and days like years. The longer she remained within the walls, the dingier the place appeared. Stuart didn't let her out of the room, not even to relieve herself. Serilda served as her handmaid, though the woman was hardly a dependable servant.

It was impossible to judge the number of days that passed by the meals they served her, for the food was scarce and unpalatable. She was weak from the lack of nourishment and sleep, but clung to the faint hope that she would someday see Brant again. It gave her strength like nothing else could.

Stuart did not order her legs pricked with the witch's powder again and she was slowly able to walk. But her body ached, and she was never left completely alone, not even to sleep. If Stuart was not with her in her chamber to keep her in distressed company, then Cedric or Serilda were just outside her door. Any little sound she made, whether it was to stand or simply turn over too loudly on the cot, they were in her room eyeing her like she was trying to escape.

Unable to rest, Della spent hours staring into the orange flames of the fireplace. They reminded her of her fiery husband. She replayed every moment with him in her mind, until each detail was remembered and every memory was emblazoned on her heart. When she closed her eyes, she saw his piercing blue gaze and the slight curl of his half smile.

The more she thought of him, the more she knew she had been wrong about everything—her view on their marriage, her esteem for her cousin, her blind hatred of his people. Brant had been nothing but understanding and kind, and she'd repaid him with every cruel insult she could think of. He'd given her space after her father died, had taken care of her and, when she was ready for him to be, he'd been a gentle lover. And how did she repay him? She'd banished him to Blackwell for it.

Although the image of him was always in her heart, she forced it from her mind. She could not think of him when Stuart was near. Her cousin would see the sadness and would know she longed for Brant. If Stuart suspected the truth of her heart, then she would not be able to save her husband or their child.

Another chair had been brought in and placed next to the table. As Stuart set yet another trencher of unsavory food before her, Della couldn't help but eye the excessively molded cheese in disdain. She strained to smile, though the motion was tight and felt as if it might crack her face. Her forced pleasantry drained her senses and she was frightened she might make a mistake.

"Stuart?" Della looked at her cousin.

He took a seat across from her, smiling as if they dined like royalty. His eyes glimmered with an innocent light, which still amazed her with its clarity. He nodded gallantly at her, permitting her to speak. "Yea, Della?"

"Did you deliver the missive?" Della refused to look into his eyes for too long. The brown orbs were so familiar and it pained her greatly to gaze into them. They were the same eyes he had turned to her as a child and she wanted to hate him, but she could not find it completely in her heart to do so. There was a deep past between them, so many tears and so much pain. Della wanted to reach into his soul and find the scared, half-starved little boy who'd come to her so lost. She hoped to see a glimmer of that lonely child within the man. Everything between them couldn't have been an act, could it?

Seeing that he watched her closely, she busied herself by tearing the green and white mold off the cheese. She set it aside on the trencher, forming a small pile. Deciding she was too squeamish to eat, she set it down and picked up her goblet of sour ale.

"Yea." He took a contemplative bite of bread, frowning slightly at the pile of torn cheese mold. His gaze hardened and his mouth formed into a grim line of hatred. "It was delivered this morn."

"How did you do it? What if he does not see it?" She didn't want to seem overly anxious so she took a small bite of the exceedingly salty venison. The meat was dry and hard to chew. Della looked for a way to spit it out without being obvious. Finding nothing, she was forced to swallow the offensive morsel with a gulp of the sour ale.

"Serilda used the secret entrance. She said it was easy, for none of the men were about the bailey yard. Methinks they must be looking for you." Stuart suddenly frowned and fingered his goblet. "Do not worry your pretty head about the details. I will protect you. It will be over tonight."

"But what if Brant, uh, Lord Blackwell is not back from the king's campaign? We should give him more time."

"He is back. Cedric watches the castle." Stuart took another pensive bite. He narrowed his eyes as he watched her for any sign of disloyalty. She concentrated on keeping her face icily calm.

Della nodded slowly and forced a smile, praying he could not read the pain in her heart. "You have thought of everything. So, when do we leave for the large oak?"

"We?" Stuart laughed. Leaning over, he patted her hand, which had fallen indifferently from the food to the table. "Oh, Della, do you think I would put you in harm's way? I love you too much for that. I am sure everything will go as planned, but I will not risk you."

Della tried not to visibly gag. She pulled from his grasp and moved to take another bite. Her hand trembled violently and she buried it in her lap. "But methought you wanted me to see——"

"You will not see him alive again." Stuart interrupted her with a silencing wave of his hand, leaving no room for argument. "I merely said you would see his severed head. I would not force you to watch anything as atrocious as a beheading. I know well how such things have hurt you in the past. Your heart is too soft for this world, so I will protect you from it."

All I need protecting from is you, dear cousin.

Della cringed inwardly, drawing her emotions as far away from him as she could until her mind and body became numb to the pain he caused her. She hated how he claimed to be protecting her. Acknowledging him with a curt nod, she suddenly wished she had been more conscientious of the secrets she told him as a child.

Stuart looked at her side of the trencher. "Of that you may be certain."

"Then you will face him alone?" Della leaned over, trying to draw his attention away from her uneaten meal. He had already threatened to force feed her if she continued to starve herself.

Breathless, she waited for him to answer her. If Stuart was to fight Brant, fair and alone, there was a small hope they both would come out of the fray unharmed. Her cousin would be no match for her husband with the sword and Brant, being merciful, might let Stuart live so she could get him help. Even now, she did not wish her cousin dead.

"Nay, I will send Cedric and William. They are

warriors and know naught else. I am a nobleman of cunning and wit. There is no need for me to fight. Battle is for the mindless drones who cannot think for themselves. This is a new age we are upon, Della. There is no need for leaders to fight." Stuart rose from the table, stretched his hands over his head and yawned. "Yea, they will go. I will stay with you, for you might have need of me as Serilda works."

Della shivered, getting his meaning. Tears threatened her eyes and she rubbed them viciously with the back of her hand. She forced herself to yawn so she might hide her face. They meant to take her husband and baby at the same time. "William?"

"You have not been introduced to him." Stuart dismissed. "There has been no need for it."

Della nodded, afraid to ask why. She said no more as she turned solemnly back to her meal. Under Stuart's probing gaze, she took a bite and then another until he finally left her alone in the chamber. When he was gone, she vomited into the corner, sobbing silently. Then, falling to the floor, she hit her fist against the dirt, unable to fight, unable to push her body up.

May God be with you, Brant, and my heart also.

24

DELLA SENSED, without looking, that the evening would be wet and gloomy, just like her soul. She rubbed her stomach, trying to keep from resting her hand protectively over her child when Stuart was around. His eyes were always on her and a few times he'd even asked about it. She put him off the best she could with a halfhearted smile, but could tell he was suspicious. He refused to leave her alone and there had been no chance of escaping within the last hours of waiting.

"Stuart?" Della inquired, disturbing him from his preoccupation with the fire. They had both been silent for so long, her voice cracked.

Stuart turned to her and smiled pleasantly. He rested against the back of the chair, his feet upon the table. "I was thinking of the time I convinced you to pour a bucket of water on Edwyn from the wall. Do you remember?"

"Yea, you had been at Strathfeld for only a few

years. You said he was afraid of water and I was to help him with that fear, going so far as to help me haul the bucket up the ladder. Then you put a clump of mud in it and I doused him in muck instead."

Stuart laughed and his feet landed with a thud on the floor. "You were so mad at me you swore you would never talk to me again."

"Yea, Stuart, I remember it well. You pestered me for hours until I was forced to forgive you and I only relented to quiet your persistence."

It was only one of the many pranks her cousin had played on her and the other hapless inhabitants of the keep, but the jokes had been the harmless antics of youth.

"And, if I remember correctly, Edwyn did not get mad at you either." Stuart sighed, his mind on the past. He chuckled to himself.

"Nay." Della watched him carefully. His eyes were distant, frighteningly so. "But my father was livid when he found out all we had been up to. He came home a few days after it happened."

Stuart's eyes clouded at the mention of the late Lord Strathfeld. "Yea, you were about seven years, were you not? Your father locked you in the tower and sent me away to my training."

"I was eight," Della said. She remembered the night her father sent him away. Stuart had already been in his teenage years. She'd cried endlessly at the unfairness. It was also around the same time she'd taken complete control over the duties of the manor. To cheer her, her father thought to put her in charge of the keep. Della wondered if the responsibility had done more harm than good, though she'd been grateful to be kept busy. "And he did not lock me in a tower, only my bedchamber until you were gone."

"Your father hated me. He banished me from the only place I was happy as a child. My father didn't want me. I could never please the man before he died."

"My father claimed it was not for the pranks that he sent you to your training, but because it was time for you to learn to be a man. You would not become a man hanging about a girl child all day. He did not hate you. In fact, you were only gone from Strathfeld for a short time. You came back oft to visit us and methinks your father bid you home on several occasions."

Stuart growled in the back of his throat, obviously not believing her. He stared back into the fire.

"Stuart, I need to go outside. I need to walk." Della spoke softly, drawing him gently back to the conversation.

"Nay. It's not a good idea for you to be out."

"Cousin, you don't understand." She hoped the heat coloring her features would be mistaken for a blush and not apprehension. "I have to get out of this chamber. I have to walk outside. In private."

"Nay, I see no need. If you must stretch your legs walk about the chamber. You will not be here much longer." Stuart waved his hand in the air to dismiss her request. "The feeling should have completely returned to them. I didn't order Serilda to prick them again."

Della tried not to scowl, wanting to spit in his smug face. He acted as if he bequeathed her with a gift. "I must relieve myself, dearest cousin. Please don't make me go in that dirty chamber pot again. Serilda does not wash it. She hates me and I must have some fresh air. Please."

"Oh." Stuart sat up. "I do not think I like you calling me dearest cousin."

"What would you have me call you then?" Della asked, surprised at the admission. "Lord Grayson?"

"Dearest husband," Stuart corrected. "Yea, let us pretend that we are already married. It will make the eve go by faster."

Her gut twitched as he stood and moved toward the bed. He smiled down at her, holding out his hand. She looked at it warily, unable to force herself to take it. Her eyes watered.

"Stand," he ordered.

Her gown was dirty, tattered, and stained to the point it no longer looked to be blue. The bruise on her cheek was still swollen and her tired eyes undoubtedly red. Yet he smiled at her as if he pictured her as the grandest of ladies in the most favored of places. Della wondered if he even really saw her.

"Stuart," Della began, only to be cut off by his hush.

"Stand," he commanded again. His voice lowered.

Della held out her shaking hand to him, unable to control her trembling.

Stuart, what has happened to make you so crazed? For surely madness affects you.

"You shiver at my touch," he whispered when she didn't speak. He lifted a finger to run along the length of her collarbone. "Do you know I have dreamed of possessing you since I first saw you? I knew then you would grow to be my wife and I waited for you. I bided my time until you were grown into womanhood."

Nausea fought its way up from her stomach, choking her. She coughed. Part of her still cared for her cousin, but not in the way that he did for her. She'd been a fool to think of marrying him, naive in her beliefs of what a marriage should be. Brant showed her there could be more than family alliances and the merging of property and fortune. "I shiver because of the draft."

"Still my shy little Della." Stuart chuckled. "Mayhap the barbarian did not poison you as much as methought. Could it be his tastes in the marriage bed are exaggerated?"

Della watched him carefully and didn't answer.

"I went to see your father on your fifteenth birthday. I asked him for your hand." Stuart's fingers had reached the opposite shoulder and began the languid journey back. He leaned closer. "He refused me."

"He did not tell me."

"I asked him again, each year after, until your seventeenth birthday. He refused me each time. I told him he would never keep us apart. I told him I would run away with you if he did not allow it. That is when he asked me to leave Strathfeld and never come back. He said he would kill me if he saw me near you again. I wasn't allowed to write to you."

"I swear he didn't tell me." Della tried to turn her face away, but Stuart grabbed her by her jaw. His grip bit into her bruises, forcing her to be still as he leaned forward to kiss her. She gasped, turning her lips from him as his hand traced along her cheek to cup her neck. His lips were cold and she felt the tip of his tongue brush her cheek. "We cannot."

"Why?" Stuart demanded in outrage. His grip tightened. "Am I not good enough for you? You would give yourself like a whore to that Viking—"

"Nay, it's not that." Della's mind raced for the right words. She stood frozen in place, too afraid to move completely away, of saying something he would deem inappropriate. The smallest insult would surely set him off. "It's you who are too good for me."

Stuart's surprise was audible as he pondered her reply. The heat of his breath hit against her neck. Finally, he leaned away and nodded in agreement. Giving her one last painful squeeze, he dropped his hand and took a step back.

"Stuart?" Della released the breath she'd been holding. "May I walk outside now?"

"Yea, let us stretch your legs. Serilda should be arriving back anytime." His expression saddened. "Methinks it might be awhile before you are able to walk again."

Her insides crumbled in despair and her breath quickened of its own accord. She could not control the shaking of her limbs. Until that moment, she'd somehow managed to remain calm. But as the minutes passed, she felt more and more helpless. Then she realized, with no small amazement, that she'd waited for Brant to save her. It hadn't occurred to her that he wouldn't.

"It will be all right, Della. After tonight you will no longer feel the pain of that heathen child in your belly." He picked up her hand and laid it on his arm. His arm flexed under her hand, but the press of his muscle left her feeling hollow and cold. He walked toward the door, escorting her out of the room, through a dingy front chamber and out into the small yard.

The outside light, though diffused in softness, hurt her eyes. Della squinted until she grew used to the brightness. Moist earth squished under her feet, causing her to slip in the dampened soil.

The cottage stood alone in a small valley, surrounded by nothing but forest and prairie. An overgrown garden grew near the front door, but looked to be unattended for several seasons. The air was thick with the threat of rain, though the darkest clouds were still far off. For a moment, Della just stood and breathed deep, cleansing pants of air.

From the corner of her eye, she saw the tree line. It was too far to chance running away. Already she felt a twinge in her abdomen and knew that Stuart would overtake her if she were to try.

A humid breeze stirred around them, sticky and moist. Her linen gown molded to her skin and the wayward strands of her hair stuck to her face. However, the air was fresh and Della found herself gratefully taking another deep breath. It was a blessing compared to the dank smell of the cottage.

Sighing, Della tried to slip her arm from Stuart's grasp. He didn't relinquish his hold. "Stuart, I should have some privacy for what I am about."

"Nay, methinks it's still too soon to risk—" His mouth snapped shut and he quickly turned his head to the sound of two approaching horses. The grip on her hand tightened as he pressed her more firmly against his arm.

Brant!

Her heart soared in hope only to have it fall again as she recognized Cedric and not her husband. He galloped to them, swinging off his horse to land on the ground with a heavy thud. Seeing her, Cedric gave her a mocking bow and quick smirk before turning to Stuart.

"You are late!" Stuart growled. His grip on Della's hand loosened somewhat as he jerked her forward, forcing her with him toward the dismounted knight. "What news do you bring from the castle?"

"We are here now." Cedric spat next to Della's feet. She jumped out of the way, pulling as far back from the man as she could manage. She watched the tree line, hoping to see Brant hidden within it, but found nothing.

"What are you letting her out for?" another man interjected. "She should be tied to a bed."

Della turned sharply toward the voice. She could not see the man's face for he was hidden behind his horse. A chill worked over her spine at the sound.

"William's horse lagged behind," Cedric complained. He ignored his riding companion's growl. "I told you that nag you stole would slow us down."

Della watched carefully as the man, William, came into view. He was large and dark, with a pointedly devious gaze. She felt the blood run from her face and her stomach lurched. Terrified, she tore her arm from her cousin's grip. Stuart let her go. Suddenly, a rush of memories flooded her, memories from the night of her mother's death. She backed away from them.

Della remembered William's face. He had been there. He'd spurred the other men on, leading them and encouraging them. How could she have forgotten it? She remembered his long black hair, how it framed the hard plains of his face, giving him a demonic cast in the orange firelight.

Black! They all had black hair and looked like foreigners from the far south! They were not Vikings. Why would my father tell me they were Vikings? No wonder they were not caught. They looked for the wrong men.

"Della?" Stuart asked, at her horrified gasp. He studied her face grimly. Reaching his hand to her, he curled the tips of his fingers as if to beckon her forward. Della denied the offer with a terrified shake of her head. She felt like a small child, cowering in the corner of her nightmares. Stiff and helpless, a flood of horror gripped her heart and pumped fear into her very being.

"He was there," Della whispered when she was able to utter a sound. She continued to back away. Her eyes stayed fixed on William, afraid if she blinked he would disappear and would never be caught. She pointed at the evil man. "You are the one. You tied my head to the post. You made me watch."

William glared at her, his expression confused. Her breathing quickened. How could he not know? Not immediately remember? Had his deeds over the years been just as bloody? Had they not marred his soul as they had hers?

Slowly, a smile of recognition crossed William's face. He nodded in remembrance before calmly stating, "The child we let live."

"You made the others... You murdered my mother. You killed her. You raped and burned her." Tears rushed down her face. Bile rose in her throat as the screams from the past echoed in her ears. She turned her desperate, pleading gaze to Stuart. "Stuart, it was never the Vikings. It was him. He did it. You must—"

"You have grown well, child," William broke in with a delighted laugh, his voice crackling in darkness. He didn't look as she imagined a villain would. His face was broad and proud, scarred only a little by pockmarks. His teeth, though a few were missing, were only slightly yellowed. But his eyes were deadlier than she could have ever recalled. He watched her closely and her panic only made his eyes glow in pleasure. "Methought I should see you again. You look like your mother. You have her eyes, as did I for a time—until they rotted."

"Why?" Her hand went to her throat. "Why did you kill her? She was a kind woman."

Stuart's stunned expression turned to a scowl of fury as he hissed at William, "I told you to stay out of her sight. I warned you. You have ruined everything!"

"Tell her, Stuart. Tell her why her mother died. Tell her of your father's greed for land. Tell her why I tied her head so your father could watch and command us from behind her. Tell her how he drank her brother's blood to seal his pact with hell." William laughed in wicked satisfaction, thoroughly enjoying the moment. He didn't take his eyes from Della as he spoke. Stuart's face turned dark in his fury.

"Stuart?" She eyed her cousin, hurt that his treachery could have gone so far. "You knew? All these years you have known? You knew and you tried to make me believe that Brant's father…"

Della couldn't continue. Tears blinded her to reason and her heart ached at the true depths of her cousin's betrayal. She started to turn, intent on getting away. Her feet slipped in the mud and she landed hard upon the earth. Pushing desperately at the slick ground, she righted herself, not knowing where she would run only that she must try. She took a hasty step toward the forest, but before she could get away something hard crashed against her temple.

Della stumbled, falling in a daze. She landed roughly on her hands and knees. Her fingers gripped the ground in pain. Through a fog, she heard Serilda cackling above her.

"I told you she wasn't changed," Serilda gloated. Della heard the woman circle her like a hunting beast. The salty flavor of blood filled her mouth and dripped to the ground. "We should kill her and be done with it. Then there will be no one left to naysay yer claim. You will be the only heir to the land."

And that was the last Della heard. Her limbs trembled as she tried to stand, wanting to defend herself against the treacherous midwife. She never reached her feet. Serilda leaned over and hit her head again, causing her world to go black.

STARS PEEKED through the purpling sky as the orange glow of the sun set against the horizon. The threat of rain was over for the moment, but the humidity the dark clouds brought was not. Brant listened to the forest. No animals made noise and even the insects were quiet. The wind picked up, blowing over the land, crashing the leaves together in a natural melody on the trees.

Brant slowly urged his horse toward the large oak. The old tree bent naturally to the east, just as Della wrote. He knew in his gut that his wife was not there, felt that she wasn't. He wasn't surprised, for he hadn't expected her to be.

Brant watched the trees, not knowing what to believe. He was no fool to think Della had meant it when she wrote she loved him. She'd said just the opposite to him on many occasions. But why the deception to gain his trust? Was she really so heartless as to throw his words of love into his face now? Or was it because she loved Stuart still? For it was with the help of Stuart and Serilda that she had her message delivered. He knew Edwyn played no part in his wife's deception, only that Rab had no knowledge of the secret passage. That was why the boy thought the elderly man helped the midwife.

Suddenly, an arrow whizzed by his ear, missing the lobe by less than an inch. Brant responded with an instinct born from years of combat. He charged his horse behind the protection of the oak's thick trunk before swinging swiftly to the ground. He landed silently on the moist earth and drew his sword as another arrow hissed by to land near his feet. He heard a string of curses before the forest went silent.

"Blackwell!"

"Yea," Brant yelled tersely. He straightened and relaxed his sword a bit, angling it toward the ground. "What was that all about?"

"Methought to give you at least a bit of sport this day," Gunther answered in return. Brant heard the smirk in his friend's voice. "Are you hit?"

"Nay," Brant growled. "Did you find the archer?"

"We got him," Roldan answered. Another curse echoed the forest and then a loud, pained grunt.

"Yea, his manhood fell on my foot. He will not be moving fer awhile."

Brant relaxed his guard and glanced around the wooden trunk of his sanctuary. He was barely able to move his head when a sword thrust deftly near his face. He struck up with his blade in one fluid motion to block the attack, returning the man's paltry blow with one of his own more powerful ones. Brant forced the hidden attacker to stumble away from the protection of the tree and into his view.

"Cedric," Brant acknowledged with a sharp growl. He shook his head in mocking amusement. The knight righted himself and swung around with a lift of his smaller sword. Brant once again deflected the blow. "Give this up, boy. You are no match for me. I have seen you practice. I know all six of your moves."

"Blackwell," Cedric spat in ire. His face turned red at the insult. "How is it I should be frightened by an old man who fights with the skill of a crippled elder woman?"

Brant grimaced at the poorly delivered slur as he blocked the man's assault. His broadsword dwarfed the man's smaller, slender Anglo-Saxon weapon. Cedric dashed his blade forward several times and each time Brant expertly countered the blow. The younger man lacked the skill to thrust his weapon close to the more experienced fighter. As Brant thwarted another attempt, Cedric turned quickly and took him by surprise. His blade glanced off Brant's unprotected arm, nicking his flesh enough to draw blood. Determined, Brant held back though he had perfect opportunity to kill the knight.

"Tell me where Lady Blackwell is," Brant commanded, as he darted away from an unsuccessful attempt. The metal of their blades met and clanged several times, drowning out any response. Brant ducked as Cedric swung wildly for his head. With each passing second, the traitor became more desperate.

"She is with her true husband, Blackwell. The true Ealdorman of Strathfeld."

"So you are loyal to Stuart, that son of a pig," Brant deduced with little surprise, getting more aggressive, pushing the man back toward the trees. His sword moved with such skill that the knight could do nothing but block the oncoming blows. "Where has he taken my wife?"

"She is not yer wife fer long. Not after I take yer head and collect my reward." Cedric tried to assault Brant from one direction and then the other to no avail. He backed his body closer to the forest. Sweat beaded on his worried brow. "And she was not taken anywhere she did not want to be. She begged me to take her to Stuart!"

Cedric's feet crunched on the dampened leaves. He saw red at the man's implications. It was as he feared. Della had gone willingly to her cousin. She had tried to set Brant up to die and she used his own words of love against him.

Cedric smiled at his opponent's fallen look and charged, angling is sword toward Brant's chest. A look of sweet victory crossed his mouth, but he was mistaken in thinking the pain of his words would lessen the ealdorman's guard. The anger only drove Brant onward, determined to live so he may find his lovely wife and strangle her. Brant moved from the inept knight's path, instead sinking his blade into the soft skin of Cedric's stomach.

Cedric gasped in surprise. Brant grunted as he forced his blade deeper. Blood ran thick from the stricken knight's mouth. Cedric's sword clanked awkwardly to the ground and he grabbed the sharp bladed edge of Brant's sword and tried to pull it from his body. The sword didn't move and Cedric lost a finger trying.

Brant watched the life drain from the man's eyes, unmoved by Cedric's silent plea for mercy. Cedric could not speak and when he opened his mouth, he choked on his own blood. It was too late for compassion, even if Brant had wanted to give it. Kicking the man from his sword, he turned his attention to the forest. The man fell to the ground, forgotten.

"Gunther! Roldan!" Brant ordered. Tortured, the pain in his chest was unbearable as he choked it down deep, trying to bury it.

"Yea." Gunther came forward.

"Stuart?" Brant asked.

"Nay, it was only Cedric and this one." Gunther helped Roldan drag a prisoner between them, each grasping one of the man's arms. The prisoner's legs were bound tightly together and his wrists were tied in the same fashion behind his back "We did not see

Cedric hidden behind the oak. Otherwise, we would have stopped him before he attacked."

Gunther dropped the man to the ground and Roldan let go soon after. The dark captive fell with a snort, hitting the dirt with his face. Rocking up, he spit out a tooth with a defiant look up at the men.

"He is William," Roldan said as the man thudded his feet hard on the ground next to Cedric's body. "He is willing to make a deal fer his life."

Brant nodded and stepped forward. He glared down at the man before nudging the prisoner's chin with the tip of his shoe. William's hands strained against the rope as he twisted to look up. Brant angled his toe so that it embedded in the tender part of the man's chin. A large, angry welt was on the side of his temple, showing through a tangle of his long, black hair.

"Let him speak," Brant ordered. The entire time, he didn't take his eyes from William. He dropped his boot and took a step away. Motioning his head, he ordered Roldan to flip the man on his back.

The knight obeyed, kicking William over before saying, "Speak."

"I will tell you where Stuart is," William panted. He looked at Brant and smiled. "I have no care who is Ealdorman of Strathfeld. I was hired only to do a task."

"A mercenary," Brant concluded with a frown. "An untrustworthy cur."

"Nay," William protested, not showing fear as he negotiated for his life. "That is why you can trust me.

I owe no allegiance and now have reason to betray him."

Brant nodded, bidding the man to continue. William might be his only hope of reaching Della and his unborn child. Listening, he made his way to gather his horse's reins. The well-trained animal hadn't moved.

"I will tell you where they are, in exchange fer my freedom," William offered.

"Tell me," Brant conceded, "and I will have you taken as prisoner to my castle. Do not and I will have you slaughtered like a sow right here and now."

"Then no deal," William said.

"If you tell me, I will have you taken prisoner until I have retrieved my wife," Brant paused, and enunciated in words this kind of man could under-stand, "my property. She is mine and I will have her back."

Brant raged inwardly, but his expression remained eerily calm. Even through his anger, he wanted Della safely home. He refused to say her name and it pained him to call her wife.

William grunted, starting to deny the claim. "She is—"

"But," Brant continued, "if you have harmed my property and thus insulted me in any way, I will have you killed for your offense to me."

William didn't move as he contemplated his options.

When the man didn't readily agree, Brant tossed his head to Gunther. "Gut him."

"Nay!" William denied, as Gunther reached into his belt for a knife. Gunther leaned over him with the blade and paused to look at Brant. William gulped, showing his first sign of fear. "I will tell you."

Brant tilted his head to order Gunther back.

"That is what methought." Gunther chuckled darkly. His hand rested on his knife.

"Speak," Brant ordered. "And make it good, lest I change my mind and kill you."

"Be still, Della." Stuart dug his fingernails into the soft skin of her inner elbow, holding her still.

Della struggled in protest. The ropes binding her arms above her head bit into her wrists, digging painfully into her flesh until she felt a raw sting with every jerk. Wrenching away from Stuart's touch, she shot him a deadly glare. Her cousin flinched at her blatant hatred, but soon found his composure.

She'd regained consciousness only to discover that she'd been gagged and bound to the cottage bed. Della paid little mind to the throbbing in her temple. Her fear outweighed any physical discomforts.

Serilda laid out devilish, gruesome instruments along a table, deliberately placing them within Della's view. A large, thin knife glinted in the firelight, as the midwife held it up. Della closed her eyes and looked away. Serilda chuckled. Stuart said nothing.

Pulling frantically against the ropes at her ankles, she found they too were strong. Desperate tears stung her eyes and her heart pounded so hard she felt it throughout her body. She muttered curses against the gag in her mouth, breathing heavily through her nose and refusing to look at Stuart. Pleading with him would do no good.

It hadn't taken her long to realize Stuart had known the truth behind her mother's death and of William's part in the deed. She'd read the hardened reality in their eyes before Serilda struck her.

Please God, don't let them take my baby. Don't let them take Brant from me. By all the Saints, don't let them harm my family.

Glaring at her cousin, she struggled against his hands on her shoulder. His touch repulsed her. She screamed against the gag.

"Quiet," Serilda said.

Della closed her eyes and continued to mutter every obscenity she could think of. She even found use of a few Nordic curses she'd heard from her husband when he didn't know she listened.

Serilda sharpened the gruesome knife against a grinding stone. "M'lady, it will hurt less if you do not move. I should hate to see you bleed to death."

"You will not cut her unnecessarily," Stuart told the midwife. "If she dies, you die."

Serilda paled and said nothing more, but her hand shook at the warning. Della whimpered, remembering the rough treatment she'd been given during the checking. With mounting fright, she realized Serilda planned on sticking the knife inside of her. She fought harder against the press of Stuart's hands, but her bonds held her fast to the bed like a metal vise.

She closed her eyes, too scared to watch as Serilda stopped grinding the blade. A tear trickled over Della's face and her heart yelled for Brant. She heard the midwife step toward the bed, her footfalls were the ominous sound of defeat. Della braced herself for what was to come. Fear welled inside her. The only thing she could think of was Brant and his smiling face. And she knew she would sooner die than live without him.

NIGHT WAS FAST APPROACHING and the evening sky blanketed the ground in its darkness. Brant sent Roldan back to Strathfeld with the prisoner before making his way to the abandoned cottage with Gunther. Everything was like the man had said. They had no trouble finding it and Stuart obviously hadn't expected his plans of an ambush to go awry because they had no difficulty sneaking inside.

As Brant stepped silently across the threshold of the cottage door, he lowered his drawn sword. The small room was musty and abandoned, and the fire pit was cold. Brant sniffed and could detect nothing that proved his wife had been there.

Turning, he motioned Gunther from the doorway, signaling his friend to check around the cottage before coming inside. Gunther nodded and ducked out into the shadows. Brant stepped into the room, worried he'd misjudged William's fear and that the man had lied to him. Then, out of the silence, he heard a muffled scream. Tilting his head to the side to better listen, he hardened his stance. A shuffling sound came from the back of the room. That is when he noticed the small door in the side wall of the front chamber.

Della! He began to rush forward, but then held back as heard the voices from the other side. Bile rose in his throat.

"Get on with it, Serilda." Brant recognized Stuart's voice. "It's taking you too long."

"Keep her still," Serilda answered. "Hold her legs open."

"It would be better if we could give her something for the pain. Did you bring none of your potions?" Stuart again.

"She had me tossed from the manor before I could gather my draughts. It's her own fault," Serilda returned, her tone harsh. A muffled sound followed the words.

"Della." Stuart's voice was strained, but then softened. "Keep still lest we are unable to get that heathen brat from your womb. It will only hurt for a moment and then you will be free of it."

Brant was sure his heart stopped beating as Della's stifled response answered her cousin. He hadn't wanted to believe that Della betrayed him. He didn't want to believe that she plotted to have him killed. But the evidence was too overwhelming.

And now she is killing my child, just as she first promised to do.

Without thought of his own safety, Brant smashed through the door in a violent rage. All he saw was his murderous anger as he glared at the chamber's occupants, taking it all in within a second. His wife was bound to the bed with a bit tied in her mouth to help with the pain.

Her skirts were thrown over her waist, lying bare her thighs and stomach for all to see. At his entrance, her eyes grew round. Stuart sat by her shoulders, possessively caressing the soft skin of her neck and Serilda kneeled between her thighs with a crude knife and a forked metal spike. Disgusted, Brant's blood ran cold.

"Blackwell," Stuart squeaked, his face instantly pale. "It's not possible. You should be dead!"

Serilda dropped her knife. The crude weapon landed on the dirt floor with a thud and she scrambled off the cot to retrieve it.

Della groaned and struggled against her ties. Tears fell from her eyes to leave clean trails on her dirty face. She stared at him, pleading with him. But for what? Mercy? Brant couldn't give her that. After her betrayal, he had none left. He had nothing left.

"Yea, it's very possible," Brant said, the words dark and passionless. "You sent a paid fool and a boy to kill me."

Stuart shot to his feet and looked hastily around the chamber for a weapon. His hands visibly shook as he didn't find one. Serilda lifted her knife and backed away slowly, refusing to give it over to him when he motioned her to come nearer.

"You would dare to kill an unarmed man?" Stuart asked weakly. "Think of your honor."

Brant didn't answer. Instead, he glared briefly at Serilda and then back to Stuart. "Serilda, drop your weapon and move away from her ladyship. Back yourself into the wall and do not move lest I be tempted to kill you as well."

Serilda did as he commanded. The long knife thumped on the floor. Out of the corner of his eye, he watched her as she moved around to the other side of the cot. Brant kept his raised sword trained on Stuart, making his way to the end of the bed.

Then, taking a deep breath, his insides trembling with apprehension, Brant glanced between Della's legs. A dirty handprint marred the white flesh of her thigh where the midwife had touched her. But he found there was no blood.

They haven't harmed the child.

Bittersweet relief flowed over him. Catching the frightened gaze of his wife, he had to look away.

Yanking at Della's skirt, Brant covered her sex before kneeling to retrieve the discarded knife. Tossing it at Stuart's feet, he motioned for the man to take the blade.

"Nay, it is not fair," Stuart whined. He side-stepped the knife, refusing to pick it up. "You have a sword."

Fury rose inside Brant. He gripped the hilt of his broadsword, wanting desperately to slay the man. His arm tensed and urged him to lift it. But, in the end, he could not bring himself to do it. He could not kill a defenseless man in cold blood. The deed would go against everything in his nature. He glowered at Stuart, willing the man to try anything that would justify his slaughter. Just as Brant was about to throw down his own weapon and beat the man with his bare hands, he heard Gunther's voice. It was calm as it drifted into the chamber from the door, and his words were the answer to Brant's bloody prayer.

"Then use this, you sniveling goat," Gunther shot in disgust.

Brant glanced at Gunther as he blocked the frame of the broken entryway. There was no other way out of the chamber. He held up his sword and waited for Brant to nod his approval before tossing it over. Stuart jolted away from the weapon as if it were a striking snake. The blade skidded on the floor, stopping as it hit his feet.

Stuart took a deep breath before leaning to pick up the weapon. He raised the blade as he stood, moving to lunge at Brant with a brutal yell. Brant knocked the effort aside and quickly thrust his sword into Stuart's gut, severing his spine with the force of his anger. Brant let go of the hilt as it stuck into the man's flesh.

The wounded Stuart sputtered and grabbed at his midsection as the sword he held once more tumbled to the ground. His legs weakened and became lifeless as his knees folded under his mass. Clutching his fingers around the hilt of Brant's sword, he tried to pull it from his body. His fingers weakened and he fell lifeless to the floor. It was over. Stuart was dead.

Brant leaned to pull his blade from the dead body, looking at the man's lifeless form in disgust. As he did, he heard Della's scream muffled by the bit in her mouth. He turned quickly to her. Serilda was poised above her, a vial of poison in her hand.

"Nay!" Brant exclaimed, recognizing the venom. From the corner of his eye, he saw Gunther's knife fly over his head to land in Serilda's shoulder. The vial flew back to avoid Della and the midwife fell wounded to the floor.

Brant gave Gunther a nod of grim thanks as he stood. After many breathless, silent moments, he looked at his deceitful wife. He stared furiously at her, tortured by her panicked face, her amber eyes glowing with a force he could not look away from. Her golden hair was matted and dirty, her skin was caked with mud and grime, and her blue dress was torn and stained. Brant didn't care about all that. He only saw the deceit he believed her capable of. He didn't trust himself to deal with her quite yet, and so turned to Serilda, who lay gasping on the floor.

"M'lord," Serilda panted. Her pale face was taut and her eyes narrowed with pain. Her lips moved as if to plead with him, but she would find no sympathy in the ealdorman.

Brant nudged her with his foot. Her injury was superficial, but for the vial of poison that had landed atop her. The thick liquid soaked through Serilda's overtunic, spilling forth into her wound and then to the dirt floor. She chuckled, her eyes glittering in the irony that her death was by her own hand. Her arms began to shake as the venom coursed through her veins.

"You will die by your own poison, Serilda," Brant stated flatly.

The woman made a strange noise in the back of her throat. Brant didn't help her. The midwife's gaze clouded over as a spasm of pain racked her body. Spit trailed from her mouth to kill off her laughter.

DELLA STRUGGLED against her restraints as she watched Brant in horror. He made no move to help her. Finally, he turned from her, as if wiping her from his sight in disgust. Tears of anguish attacked her heart and shook her body with his rejection. His handsome face held no tenderness for her, no relief, no hope. It was her worst fear. He didn't care for her, and only came to her rescue out of pride and mayhap a sense of duty.

Brant motioned Gunther to wait outside the chamber. When they were alone, he turned back to her. His stare was detached as he walked to stand over the bed.

Della fought her restraints, desperately wanting to hold him. Tears coursed down her reddened cheeks. She mumbled incoherently through the stifling piece of cloth bound to her mouth, glancing a few times at Stuart's dead body as she tried to explain. Brant shook his head, his look stopping her words. It didn't matter. He couldn't understand them anyway. She barely understood them.

"You are lucky I do not kill you, lady wife." Brant said calmly. Della made a weak noise and he narrowed his gaze in warning. She quieted. "I will leave you alive to live with your failure and the knowledge of what you tried to do to our child. You will carry the child, of that you can be certain, but you will never raise it. I'm taking the babe from you the moment the child is born. You will never be his mother. You will never look upon him or hold him. You will not even be told his name."

Della saw the hard set of his beautifully chiseled face as he turned away. His eyes were cold and dead. Not even anger showed through their depths. She screamed against the gag, yelling at him to stop, straining unsuccessfully to free herself.

BRANT IGNORED her cries as he walked silently out the door, his shoulders hunched in disappointment. Closing her in the chamber, he didn't look back. As he strode out of the cottage, Gunther stopped him near their horses. He couldn't look at his friend, choosing instead to stare off into the night. When he spoke it was in low, dark tones commanding Gunther in their shared Norse tongue. Gunther froze at what his lord asked of him, but Brant didn't wait to hear his man's opinion of the order. Swinging onto his horse, the ealdorman galloped away into the night.

DELLA WATCHED BRANT GO. Her heart leapt wildly into her throat to choke her more effectively than the gag.

He thinks I had something to do with this. He doesn't care for me. Brant, come back, don't leave me, let me explain.

Her limbs shook. The gag made it hard to breathe. She panicked when several minutes passed and he didn't return. Then, finally, she heard footsteps coming back to her. She looked hungrily at the door, waiting for her husband to reappear. It wasn't to be. In his place stood Gunther, a frown marring his brow.

Gunther pulled the gag from her mouth and then moved to slowly unbind her wrists. His actions were distant, as he made no sign of pleasure at her recovery.

"Brant!" Della yelled, her hoarse voice barely audible. Her dry mouth made it hard to speak, but she tried anyway. Screaming louder, she croaked desperately, "Brant, come back. You don't understand!"

"M'lady," Gunther stated calmly. She kept straining to be free and it halted his progress to untie her wrists. "Let it be fer now. He cannot hear you anyway."

"Gunther, you have to get him. You don't understand," Della pleaded, trying to jump from the bed even as he untied her feet. She sat up and grabbed at his arm. "Please. You must stop him."

Gunther took in her pleading face. "He will not listen to me. Besides, he has already ridden back toward Strathfeld."

"Nay," Della wailed. She pushed from the bed as he finally finished with her ankles and stumbled toward the door. Her feet had been bound so tight they stung as blood rushed into them. Her legs weakened and she stumbled into Gunther's chest.

Gunther held her slight weight against him. Her eyelids lowered as blackness threatened to consume her. Della's head rolled slightly before she caught it. Taking a deep breath, she fought the oncoming swoon. "Gunther, you must believe me. I had naught to do with this. Stuart kidnapped me. He was the one trying to rid me of our child. Gunther, I love Brant. I could never kill—"

"Wait." Gunther broke into her tearful confession with a frown. A look of bleak understanding came across his face. "You carry Brant's child?"

"Yea. Methinks he may not have known until he saw Serilda with the knife. But I told Rab, and the boy surely must have told Brant." Della trembled, her words rushed and incoherent in her desperation. "Did he not tell you?"

"Nay." Gunther moved out of her way, nodding as if in understanding. Della sank wearily onto the cot. "It is why he thinks you are to blame fer this treachery. Did you not tell him once that you would... It doesn't matter."

"Gunther, please," Della began desperately. She collapsed back on the bed as tears streamed down her face in despair. Her hand jerked into her long hair, pulling it roughly from her face. Then, sitting, she looked at the splintered chamber door. "I need to tell him."

"Hush. I know well, Della, that you had naught to do with this. I have seen you with Rab. You have too big of a heart to murder a child before he takes his first breath."

Della again stood as her world stopped spinning. Her feet wobbled under her weight and Gunther lifted a hand to her elbow for support. She was too tired to wipe the tears from her eyes. Seeing Stuart's dead body, a wave of nausea rushed over her. The fact that she was free finally hit her and she shook violently.

"Oh, Stuart," Della whispered in grief. Her face paled and she shook her head sadly. In death, he resembled the boy she loved so much, and her heart ached for him. But, even as she mourned him, she knew his death was the only way she would be free of him. "You were the foolish one, dear cousin. Mayhap death will bring you a peace life could not."

Gunther let her go as she shrugged out of his grasp. He moved to the door and waited patiently as Della kneeled by her cousin to close his eyes. Then, taking the satchel at Stuart's waist she searched for the ring he had taken from her—her wedding band. In the pouch, she found a white square cloth with a spot of blood. Inside it was her ring.

"What is that?" Gunther leaned over to see.

"My ring," Della said. "Methinks this must be Stuart's blood."

"Nay."

Della gasped at Serilda's voice. She'd forgotten the woman was there.

"It's yer maidenhead from yer checking. I gave it to him so he would be the only man to possess it." Serilda's pale lips barely moved as she said the words. Her eyes turned to the dead man and a light smile entered her troubled gaze for a passing moment. Then, as the breath hissed from her lungs, she stopped moving.

Della dropped the cloth onto Stuart's chest and slipped the ring onto her finger. Her body ached, her feet and hands tingled with feeling, and she was so tired she could barely stand. Closing her eyes, she whispered, "Just take me home, Gunther. Please, I just want to go home."

Gunther led Della from the room, awed that after all the man had done to her, she still had enough heart to forgive Stuart. Swallowing over a lump in his throat, he knew Blackwell was indeed a lucky man to have such a selfless wife. And for the first time in his knighthood, he debated the wisdom of the orders his friend had given him.

DELLA BEHELD Gunther as he formed a makeshift torch out of a branch and some dried grass. Taking his flint, he easily lit it with two flicks of his wrist. Della watched the torch blaze, her heart numb. Gunther shielded the flames with his hand. Then, when it burned steadily, he drew it along the cotter's hut to alight the roof. Even with the recent rainfall, the old roof was dry enough to catch fire. Gunther threw the torch inside.

Della watched, dazed, as the flames consumed the old building, burning the cottage to the ground and burying her cousin and Serilda within the fiery tomb. Gunther led his horse to her, handing her up silently before seating himself behind her. They didn't speak as they rode and Della didn't look back, not even when she heard the structure fall.

Rain descended, and through the moonlight, the land became more familiar to her. Gunther traveled back to Strathfeld. Della sat stiffly before him, her head held proudly against the elements. Then, as they neared the great oak where Della had bid Brant to meet her in the missive, she asked Gunther to stop. He reined in his horse and she slipped to the ground. Paying little heed to Cedric's dead body as she stepped past it, Della made her way to stand before the tree.

For a long moment, her form was unmoving in the shelter of the tree's large limbs as she looked up into its great branches. Lightening crashed across the sky as if answering some silent whisper she'd given it. Then, kneeling, she grabbed a handful of weeds at the tree's base. Pulling hard, she tossed them behind her, so she may touch a small heart carved in the exposed bark before coming back to the horse.

Rain poured on her face, washing away the grime of her imprisonment. Her tired eyes lifted to him and he helped her back up without question. They rode on, neither one of them complaining about the weather. Gunther didn't slow his steady pace, didn't offer to find her shelter, and Della never thought to ask him to do so.

The sky was dark with the nearing of the midnight hour as Strathfeld came into view. Gunther reined his horse so that they could see the magnificent keep from atop the nearby hillside. A light came from the direction of the hall. If Brant rode full gallop, he would have beaten them by little more than an hour.

Their bodies were soaked and cold, as they watched the manor. She sighed as Gunther spurred the horse onward. The animal hung his head low, trying to avoid the onslaught of rain. Finally, Della turned to Gunther and gave him a brave smile. They both knew what anger awaited her below.

"M'LORD, might I have a word with you?" Della asked from her place on the main hall floor. Her voice was docile as she looked up to the head table at Brant. Her gown was drenched, her hair falling in a heavy wet mass to her waist. She hadn't stopped to change from her rain-soaked clothes before heading straight to the hall from the stables. The bruise on her cheek had begun to yellow and heal, and the knot on the back of her head had all but disappeared.

The hall was filled with soldiers, weary from the last several days spent searching for the countess. Hearing the news of her imminent return, they waited to see her, drinking to warm their blood against the chill of night. Brant told them nothing but the fact she was alive and would be arriving soon. A few of them dared to smile at her, but she didn't return the look.

Brant sat handsomely above her. His regal face motionless as he kept his eyes on her. She stood before him proud and tall, awaiting his answer, but inside she trembled with the importance of the moment and her flesh tingled with a need to hold him. Dried blood stained the sleeve of his tunic. Her heart leapt in worry at the sight, but she stilled it. His hair was wet, but not nearly as drenched as hers.

And, to Della, he was the most beautiful sight in the world.

Now that she faced him, a chill overtook her damp body. She didn't know whether or not it was from the cold, drizzly weather or from Brant's angry stare. Courageously, she insisted, "Please, m'lord."

Brant raised an eyebrow in her direction. She could tell he was still mad. His fists shook as he wrapped them around a goblet in what looked to be an effort to control his rage. His glare bored dangerously into her.

"Methought I gave you an order, Gunther. I want this treacherous woman forever banned from my sight," Brant commanded. "You are to take this prisoner to her chamber. She is to be tied to the bed."

A murmur rose over the hall at Brant's decree. Gunther didn't answer. Della knew he was seated behind her at one of the tables. Scared, she forced herself to continue.

"M'lord, may I please have a word with you?" The words came more forcibly this time and the hall stayed silent. Servants stared in bewilderment, pausing in their duties to watch the reunion. Some of them yawned, having been awakened from their sleep.

Brant's breathing deepened notably. The men watched with avid attention, not even lifting their goblets to drink. She felt their eyes on her, waiting.

"M'lord, I would explain how you are wrong," Della persisted, never having seen him this distant.

There was a terrifying quality to his controlled temper.

"How I have wronged you?" Brant fumed, incredulous. Suddenly, he shot to his feet, darted around the table, and moved swiftly down from the high platform. He grabbed the hair at the nape of her neck and pulled her head back until she was forced to look at him.

"Even now your beauty is treacherous," he whispered. Then, louder, he said, "You, *Della the Cold-Hearted*, are fortunate you still carry my child in your belly lest I be tempted to beat you now for your daring."

Della shivered at his passionless voice. The onlookers gasped, eagerly spreading the news of her condition. Brant took a deep breath and turned to the main hall. He still held her firmly in his grasp as he led her by her neck. Her feet shuffled through the rushes leaving a trail behind them as they moved, but he did not hurt her.

"Blackwell." Gunther stood from one of the back tables where he had been sitting quietly with Roldan and a dozen of the men. He slowly moved forward. When he was in whispering distance, he said, "Mayhap you should hear m'lady out."

Brant glared at his long-time friend. "Nay, I want her locked in her chamber, tied to her bed until she births this child. I want her kept prisoner. I want her forever out of my sight. And then I want her hanged for treason."

"Blackwell," Gunther tried again.

"I will be leaving at dawn to ride with King Guthrum. I will be back with the news of my child's birth," Brant finished.

"But the king bid you home." Gunther insisted with a look of warning to lower his tone. "Please, let us retire to chambers where this may be discussed in private."

"I would rather be on a political campaign for the rest of my life than to live one minute more in this woman's cold presence," Brant argued. He ignored his friend's plea for privacy, beyond caring. "Gunther, I am asking you as my long-time friend. Don't naysay me now. Not in this."

Gunther sighed and looked apologetically at Della. She didn't move, Brant's grip still on her hair and neck. Gunther said, "Don't be unreasonable, m'lord."

"Unreasonable?" Brant let go of Della. "You dare to call me unreasonable when you saw with your own eyes her treachery?"

Della frowned meaningfully at Gunther, bringing her hand protectively to her stomach. The man nodded at her in understanding before saying, "Brant, you are too angry."

"*Blessed Saints!*" Brant yelled. "Roldan, see to it!"

Gunther turned to Roldan and nodded. Roldan in turn motioned sternly to the table of soldiers.

"I said see to it, Roldan. You do not need this man's permission." Brant waved his arm toward Gunther, his face purpling in his outrage. "Take m'lady to her prison."

The soldiers stood up and moved cautiously forward. They looked to each other, as if unsure what to do.

"Now," Gunther yelled. "You have your orders!"

The men sprang forward, grabbing their lord about his waist and tackling him to the rushes. Brant fought their grasp, landing a few good punches to some of the men who were unlucky enough to be close to his fists. But the dozen soldiers were too much for the ealdorman, and they quickly had him subdued under their combined strength.

"Gunther," Brant shouted in disbelief. "What treachery is this?"

The servants gasped in chaos and more came from the kitchen at the commotion. The men not involved hung back, unsure what to do. None of them were armed. Della lifted her hand to hold any would be rescuers back, thankful that they obeyed.

"Secure his legs," Gunther ordered, before pointing to the stairwell. "Carry him abovestairs to his chamber."

"Gunther, I will see you hanged for this betrayal." Brant yelled viciously. Curses, Saxon and Norse, flew from his lips. The men bound his strong limbs together with rope and hauled his massive body abovestairs as instructed. Brant kicked and hollered profanities the entire way.

When her husband was out of sight, the hall burst into an uproar. Gunther waved the knights back and harshly ordered the servants to bed.

"You all saw how he is changed. Lord Blackwell

has been ensorcelled by the witch, Serilda," Gunther explained before promising to give a much better account of all that had happened later. He turned to the countess. Della nodded at him. With a rueful smile and a solemn shake of his head, he held out his hand. "M'lady."

Della took his hand and smiled sadly. She brushed the skirt of her stained, damp gown the best she could and then rubbed the back of her neck. "I should have known he would fight me."

"I have kept my end of the bargain, now it is yer turn." Gunther slipped her hand onto his elbow. He guided her to where the men disappeared with the still-yelling Brant. "And may all the gods be with you."

"Mine or yours?" Della asked with a wry grin.

"Methinks you will have need of them all," Gunther answered as he led her abovestairs to face their outraged captive.

DELLA PUSHED OPEN the door to the bedchamber she shared with her husband. Pausing, she stepped back to let some of the men out of the room before she entered. Brant was tied to the bed, his arms and legs each strapped to a corner. Though he glared ferociously at her, he was still ravishing to behold and her heart did little flips in her chest. Della bit the inside of her lip, so happy to be home, to see him alive, yet nervous about what she was going to say to him now they were alone.

She had quickly changed into a simple, dry gown before coming to join them in the room. The blue wool was thick and warm. Her hair still hung damp around her shoulders, but at least now she wasn't freezing. Unable to hold it back, she smiled at him, unfazed by his irritated expression. As all the men finally left, she shut the door behind her.

Going to his side, she laid her hand soothingly on his forehead, trying to smooth away the crease of his frown. There was a cut on his head from the effort it took to get him abovestairs and she wiped the blood with the edge of her tunic sleeve. Her tone gentle and tender, she said, "You are bleeding."

"It is your blood that will spill in the end, treacherous woman!" Brant snapped his head away from her light touch.

"Quiet." Della refused to be baited into another fight, but would also not back down. She stood from the bed and placed her hands on her hips. "Don't make me call the men back to have you gagged. You will hear what I have to say to you, even if it takes me all night to say it. So, the sooner you stop being mean, the sooner I will have the nerve to speak."

Brant glared at her, but kept his mouth shut. He worked his arms against the constraints of the rope, but they held tight.

"Where to begin?" Della thought aloud. She'd rehearsed the words endlessly in her head on the way home, but now they would not come to her like she'd planned. "Foremost, I'm sorry to have to bind you like this. But, in many ways, it's your own fault. I asked nicely to speak with you belowstairs, but you would have none of it."

"You had best keep me bound here, for the second I'm untied, I'm going to kill all of you." Brant's whisper was deadly. His muscles tightened into hard bulges. "I shall see you hanged."

"I said to keep quiet! We both know you will do no such thing. Must you always have your say first?" Della shivered, forced to concentrate past the sudden arousal she felt from watching his body. Sighing in frustration, she began to pace. "You are a fiery tempered oaf. You do realize that, don't you?"

Brant narrowed his gaze at the insult, but kept his mouth shut.

"All right. I am sorry for blaming you and your people for my mother's death. I was wrong. But, before Stuart *abducted* me, I came to realize I did not blame you for the crime. That, in fact, I could not blame you." Della took a deep breath as she paused. Her heart pounded at the distant memory and she blinked back tears. "The man you have in custody, William, is responsible. He admitted as much to me. Then I heard him arguing with Stuart. He said that my uncle, Lord Grayson, paid to have my mother, his sister, killed. He worried she carried a male heir. My uncle wanted Strathfeld. He'd squandered his fortune and was close to losing his land.

"I know I was harsh to you, but you must understand. My brother was alive when they cut him out of her. They gave the child to my uncle to dispose of. He put on a mask so I would not know it was he who slit," Della paused, taking a deep breath, "who killed him. But he was there watching the whole time. They tied me to the bed so I would not see him behind me.

"In doing this, my uncle thought to secure this land and title for his son. Soon after my mother's death, Stuart's mother died and he came to live with us. While they thought I was unconscious, I heard Serilda whispering about Stuart's mother. Lord Grayson strangled his wife and told everyone it was an accident. Stuart was there when it happened. My uncle must have forced his son to Strathfeld to befriend me. Only, after Stuart got here, he came to like it. He always said he was the happiest when he was here. Methinks in some way, he did come to love me, but didn't know what love was. His father didn't teach him to love. Stuart could never please the man.

"Lord Grayson died before he could complete his scheming and Stuart continued on as he had been raised to do. After the news of our unexpected betrothment came to light, he had Serilda tend to my father's wounds with poison."

Della clutched her hands nervously together when he said nothing to her. Then she realized he was listening. She continued to pace back and forth. "It wasn't even the Vikings who attacked my mother. It was the foreigners from the south. I don't know why my father told me it was the Vikings. Mayhap it was something they found later. But they were looking for the wrong men. I don't know why my father was convinced, but he was distraught, and Lord Grayson helped in the search. In fact, my uncle did most of the investigating. And William is just as responsible. Aside from my uncle, he was their leader."

Della turned pleading eyes to her husband. "I must make you understand. They tortured her for pleasure. They could have just killed her and been done with it, but they tortured her."

"If this is true, he will be hanged for the crime." As he spoke, Brant's words were low. He still hadn't moved.

Della took a deep breath and forced herself on. "I wish to forget what happened. Forever. But if I must tell you everything, I will. I want there to be no more secrets between us. No more deceptions of any kind."

"Della, untie me," Brant said calmly.

"Nay." She shook her head. "I have more to say to you and I cannot guarantee you will listen unless I make you. And you must listen."

Della went to the bed and sat beside him. She laid a tender hand on her stomach. "I swear on all that is sacred to me—my mother, my father, our child. I did not plot with Stuart to have you killed. I *did not* plot to kill our unborn child. From the missive I wrote, you should have figured that out, but I understand why you doubt me and I forgive you for that doubt. I have said many harsh things and I hope in time you will be able to forgive me."

Della prayed he understood. Looking at her stomach, she rubbed it gently. Tears fell from her tired eyes, for what had almost happened, and for what she'd almost lost. Unexpectedly, Brant's strong fingers clasped her side. She gasped in surprise. He'd managed to free a hand. Pulling her, he swept her onto the bed so she rested on his restrained arm. His fingers curled around her throat, holding her down, but applying no pressure.

"Tell me why I should listen to you." Brant brought his face close to hers. She trembled in his arms as his warmth invaded her throat. Her pulse raced beneath his strong fingers. His hard length pressed her into the bed. "Tell me why I should believe you."

The fingers around her neck tightened slightly, but not enough to cause her harm. She swallowed, looking deep into his clear blue gaze. She shook with insecurity, even as her insides seemed to melt at his nearness. She ached with longing, wanting to stay forever in his arms, and she filled with the fear that he could not love her nor forgive her.

"Because," Della whispered.

"Because, why? Because you have been so truthful in the past?"

"Nay." Della pleaded with her eyes for him to understand, begging silently for him to believe her, to trust her. "Because I love you."

"What?" Brant froze above her.

"I said you should believe me because I am in love with you. I have been since I first saw you, only I was too blinded by hatred to realize what I felt. And you were just so... aggravating. But I fell in love with you. I love you still." Della inhaled sharply. Her body continued to quiver at his nearness. She'd said it, finally.

"I don't believe you." Brant looked like he wanted to trust her, but couldn't. "You claim to have sent the missive to warn me, but how is throwing my words back at me a warning to me. You are a deceitful wench."

"Your words?" Della repeated, confused. "Stuart must have switched missives. Nay, the missive I sent said that if the words of love you declared were true then to come alone. You never declared words of love to me. Thus you should have known I was lying. You should have known it was a trap. That's why I sent you to the tree where my mother is buried. Surely, Roldan told you as much. I told you to ask him. So you would know that danger awaited you."

"Your mother?"

"Yea. That is the tree where she first laid eyes on my father. She loved that oak. It is where he buried her. My father carved their initials at the base. It is still there, I saw it tonight. It was so, in the afterlife, they would be able to find each other again." Della blushed. "Methought Roldan would have told you and you would have concluded that, in being a trap, you would eventually find me if you went there. And you did."

"Roldan said naught about it." Brant shook his head. A look of amazement came over his features. "I didn't show him the letter. I only asked him how to get there."

"Wait," Della furrowed her brow. "If Stuart sent

the missive I wrote, then what words did I throw back at you?"

Brant smiled down at her, caressing his finger against the pulse at her neck. "That day, when you thought to have caught Serilda and I in the bath together—"

"I already know naught happened between you." Della liked the way Brant's fingers felt against her throat. "Gunther told me."

"Yea, Gunther," Brant mused, frowning a bit.

"Do not be harsh with him. I made him help me. And the others believe you to be under the spell of a witch. You didn't look like yourself when you came back."

"Hmm." With a preoccupied smile, he continued on as if she hadn't spoken. "The day you thought to have caught us, Serilda was applying healing draughts to me. I feared I had lice from Blackwell Manor and methought to be rid of them before I infested the whole of Strathfeld. Blackwell Manor was a sty and made me appreciate the cleanliness of your keep, wife. Or, let me amend, the keep of the cleaning spirit."

Hope curled within her at his lighthearted banter. "Pray tell, what words did you think I threw back?"

"Now it is your turn to be quiet, wife," Brant said. "I am coming to that."

Della nodded.

"After Serilda left, I told you how I felt. You did not answer me. Why?"

"You did?" Della wondered what he'd said to her

that day. "I was so tired and I fell asleep before you left. I had been ill every morn and night for several days, as you well witnessed. When I awoke, I found you feasting belowstairs with that harlot on your lap. Tell me, what did you say?"

"You didn't hear me? It never occurred to me that you fell asleep and did not hear me. You rarely sleep."

"What did you say?" she insisted, pleading for an answer.

"I said I love—"

Della sprung up, effectively cutting him off with her lips. She kissed him, unable to hold herself away a moment longer. Pressing into his warmth, she never wanted to let him go. He loved her. She could never have imagined such a wondrous feeling. He loved her.

Brant chuckled and lifted up, pulling her mouth unwillingly away. "I love you."

"As I you," Della said. "You believe me? You believe all that I have said?"

"Yea." Brant's voice was husky as he nodded and she could see in his eyes that he meant it. It was more than she had ever hoped for. "And do you know what else I believe, lady wife?"

"Hmm?" Della ran her hand over his whiskered cheek, only to move down over his neck. She loved the feel of his skin, wanted to feel the press of it against her for all time—that and his love.

"I believe we both are badly in need of a bath." He kissed her nose.

Della's chuckle joined his. "That is easily taken care of. But what of the lice? Are they gone?"

"Yea, I had Blackwell Manor burned to the ground soon after I left it. Methought it would be easier to build anew then to fix what was there."

"Oh, no," Della laughed harder, looking guiltily at the chamber door.

Brant raised his brow in question.

"I had to promise that I would talk you into giving Gunther permission to live at Blackwell in your stead for his loyalty and his help this day."

"Gunther is the one who burned it down for me," Brant interjected. "No doubt he thinks to get a new manor out of the bargain."

"Are you angry? I was desperate to have you believe me and could think of no other way to make you hear me. I was afraid you would leave and never come back. Edwyn really has Strathfeld well in hand and Gunther is not needed here as seneschal. And, if he is there, then you…" She touched his face, pushing back the long locks of his hair. "I could not have survived it if you were to leave me."

"Methinks it is a good idea," he said thoughtfully, only to laugh when she panicked at the thought of him leaving her. "I mean entrusting Blackwell to Gunther. You are right about Edwyn, and Roldan is competent with the guards. It would make much sense to give Blackwell to Gunther…after I punish him for his treachery."

Della froze at Brant's mischievous smile. "What would you do to him?"

"Methinks I will not have to punish him much at all. I will make it conditional upon his receiving

Blackwell that he brings us home a wife. That will be punishment enough." Brant leaned down to kiss his wife more fully.

"Punishment?" Della said against his parted lips, pretending to be offended.

"Yea." Brant fingered a lock of her damp hair. "But if it is given by those pink lips, I would gladly die by such punishment, for it is most sweet."

"It would seem your fire has melted my ice after all." Della rubbed her hands through his dirty hair, moaning softly as his fingers rested possessively on her stomach. She placed her hand over his, leaning up to sprinkle his face with kisses.

"Wife?" Brant asked in between kisses.

"Yea, husband," Della answered, completely enamored by him and awed by the strength of his gentle presence.

"Do you think you could untie me now?" He chuckled against her mouth.

Della fervently shook her head, denying his request as she continued to kiss him. "Sorry, my love, but you will forever remain my fiery captive."

"Yea, my sweet princess. Forever."

The End

About Michelle M. Pillow

New York Times & *USA TODAY* Bestselling Author

Michelle loves to travel and try new things, whether it's a paranormal investigation of an old Vaudeville Theatre or climbing Mayan temples in Belize. She believes life is an adventure fueled by copious amounts of coffee.

Newly relocated to the American South, Michelle is involved in various film and documentary projects with her talented director husband. She is mom to a fantastic artist. And she's managed by a dog and cat who make sure she's meeting her deadlines.

For the most part she can be found wearing pajama pants and working in her office. There may or may not be dancing. It's all part of the creative process.

Come say hello! Michelle loves talking with readers on social media!

www.MichellePillow.com

facebook.com/AuthorMichellePillow

x.com/michellepillow

instagram.com/michellempillow

bookbub.com/authors/michelle-m-pillow

goodreads.com/Michelle_Pillow

amazon.com/author/michellepillow

youtube.com/michellepillow

pinterest.com/michellepillow

Complimentary Excerpts
TRY BEFORE YOU BUY!

Maiden & the Monster
BY MICHELLE M. PILLOW

*Winner of the 2006
Romantic Times Reviewers' Choice Award*

Medieval Historical Romance

Vladamir of Kessen, Duke of Lakeshire Castle, is feared as a demon in the land of Wessex. The Kings have granted him a title of nobility in exchange for his part as a political prisoner. Discontent, he bides his time in his new home until war will once again rip through the land. But boredom soon turns to devious pleasure as the daughter of his most hated enemy is left for dead at his castle gate. Now the monster bides his time plotting revenge.

Lady Eden of Hawks' Nest doesn't know what to think of the man who saved her life, but she can't wrench her thoughts away. His words are those of a tyrant, true to his vicious reputation, but his touch is that of a man, stirring passion and lust when there should only be fear. It would seem the infamous monster is not as monstrous as he appears.

A Romantic Times Magazine TOP PICK!
"4 1/2 STARS! This is a perfect blend of history, emotion, tension, hot sex and fascinating and sympathetic characters, and the writing is superb. Pillow chooses magical details to set the scene, and they add to both the history and the emotion."

Page Traynor, RT Bookclub Magazine, April 2006 Issue

Extended Chapter One Excerpt
Lakeshire Castle, Wessex, 879 AD

"God's bones, Ulric! Methinks this land of Wessex is making you soft!"

Vladamir of Kessen, the Duke of Lakeshire's voice was hard due to his exasperation. He knew his tone had a gravelly quality, which reflected a Baltic culture far to the northeast of the Saxon manor of Lakeshire. The heritage gave his softened words a hard bite as the harsh press of his lips gave his features a merciless appearance. Vladamir did it on purpose.

"'Tis irrational, foolish old man, for you to insist I stand downwind of that rotting pile of animal carcasses for nary an instant more. I don't know why you thought I'd be interested!"

His accent frightened the people under his rule. In fact, everything about him scared these people. He wanted the Saxons afraid of him. If they were afraid, they would follow his orders and leave him alone. He'd been in Wessex for a year and the plan had worked so far. It wasn't like he'd been sent to make friends.

Vladamir was the very first Duke of Lakeshire. It was a position he didn't relish. If he had his say, he'd live out his miserable days alone in a castle far away from everyone and everything. Either that or he'd gladly ride into another war.

Frowning sternly, he narrowed his eyes in annoyance and made no move to leave for his training exercises, though his fingers itched to grip his sword. Instead, he swept the fur lining of his cloak off his shoulder. The breeze lifted the weight of his unfashionably long, straight black hair off his shoulders and he absently watched the strands trailing away from him. He purposely wore the heathenish attire of those who lived in the Danelaw rather than to adapt to the more *civilized* dress of the nation of Wessex. He did it to irritate the Christian sensibilities of his Saxon neighbors and to drive fear into those men who were made to unwillingly serve under his rule.

Yea, everything about me is different than this accursed

land. I'm a man without a country. I hate Wessex and I hate the land of my father. And I hate the peace between them both.

Tense, Vladamir raised his arm, motioning to the guard who stood above him on the dark stone of the bailey wall. A black onyx ring glinted on his finger, shining like a beacon the guard would be able to see. With a deft flick of his wrist, the duke silently commanded the knight to raise the outer gate.

The young, fair-haired Saxon didn't hesitate to follow his barbaric lord's order. Like all his subjects, Vladamir knew the guard watched him intensely for any sign of movement, no matter how small. It wasn't out of respect for him that the man instantly obeyed. It was out of fear. Fear was the reason all the Saxon warriors residing at Lakeshire Castle followed his command. They'd all heard the sinister rumors that followed him from his homeland, and he'd never tried to earn their respect or change their opinion of him.

Angrily, he jerked his arm, letting his irritation show. Vladamir knew what he was, knew what he looked like, and it was his intent to appear monstrous in both mannerisms and appearance. His linen undertunic was dyed to the pitchest of blacks. Although the material was of obviously rich quality, it lacked the perfected embellishments that frivolous nobles prided themselves on.

The sleeves of his tunic hung over his wrists and settled over the backs of his hands in long rolls. The undertunic fell loosely over his tightly fitted black braes, the long slit down the side showing a hint of his thighs. He fastened the material of the braes into place with laces that joined at the side and wore a plain, thick leather belt over them. From this belt hung an imposingly sharp knife and a modest leather pouch, which contained small pieces of flint for starting a fire and an iron key that fit a door the servants didn't even know existed.

"Clear it away at once. Methinks you have interrupted my morning training for naught more than fetid garbage!" The duke ordered Ulric, only to growl in anger when the gate didn't rise fast enough to suit his impatience. He rested his hand on the hilt of his sword in warning. The action wasn't missed. Another knight disappeared off the wall, obviously going to hurry the man lifting the gate. Vladamir relished his ill humor, wallowing in it. "Argh!"

He sighed as the gate finally squeaked on its iron hinges, making the slow trip up. Gripping his sword, his scowl deepened. Instead of watching the gate, he stared at the hilt. The monstrous broadsword at his waist was in a leather scabbard, hanging from a leather shoulder baldric. The strap crossed over his chest so he could easily draw the weapon at the slightest provocation.

Still irritated, he glanced back to Ulric as the man tried to get a good view of the rotting animals through the gate's crosshatching. The servant turned to the duke, eyeing the nobleman's attire. Vladamir glanced down at his clothes, again thinking of how different he was from the Saxon men.

Over his tunic he wore a woven cloth belt of black and silver. It wrapped about his waist and knotted on the front right. He left the unadorned ends to drape freely about his thighs. The undertunic's oval neckline was laced high and tight against his thick neck, hiding the entirety of his chest from view. It was only on the rarest of political occasions that Vladamir was obligated to don an overtunic. He didn't feel the need of such formalities in his life when it came to dress. But, on those rare occasions, the overtunic was also black with very little silver embroidery.

The only relief to the investigating eye that Vladamir allowed was the lighter colored *rocc*, his fur cloak that was constructed of the skinned hide of several gray wolves. He would've dyed the fur black as well, if not for the ample waste of time and resources the project would consume. He wore the fur side inward for warmth as was customary among his fellow pagans.

"By all that is hallowed!" Vladamir growled, not caring who heard his cry. Many of the servants milling about the yard skidded to a stop at the sound. A small smile of devious pleasure automatically curled the sides of his mouth. It took a few seconds, but soon the servants were hurrying away in relief when they realized they weren't the cause of his present anger.

It was a well-known and accepted fact to the people of Lakeshire Castle that Vladamir had converted to Christianity solely to please King Alfred of Wessex in accordance with the Treaty of Wedmore. The duke did nothing to dissuade their beliefs or make them think that he was sincere in his conversion. Let them believe he was a devilish monster sent by King Guthrum to torment them.

In truth, Vladamir didn't much care for the Christian God, nor had he cared for the many gods of his ancestors. He lost faith when his wife died six years before. As he thought of it, it was quite possible he'd lost his faith before then.

Lowering his chin to glower down from his towering height, he curled his nose in disgust as another gust of wind assaulted him. The air carried a stench so severe that, even with his war-hardened training, Vladamir couldn't ignore the putrid smell. His expression turned quickly into a snarl. For all his rough appearance, Vladamir was a clean person, having been influenced by the peculiar bathing rituals of his father's people, the Vikings. He even insisted his household followed suit and bathed at least twice a sennight. It was a completely pagan routine little heard of in the dwellings of the Saxons. He'd received some protest over the decree, but it was necessary to keep such smells as these rotted animals out of his home.

His forehead wrinkled in irritation and tried unsuccessfully to determine what exactly emitted the foul odor. "What is it, Ulric? It smells of decaying flesh. Who would dare to lay carcasses afore my gate to rot?"

"Mayhap, 'tis a sacrifice in honor of the castle," Ulric offered with a grave shake of his head. The manservant's expression said he highly doubted it.

Ulric had traveled with the duke to Wessex the year before. A short man with a balding head, he had a pleasing face hidden under his trim beard. His jaunty nature was a direct contrast to that of his dark, forbidding lord—just as his rounded frame was opposite Vladamir's sinewy one. He wasn't only the duke's seneschal but was also the closest thing Vladamir could call friend.

"Nay, 'tis not the season for sacrifice," Vladamir answered as he looked up to the changing sky. It was early morning, yet the sky darkened to purple. He pulled the broadsword from his waist in one smooth motion and flexed the muscles of his sword arm in distraction, scuffing the tip across the dirt in a lazy stroke. Smirking, he said, "Besides, the prelate has forbidden such practices. 'Tis too barbaric a custom according to the church."

He sighed, fisting his hands as he pressed his lips tightly together. Upon closer examination, he discovered that the rotting bundle was actually an oddly shaped mound of pelts. Resting his fingers firmly upon his hips, he was mindful of the tip of the broadsword that still rested on the ground.

The stronghold's gate stopped above him, but he didn't bother to move. The gate was constructed of thick English oak and bound together with iron strips. The pointed ends at the bottom of the gate were wood reinforced with iron, causing them to act like metal teeth if lowered too quickly. Eyeing the spikes, he morbidly thought of how effectively they could sever a man in two.

Ulric rushed forward to the pile as soon as the spikes were out of his way. The seneschal's wider frame lumbered with the effort it took him to kneel and he grunted under the strain. Swiping the sleeve of his brown tunic across his forehead, Ulric placed his arm before his nose as he leaned closer to the pelts.

Impatient, Vladamir watched Ulric pick through the skins. He followed silently behind, refusing to sheath his sword. The seneschal sat straight up in surprise.

"M'lord, it would appear to be a maiden amongst these pelts. Methinks I see the entrails of a rabbit in her hair," Ulric yelled through the sleeve of his tunic.

The servant again wiped his sleeve across his brow before returning it to his nose. His small brown eyes shone with concern. With a grumble of disdain, Ulric lifted entrails from the maiden's hair and flung them aside, only to gingerly remove a rabbit carcass the same way to reveal the bloodied lines of her swollen face. It was impossible to see whether she breathed.

In the distance, the sounds of fighting men and clashing swords filled the air as the knights competed in mock battle. A flock of wild birds flew high above to seek shelter from the changing sky. Their song softly drifted downward. None of the sounds pleased the duke as his eyes stayed trained on Ulric.

"A maiden? Out here? And scented with festering carcasses?" Vladamir searched the forest that surrounded his castle. The hum of insects was quite clear on the morning air, and he noticed that the red bristled pigs grazing just beyond his walls were undisturbed. Nor could he detect movement within the barren limbs of the trees. Finally satisfied that the girl was alone, he turned his attention back to Ulric. He refused to show any interest in the maiden.

"Wake her and send her on her way." He kept his voice passionless and made no effort to help the woman. "If she is dead, burn her, for I won't tolerate that wretched smell in my bailey."

"Should we not try to find out who she is first? Mayhap there are those who search fer her even now. Would you deny her kinsmen a proper burial?" Ulric protested quietly.

"Do as I command!" Vladamir insisted in a low growl. Even as he did so, he saw the knights that manned the wall look over the girl with curious stares. He heard their whispering as it drifted down, though he couldn't make out their hasty words. He didn't need to. The woman was more than likely a Saxon wench and they would wish to know whom, for none in the manor were missing. If she was dead, there was nothing he could do for her. He didn't need this headache. His life was stressed enough.

Through his irritation, Vladamir saw hesitation on the older man's face and quieted his tone to a logical murmur. "Is she dead?"

"I know not, m'lord." Ulric leaned to touch the girl and then turned back to his lordship. "She is not responding."

Vladamir tried to control his exasperation and

repeated his original command, intentionally raising his voice to quiet the knights on the wall. His harsh accent made his words all the more lethal as he ground out, "Then she is dead. Burn her. I won't have her corpse carrying disease to the manor."

Ulric looked to him, searching the duke's face for a sign of compassion. Vladamir didn't give him one, refusing to be stirred to pity. It was easier to be feared than loved. It was easier to be dead inside than to feel.

Sighing heavily, the servant crouched over the girl. The duke stepped to the side, getting a better look at her. She was young and it was clear she'd been beaten. Her clothes were torn and her hair was matted with dirt and possibly blood.

Ulric yelled over his shoulder, loud enough to make sure the watching knights also heard his reply, "Nay, methinks she takes breath. She is not dead, merely insensible."

The duke frowned, knowing the servant hoped he wouldn't dare to leave a Saxon girl for dead, especially with so many soldiers to bear witness. If it had been a decade earlier, Vladamir would've carried the injured maiden into the castle to care for her. He'd have tended to her wounds, oversaw the physicians, stayed by her side until she was better. But the time was now and the duke would never allow himself to care like that again. Life had taught him some hard lessons.

Rubbing his brow, he then ran his fingers through the long locks of his tangled hair to brush it from his eyes. He shifted his weight from one leg to the other and didn't answer the servant. Scowling, he willed the maiden to disappear. He didn't want her in his home.

"Would you like me to leave her afore yer gate to rot? Or would you like to bring her in?" Ulric stood up and boldly matched his lord's stare, his thick jowls quivering in irritation.

Vladamir didn't like his servant's impudent tone and the man's sarcasm didn't go unobserved. He gritted his teeth as he asked with a sullen glimmer of hope, "Is she near death?"

"I know not." The servant once again turned from his overlord back to the pitiful girl. Thunder stuck in the horizon, beating its violent rhythm across the purple sky. The man pulled another carcass from her and tossed it aside.

"Check her." Vladamir purposefully sounded bored as he sheathed his sword. Anger was the easiest of all emotions and he clung to it. His gut tightened and he raised his eyes briefly to the heavens as a droplet of rain fell across his nose. "Be quick, Ulric."

Ulric felt the girl's pulse. "She has a good chance to recover if we move her indoors now."

Suspecting that the man might be lying, the duke paced in a frustrated circle, his hands fitted firmly at his waist. He rolled his neck until it cracked, debating the fate of the girl.

Those who moved about the bailey made their way toward shelter. A small page ran close to Vladamir, a pack of mongrel dogs quick on his heels. The boy laughed as a particularly ugly gray dog tripped him about the legs and sent him sprawling to the ground at the duke's feet. The page's face became wrought with fear as he looked up from the ground. The duke growled at him and the boy scurried away from him as the rain fell harder, hammering the ground with its loud music.

"It would appear she has been badly beaten," Ulric said. "Methinks it would be wise to move her inside, out of the rain, lest she is not like to live through the night. I can have a chamber readied for her abovestairs if you wish."

No matter how badly he wanted to give the order to leave her outside, Vladamir couldn't do it. He silently cursed himself for a fool and gave a self-depreciating laugh.

So much for being a complete monster.

"Yea," Vladamir conceded reluctantly. He stopped his pacing and turned to go, intent on leaving Ulric to tend to the woman.

"M'lord, wait." Ulric's urgent voice stopped him.

"Yea?" Vladamir gripped the hilt of his sword.

"M'lord, it would seem the maiden is a lady."

"Who is she, Ulric? Why has she come? Methinks 'tis a bad omen." Vladamir paced over a quarter length of his main hall only to turn and walk back in agitation. He always paced when he was unnerved. His arms held strong to his sides and he moved with circular purpose, his feet not stopping in any one place.

Who would leave a lady afore my door to die? Who would dare to conspire against me?

Narrowing his eyes into slits, the duke impatiently brushed back his hair only to slash his hand through the air, striking his palm with a hard crack against a table.

"M'lord doesn't believe in omens," Ulric said logically. The duke growled. Only after Vladamir had finished his small tirade, did the man continue, "So, 'tis impossible fer her to be a bad one."

Vladamir grumbled in response and continued to pace. His feet crushed the matted rushes into the stone floor and he touched the knife at his waist.

"I had Haldana look to her ladyship. It would appear she was badly beaten and it may take many days fer the wounds to heal. But Haldana is most hopeful in the recovery." Ulric's bemused statement wasn't the one the duke sought. Sardonically, the man added, "With yer present generosity, m'lord, she should mend quite well."

Ladyship? This woman is no more a noble than you are, Ulric.

Vladamir turned to glare at the impudent man. Sliding the knife swiftly from his belt, he flung it through the air, embedding the blade into a small knot of wood in a nearby table.

Ulric looked unimpressed as he reached for the weapon. With a jerk, he pulled it from the wood and handed it back to his lordship. Vladamir took it without comment and sheathed it at his waist. If he hadn't been in his service for so long, the duke might have considered turning Ulric out of the castle. But, instead, he tolerated the man's careless smirk and paced once more.

"It would also appear that m'lady has either fallen or has been carted in dung. Methinks it would be wise to question the peasants who work with the pigs," Ulric advised. "I instructed that her ladyship should be bathed at once and a new garment sewn fer her."

"Nay, don't waste time sewing for the intruder. Only mend the clothes she has brought with her," Vladamir commanded with another aggravated slash of the hand.

The duke thought of the odorous cloak she wore. As she was carted inside, he could tell the fine cut of the garment, though it was matted. He hadn't wanted to get too close to her and so had refrained from intimate inspection—for not only had she fallen in pig dung, but she'd been covered with the rotted carcasses of gutted rabbits. The rabbits were set ablaze as soon as she was free of them. He imagined that he still detected her awful smell in the keep from when the knights carried her abovestairs.

His voice was abnormally loud in the empty hall and he turned to glare at the servant. "'Tis not my place, nor my desire, to care for her. As soon as she awakens, I want her gone. She has already outstayed her welcome!"

"M'lord." Ulric nodded, not liking the decision to turn the maiden out, but he wisely refused to press the issue.

The servant was unimpressed by the great show of fury coming from the duke. He was well used to the nobleman's moods by now. None who saw the nobleman would know he was unsettled as he paced the floor, for Vladamir appeared to be and was accepted as, a ranting monster. But Ulric knew better. The nobleman might appear to be brooding in his ruthlessness, but really he was just scared of anything disrupting his angry world.

"Argh!" the duke yelled in anger.

Just then, Ulric noticed one of the Saxon maids entered the hall carrying a tray laden with goblets. Lizbeth was a beautiful child and so full of life, though she was very demure in her carriage. Her willowy frame swayed and she halted to a nervous stop. She diverted her round eyes from the tempest of straw and dust that his lordship kicked up from the floor in his frenzy. Taking a hurried step back, she disappeared into the kitchen clearly unaware that Ulric had seen her hastened retreat.

Ulric shook his head in pity, hating the way the people of Lakeshire feared the duke. Most of the time, the servants tiptoed around him, endeavoring to accomplish their duties when he wasn't present. Like Lizbeth, trying to set the high table for the morning meal while the duke was supposed to be out of the castle.

Ulric knew all the whispers, knew that Vladamir earned those whispers because he had an exalted temperament. Just as he realized that if the duke would stop in his self-pity, he would grow to be an even greater leader. Ulric had become used to his overlord's ways in his many years of loyal service. Just as Vladamir was now feared, Ulric also knew it hadn't always been so. There had been a time when the duke had been quite charming in his ways, but those times were gone forever, and in the charming man's wake was a self-proclaimed monster.

Ulric shook his head, drawing his eyes away from where the maid retreated into the shadowed kitchen. He returned his attention to the discussion at hand.

"Who is she?" the duke demanded. "Do you not recognize the crest on her cloak?"

Ulric was happy Lord Kessen conceded to letting the woman stay long enough to recover, knowing he could deal with Vladamir's desire to banish her from the castle when the time arrived. Instead, he was more alarmed that the duke acted so merciless in public view, though none were there to witness the tirade. Seeing his lordship desired an answer, Ulric sighed.

"I know not, m'lord. The crest has been torn from her cloak. I cannot see what family she is from." Hiding the mischievous glint in his expression, the servant added, "It would appear m'lady is quite beautiful."

"With welts on her bloodied face?" Vladamir asked, his brow rising to a severe arch, before he waved a dismissing hand. Then, stopping in his restless pacing, the duke took several steps forward so he could face the manservant. "I care not what the lady looks like. I would that she was dead so I could burn her and the offending smell she brings with her."

"M'lord." Ulric nodded again in understanding. He easily dismissed the scathing look directed him and concealed his smile.

"Mayhap her garments are torn because she is a thief. She stole the cloak from a noblewoman she did to death. Ealdorman Baudoin, the incompetent goat, will no doubt commission the Witan and blame us for giving her aid. No doubt Alfred's fyrd will hang us next to her in the gallows." Vladamir's look scathed in its intensity as he narrowed his eyes, appearing to contemplate his actions. "I have changed my mind, take her to the countryside and leave her. We have done our best by her."

"That would be murder. She couldn't survive unattended in the country," Ulric protested in the reasonable tone he knew aggravated his lord. He wouldn't be bullied to anger or driven into fear and had no intention of following the cruel decree given him.

"Very well," Vladamir conceded with an aggravated sound of contempt. He gave Ulric a vicious growl before his mouth curled in a mischievous grimace. "Give her food and water. Then take her to the country and drop her off at some cotter's hut. Let someone else take care of her. I won't have a murderous thief in this keep. I have no wish to be involved!"

"Have you thought that, perchance, m'lady is the victimized noblewoman? Would you have her point the king's gauntlet at you fer not helping her? Would you dare to bring the wrath of Alfred on our heads? And fer what? The paltry cost of a little meat and ale? The insignificant time it takes Haldana to look in on her? 'Tis not as if you need to be bothered with her care. You have no need of even seeing her." Ulric smiled as he saw he had his lord's attention. He scratched his balding head before turning an audacious look to the taller man. "Mayhap, m'lady is innocent."

The comment received the wrathful snarl Ulric expected. He flinched at the pain that flickered over the duke's face. However, the emotion was so brief that Ulric wondered if he'd witnessed it at all. Over the years, Vladamir's emotions had shown less and less, until the servant was left with only an impression of the deeply seated pain he knew to reside within the duke.

"No woman is innocent, especially not one of noble breeding. 'Tis not in their devious natures. Methinks the treachery they are capable of must far surpass that of a man," Vladamir stated. His eyes appeared to turn a supernatural black in his rage and his voice crackled in its low tonality. As his chest heaved, he continued under his breath, "If she is not guilty of murder she is guilty of something. All women are. Mayhap, 'tis why she was banished to die."

"Perchance this one is innocent," Ulric persisted, softening his tone. "Besides, would you dare to anger King Alfred while we are living in his land on his good graces? You should at least find out who she is afore you sentence her to death. Mayhap the king will reward you fer yer chivalrous deeds."

"More reward than this?" Vladamir snorted as he lifted his hand to encompass the main hall of Lakeshire Castle. He swept his fingers past the line of his vision to move over the dusty black stone of the wall and the dirty straw rushes of the floor. The hall was undusted and unkempt, just like Vladamir ordered it to remain. "Methinks I don't wish for more reward from the king. The empty title and foreign land, 'tis enough while I reside peaceably in Wessex and await the war that is sure to come."

Ulric gave a wry laugh and tried to hide his disappointment in the duke's attitude, but the man's disposition was getting harder and harder to put up with. "These times of rest cannot last forever. The killing will soon start again. And then, perchance, you can find yer own peace as you bloody yer sword with the Anglo-Saxons' fluids. Never mind that you have lived amongst them fer a year."

"Yea, soon we will be fighting our way back to the border or dying in the try." Vladamir smiled at the prospect. Ulric grimaced. The duke didn't notice. "Though, I don't care much for going back. What says you? Shall we head south instead and join the Franks or even the Moors? Do you think Guthrum will notice if we were to leave tonight?"

"Yea, if his peace treaty is broken because King Alfred's most prestigious hostage disappears, methinks he might take note." Ulric shook his head in denial. "I won't be the cause of war."

"Yea, but I must be the peace of it," Vladamir grumbled in anger. The duke had said on many occasions that anything would be better than wasting away in a place he had no liking for. Pointing his finger at Ulric, Vladamir asked, "Do you think it would matter if one of the other hostages disappeared? Methinks the kings wouldn't even take notice. By hell's fire, the others are probably returned home as we speak."

"'Tis no one's fault but yer own that you are here. You asked to be sent as a prisoner. 'Tis a prison of yer own making." Ulric had little sympathy as he reminded the duke of their situation. Vladamir flung his hand with a sound of annoyance. Unlike Ulric and some of the others who felt they had no choice but to come to the foreign land, Vladamir had been given an option. Albeit, a narrow one. "You made yer deal with the king, now 'tis you who must live with it and the responsibility it bears. And if that responsibility means you are to reside here in peace, then 'tis what you'll do."

"Argh!" Vladamir fumed as he again pointed a long fingernail in the manservant's direction. His eyes darkened and shot out with a vaporous light. Snarling, the duke's face contorted into that of a great beast. For a long moment he didn't move from his pose. Then, whipping his finger back toward his chest, he said, "Fine! She can stay. But you mind after her care and alert me as soon as she awakens or when she is dead. I don't wish to be bothered with her afore that time."

"Yea, m'lord." Ulric hid his smile by scratching his whiskered chin. He took a deep breath, pleased with the small victory.

"And clean her up! I won't have her filling the manor with her stench." Vladamir's voice crackled through the air as he glared at the stairwell.

"Yea, m'lord as you wish." Ulric bowed, wiping his sleeve over his forehead.

"Nay, if 'twas as I wished it, she wouldn't be here at all." Vladamir stormed from the room, only to bark over his shoulder, "I go back to my exercise!"

"But, m'lord, the storm," Ulric called after him. It was too late. A blanket of rain emerged behind the duke as he passed through the open doorway. Within a blink, Vladamir disappeared into the thundering morning air.

Ulric's smile didn't fade as he turned to the stairwell. His steps were light as he made his way up the narrow stairs to the maiden's chamber. The ring of keys on his belt clanked a merry tune with each bounce. It had been a long time since he'd seen Vladamir unsettled and the old seneschal knew that the duke was well overdue.

End Excerpt

For a complete, up-to-date booklist, visit www. MichellePillow.com

Emerald Knight
BY MICHELLE M. PILLOW

Medieval Historical Romance

Since birth Lady Ginevra has been betrothed to Lord Wolfram, second son to the Count of Whetshire. There was never any question as to whom she would marry or who she would be. Life has been mapped out for her and she's going to live happily ever after as a Countess. However, there is one complication to her plans. Her rogue of a future husband isn't taking to their life together with open arms. In fact, he seems to enjoy finding reasons to put the nuptials off.

For some, love comes swiftly at first glance, for those most stubborn it can take a lifetime...

Extended Excerpt

Prologue
Whetshire Fortress, Wessex, 1171 A.D.

Baron Southaven raised his proud blue eyes from the sheepskin parchment. His quill dripped with ink as he set it aside. As he blew lightly over the bold flourish of his signature, a satisfied smile lined his mouth. Then, dripping wax onto the paper, he slipped his ring from his finger and pressed his seal onto the agreement. Next to him his wife, Lady Southaven, clapped happily. He placed the crest back onto his hand. It was done. The endless fortnights of negotiation since the birth of his daughter had finally ended to the satisfaction of both houses.

"It's decided then," the Earl of Whetshire announced with a solemn nod.

Wolfe's head snapped up. In all his eight years he had never been so mortified. His father's stern voice expressed neither anger nor pleasure at the decision. Though, by all indications, the man was pleased with the match. Turning to look down the floor of the main hall, the earl squinted in the dimmed torchlight. The hour was late and the fire had dwindled to a soft heat.

Wolfe stood dutifully with his two brothers awaiting his father's command. Thomas, the oldest, held his head high and proud. Wolfe, standing next to him, swallowed nervously and kicked at the floor. William, the youngest, grinned sheepishly as if nothing concerned him. Their sister's giggle broke the silence, as she sat on the lap of the baron's only son. Robert's gentle laugh followed hers.

The earl sighed as he watched his sons. Motioning

to Wolfe, he commanded gruffly, "Wolfram, come kiss your betrothed's lips and seal this match."

Wrinkling his nose and stiffening his legs, his feet refused to move. His brothers chuckled mockingly behind the backs of their hands. Thomas knocked him forward with a swift punch to his back. Wolfe spun to his older brother with a fierce growl.

"I'll get you fer that, Thomas!" Wolfe hissed, raising his fists in warning. "I'll wallop you good!"

Thomas just laughed harder. Being the oldest and the heir, he wasn't too concerned. Even though he was only two years older, he had grown well over Wolfe in size. He smiled confidently down from his impressive height. "Yea, Wolfe, go kiss your bride."

"*Wolfram?*" Lady Isabella called when her son hadn't moved. The countess' voice was loud and booming compared to the stern tone of her husband. She pushed her flaming red hair back from her forehead as she watched her children expectantly.

"Yea, you'd better hope she don't spit up on you!" William chimed in. He too was rewarded with a dark scowl.

Slowly, Wolfe stepped forward. His dark brown hair fell in front of his eyes as he looked solemnly up at his parents. Both the baron and baroness watched him expectantly from across the hall. Before having taken two steps, a foot jutted in front of him. He tumbled to the ground. Glancing up from the straw rushes in anger, he glared at his snickering older brother.

"I warned you, Thomas!" Wolfe hollered. He

forgot his father's command as he glared at his attacker. Jumping to his feet, he charged Thomas in the waist. He rammed his head into his brother's chest and knocked him to the ground with the unexpected force. Thomas slid across the straw rushes that lined the hall floor, as Wolfe howled atop him.

Wolfe swung for his brother's jaw, his fist glancing off Thomas' cheek with a reverberating smack. William shouted in pleasure. Thomas fought back. He rolled Wolfe amidst flying fists that quickly found their mark. Wolfe grunted as Thomas clapped the side of his head and Thomas protested loudly when Wolfe tried to bite his finger off. The digit had strayed too close to his younger brother's opened mouth.

The battle ended as fast as it begun. Wolfe grunted in protest as he was lifted off of Thomas. His feet kicked in the air only to land with a heavy thud on the stone floor. Neither boy was badly bruised, only disheveled from the fray. Guiltily, Wolfe wiped his bloodied mouth and looked at his father, his eyes pleading for parental mercy. It was not to be.

"Attend your duties, son." The earl pointed to the head table where the adults waited patiently. Wolfe kicked the ground in anger, as he was made to kiss his future bride. Thomas and William laughed in delight as he was made to walk up to the platform. The earl ignored his snickering sons and followed closely behind Wolfe.

As he stepped up to the head dining table, Wolfe ignored the rolled parchment next to the small wooden bassinet. The paper served only as a reminder of things he couldn't control. Frowning, he glanced at his sister Helena. She had crawled off Robert's lap and played on the floor near his feet. She looked up at him and giggled in childish amusement. His frown deepened into a scowl.

"Go on," Robert encouraged in a whisper. His young green eyes shone with understanding, as Wolfe leaned over the cradle to see his sister. It was obvious he didn't think much of kissing Ginevra either. "Hurry, afore she wakes up and starts to bawl."

The boys' mothers shared modest smiles. Wolfe gulped. Leaning over, he studied his future wife--a round baby clad in soft yellow. She was only as long as his arm, with pudgy, pink cheeks that puffed out from her tiny nose. Her lips puckered to suck in dreamlike abandon. Grimacing, he shook his head in denial and took a defiant step back.

"Why do I have to marry 'er? Why can't I give 'er to Thomas? He's the oldest. He's the one who's goin' to need a wife." Wolfe glanced dejectedly to his mother, who only smiled and nodded her head for him to follow his father's order. Already he knew the answer. Thomas wouldn't be bound by such an agreement because he was the oldest. The earl wanted to be sure they left Thomas' option open in case there was a shift of politics. And Wolfe, being the second oldest, was the most logical of choices to unite the manors of Whetshire and Southaven. It would strengthen the ties of the land and help to build a secure future for all those involved.

Understanding didn't make it easier.

With a sigh, he glanced back down. Ginevra's eyes opened. The round green orbs looked at him curiously from underneath silky black lashes. Quickly, he puckered his lips as he leaned over to kiss the baby's soft cheek. The baroness flushed and laid her hand proudly over her heart. The men nodded in satisfaction as they clasped hands.

Ginevra gurgled and her lips twitched into a softened, toothless smile. Drool spilled over her lips and chin. Wolfe felt himself melt a little as he looked at her. But, then, he hardened as he heard the snickering laughter of his two brothers behind him. His face turned into a disgusted scowl.

"She smells!" he exclaimed loudly with an offended wrinkle to his nose. Ginevra began to cry, her tiny fists pounding her displeasure into the air. Her shrill voice rang over the hall, as her mother rushed forward to lift her into the protective enclosure of her arms. Wolfe ignored his bride and stalked from the table to once again pummel his brother.

Chapter One

Southaven Castle, Southern Wessex, 1179 A.D.
Ginevra 8 years of age, Wolfe 16 years of age

The sprightly, young girl ran through the bailey courtyard, curving around the bodies of peasants and servants as they went about their chores. Her long, white-blonde hair flew about her shoulders as a beacon of warning to those who would get out of her way. Her legs were clad in a pair of old breeches and a large tunic shirt hung loosely on her thin frame. Her arms pumped faster as she raced forward through the clasped hands of young lovers and under a woman's basket of turnips. And then, with a strong leap from bared feet, she flew over a pile of loose hay being pitched near the stables.

The stable lads looked up from their duties to smile after the castle nymph, as she raced beyond their tedious work. It was always so at the peaceable Southaven. As they turned back to scoop the horses' morn meal into the stables, they could hear the merry tune of her laughter tinkling from afar.

The sun was just beginning to peak over the thick wall of the bailey. Ginevra let her lips curl in a triumphant smile as she looked over her shoulder to gloat at Robert. Then, unexpectedly, she crashed into a warm body, tumbling over. The young boy, whose chest rudely halted her progress, stepped aside and let her fall to the ground. Panting, she looked up to glare at whoever had gotten in her way. She heard Robert laugh as he flew past her to touch the gatehouse.

"Watch it, urchin!" the older boy said in amusement with his hands on his hips. Brown eyes laughed mischievously down at her as she huffed in fury.

Ginevra hiked up the sleeves of the undertunic she'd stolen from her brother and shot the obstacle her nastiest glare. His thin body was framed by sunlight, but she could see the fine cut of his expensive linen tunic and the proud tilt to his aristocratic head. Not stopping to think of who he might be, she pushed herself up from her backside onto her feet. Her chest rose and fell as she pushed her finger into his chest. The defiance only made him laugh harder. An easy smile came to his lips, but his charm was lost on her.

"I should thump you fer makin' me lose!" She stiffened in anger and placed her hands on her hips, widening her stance. Her hair was wild about her shoulders, her face was smudged with dirt, and she was dressed as a lad in a wool tunic.

"Thump me? You're just a babe." The boy studied her for a moment with cool brown eyes that sparkled in his impishness. "From the tips of your toes to your rosy round cheeks."

Ginevra gasped.

"Get to your cottage, peasant babe." The boy laughed harder. "I think your wet nurse must be looking for you."

Ginevra's mouth dropped open at the insult. The boy didn't wait for her to reply as he held his hand up in familiar greeting to her brother. Robert was fast approaching from the gate. She frowned as Robert clasped the boy on the shoulder in friendly gesture.

"Robert!" The boy gave an arrogant toss of his chin length hair. "I hoped you would be here! I brought a new palfrey my father bought me to breed with your father's mare. It's of the finest stock. I thought we could ride him later."

"Ho, Wolfe," Robert answered with a wave of greeting. Ginevra felt the color drain from her cheeks at Robert's words. "Is he in the stables?"

"Yea!" Wolfe paid her no mind, not even to glance in her direction as he walked to the stables. Yelling over his shoulder, he cried so his friend could hear, "My father's in there now! I think they are going to breed them. Want to watch?"

Robert nodded in boyish mirth at the prospect. Leaning over to her, he whispered, "Now you have to wear a tunic gown, Gin! And do your hair like a lady."

"It would be you wearin' the gown, Robert, if not for him knocking me over! I had you beat better than a fur rug set for cleanin'!" Ginevra stuck her tongue out at him as he swaggered toward the stables. Crossing her arms over her chest, she pushed her lower lip into a pout. Inside her heart pounded wildly. Her chest lifted in angered pants. In all the eight years since her father betrothed her to Wolfram of Whetshire, she had never seen him and rarely thought of him. And now that she met him, she was fighting mad.

Ginevra glared in defiance, making a face at the back of her mother's perfectly wound hair as the baroness led the way down the stairwell to the main hall. She nearly refused to move under the weight of the tunic gown. Her mother had ordered the gown sewn especially for the occasion, since Ginevra had cut up all her other dresses into shreds and used them as ropes. For that reason alone, she hadn't been told about the gown until a moment before she was to put it on, and she hadn't been told about her intended's visit until it had been too late. But Ginevra didn't care. She hoped she scared the horrible boy away.

The gown hung loose on her girlish frame with feminine embroidery at the simple rounded neck. It was made of the finest cream-colored linen with sleeves that fit down to her wrists. Her mother lent her an elongated fabric belt that hung to her ankles. She pushed the belt to swing with her knees as she walked. Her hair hung loose in whitish waves down her back. Ginevra had fought it, but in the end her mother had combed it free of tangles.

Taking a grudging step down, Ginevra spied the banner hanging on the edge of the great hall where everyone would later gather to dine. The banner was of her family's crest--the bright golden cross over a slash of blue on a sea of orange.

Her mother led her forward insistently, past the opening of the stairwell to the dining platform where the Earl of Whetshire and his family gathered. Ginevra grunted, digging her finger inside her ear to poke at an itch.

"Ginevra!" the baroness scolded softly in aggravation. She jerked her daughter's hand down. "Stop that at once. Act like a young lady!"

"No one saw," Ginevra grumbled, rolling her eyes.

She turned her attention to the head table. Spotting Robert, she braced herself as she watched her brother's face. As soon as he saw her in a dress, he grabbed onto his sides and laughed dramatically. The baron shot him a look of warning before cuffing him soundly over his head. Robert only laughed harder, all but tumbling to the hard stone floor in his exaggerated merriment.

Ginevra stuck her tongue out at her brother and narrowed her eyes. Her mother pushed down on her arm to get her to stop. Scornful, Ginevra lifted her chin as she turned to the three boys and one girl sitting near Robert. Already, she knew Wolfe from their earlier encounter. She ignored him and the bemused expression he had on his face when he recognized her.

"Ah, Ginevra!" the countess exclaimed with a smile. Her easy manner was warm and her pleasant green eyes shone with approval. She stood from her seat and moved down the platform. Touching Ginevra under the chin lightly, she smiled as she dusted a smudge of dirt from her cheek.

Lady Jayne made a small sound of displeasure. Ginevra glanced up as her mother pushed down on her shoulder, reminding her to curtsey. The baroness shot an apologetic look at her guest with a dignified nod of her head. Ginevra curtsied dutifully, feeling awkward in the gown.

"My how you have grown child! I haven't seen you since you were a wee babe." Lady Isabella grinned, as she let go of her chin. Then, turning to face her own children, she beckoned them forward for quick introduction.

Thomas was heir to the earl's title and lands, and

was a year older than Robert. His green eyes shown with disinterest as he expertly bowed over her hand. Except for his eyes, which he received from his mother, he looked like his father's son.

Next was William, the youngest. He had flaming red hair and an easy smile. He looked like his mother, except for his father's eyes. He was a strange opposite to Thomas. He carried himself well, but shot her an inoffensive smirk as he bowed over her hand. Ginevra smiled back, instantly liking the boy.

Then came Helena, the youngest of all the children, with the same coloring as William. She curtsied politely. Her tunic gown was impeccably smoothed and her hair curled over her shoulders with girlish perfection. She stepped back without comment. Ginevra decided she didn't care much for the snotty Whetshire girl.

And finally, Wolfe was called forward. He frowned at her, not bothering to take her hand as she curtsied before him. Her dirty bare feet poked out from underneath the dress as she did so. As he witnessed her bare feet, he stated loudly, "I can see your dirty toes."

Ginevra shivered, struck speechless by the unexpected jibe. Lady Jayne gasped, instantly looking at her daughter's offending feet. The boys, along with Lady Isabella, giggled. Helena pressed her hand to her chest in feminine amusement and unconcealed disdain. The earl sternly frowned and the baron covered his smile as he studied his little hoyden.

Ginevra pressed her trembling lips together,

staring down the calm look of her future husband. His eyebrow arched in silent challenge and a smile slid to the side of his mouth. Then, as tears silently welled in her rounded eyes, she ran from the hall.

***

A gentle spring breeze flitted over the courtyard while sprinklings of sunlight danced through the thick blanket of clouds stretching majestically across a pale sky. The warm earthen floor of the courtyard was alive with activity as servants scurried about their business. Some women hauled baskets of laundry and others carried vegetables from the garden to the kitchen. One kitchen servant carried live chickens, two pairs of legs gripped in each of her weathered hands. The fowl jerked and squawked resentfully against her hold as they fluttered about to be free.

The morning drew to a close as the sun pushed higher over the bailey wall. The raised stone surrounded the courtyard, looping about from one side of the main castle to the other in an oval shape. Built into the inner face of the stone ring were the living and service quarters. Some quarters were made of stone, like the main castle and hall itself, but mostly they were built of timber. Atop the wall that stood several feet wide was the walkway surrounded by battlements. Going up any of the corner spiral stairwells one could reach any of the various floors, go to the roof, or to the battlements to walk the entirety of the wall in a complete circle with it dipping under an arch as it passed by the main castle.

A small chapel built of dreary gray hosted a separate courtyard. This courtyard lay dormant with a floor of hard stone and housed a circular bench where Ginevra often came to sit. Sniffing, she hiked her skirt up to expose her dirty feet and the pair of breeches she wore underneath the gown. Setting her feet next to her on the bench, she lounged back and curled her toes against the rough texture of the stone.

"I told you she'd be here," Ginevra heard her brother whisper. She pushed her chin further in the air, refusing to cry and pretended not to hear him.

Someone cleared his throat behind her. She swung around until her feet landed neatly on the ground. Seeing Wolfe, she scowled. "What do you want? I hope it's to call off our betrothal."

Wolfe looked uncomfortable as he held out a flower to her. At her words, a frown creased the sides of his mouth. Not sounding at all convincing, he said, "I'm sorry for looking at your feet."

Ginevra nodded and took the flower with a trembling hand. Not even her own father had given her a flower before. Hating the blush that threatened her cheeks, she looked at the pretty token with its yellowish center and pretty pink petals. Sighing in forced disinterest, she tossed it over her shoulder and stood.

Wolfe stared at his rejected token in displeasure. He opened his mouth to speak, but she ignored him by whirling in the other direction. As she stormed off into the chapel, he followed her. His father's order had been clear. Either he made up with the girl, or the new palfrey would be given to her as a gift.

"I said I was sorry," Wolfe said as he followed her under the drab gray archway. Jogging, he caught up to her just in time to be scolded.

"*Shhh!*" Ginevra hissed with a wave of her hand. They were alone in the chapel. She looked up at the narrow window filled with thick colored glass in the shape of her family crest. A streak of blue light fell across her pale childish face. Whispering under her breath, she said, "We are in a chapel! You have to be quiet or God won't hear you."

"I don't want God to hear me. I want you to." Wolfe sighed in exasperation before crossing over to her. Taking her by the arm, he tugged her gently. Ginevra looked at his hand. Whispering in her ear, he said, "Come on, then. Let's go to the yard."

"Don't you like chapels? Or do you worship the devil?" Ginevra asked with a toss of her white-blonde hair. The tresses reached down her back to her hips. The taller frame of her intended dwarfed her slender body as she looked boldly up to him. Her emerald gaze showed no fear.

"Come on," he grumbled as he pulled her back out into the sunlight. Shaking his head, he frowned at the young girl. When they were free from the solemn chamber, he said, "I don't worship the devil. Someday I'll go to the Holy Land to fight the devil. I'm going to reclaim Jerusalem from the heathens just like the first crusaders."

"I didn't know you were a knight yet," she stated with a touch of awe. Quickly, her opinion of him changed. They had all grown up hearing tales of the Holy Crusades. It was whispered that Richard, son of King Henry, was going to someday finish what the other crusaders had started. "Will you teach me to use your sword? Can I be your squire and ride with you to the Holy Land? I should very much like to fight the heathen devils."

"I'm not a knight, yet," Wolfe answered, falling into stride next to her. "But I will be after the king comes. And then the whole lot of us will go--me, my brothers and even Robert!"

"Robert won't go," Ginevra returned with conviction. She didn't like the idea of her brother leaving for so far away. Already he had been gone for a long time to the earl's to train for knighthood. Even if the earl let him come home for the winter feast, it didn't make up for the rest of the year. "I don't want him to."

Wolfe chucked at the certainty of her words but said nothing.

"So will you take me with you there?"

"War is no place for ladies," he answered.

"I'm no lady." Ginevra wrinkled her nose. Her tone dared him to disagree with her. "I'm your squire and I wish to go with you."

"All right, squire," Wolfe said obligingly. "What skills do you have to prove you are worthy of such an arduous journey?"

"I can run faster than any boy you e'er saw. And I

can ride my father's horse, bareback. Well, he thinks he has to hold the reins for me, but he doesn't. I could do it by myself!" Ginevra beamed with pride. Wolfe nodded his head in approval, but his eyes sparkled with merriment. Lowering her voice, she said confidently, "And I can spy for you! I'd be a very good spy. Once, I made a rope and hung outside my window and I saw Cook kissin' a knight that weren't her husband. Now, I get all the tarts I want from the kitchen and she can say nary a thing to stop me. Come on, I'll show you!"

Grabbing his hand, she pulled him toward a narrow door. Then, stopping, she peeked around the corner. Wolfe could hear the faint sound of muttering as someone moved about inside. Putting her fingers to her lips, she motioned for silence. Wolfe watched in amusement, as she slipped around the corner only to return a second later with two fistfuls of apple tarts still hot and steaming from the baking table. Handing him two, she smiled triumphantly.

"Very resourceful," Wolfe said, impressed. Biting into one of her ill-gotten treats, he smiled in satisfaction.

Ginevra led him to a narrow tapering in the wall. Inviting him to sit by her, they ate in silence. Then, licking her fingers as she finished the tarts, she sighed and lay back along the ground not caring if her gown was soiled by the loose dirt. Her breeches-covered legs poked out from beneath the voluminous folds.

"Do you remember our parents signing the agreement?" she asked, curious. She sat up and hugged her knees to her chest. "What did they do?"

"Not much." Wolfe's eyes narrowed in concentration. He knew she spoke of their betrothal. "They sat at the table in our main hall for a long time deciding how much they would give each other and who would live where and which one of us sons would be trained in knighthood at Southaven and that Robert would train with me at Whetshire. Really, it was a fairly dull dealing."

"And that was it?" She frowned. "They just talked and said, 'All right, Wolfe will marry Ginevra and that will be the end of it'?"

Wolfe laughed at her perfect imitation of her father's voice. "Yea, that was most of it. After they talked, they signed the parchments and then--"

"What?" Ginevra questioned when he paused with a bemused glance at the ground.

"Then they made me kiss you," he stated dryly.

"You kissed me?" she asked in wonder. She had never been kissed before, or at least she thought she hadn't. Lightly, she touched her lips. "Where?"

"On the cheek," he answered. His face became blank. "It was only to seal the agreement. My father made me kiss you."

"And did I cry when you did it?" Ginevra persisted. "Did I try to strike you?"

"Nay, you smiled at me and drooled all over your chin." He laughed, vaguely remembering the little baby he had been made to kiss. He hated to admit that the image had floated through his mind often over the years. "Though, it was supposed to be on the lips. I cheated."

"And after?"

"After, I fought my brothers for teasing me about it," Wolfe chuckled. "And I won too."

"Well, at least someone got to fight over it."

"Yea," Wolfe agreed. Already, he could see Ginevra wasn't like most girls he'd met. His sister would never sit in the dirt and talk of fighting. He hated to admit he was glad for it.

"So, if you didn't kiss my lips, then we don't have to be married?" she inquired. Wolfe thought he detected a hint of disappointment in her voice. "Did you not want to kiss me? Was I ugly? Or were you ashamed of me because of your brothers?"

"You were a babe," he said, discomfited by her reasoning. When her sad emerald eyes turned up to him, a small part of him became lost.

"So, then you won't train me to be your squire?" she asked in dejection. "Who will you marry instead? A lady who knows how to sew?"

"Nay, *simpkin*, I'll have to marry you," he whispered, coming to sit by her. Laying a hand on her chin, he turned her face to him. Very seriously, he explained, "Duty demands that it be so. Duty and honor are all that we are in this world."

"But--"

Wolfe leaned forward and pressed his lips quickly to hers before drawing them away. With a smile, he said, "There, now you haven't a thing to worry about. It's sealed."

Ginevra gasped in shock. Her face lit with a hesitant pleasure before quickly dropping into a dark scowl. "Why'd you have to do that?"

Wolfe laughed at her as they stood. Absently, they made their way along the wall until they neared the weavers. Suddenly, he stopped and looked at her. "Why did you throw my flower away?"

Ginevra gazed up at him in surprise as she felt herself softening toward him. She didn't like it. Imagining her lips were still warm from his quick kiss, she pressed them together. "I don't like flowers."

"All girls like flowers." Wolfe put his hands on his hips, daring her to disagree.

"I don't!" Ginevra spat, her eyes sparkling with defiance. "And I hate wearing gowns and sewing and singing and dancing. If you don't take me with you to the Holy Land, I'm going to be an acrobat and travel with gleemen."

"You can't do that," he said. "Not if you are to marry me."

"Well, mayhap, I don't want to marry you," Ginevra smiled at his stunned face.

"All girls want to get married," he countered. "You have to. The bargain is sealed."

"Not me. I'm going to see the world!" she said with confidence.

"Ladies don't travel," Wolfe argued in frustration. Suddenly, a superior grin spread over his features, as he stated, "They stay at home with the children!"

"I'm not going to have children," Ginevra said,

appalled by the very idea. She tapped her foot in anger.

"You have to. My father says that all men have to have heirs." Wolfe grinned as her face turned white enough to match her hair. "And I want six of them, at least--five boys and one girl."

"Then I'll let the nursemaid tend them. When you bring them home they can go to her. I won't even have to see them."

"You don't just bring children home, *simpkin*. They have to grow in your belly."

Ginevra looked at her flat stomach, poking at it before wearily shaking her head in disagreement. "You're not puttin' a babe in my belly! I won't eat one. And you won't be able to make me. And if you try, I will wallop you good and make you eat it. Then you can get fat and I can travel without you!"

Wolfe chuckled, annoying her with his confidence. "I think you don't like flowers because you are not a girl, but a little urchin."

"Well," Ginevra faltered with an exasperated huff. "You are named after a mongrel dog! Your parents probably found you in a forest somewhere being raised by wolves and felt sorry for you and took you in. Yea, you look like one of 'em too."

"Take that back!" Wolfe demanded, rushing at her. She sidestepped his arms with a skillful dart to the right before making her way to the stone pool used to dye the cloth.

"You take it back, wolf boy!" she hollered obstinately as she stuck out her tongue. Her childlike voice echoed off the stone to draw the attention of a few of the servants. "Wolf boy! Wolf boy! Smelly mongrel wolf boy!"

Wolfe circled her, a smirk lining his lips as he crouched and raised his hands into threatening claws. Ginevra grunted at the silent challenge. She lowered her head like a charging bull and screamed as she ran forward to ram his stomach.

Wolfe growled, stepping out of the way at the last moment before impact. Ginevra flew past him, tripping over the stone ledge into the dye bath. Her scream turned from fury to surprise to outrage. She landed in the purple water with a mighty splash. And, as her head ducked under the dye, she heard Wolfe's hearty laughter reverberating from above.

"I may be a wolf, but you're a grape!"

***

Wolfe trailed silently into the main hall, kicking at the rush covered stone. Woeful, he thought of his new horse belonging to Ginevra. He looked up at the head table and swallowed in remorse, knowing he was going to get into trouble. His father noticed him immediately. The earl waved him forward to where the nobles were visiting.

"Well, boy?" he asked in his gruff voice. His brown eyes narrowed questioningly as he studied his young son. Wolfe's face drew blank, an exact match to his father, as he guiltily shifted from one foot to the other. "Did you make amends with the girl?"

Wolfe glanced over his shoulder. All of a sudden, he noticed he was alone. With an exasperated sigh, he turned and walked to the kitchen entryway. Reaching around the corner, he tugged at Ginevra's arm pulling her forward. The girl resisted.

"Nay, Wolfe," she protested, looking mournfully at him. "My mother will be cross."

"Come on," Wolfe ordered as he pulled her forward into the hall. "Let them see you."

Lady Jayne gasped and grew faint at the sight of her only daughter. She fell back into her chair. The countess fanned her dramatically and called for mead. The earl stared in quiet amazement and Lord Richard began to chuckle.

Ginevra studied her bare feet. They were stained as purple as her mother's dark wine. It was the same shade as the wet, formerly cream, tunic gown she wore. Lifting her head at her mother's exclamation, she let her mouth curl into a guilty smile. Her teeth shone white underneath her grape-colored skin. At the look of her face, even the earl hid an amused smile behind his hand.

She knew she looked bad. Her skin had turned a light shade of purple and the white blonde of her locks had stained to a bright purplish-pink. Her green eyes clashed and glowed dramatically from beneath her dyed skin. Pursing her lips together, she glanced at Wolfe who only shrugged.

"Oh!" The baroness gasped coming out of her initial shock. She looked helplessly about the table. "Oh!"

Lady Isabella waved to a nearby servant to order a scalding hot bath brought to the girl's chamber. Standing, she pulled Lady Jayne with soft insistence to her feet. "Come, Jayne. Let us get her cleaned. And I am sure that Helena has a gown she can borrow for tomorrow eve."

"But, mother!" Helena protested.

"Helena!" the earl quieted the girl with a stern growl. He frowned at his daughter with displeasure.

The baron's laughter only grew, earning him a tight-lipped glare from his stricken wife. Lady Jayne's lips pressed harshly against the taut skin of her cheekbones. To her justice, the nobleman's laughter lightened into chuckles.

"But King Henry will be here on the morrow! And there will be all his knights and the--" Lady Jayne's protest trailed off. She swept forward to her daughter. Her hand moved as if to touch Ginevra but withdrew just as quickly. "Whatever will we do with her?"

"I like it," Ginevra said softly, as she touched her colored locks. She shared a small smile with Wolfe before hiding it under a mask of penitence.

The baroness shook her head as she glanced heavenward. Her lips moved as if she muttered a prayer. Lady Isabella motioned to Ginevra to follow her, but Ginevra was never given the chance to walk on her own. Her mother finished her entreaty with the motion of a cross over her heart before turning determinedly to her purple child. Lady Jayne stepped to her daughter, careful to keep her distance from the dripping wet gown, and led her from the hall by the top of her small ear.

Wolfe looked miserable as he eyed Ginevra's pink hair. It was wet and combed straight back from her face to dry. Her skin was scrubbed back to normal, albeit a little red from the hot bathwater she had been made to soak in for an hour. She again wore breeches and a tunic shirt, as she waited for her mother to finish the alterations on Helena's gown.

Kicking at the dirt, Wolfe handed over his palfrey's reins. "This is for you."

Ginevra looked at the small tanned horse in surprise. Lifting her hand, she patted the peace offering on the nose. Instantly the horse snorted and rubbed against her palm. She flashed a smile as she cooed to the animal.

Behind her, Robert snickered. Turning to glare at him in amusement, she knew she couldn't be mad at him, not when he was going to leave on the morrow with the earl. Grinning, she asked, "Did you see what Wolfe gave to me?"

"Our father made him," Helena stated with a pretentious grin as she came around the corner. Still obviously upset that Ginevra had been given her favorite gown, she huffed disdainfully in the child's direction.

"Quiet, Helena." Thomas purposefully bumped his sister on the arm as he passed. He walked over to the horse and patted its back. "It's a fine animal, Ginevra."

"You look like a purple urchin," Robert said as he eyed her dyed tresses. He ignored the young Helena, who tried to take up his arm, by moving forward. "Did mother faint?"

"Hey, she's a *Pur-chin!*" William called with a smile as he too walked into the stables.

Ginevra frowned slightly at the nickname as she leaned into the horse. Nuzzling the palfrey's soft coat, she patted its lean neck in long strokes.

"*Purch*," Wolfe muttered absently at her side. Sadly he eyed the horse, as it took a liking to its new owner.

Ginevra looked at him. Then, chuckling she said, "That is what I'll name him. Purch."

"That's a stupid name for a horse!" Helena announced in contempt. She glanced at Robert to agree with her. He rolled his eyes and made a face so she couldn't see.

"How would you know?" Thomas shot in defense. "You can't even ride."

"Can so," Helena pouted with another longing glance at Robert. The boy still ignored her and she frowned. "Lady Jayne says proper ladies don't have to ride."

"Better the horse than me," Ginevra grumbled under her breath, ignoring them all. Wolfe was the only one who heard. He shot her a bemused smile.

"Come on," Helena stated in annoyance. "Mother said we were to get ready to dine."

William and Thomas followed her as she left the stables. Lingering as Wolfe walked Purch to his stall, she watched as he bolted him in. Ginevra turned a frolicsome grin to her brother.

"Our lady mother did almost faint," Ginevra divulged. With an impish smirk, she rubbed her ear. "And she pulled my ear almost off my head. It still burns."

"What's she going to do about your pink locks?" Robert fingered a wet strand before shaking his head in amusement.

"She is going to make me wear a headdress and veil tomorrow in front of the king," Ginevra said with a sulk. "I hate veils more than I do gowns."

"You are lucky your eyebrows scrubbed clean," Robert said. He glanced at Wolfe as he came back. The younger boy said nothing.

"Do you have to leave on the morrow, Rob?" Ginevra asked, disheartened by the thought.

"Yea, Gin. I will be sworn into knighthood tomorrow by the king. Wolfe, too. We will become men," he responded with a brotherly pat on her head. Ruffling her moist hair, he smiled. "I expect you to be good for mother. And mind your lessons while I am gone."

"But I don't like to sit indoors," she protested. "It's boring! And mother makes me sew. I hate to sew."

"Ah, but Gin you are so bright. Don't become one of those simple-minded maids. If you promise to study, I promise to write to you oft while I am away. I might even send you a trinket or two. As a knight, I will travel many places with the earl. Yea, he might even take us to tourney with him. There I will make a name for myself." He glanced up from her as Wolfe joined them. He gave his friend a slight smile over the child's head as he nodded to the downhearted girl. "And someday you might come to watch me and I will be your champion and wear your glove upon my chest."

"I don't want jewels, Rob. Don't send me girl trinkets." She sniffed, tears lining her eyes. "Send me boy things. Like a sword or something."

"Yea, Gin," Wolfe said easily at Robert's insistence. "I'll write you too. That is, if you want."

Ginevra nodded half-heartedly. Sniffing back tears that she didn't allow to fall, she kept quiet. The boys solemnly walked by her, as they made their way inside.

Ginevra peeked around the empty passageway, a smile on her lips as she stealthily walked the corridor to Wolfe's guest chamber. Hearing a maid approach, she ducked into an inlet built into the wall. The servant gripped an empty bucket used for hauling bath water in her hands. She hid until the maid passed. Slipping past the maid unnoticed, Ginevra squeezed the bottle of green dye firmly in her hand. Pushing open Wolfe's chamber door, she slid inside.

And, as she shut the door behind her, an impish smile shone from her disobedient face.

That night King Henry came to Southaven. Ginevra's locks were hidden well underneath her simple veil as she was presented to his royal majesty. Her gown was sewn from the finest silk and her escort's the finest of linen. Robert and Wolfe were to be knighted that night to join the ranks of men.

The young girl was led forward on the arm of her future husband. The hall was silent, in awe as they watched the young couple who carried themselves with such reverence. As Ginevra curtsied beautifully before the king, a hand gently knocked the top of her headdress so it tumbled to the rush-lined floor.

Lady Jayne gasped and fainted, caught at the last second by Lady Isabella. King Henry laughed heartily, unable to make his words to bless their future union heard over the mumbling hall. Ginevra turned to Wolfe, a sweet smile lining her mouth as she looked at his humor-filled eyes. And amidst much fuss and formality stood two odd children, one with hair as pink as a spring flower and the other with locks the shade of a grassy summer field.

End Excerpt

For a complete, up-to-date booklist, visit www. MichellePillow.com